Joanna Bourne has always l[...]e. She's drawn to Revolution[...]d Regency England because, as [...] a time of love and sacrifice, daring deeds, clashing ideals and really cool clothing.' She's lived in seven different countries, including England and France, the settings of the Spymaster series.

Joanna now lives on a mountaintop in the Appalachians with her family, a peculiar cat and an old brown country dog. Visit her online at www.joannabourne.com, and connect with her via Twitter @jobourne, www.facebook.com/joanna.bourne.5, or www.jobourne.blogspot.co.uk.

Irresistible reasons to indulge in a Joanna Bourne historical romance:

'Joanna Bourne is a master of romance and suspense' Teresa Medeiros, *New York Times* bestselling author

'Bourne is an undeniably powerful new voice in historical romance' *All About Romance*

'Destined to be a classic in the romance genre' *Dear Author*

'Exceptional characters, brilliant plotting, a poignant love story' *Library Journal*

'Unusual, resourceful, and humorous heroines' Diana Gabaldon, *New York Times* bestselling author

'Distinct, fresh, and engaging' Madeline Hunter, *New York Times* bestselling author

'Addictiv[...]

By Joanna Bourne

Spymaster Series
The Forbidden Rose
The Spymaster's Lady
My Lord And Spymaster
The Black Hawk
Rogue Spy

The
Forbidden
Rose

Joanna Bourne

headline
ETERNAL

The right of Joanna Bourne to be identified as the Author of
the Work has been asserted by her in accordance with the
Copyright, Designs and Patents Act 1988.

Published by arrangement with Berkley,
a member of Penguin Group (USA), LLC,
A Penguin Random House Company

First published in Great Britain in 2014
by HEADLINE ETERNAL
An imprint of HEADLINE PUBLISHING GROUP

1

Cataloguing in Publication Data is available from the British Library

ISBN 978 1 4722 2243 5

Offset in Times Lt Std by Avon DataSet Ltd, Bidford-on-Avon, Warwickshire

Printed and bound by CPI Group (UK) Ltd, Croydon, CR0 4YY

Papers used by Headline are from well-managed forests
and other responsible sources.

HEADLINE PUBLISHING GROUP
An Hachette UK Company
338 Euston Road
London NW1 3BH

www.headlineeternal.com
www.headline.co.uk
www.hachette.co.uk

Acknowledgments

This book is dedicated to Lily and Maya.

I would like to thank my wonderful editor at Berkley, Wendy McCurdy, and my agent, Pam Hopkins, of Hopkins Literary Associates.

I am endlessly grateful to my tireless and patient beta readers: Leo Bourne, Mary Ann Clark, Laura Watkins, and Wendy Rome. I thank the Ladies Who Drink Coffee for support and friendship. I owe much to the excellent folks at the Compuserve Books and Writers Community: Diana Gabaldon, Deniz Bevan, Beth Shope, Jenny Meyer, Jennifer Hendren, Donna Rubino, Susan Adrian, Julie Weathers, Linda Grimes, Tara Parker, and others too numerous to mention.

I would not have written this story without the expert advice of David Barnes and Hugo Clément, who know much about geology and caves, and Linda Weaver, who knows much about donkeys. The Beau Monde, a special interest chapter of RWA, has provided endless expertise on all things 1800-ish. Anything I got right is because of these wonderful people. All mistakes are my own.

A special thanks goes to Franzeca Drouin, researcher, editor, and general all-round expert on all things having to do with history and historical language.

One

"YOU HAVE NOT BEEN FOOLISH," SHE SAID. "BUT YOU have been unlucky. The results are indistinguishable."

The rabbit said nothing. It lay on its side, panting. Terror poured from it in waves, like water going down the steps of a fountain.

Her snare circled its throat. She had caught it with a line of red silk, teased and spun from the torn strip of a dress. It could not escape. Even when it heard death coming toward it through the brush, it didn't struggle. Being sensible, it had given up.

"The analogies to my own situation are clear. I do not like them." Marguerite de Fleurignac sat down and pulled her skirts to lie smooth over her knees. The grass was slick and sharp-edged on the bare skin of her ankles. Behind her rose the ruins of the chateau. She did not look in that direction if she could help it. "I am starving to death, you know. Not as one starves in stories, nobly and gracefully. I starve stupidly. I scrape up oats from the bottom of the feed bins and pick berries. I pull wild carrots from the earth and gnaw on them in my cave under the bridge. None of this rests easily in my stomach. It is very sordid. I will not share the details with you."

The rabbit's eyes stared beyond her.

"Life is not like the fables. No magical bird alights on the rooftop, bearing messages. You do not offer me three wishes in exchange for your life. No prince rides up on his white horse to rescue me."

Rabbit fur was a brown made of many shades, like toast. The guard hairs were darker than the down that clung close to its body. Inside its ears was a delicate velvet, pale as cream, and she could see the pink skin underneath. Its eyes were fringed on top with a row of short, thick hairs. It had eyelashes. She hadn't known rabbits had eyelashes.

Terror terror terror.

It had been a mistake to look so closely at the rabbit. She should not have talked to it.

When she was five or six, Old Mathieu, the gamekeeper, had let her tag along behind him through this wood. He set snares and made great slaughter among the rabbits and put them in a big leather game bag to carry home.

He had been dead fifteen years. In his last illness, she'd visited him every day in his dirty, crowded hut by the river. She'd brought him the best brandy from the chateau cellars to ease the pain.

Uncle Arnault, who was marquis then, had scolded and given orders, which she had ignored. "You spoil these peasants. You make pets of them." Papa had pointed out that spirits were not good for the humors of the body. She should take the man seawater and a mash of beets. Cousin Victor sneaked after her and pushed her down and spilled open the basket and broke everything inside.

Uncle Arnault was long dead, having discussed politics with the guillotine. Papa was marquis now, inasmuch as anyone held the empty title. Victor had joined the most radical of the revolutionary groups, the Jacobins. The casks of brandy had exploded in a ball of blue flame when the fire fingered down to the wine cellar. It had never mattered a bean that she had given brandy to a dying man.

Old Mathieu's sons had been in the mob that came to burn the chateau. She'd seen them with the others on the lawn in the light of torches.

A pulse rippled in the rabbit's throat, under the fur. That fluttering beat, in a hollow the size of a copper sou, was the only sign of life.

"I make up stories in my head and I am always remarkably heroic in them. When men actually came to destroy me, I ran like a rabbit, if you will forgive the comparison." She wiped rain from her face. Her forearm was gritty and smelled like crushed grass and sweat. And smoke. "You are doubtless stultified with boredom to hear my problems. One's own disaster is of compelling interest. The disasters of others, less so."

Clouds hung flat and close overhead, the color of old bruises. A few sharp tiny points of rain hit her face when she looked up. Even this far from the chateau, thin black flakes of ash had caught in the leaves of the trees. The rain fell with ash in it.

"Here is the story, if you wish to read it." She caught drops on the palm of her hand. "This," she lifted one speck of black onto her forefinger, "came from the destruction of curtains in the blue salon. And this," another bit of ash, "was a page from a book in the library. A mathematics text. This . . ." She picked a fleck of ash from her forearm. "This is the period at the end of a sentence in one my notebooks. That was the only copy of an old tale of the people. It is lost now."

She let the drops of water run away. She was very tired. She had been up all night, two nights in a row, walking the last shipment of sparrows to safety. She had taken three men, three women, and a child through the dark fields to the deserted mill that was the next waystation. She'd waited with them till Heron's son came to take them onward. Then she had trudged the long way back. Because Crow—careful, reliable Crow who never missed a meeting—had not yet come. He was late, and she worried.

The sparrows had complained a great deal that she had no food to give them. No one had asked what had happened to her in the burning of the chateau.

They would go to London, those sparrows, and tell everyone how brave they had been and what dangers they had undergone, fleeing France. None of them would speak of the bravery of Heron's young son who came at night, alone, to lead them onward. Or of Jeanne, who was the Wren, who risked death to smuggle them out of Paris. Or of Egret and Skylark and the others who hid them along the way. The sparrows would take it all for granted.

She shivered, which was what she deserved for sitting on the ground in this small rain, talking to a rabbit. "I will tell you what I should do. I should go deep into the woods, carrying—you will forgive me for being blunt?—carrying your dead corpse, and light a fire and put you on a spit and cook you. Then I should begin my walk to Paris in the dark of the night." Rubbing her arms did not make them any warmer. "Crow is more than wise. I should leave him to take care of his own sparrows and go warn the others."

The rabbit's fear was like the whine of iron on a grindstone. *Terror terror terror.*

The wind coming from the chateau pushed at her back, smelling of smoke, ugly and somehow metallic. "Do not expect pity, Citoyen Rabbit. I am without a heart. It was the first thing I ate when I became hungry."

The rabbit did not flinch when she laid hands upon it, but inside its fur, it shivered. The knife in her pocket was sharper than it had been four days ago when it lived the placid life of a letter opener. She worked a finger into the snare of silk that held the rabbit. "Instead of being sensible, I will chew on parched grains that do not agree with me and let you go free." She cut the red thread. "You will not be grateful. I know. You will come back tonight with a hundred rabbits and burn down the bridge and me underneath."

It did not move.

"Go. Go. You annoy me, lying there. Go, before I change my mind and eat you with wild onions and watercress."

The rabbit shook from end to end and wobbled to its feet. It lurched off into the drab grass of the drainage ditch. The waves of terror departed with it.

It was a relief to be free of that. "It would have made me sick, I think, to eat something so afraid."

Two

She was a little dizzy, so she sat a moment longer, looking down the parting in the grass where the rabbit had disappeared, wondering whether it would live to a ripe old age and become a patriarch with grandchildren at its knee or be eaten, almost immediately, by a fox.

Then, from beneath the rustle of rain, voices slid like snakes. Men's voices.

She grabbed up her skirts and ran.

There was no time to get to the woods. She ran toward the chateau. Down the long path of the flower garden, lavender and foxglove and marigold caught at her. Pebbles scattered under her clogs. She was making noise. Too much noise.

It wasn't men from the village walking up the back lane. Men from Voisemont wouldn't come this late in the day, in the rain. They could pick better weather to loot the chateau. They'd roll up in squeaking carts she could hear a hundred yards away. Crow's messenger, when he came to find her—if he came—would be silent.

She ran across the courtyard to where the stable door hung open and ducked inside. Her sabots clicked down the rank of stalls where each window stood open to the gray outside. No whicker came. No click of a hoof. Only the dry commentary of barn swallows, nesting in the eaves. The stable was empty and desolate under the high roof. The heart had gone out of here with the horses.

The villagers had come, thrifty and sharp-eyed and acquisitive. There was not one small valuable object left in place. Not a blanket. Not a jingling bit or rein or a braided rope. Not a scrap of worked leather. They'd even emptied the feed bins into sacks and carted the oats away, all but a handful in the bottom of the bin. The chickens of Voisemont would eat well this summer.

At the last stall, she stopped below the hayloft where the ladder slanted down. She stood ankle deep in straw, well back in the shadow. The shutters were open everywhere, creaking in the light wind, dripping with the damp congealed on the boards. It would have taken three minutes to close them, but no one had bothered. Perhaps it was a revolutionary principle that good straw should spoil in the rain.

There was a clear view of the courtyard. She would make certain this was not the messenger from Crow. Then she would slip away out the back door and leave them to occupy themselves with looting.

In the courtyard, voices separated into a deep, heavy rumble and answers, lighter and higher. Two men, at least.

They could be chance travelers, looking for a dry spot to spend the night. They could be philosophers or scholars, knights-errant, pilgrims, heroes in disguise, wandering minstrels. They might be veritable princes among men, bent upon good works, full of benevolence.

She had become skeptical of benevolence.

The high bushes of the lane were hazy under the desultory scatter of raindrops. They emerged. A tall man, dressed like a prosperous tradesman but brown as a farmer, strode ahead. His servant boy lagged behind, struggling with a pair of donkeys.

The big man stopped in the center of the courtyard and stood with his back to her, his head tilted to look up at the streaked black and gray facade of the chateau. He was not a man of fashion, certainly, but he was no shabby vagabond. He dressed substantially and practically, outfitted for hard travel with a plain coat and high boots. His hands, heavy and motionless, hooked into the waist of his trousers. His wide-legged stance was calm and meditative.

He could have been a soldier, surveying a captured city, preparing to raze it and salt the earth, or a builder, inspecting the blocks of a fallen Roman villa, calculating tonnage, planning to buy and transport the marble. As she watched, he pulled his hat off and slapped it against his thigh. There was decision in that motion. The whisper of great force, held easily in check.

I do not like this at all.

He carried no sign to say he was Crow's messenger. A red ribbon with a knot in it, any bit of red cloth, knotted, would be enough. He was only a stranger in her domain, pointless and useless to her.

You have no business here. Go away.

He did not, of course. He set his hat back, low over his forehead, and flipped the collar of his coat up. He turned slowly, taking in the dairy house and the coach house, working his way around. At this distance, she couldn't make out his features. Weak, gray light slid across his face, drawing a suggestion of high, flat cheekbones, a jaw dark with stubble, a jutting nose. His hair was brown and hung raggedly on his neck.

If he had inhabited a fairy tale he would have been the giant, not the prince. Giants are more chancy to deal with than princes.

This was what came of clinging to the stones of the chateau like damp moss. She had not gone to seek danger on the Paris road, so danger had come to her, stalking her right to her own doorstep. She was like the man who ran away from Death, all the way from Baghdad to Samarkand. Death found him anyway, because it was his fate.

The stranger surveyed his way around the outbuildings. When he came to the stable, for an instant he seemed to look directly at her. The force of his concentration grabbed her breath and twisted it in her lungs. Knowing she was invisible, knowing she was wrapped in shadow, she froze.

His attention moved on. To the stone wall that hid the fishpond garden. To the tall iron grille of that garden, standing open. To the kitchen plantings beyond, with that gate left open as well. Perhaps there was some unwritten rule that mobs and looters did not close doors after themselves.

The servant boy tied the donkeys to a post, swearing a staccato chain of annoyance. A trick of wind blew the words to her. "Donkey feet in butter. Donkey *en croûte*. Donkey soup. You just wait."

He spoke with a Gascon accent. He looked Gascon also, dark haired, with the smooth, dark skin of the south of France. He was a servant many miles from home.

Master and servant were occupied with their own business. She could slip out the back door of the stable and crawl in the direction of the garden shed, pretending to be something unnoticeable. A hedgehog perhaps. Or she could wait. This pair might gawk at the chateau for a dozen moments, then leave for a warm fire and dry, comfortable beds in the village. She could climb to the stable loft and watch from there. There was always the chance they might call out and identify themselves with one of the passwords.

Or she could stand here like an idiot. She was a battlefield of possibilities.

The big man said, "There's broken glass all over. Watch your feet. And don't bring the donkeys in." A Breton voice. This was a man from the oldest, the least civilized, province of France.

He didn't start poking through the ruins. He stood and thought a great deal about what he was seeing. She did not wish to deal with a man who came here with more in his mind than straightforward looting.

WILLIAM Doyle, British spy, stood in the French rain and thought about destruction.

Decorum and Dulce balked at the gate. Laid their ears back and refused to set hoof on the open gravel in the courtyard. They didn't like the stink of burning. They smelled death, maybe. Something they didn't like, anyway.

Wise as cats, those beasts. The boy hadn't learned to appreciate them.

There weren't any remains lying about in an obvious way. No bodies hanging from the trees like ripe fruit. Always the possibility somebody was tucked away in a corner, dead.

Dulce snaked out to bite Hawker. Missed him by a hair. The boy was getting downright nimble, wasn't he?

"Rutting bastard of a—" Hawker dodged, "sodomite monk."

He learned that one from me. I am just a shining example to youth. The boy had come to him speaking some French. He was improving the lad's vocabulary.

The donkeys were what he'd call a pointed lesson in how to deal with a problem you couldn't out talk and couldn't stab in the jugular. Sometimes it was a real pleasure to educate the lad.

Hawker hanked the reins up with a last jerk, looking like he knew what he was about, which was a tribute to his acting skills. "I'm going to boil your entrails down and make goddamn donkey *glue*."

"When yer through chatting with the livestock, maybe we can reconnoiter a bit. Take the back garden, down to that shed. Then go round the west side." He did a slice and circle, saying the same thing in hand-talk. After this, the gesture would be enough. Hawker learned the first time.

The boy stuck to the wet grass where it was quiet and let the boxwood hedge screen him from sight, taking city skills and applying them. He was beginning to move like a countryman.

They had Chateau de Fleurignac to themselves. No Jacobin radicals waved official papers. No servants clacked buckets at the well or broke dishes in the kitchen. No chickens underfoot. No horses in the stable. Not even a dog came out to discuss meum et tuum with trespassers.

No sign of the mad, old Marquis de Fleurignac or his daughter.

In the tavern in Voisemont, they said the old man had escaped before the Jacobins came to arrest him and drag him back to Paris, to the guillotine. He'd driven away in a coach and four, his pockets stuffed with jewels. He'd been seen going north to join the armies attacking France.

Another contingent claimed he'd been spirited away by one of the fraternities of heroes and fools who flipped a finger at the Revolution and rescued aristos. He was hid in the false bottom of a wagon, joggling along the road to the coast.

Then there was a lively group that said the marquis had been trapped in the fire. Oh, yes. They'd seen him with their own eyes, beating at the windows to get out. Burning like a torch. He was buried under eight feet of ashes with a fortune in gold clutched in his charred, bony fists. All a man had to do was dig him up.

Himself, he thought de Fleurignac had never been at

the chateau. De Fleurignac was a city man. He'd gone to ground where he felt safe. Paris. That's where he'd find him and his damned list.

But De Fleurignac's daughter had been here. In the tavern there was complete agreement she'd been in the house when the Jacobins came. Nobody speculated on what had become of her. They passed quick glances back and forth and said nothing. Always interesting, what people didn't talk about.

He looked around, writing his report in his head.

Chateau de Fleurignac was the size of his father's house, Bengeat Court. It was the same age as Bengeat, too. Sixteenth century. Built with the local granite they'd been passing in every field all the way from the coast. The roof had caved in unevenly when the timbers went, making a gray hunchback of a ruin. Every window was topped with a fan of black soot.

They burned the hell out of this place, didn't they?

Statues had toppled from their niches at the roofline. A stone hand, holding a scroll, lay in fragments at his feet. The broken line of marble over there was the drape of a toga. Late classical work. Roman, not Gallo-Roman. Emperors and poets, brought crashing down by the farmers of Voisemont-en-Auge. A lonely end, a long way from the sun of Italy.

In the neat formal gardens, the marble statues of nymphs had been systematically beheaded. That was the fashion in France these days. Beheading.

Hawker threaded his way across the rubble of the courtyard, deft and fastidious about where he put his feet. "What's the word . . . that long animal?" He slithered his hand sinuously. "On the ground. With fur. The mean one."

He meant weasel, probably. *"Belette."*

"That's it. I'm going to drop weasels down their long, furry donkey ears. Let them chew on their brains."

"That'll work."

"I want 'em to die slow, so I can take my time and savor it. There's nobody in the gardens, alive or dead. The grass is all churned up with carts and horses. Four different carts, since you're going to ask. And there is nothing anywhere here worth stealing." The broken chairs, muddy silk, and torn paintings got a scathing appraisal. "I will give you my expert opinion. You can loot a place or you can burn it to the ground. It's a mistake trying to do both at once."

"Bad planning on somebody's part. See that, up there?" Lead had melted from the roof and cooled into thick black icicles.

"That's . . . ah . . ." Hawker rubbed his forehead, tracking down the French word. "Lead."

"Right. Lead. That's about the third most important thing here, so I'm taking an interest in it. Why?"

Hawker didn't know. He hated not knowing. "Reminds you of the lead soldiers you played with as a nipper?"

Very funny. "There's a shortage of lead in France. That's three—maybe three and a half—tons of it. They'll hack that down to make bullets for the Republic. We'll be dodging that lead, one of these days, on some battlefield."

Cold eyes looked out of an unlined face. "You, maybe. Not me. It's stupid men who die on battlefields."

Not an ounce of patriot in you, boy. Considering the hellhole you come from back in London, I can't think of any reason there should be. "I'd be careful, saying that. The gods have a sense of humor. Not a nice one. We'll camp here tonight."

Fire had played favorites with the outbuildings. The dairy house was intact. The carriage house, burned out completely. The carriages, hauled into the open, overturned, and set on fire. Nothing left of them but the wood frame and hanging leather straps. The stable was untouched.

When his father was angry with him or his brothers

were on a rampage, he'd slept in the stables at Bengeat. But he didn't like to sleep closed in, in hostile country. The orangerie was a better bet. "That way. Let's get in out of the rain."

The orangerie was open to the wind, a disorder with a roof over it. Every window was broken, the orange trees trampled, the planters thrown down on their sides. The hothouse plants had been stomped into the tiles. Glass covered the ground, thick near the walls, and scattered out in every direction for a dozen yards, glinting.

He made a circuit of the place. Open space on three sides. He'd see visitors coming through those big, naked windows and hear 'em walking on glass. He hated getting sneaked up on.

Hawker followed him, crunching glass into the gravel. "The boys in that stinking little village waited years to do this."

"Did they?"

"They dreamed of it. They'd sit in those pig houses in the village with the shutters closed and the wind leaking in. They'd think about these fancy weeds in here, being coddled, all warm and happy behind glass. Down there, they were freezing in the dark. Up here, they were growing flowers."

"That's fixed, then. No more flowers."

Out of the corner of his eye, he saw Hawker stoop and pick up a rock, draw back and throw. Glass fell with a thin, silver discord. The heroic revolutionaries of Voisemont had missed one pane. Destruction was now complete.

"It would have bothered me all night, knowing there was one window left," Hawker said.

"Anything else you need to break to make it homey in here?"

"That'll do." The boy poked at pottery pieces where somebody'd beaten an orchid apart, pot and all. "They

hated this place. Hated it more than the big house. I'm surprised they didn't take it down, stone by stone."

"They may yet. It's early days." *Lots of hate in you, isn't
there? But you're worth trying to save if you see things
like that.* "Put the animals in the kitchen garden. If you
walk them through any of this glass I'm going to make you
pick it out of the hooves with your teeth. And fetch some
straw. We'll put it between us and the ground. No reason
we shouldn't sleep soft tonight."

"Straw. I love luxury."

Three barn swallows shot out of the gable end of the
stable, sudden as arrows. If he'd been facing the other way,
he would have missed it.

It probably didn't mean a thing. Birds pick any odd minute to get spooked. But the hairs stood up on the back of his
neck. And the donkeys were nervous. *Somebody's watching us.*

"What?" The boy's hand hovered over the knife he kept
hidden under his waistband.

"Don't turn."

"Where are they?"

"The stable. Far left end. You walk off slow and get out
of the line of fire. Go busy yourself with our four-footed
brothers."

"Your brothers, maybe. Not mine." He gave a fluid
shrug for anyone watching—that was a damned eloquent
French shoulder he was developing—and sauntered off,
whistling, without a backward glance. The boy was born
for this work. He'd make a spy of him yet. If he didn't have
to kill him.

He strolled out to the six-foot stone wall that edged the
kitchen garden, adjusting his trousers like a man picking
a good spot to piss. When he had a substantial boxwood
between him and the stable, he boosted himself up and over
the wall and dropped into an herb bed on the other side.

Basil crushed underfoot when he landed. He was going to smell like basil. Going to yell his approach to all and sundry. Couldn't be helped. He loped along the garden wall, keeping in its cover, staying on the dirt so it was quiet. Thirty feet, and he was coming up behind the stable. He went back over the wall again. Nobody on guard. All quiet. All deserted.

The feeling that somebody waited inside got stronger and stronger.

The back door to the tack room was open. He stalked forward, hunting whatever waited for him in there.

hree

SHE KNEW HOW TO STAY STILL. THAT WAS THE FIRST important thing Doyle learned about her. She had a controlled patience that made her just about invisible. Most people couldn't pass two minutes without fidgeting.

The woman stood in the shadow under the stable loft, outlined against the window, watching the courtyard. Breaths slipped in and out of her body like ghosts. Her face was turned away from him. She wore country clothes, like an upper servant or a farm wife. Dark blue skirt. White apron. A plain linen fichu tied around her shoulders. She had clogs on her feet. Her hair was pulled back from her face and braided in a thick tail that hung down her back, tied at the bottom with a scrap of bright red cloth. Her arms crossed her chest, one over the other, hugging tight and protective.

The smear of mud on her skirt and the scratches on her arms said she'd been hiding in the woods, living rough. She'd be one of the household—a lady's maid or seamstress or the wife of the steward.

The stable window she'd picked had a wide, unobstructed view of the chateau and the avenue between the coach house and the back lane. By chance or planning, she'd picked a first-rate lookout post.

Even as he thought that, her hand went to the back of her neck. She could feel when eyes were on her, a skill that wasn't as common as mice in a closet.

She turned. Saw him. The instant stretched tight.

He'd put himself between her and the back door. She hadn't thought of keeping two lines of retreat. One for your enemy to block off. One so you can run like hell.

Skirt and apron whirled. She exploded into flight, down the stalls, long braid trailed out behind her. He caught her halfway to the door. Wrapped his arms around her and held on.

She twisted and tried to rake her nails at his face. When he caught her wrists, she curled like an eel and bit the hand that held her, digging her teeth deep.

Well, that hurt. "I'm not going to—" A sabot hit his shin. "God's . . . tortoises. Will you hold still? I'm trying not to damage you." He shifted his grip and she broke a hand free and pulled out a knife.

Enough. He kicked her legs out from under her. The knife bounced away. He flopped her down on her back into the piled straw.

That was the end of it, to all intents and purposes, except she was going to keep fighting for a while.

She was light for her size and panicked and dead ignorant of fighting. He'd make short work of a man her size. This girl had no chance at all. She kneed him in the belly, missing the vital goods by a margin narrower than he liked. That seemed to be sheer luck. None of the men in her life had taught her how to do damage to the male of the species. That was a pity because she was approaching this business of hurting him with lots of enthusiasm.

He didn't blame her for trying. He'd do the same himself. He climbed on top and held her down. "Biting everything in sight don't do you any noticeable good, and it's annoying the hell out of me."

The ending was abrupt. She gave up, all at once, all over. She lay under him, looking up. They were wrapped together like lovers. But this wasn't even the distant cousin of lovemaking.

I am scaring her to death.

Then she got a good look at the scar on his cheek and stopped breathing.

That scar was a work of art, seven inches of grotesque, running from his eyebrow to his chin. The major geographic feature of his face. It made him look fairly depraved.

"This face of mine's always been a great trial. I'm lucky I don't have to look at it." He stayed as he was, still and heavy, on top of her.

Her eyes were the color of coffee pouring from the pot—intensely brown, translucent. She was pale under the sunburn, and scratched and dirty. Her muscles, hard with fear, vibrated in his hands where he had her pinned down.

"Let me go." Her throat clenched and unclenched.

The fichu kerchief around her neck had got itself pulled loose. Her breasts were nudging out of her bodice. And . . . he had his hand on one of them. When did that happen? God. He jerked away fast and took hold of her shoulder instead. That was neutral ground up there. "Sorry. Don't mean anything by that. An accident."

Fine pair of breasts she had. White as split almonds. Round as peaches. The nipples peeked out, since the fichu wasn't doing its job. A pair of dark little roses, pulled up into buds. Tasty looking. And if he got any closer he could put his mouth down and lick them.

That's going to reassure her—you slavering at her tits.

He levered himself up some, so he wasn't crushing her. "I wanted to know who's spying on me. That's all. I'm not going to hurt you. See. I'm letting you go. What you do is, you don't hit me. You might hold off on that biting, too."

He watched a bit of rational thought come tiptoeing into her mind. Watched her turn his words over, considering them from all sides. She unfroze, muscle by muscle.

He shifted back farther. "I didn't expect to find anyone. In the village, they say it's deserted. What are you doing here?"

"That is not letting me go." She looked at the scar on his face and away, quickly. "If you are going to not hurt me, you may do it at a greater distance. You are very heavy."

He could get to like this woman.

He rolled to the side and got up to his knees. He didn't need to keep hold of her. He could snag her if she tried to run.

"That is somewhat better." Her voice shook. "Nonetheless, I would prefer more space between us. The space of an entire stable perhaps."

Oh yes, he could like her very much. "Sit up and talk to me. Who are you? Why were you spying on me?"

She pushed herself upward and began tucking her fichu in at her neckline, covering up. "I was not spying. I was avoiding you. There is a significant difference."

Her accent was the Paris of coffeehouses and boulevards and salons. No trace of the Normandy patois. This wasn't a fancy lady's maid or the bailiff's wife. He'd netted himself the daughter of the house. De Fleurignac's daughter.

"You're being cautious." She was going to lead him to her father. All he had to do was hold on to her.

Maybe what he was thinking showed. Her eyes skittered away from him. "I am wary of strangers lately."

"And I don't look particularly benign." He ran his thumbnail down the scar on his cheek. His masterpiece of a scar. He'd be a nightmare to a woman, alone, in a deserted stable. "Not pretty, is it?"

Fear shifted behind her eyes. That would be one more affront to this woman's dignity, that she couldn't keep herself from being afraid of him.

"It is not pretty." This time, she looked steadily at his face. "But also not a countenance to stop the hens from laying. One sees worse in any village. You need not feel slighted because you lack beauty. I hid from you before I saw your face."

"That's putting me in my place." He leaned back on his heels. "I don't look like much, but I'm respectable, back at home."

"When you are at home, perhaps you do not chase women and fling them to the ground like so many sacks of meal." She pulled her knees up and twitched at her skirt to cover her ankles. A graceful, lovely little gesture. The muddy dress could have been silk brocade at Versailles. "At home, perhaps, you introduce yourself before you assault women."

"I don't assault women at all, generally speaking. I'm Guillaume LeBreton, once of Brittany, living in Paris now. I'm not the one sneaking around, spying and biting all and sundry, now am I? Who are you?"

She drew a deep breath. Everybody drew in a deep breath before they started telling lies. "I am Margaret Duncan, *dame de compagnie* to Mademoiselle de Fleurignac."

"You're English, then."

"Scots."

If she was Scots, he was Robert the Bruce. "You're a long way from home, Maggie Duncan."

"On the contrary. France is my home. My family lives in Arles. My father is a colonel of infantry."

France was full of the red-headed grandchildren of men who'd followed the Stuart king into exile. A good many of them were in the French army. But that wide and witchy mouth didn't come from Scotland. She was pure French.

She looked to the window of the stable and beyond, to the shell of the chateau. "Mademoiselle escaped. I was left behind to hold this delightful conversation with you."

Just a dish full of cleverness, this Maggie.

Four

IT WOULD BE POINTLESS BEYOND MEASURE TO KICK
at this walking monolith, so Marguerite did not. She would
find a way to checkmate him, eventually.

Or he would kill her. He could do that at any time.
He need only choose among several methods and get on
with it.

Monsieur LeBreton pulled her to her feet. He took the
letter opener from the straw and studied it on both sides
before he slipped it into a place inside his jacket. He then
suggested, by his hand upon her arm, that she accompany
him out the door of the stable, into the wide-spaced drops
of rain. He was not cruel or hurtful about it, but he was
very determined. It was like being carried off by a huge
bird of prey that was on its best behavior. A roc perhaps,
as in the fable of Sinbad. One does not discuss alternatives
with a roc.

She was not to be abused and strangled in the open air
of the garden, it seemed. He dragged her to the greater discretion of the orangerie.

Her journey across the courtyard concerned itself with small practicalities. She hooked her toes into the sabots so she wouldn't lose them. If she was not to be killed, she would need her shoes.

"Adrian," LeBreton called. "We have a guest."

The servant boy stepped from between white planters and disheveled palm trees. He was dark and lithe and sullen, grumpy as a genie called forth by an impatient magician. He looked unsurprised to see his master with an unwilling woman in tow. This was probably not a good sign.

LeBreton remained a pace behind her while the boy swept glass from the tiles with a bundle of palm fronds, limping a little as he went about the work. He was a handsome boy, unlike his master who was ugly as several sorts of sin, in all of which he was doubtless proficient.

When a space was clear, LeBreton took his coat off and swirled it down on the tiles at her feet. There was a story . . . One of the courtiers of the old English queen had spread his cloak upon the dirt of the street for the queen to walk upon, a century and more ago. The queen was Elizabeth. She did not remember the name of the courtier.

"Sit. Don't faint." LeBreton pushed at her shoulders and she sat with a thump. She did not know why he bothered to give orders, if he was going to shove at her anyway.

Fear sustains one for a time, but it is a false friend. It departs, taking all strength with it. A chill spread along her skin. The edges of her sight darkened. The shush of the makeshift broom and the scratch of tumbling glass became distant. She felt as if she were falling into a dream. Not a good dream.

She had sent men and women of La Flèche into infinite risk, telling them to be strong and clever. She had promised that one may endure anything.

Now it was her turn to discover the truth of this.

LeBreton's coat was large, as one would expect. It was

a brown so dark it became black in this dim light, lined with the reddish brown of fallen oak leaves. She sat in the middle of it like a frog on a lily pad, surrounded by a desolation that had once been a garden, and shivered.

"There's no use being afraid," he said. "No need for it either. I told you that." His hand opened, as if he might reach out and touch her.

She flinched. Just a little, but he'd seen it. "I would like to leave now."

"You been hiding here since they burned the house, haven't you? I don't blame you for being scared. There's packs of scavengers loose these days. Deserters. Outright bandits. You're damned lucky it was me that came along."

"I am properly grateful."

"No. You're terrified of me. I'll fix that in a while. Stay where you are." Perhaps his words were meant to be reassuring. If so, they did not work.

She was left alone to consider the matter of who Monsieur LeBreton was, who spoke like a villager of Brittany and pretended to be a simple man when he was not in the least simple, and why he had come to peer and poke around her chateau, not looting, and what she should do about all this.

If she tried to run, there'd be another demonstration that he was larger than she was, and faster. She would sneak away when it was dark. Not now. Not yet.

Wind, heavy with mist, blew in steadily from the west. Her skin prickled into little bumps. Hunger twisted in her stomach like a live thing. If she had killed the rabbit, like a sensible woman, and taken it into the woods to cook, she would not have met Monsieur LeBreton and she would not be in this situation. *Jean-Paul always says I would get us all killed, being impractical.*

She pulled herself into a tight ball and laid her cheek upon her knees and closed her eyes. Perhaps when she opened them she would be somewhere else—Cloud

Cuckoo Land or the island of Tír na nÓg or the Atlantis of Plato. One of the mythic places of the old stories. It was not likely, but it was not impossible.

LeBreton sent the boy to fetch baskets from the donkeys and took over the task of sweeping the floor. She heard him grunting and dragging big copper planters from one place to another. She could not imagine why he did that and did not waste her energy in pointless speculation.

When the chateau burned, they came here to throw stones again and again. It was as if the orangerie were an adulterous woman, crouching in fear, and they destroyed her. How strange that it should be so cold. It was always warm here.

When she was a child, this had been her playhouse, her secret kingdom, with flowers like spears of sunlight, flowers like fans and feathers, like waxy red swords. The stoves ran night and day all winter long, keeping oranges and cyclamens and the ferocious, stubby pineapples alive.

Jean-Paul was the son of Maître Béclard, botanist of the Royal Gardens, who had come with a shipment of orchids and bromeliads and stayed to tend them. Jean-Paul told her the story of every plant in the glasshouse, invincible in his belief she wanted to know.

One day when she was fifteen he had plucked down an orange blossom for her and tucked it into her hair. "That's one less orange for your dinner, Marguerite." He had kissed her.

Boots scraped beside her. LeBreton towered over her, perhaps a mile high. He'd come carrying a donkey blanket. He flapped it out and let it fall softly over her shoulders, doing this all in one motion, without touching her. She was circled in it now, like an Arab in his tent.

If he is going to hurt me, what is he waiting for? She did not wish to imagine what complex villainies a man might approach in this leisurely fashion.

He said, "You go right on being afraid of me, if you want to. But stop shivering. Makes me chilly just looking at you."

"No one would wish you to be uncomfortable."

"That's good. That was a bit of a smile. You keep doing that." And he left her alone.

The servant boy carried in the last of the donkey baskets. His gaze upon her was neither friendly nor unfriendly, merely assessing. It did not surprise her that a man like LeBreton would employ such an unsettling servant.

LeBreton started a fire with dry palm fronds, then laid on small lengths of charred timber. The boy took the canvas off the donkey panniers and lifted out smaller baskets with lids and leather bags, cooking pans and a coffeepot. He set everything out without hesitation, having a pattern to it, as if he'd done this many times. He put water to boil in a black kettle, exactly like the kettle in every cottage in Normandy, but his firewood was table legs and broken curio cabinets.

LeBreton finished his own unpacking and came over to her. He sat beside her, tailor fashion, so close his knee almost touched her. He'd pulled his hat off and left it somewhere so she had a clear view of his scar and his various other brutal features. His dense, weighing regard rested on her. "Let's give you some coffee before I start asking questions." Probably he had no expression that did not look menacing.

The boy, Adrian, came up carrying a blue and white china cup full of black coffee. Its handle was broken off and the rim was cracked. It was from the set the upper servants used. Had used. LeBreton wrapped her fingers around it till she had it steady.

"Drink this. Then we'll talk." He had the hands of a laborer. Blunt-fingered, calloused, capable, broad of palm. Hands like well-forged steel tools that had seen a lot of use.

Hands like a treatise on engineering. "I'm not a villain, Maggie."

A man like you is anything he chooses to be. "I am Citoyenne Duncan. Or Miss Duncan. Not Maggie."

"I'll keep that in mind." He took the corner of her blanket, where it was slipping away off her shoulder, and pulled it higher. "You didn't jump out of your skin that time. We're making progress."

There was no progress. She was exhausted, and she did not wish to spill coffee upon herself. She did not feel it necessary to explain this to him.

The coffee was hot and very sweet. True coffee, from Haiti, not the brew of roots and barley that filled the markets these days. "You do not make me less frightened of you by crowding in upon me like an overgrown bush."

"Of course not. I do it by showing you how harmless I am. Look over there, Citoyenne Maggie." Over there were the four donkey baskets. "That's my stock in trade— Voltaire, Diderot, Rousseau, Lalumière—the approved instruction list from the Committee of Education. Some children's books with proper sentiments in them . . . 'C is for counter-revolutionary. May they all die. *D* is for duty to France. Let us all try.' That sort of thing. I got packs of playing cards. Those have fine revolutionary pictures on them. The single pip is a guillotine, which is just going to liven up a game, ain't it? And I got me some nicely illustrated copies of the Rights of Man, suitable for framing and hanging over the fireplace. You see before you Guillaume LeBreton, seller of fine books."

There was no slight possibility this man traveled with donkeys and sold books for his living. It was nonsense. This was the wolf who claimed he cobbled shoes. He did not fool her for even the tiniest moment. "That is a respectable trade, certainly."

"Bringing revolutionary thought to the provinces. That's

my job. When I see the schoolmasters using the old books full of superstition and lies, I haul them out and burn them. The books, not the schoolmasters. That's my little joke there."

"It is very amusing."

"Then I take orders for the approved books, which they're eager to buy at that point for some reason. With luck, the books are still approved when I get back to Paris."

"Yours is an uncertain life, citoyen."

The fire snapped and shot out sparks. The servant boy went out into the rain and came back with armloads of straw from the stable.

LeBreton shifted, so the light of the fire was strong upon the ruined side of his face. That was deliberate. He was showing her the worst of him so that she would become accustomed. It worked better than it should have. Already she was less afraid of him.

He had been unlovely even before he acquired that scar, a man of blunt eyebrows, emphatic nose, and stern jaw. She decided now that he did not look evil, only hard and filled with grim resolve. He was like one of the stone warriors laid in the vault of an old cathedral, holding the hilt of a stone sword, waiting to be called back into battle at the Apocalypse.

She drank this coffee the sly giant provided. It warmed her. The rainy dusk, beyond the sad, broken windows, seemed brighter. She raised her knees to balance the cup upon and blew on the surface to cool it and made herself take it delicately, in little sips.

They had brought a china cup to her so she would have something civilized to drink her coffee from. It was a small, astute kindness that impressed her deeply. She was seated beside a most perceptive intelligence.

"You'd want tea," he said. "You being from Scotland."

"I do not much care for tea. I have never seen Scotland

myself. It was my grandfather who was born in Aberdeen."
This was the story of her governess, the true Mistress Duncan, who was sandy and freckled and forty years old and married to a staid banker from Arles.

"But you're still Scots."

"One does not stop being a Scot so easily." He was lying. She was lying. They traded prevarications. Perhaps they would become complacent, each of them thinking they made a fool of the other.

He did not know she had learned to lie at Versailles, in the old days, when the king was alive. Lying had been an art, formal and elegant as the minuet. The proper lie, the angle of a bow tied under the hat, a message slipped from one hand to another in a crowded corridor. The air had been dense with intrigue. Uncle Arnault had been at the center of most of it. She was no amateur at reading lies.

She took another sip. The coffee was sweetened with white, clean sugar that dissolved completely. Coffee from Haiti. Sugar from Martinique. These luxuries were expensive in Paris, but far cheaper in the port towns where the ships from the islands unloaded.

LeBreton might have innocently delivered books in Dieppe or Le Havre last week. But perhaps he had visited the small fishing villages of the coast, where the smugglers pulled their boats ashore. Perhaps he was one of the men who carried contraband across France—letters from émigrés in England, foreign newspapers, bank funds, messages from spies. He might even be a spy himself, Royalist, Austrian or English. He might be an agent of the Secret Police in Paris.

He could be part of La Flèche.

The servant boy, having made three pallets of his heaps of straw, was toasting bread by the fire. She sat straight and drank coffee, holding her hands elegantly, as she had been trained to do. She was very hungry.

"We'll eat in a minute," LeBreton said. "Have you stopped being afraid of me yet? I'm hoping for that."

"I am surprisingly tenacious. This is good coffee."

"Better than the wine we have. And we are finally going to feed you, looks like."

The boy brought bread with cheese melted on it, juggling it from hand to hand because it was hot. He sat on his heels and held it out, balanced on his fingertips.

"If you think she has sense enough to eat slow," LeBreton was genial as carded wool, "give it to her. You can clean up when she empties her belly out."

Nothing changed in the boy's dark face. "You feed her, then. She's your pet." He tossed the bread in LeBreton's general direction and walked off.

They should not show her the bread and take it away. She would have clawed the world apart to get to that bread.

"I keep him around because he's so fond of the donkeys." LeBreton picked the bread up and brushed it off. Tore it into parts and laid them along his thigh. He blew on a piece before he handed it over. "Then there's his honesty. You'd look long and hard to find a lad with his kind of honesty. And that amiability of his."

She did not stuff bread into her mouth, snatching like an animal. She ate neatly. With restraint. She had been taught so well to be a lady.

When she was done, he took up another piece, ate half, and gave her the rest. "He didn't think about you needing to eat slow. Now he's annoyed at himself."

"One is sincere at that age, and easily offended." Maybe she burned her mouth. She didn't feel it.

Another morsel broken between them. Bread for her. Bread for him. They might have been friends sitting at the hearth, toasting bread and tearing off hunks to share back and forth. LeBreton kept talking, but she paid him no attention. ". . . with your mind running round and round like a squirrel in a cage. If I was going to do terrible things to you—which, I point out, I ain't got around to yet despite these numerous opportunities—there's not much you could do about it, me being twice as big as you are and strong as an ox. And that's enough for right now." He got up and set the rest of the bread on the upturned planter they were using as a table.

He was right. She was still hungry, but she should not eat more.

"You concentrate on keeping that down, just as a favor to Adrian."

He fed her and pretended to be harmless. He was subtly intelligent. He was a pillar of deception from the long, untidy hair he shook down to hide his face to the worn soles of his boots. Such a man did not wander to her chateau by accident.

Are you one of us? Are you La Flèche?

She offered the most common of all the passwords of La Flèche. "If the wind is right, you can smell roses in the garden."

"Roses? I saw some as we passed by. Pretty."

It was not the right answer. She had not expected to feel so disappointed.

"When you finish that, I'll lay a blanket by the fire and leave you to sleep," he said.

He was right in this much. If she was to escape, she must sleep first. There would be some chance in the night, when he was less attentive.

He took the cup away from her, because it was empty. "Or you can just lie awake, thinking up all the things I might come do to you that I'm not doing now."

THE long dim twilight of July was winding to a close when Doyle finished going over the grounds and got back to the orangerie. A drizzle had been coming down, off and on, for a while. Mostly on. He was damp clean through.

From every side of the garden, he'd been looking back toward the light in the orangerie. He couldn't see the woman sleeping on her pile of straw, but Hawker was there, with his back to the wall, a candle lit beside him, a book in his lap. Alert. Keeping watch. Glancing up at the end of every couple lines, walking a round of the orangerie every ten or fifteen minutes. There was something to be said for recruiting cutthroats from the London rookeries. The King of Thieves, Lazarus, trained his crew well.

When Doyle showed himself outside the windows, Hawker set the book down and came to him. They found an oak tree far enough away that their Frenchwoman wouldn't hear them talking, close enough they had a clear view of her. And they weren't getting actively rained on, which was all to the good.

Maggie was edged close to the wall, rolled in her blanket, curled up tight. She'd lived through men burning the chateau and four days of lurking in the woods. He'd wrung the last strength out of her, scaring her. With food in her stomach and being warm, maybe she'd sleep the whole night.

"Now what?" Hawker spat, accurately, hitting an inch to the side of Doyle's boot. "You bring her in and dry her off and feed her and tuck her in like a lost kitten. She's de Fleurignac's daughter. Right?" He waited for confirmation. "Does she know where her father is?"

"Most likely."

"Fine. Do we ask nicely where the old man is, or do we haul her out and torture her in the small, cool hours before dawn?"

"We let her sleep."

No way to tell whether the boy was disappointed not to have a chance to apply his skill with sharp implements. "And tomorrow?"

"We see if she'll lead us to him. He's probably not in these parts, or he'd have showed up by now."

"So he's in Paris."

"If he is, we'll take her to Paris. We have to go there anyway to drop off the money." The donkey baskets were half full of counterfeit assignats, headed for British Service headquarters in Paris. One more yapping pack of nuisance to deal with.

He'd brought a bundle back, under his arm. He tossed it to the boy. "I found this. What do you read in it?"

Slowly, suspiciously, Hawker unrolled the length of white cloth and turned it over, frowning. "A woman's shift. Blood on the front." It was marked with big, rusty-brown patches. "Some on the back of the shoulder. On the sleeve."

"We have ourselves a goodly selection of blood." It had been a jolt when he caught sight of it, tucked under the bridge, and climbed in to dig it out.

"A night shift. It's hers. Right length. Right shape to cover those apples."

"Is it, now?"

An instant of grin from the boy. "I've got eyes." He sobered, fingering the white-on-white embroidery around the neck. "Besides. This . . ."

He supplied the words. "*Piquer. Broderie.*" Stitching. Embroidery.

"This embroidery. You don't see it. You feel it. And these little pearl buttons. Not fancy. It's . . . quality. It matches her." The boy shook his head impatiently. "The blood's not hers. She's not hurt. Not this much."

"What else? What does your nose tell you? Go ahead."

Hawker held it up and sniffed gingerly. "Blood. Dirt. Some kind of . . . perfume?"

"That blood's a couple days old. Two or three weeks and you wouldn't smell it the same way. The dirt's because I found it rolled up small and hid under a bridge in the garden. That's where she's been sleeping. She left a trail back and forth."

"Under a bridge. Sounds damp." Hawker started to say more. And didn't. He fingered the cloth and sniffed again. "Plants. Dirt. I'd know it's been left outside. That's soap, not perfume."

"Lavender soap."

The boy pulled the cloth flat between his fists, stretched out. "A handprint on the back. Somebody grabbed her when he was bloody."

"And?"

"She got away. Citoyen Bloody Hand got the worst of that meeting, didn't he?" Hawker looked off in the direction of the orangerie. "In the village they say one of the men from Paris got hurt during the fire. A knife slash. She doesn't look the type to knife a man, somehow."

"The best ones don't."

"You think she's in it with her father? Part of the killings?"

"Well, somebody's hunting down young officers and murdering them. It's his list. She could be helping in a loyal, daughterly way. She's got the brains for it." Maggie was quiet in a corner, either sleeping or pretending to. "I wonder if she's got the ruthlessness. I'll go run a few errands. Always something to do when you have a woman to take care of." He tapped the nightdress. "Burn this. Stir the ash. Toss the pearl buttons down the well."

"I'll make it disappear."

"Don't take your eyes off her. Don't let her leave. Don't hurt her. Don't wave a knife in her face and terrify her."

Deep irony. "I'm not the one she's scared of."

A pebble hit her arm. She heard it skip and rattle on the flagstones. She woke immediately. She had not flung herself deeply into sleep, in any case.

She faced a low, whitewashed wall. Above that, broken

windows. She was in the orangerie. She lay on straw, on the floor, wrapped in a rough blanket.

The second small pebble bounced next to her with a clear ping. With it came, "Do not move. They can see you." The words formed themselves in the patting of the rain, a whisper made of water. "If the wind is right, you can smell roses in the garden."

The Crow's messenger. At last.

Beyond the empty windows the bushes and trees were indistinguishable in the gray evening. The voice was almost as muted. Again came, "If the wind is right, you can smell roses in the garden."

The fire made its accustomed small noises. She did not hear the boy servant breathing or turning pages. She turned a cautious inch to look. There was no one within the circle of light of the fire. No one in the open space of the orangerie, anywhere. No one in the shadowed patterns beyond the window.

She gave the reply, softly. "The roses are lovely, but it is forbidden to pick them."

Leaves crackled, as if a body moved on the other side of the wall. "Ah. You are the one, then. You are Finch." It was a child's voice. "I was afraid you'd have the sense to be gone."

"I expected you three days ago. You see the disasters here." Marguerite took hold of the blanket. "I will come—"

"Stay where you are. The two men have stopped under a tree, not so far away. They are watching."

The child was right. LeBreton would have his eye on her. He was not the man to let her just stroll away into the garden.

The whisper came again, with a child's simplicity. "I do not need to see your face, Citoyenne Finch."

The men and women and—yes—the children of La Flèche did not indulge in curiosity. No one could be forced to tell what they took care not to know. "That is wise."

"I am entirely wise. I was watching from the woods when you were captured by that man. Do you want me to help you escape? It should not be impossible. You can travel with us, if you want."

The men who burned the chateau were scouring the countryside for her. She would not lead them to the wagons of the Gypsies. To Crow's family. "Thank you, no."

"As you wish." The shrug was unmistakable in that voice. The boy—surely no one would send a girl child on this errand—said, "I would not like to disengage myself from such a large man, entirely on my own. But Crow says you are wily in the extreme. Doubtless you have a plan."

"Several. I am weaving them even as we speak."

"Then I will deliver my message and go, before it is too dark to find my way through the woods. I am charged to say this— 'Finch, I saw your signal. I can't go back the way I came. Skylark is on the run, with soldiers after him. Dragoons are stopping the wagons of the Rom everywhere west of Rouen, looking for me. It's not safe for me to hold the sparrows. What are your orders?' "

It was worse than she'd dreamed. La Flèche was in disorder all across Normandy. Wren, Skylark, Crow. All unmasked. What was happening in Paris? How many of her friends were already arrested? Or dead?

"Tell Crow this— 'You are on your own, my old friend. I sent Heron away yesterday with the last of my sparrows. There's no one left here. We are all scattered and in flight.' " She rubbed her forehead. "Tell Crow to go north and west, all the way to St. Grue. He knows the roads to the coast better than I do. I can't advise him."

"He will not like this. We do not—"

"There's no choice. Say to him, 'Pass the word every-where. The chain is broken. Everyone is ordered into hiding. Send the sparrows westward as best you can.'"

The sparrows still in Paris—men and women condemned to the guillotine, hiding, struggling to get out of France—would have to wait.

"We cannot—"

"There is no other way. Now listen. We may have very little time." She kept her voice to a bare thread. "At St. Grue, one mile south of the village, there is a shrine at the crossroads. The Lady's face is broken. You will leave three white pebbles there, in a row. Pebbles the size of a baby's fist. Camp in the dunes. Grebe will find you."

Grebe was the last link to the smuggler who carried sparrows across the Channel. If Grebe had been taken, God help them all. "Let me say this again—"

"It is not necessary. My memory is excellent." The brush outside did not quiver, but she felt a sense of readiness behind it. "You have given me a great basket of news to carry. You are sure you will not come with me to the wagons?"

"I am sure."

"Then go with all good luck, Citoyenne Finch. I think we will all need a great deal of luck in these next days."

No sound marked the transition, but she knew she was alone. "Be safe, child."

She rolled over, to keep an eye upon happenings inside the orangerie. Silence gathered around her, with the smallest murmur at the bottom of it, like a cricket deep down in the well. She had lied about one thing. She had no clever plan for disengaging herself from Citoyen LeBreton.

After a time, the boy Adrian returned. She let her lids open, just a crack. She could see him sitting cross-legged next to the fire, his head bent, a book across his lap, his fingers tracing the line of words. He moved his lips when he read.

He limped from some injury. Perhaps she could out-run him.

His eyes shifted. They looked at each other.

He said, "I wouldn't try it."

"As you say." She lay watching smoke coil and uncoil in the upper reaches of the ceiling, piled into shapes by the wind, lit red from below. LeBreton's servant boy went back to reading Lalumière.

She had taken the name of La Flèche from Lalumière . . . where he wrote of the wild geese, rising from the winter marsh, all at once, all of them knowing when they must leave and where they must go, because it was natural for them. They made an arrow in the sky, flying toward safety.

La Flèche. The Arrow.

LeBreton did not come back to the orangerie. He had wandered into the dripping evening to see to some concern of his own.

He looks at my breasts when he thinks I will not notice. After a while she slept.

Five

IT WOULD BE A DIFFICULT DAY, AND IT WAS START-
ing before the sun came up.

Marguerite sat on the edge of the fishpool and pulled
the comb LeBreton had given her—a man's comb, plain
but finely made—through snarls, not being gentle with
herself. It was a relief to accomplish something concrete.
Her braid was heavy between her fingers when she wove it,
twist by twist. Her hair smelled of smoke.

LeBreton came from the orangerie into the enclosed
garden of the fishpond, deliberately making noise to let her
know he was coming.

He carried a coarse towel and a roll of linen clothing. "There's time to wash. The boy's still currying the
beasts."

"I will groom myself while he grooms the donkeys.
There is an inherent symmetry about mornings. Have you
ever noticed?" She took the clothes from him. They smelled
of fresh washing and ironing. "That is a chemise. It is an
odd thing for a man like you to carry about with him."

"I stole it last night from that hut down by the river."

"From the laundry maids." He had made a good guess of her size, had he not? He must have sorted through clean laundry from half the village to find clothing that would fit so well. Guillaume LeBreton was a man of unusual skills. "I think I have become a receiver of questionable goods. Still, I am glad to wear something clean."

"I left a coin." He set the towel on the wide lip of the fish basin. There was more clothing wrapped in it. A clean fichu. An apron. She would wear borrowed linen from the skin out.

He stood, looking formidable. Behind him, dawn curved like a shell. The wide granite pool was white as the moon.

It was cold as the moon when she dipped her hand beneath the surface of the reflection. "Will you tell me what you plan to do with me? I am naturally curious."

"We'll talk about it when we're on the road. I want to get away from here. Soap." LeBreton laid it beside the towels. A metal box of soft and greasy-looking soap. "Probably not what you're used to."

"It is lovely. Thank you."

"Don't get any in the pool."

Fish were poisoned by soap. She liked it that LeBreton knew that, and cared. It is in such small things that men reveal themselves.

Goldfish came and nibbled at her fingers. She had named them all when she was a child. Moses—because he parted the waters—and Blondine and fat, lazy Rousseau. Once the noisy Jacobin riffraff took themselves off, Mayor Leclerc would come from the village with tubs to steal her fish for his own pond. He had coveted them for many years. She hoped he would hurry. They should not be neglected in this fashion.

"I'll leave you to it, then." LeBreton took himself off to the orangerie.

It was dawn, the beginning of a new day. It was not raining upon her. She had eaten good food and drunk good coffee. She had succeeded in sending a message to Crow. Her fish would go to a good home. She was filled with a mood of optimism.

On the other side of the wall, in the orangerie, she could hear LeBreton sweeping glass back into place across the floor where it would look natural and well scattered. The ashes of their fire had been tidied away, the straw thrown into the stable. There would be no sign that anyone had spent the night here.

The ties of her skirt had tangled into hard knots. She made herself patient, picking and tugging till the strings were free and her skirt fell to the flagstones. Her stays were already loosened to sleep in. She tugged them looser still and pulled them over her head. She slipped the shift from her shoulders and let it fall.

She wore nothing at all. It was strange to be unclothed under the open sky.

Her reflection looked up at her from the fish basin, more pale than the sky, rippling in the circles that spread where fish came to lip at the surface. The rim of the basin was gritty under her buttocks, with little puddles in every unevenness. The wind of the new day scraped her skin like a dull knife. She put her feet in the water. The slippery film of mud at the bottom of the pool crept up between her toes. Cold. Immeasurably cold.

Quickly, before she lost her courage, she wet half the towel, rubbed water down her arms, over her breasts and her stomach, hissing every breath in and out. Then up and down her thighs. She washed every scratch, every cut. There was not one of them without a sting. It was not helpful to remind herself that she was the descendent of warriors.

Moses and Rousseau and the other great rulers of the

pool held themselves aloof, but many small fish came to nibble at her calves and ankles and the knuckles of her hands with little bites, like kittens.

Citoyen Giant Bear spoke to his servant in a distant grumble.

Enough. Enough. She was done. She pulled her legs from the water. Naked, except for an extensive covering of goose bumps, she stepped into her sabots. The chemise Citoyen LeBreton had stolen was clean but old. It had been mended unskillfully. She shook it out, becoming acquainted with its many faults and limitations.

There was no warning.

LeBreton was upon her. He slammed into her and carried her with him in a great angry rush, backward, against the wall of the garden. His hand covered her nose, her mouth, and she could not breathe.

Six

HE WAS HUGE AND DARK AND SUDDEN AS A LAND-
slide. His arms closed around her, trapping her against his
chest. The stone wall jabbed her back. His hand filled her
mouth with leathery, unyielding force. She couldn't twist
away from it.

She bit down with all her strength. No reaction. Nothing could have told her so clearly that her struggles were
unimportant.

At her ear, he breathed, "Listen."

A faint, rhythmic tapping.

She stopped biting. At once, he spread his fingers so she
could breathe. The beat of blood slowed in her ears. Now
she heard it clearly. Horses walked the front drive, slowly
approaching. Two or three horses. Someone was coming.

She nodded against the hold on her mouth, and Le-
Breton loosened the grip. They both looked toward the
grilled door in the garden wall. Through that she could
see a narrow slice of courtyard. Pale gravel, scattered with
debris, stretched to the ruins of the chateau.

The village of Voisemont had become achingly poor since the Revolution. The army had come three times to requisition horses in return for worthless paper. The horses that were left plowed fields and drew wagons. Even the mayor did not ride out for pleasure these days. Who would come to the chateau at first dawn?

A scramble and scratching slipped over the wall behind them. Adrian landed beside her, softly, on bare feet. Shockingly, he came with a knife between his teeth. Then it was in his hand, held low, at his side, flat to his waistcoat. He was totally silent.

"Lead the donkeys out." LeBreton's lips shaped the words, almost without sound. "Green stuff on top. You're gathering herbs for your grandmother. Go. And hide that damned knife."

Not even a nod. The boy fitted toes into the wall and was up and over in an instant. Noiseless.

Voices pricked the surface of the silence. Paris voices, out of place against a background of country birds and crickets. They were close. LeBreton said, "Don't move."

He had done this before. He'd hidden from men hunting him. She stayed still.

He drew his coat around her. Pulled her to him and wrapped her deep in it. LeBreton was earth brown. His hat, his clothing, even his skin were the dun and buff of the trees around them and the wall at her back. He would be invisible in this corner of garden among the disorderly branches of the pear tree. And she was hidden by him. Surrounded by him.

She took fistfuls of his shirt. Pressed close. The warm cloth, the sense of his muscles underneath, the tension of his skin, his breath moving in and out, steadied her. The scar on his face was altogether harsh and menacing. But this time, all that menace and power stood between her and whatever was coming up the drive.

He settled his coat one last careful time around her and opened it a slit to let her see out. The iron grille that was the gate of this garden showed a narrow slice of courtyard.

He listened as if he were sorting a hundred sounds apart, assigning meaning to each one. He was still, the way an animal is, in the woods, when a man walks by.

They waited. One cannot stop breathing. She did it in shallow, slow breaths, very quietly.

Soft thuds and then crisp, loud scrunchings came, marking a transition from dirt paths to gravel. Adrian came out of the kitchen garden and slouched into their line of vision, leading the donkeys on the full length of rein. They were transformed, those donkeys. He'd piled the panniers and the backs of the donkeys high with great heaps of green herbage. Basil. Lavender. Rosemary. Sage. On top he'd tied bundles of long hazel poles, the ones the gardeners cut and peeled to make bean towers.

The animals disappeared beneath the load. He'd smeared dirt on their necks and legs. They were the meanest of village donkeys now, muddy, unkempt beasts kept by the lowest farm tenants. Adrian had become slovenly as well. The cheeky defiance was gone from him. Slumped, dull, placid, moving at a snail's pace, he strolled through their sight.

LeBreton set his hand on her bare shoulder, a tight, warning touch. He must have known what was coming next.

"You! You there. Halt." The harsh Parisian accent came at a distance. Hooves speeded up. "Come here."

Adrian had dallied in the courtyard in a lackadaisical way. The riders had seen him and the donkeys. He was caught.

"Who are you, boy?"

I know that voice. Edged like a razor, carrying with it the slums of the Faubourg Saint-Antoine to the east of

Paris. This was the man who'd broken into her room the night the chateau burned. The man she'd fought. The one who'd come to kill her.

"You have no business here. What are you doing?" The clop of hooves. She could see nothing, but she could hear the breath of the horses. "Explain yourself."

LeBreton's muscles registered no surprise. He'd sent the servant boy to play out this scene in the courtyard. Exactly this.

"Looting is forbidden."

The Jacobin had screamed when she slashed his face. He'd shrieked loudly enough to be heard by the mob on the lawn. His blood spilled over her hands. Covered the letter opener she held like a knife. When she fought to get away the night candle fell from the desk. Her papers caught fire. The curtains went up in flames.

He'd survived. Hidden in the dark, in the damp niche under the bridge, shaking and sticky with blood, she'd heard him howl her name.

"We will not tolerate a plague of scavengers, stealing from the people."

Crouched like an animal in her hiding place, she'd watched that man stalk through the mad carouse of the burning. She'd seen him, his head dressed in a rough bandage, going through the crowd, grabbing women to search their faces, rolling drunken couples on their backs to get a good look, yelling, "Where's the de Fleurignac bitch? She has to be here somewhere. Find her."

The servant boy whined. He had done nothing. Nothing. The people could have the greens. He didn't want them. Here. Take them. His *grand-mère* would find other herbs for her stew. Nobody told him he couldn't—

The outraged squawk said Adrian had been booted to the ground. The men snickered. That was the sport they brought out of Paris these days, bullying a farm boy.

LeBreton closed his hand on her. *Quiet. Quiet.*

Adrian had a widowed mother. His *grand-mère* was aged. She had no teeth.

"God rot your grandmother."

The boy hurriedly mentioned more destitute relatives.

The Jacobin said, "They are a plague upon us. If we tolerate vermin like this, they will strip France bare."

Adrian would give everything back. All of it. They were only herbs from the garden. He was not a plague. Please.

"Better to hang a dozen now as an example."

"He's a boy." That was the other voice. Slower, deeper, better-natured. She had seen this man as well, that night, wandering his way through the rioting, wine bottle in hand, annoying the young women. A long pole of a man with the loose jowls of a hunting dog.

"Boys his age are fighting for France. No, I don't want a load of damn weeds. What do I—" The squeal of a horse. *"Fils de salope.* It bit me!"

One of the donkeys had helped itself to a chunk of Jacobin.

A barked obscenity. Horses stamped. Gravel scattered. Adrian let loose a dozen panicked apologies, fitting them between snarls and gutter oaths from the men.

I wish I could see.

From the sound of it, the Jacobins had their hands full, keeping their horses under control. They were city men. Not used to riding.

"Get those stinking asses out of here. Out! Get out. *Allez!"*

Reins jangled. Hooves scraped iron on stone. A donkey brayed. Paris accents cursed the horses. Adrian hurried past the grilled gate, limping and bent over, being a hapless country lad. Lying with every inch of his body. The donkeys were in on it, too. They nosed along after him, heads hanging, mistreated and down-trodden. It was not altogether her imagination that they looked pleased with themselves.

Quiet. LeBreton said it through his hands, pressing the message into her skin.

The Jacobins trotted by. One man, then the other, then a horse on a lead, loaded high with bags and bundles of loot from the chateau.

They'd confiscated themselves better horseflesh than they could manage. The man in front, heavily bandaged, jerked the reins, making no impression on the mare. The other Jacobin, pale-skinned and pockmarked, followed, clinging to the mane of his horse, riding like a sack of potatoes.

They did not glance into the goldfish garden. They jogged through her sight and away.

She had learned stillness at Versailles, in the hardest school on earth. One does not fidget in the presence of a king. Hungry, thirsty, exhausted, with pins sticking into one's bodice, with feet that ached, hour after hour, one does not wriggle. Those first weeks at Versailles, Uncle Arnault stood behind her and pinched her every time she blinked.

The thud of hooves turned dull on the grass beyond the terrace. The path in the front took up the noise. Long minutes later, three horses, not matching steps, took the road that led toward Paris. A busy, rustling wind blew by and scattered the sound of the last hoofbeats.

Time lengthened. She closed her eyes and released the breath she was somehow holding and let herself relax against Guillaume LeBreton. Her cheek comprehended the folds of his shirt. A noisy little piece of her mind insisted on figuring out each line, each seam, but she ignored it. She let herself stop thinking.

Her lips were open and rested upon him. His waistcoat had a dark, pungent taste, like rye bread. In the space between them, she breathed back her own warm breath mixed with his. He was leather, and wood smoke, and a smell like morning, green and alive.

Complicated textures of his clothing pressed against her everywhere. Compelling. Overwhelming. She felt each distinct, hard button he wore and the smooth fabric of his trousers. She was naked, so she felt this with great exactness.

He was hugely erect. The hardness grew and stirred against her.

He desires me.

The moment fell between them like a ripe fruit. She felt a shock in him that mirrored the shock inside of her. He had not planned this. She had not imagined this.

She was naked, after all. She was plastered against him. It was not amazing that a man should notice.

He was not the first man to push her against a wall and shove his interest in her direction. Versailles had been a viper pit. Men with power believed they could take anything they wanted. Many of them had wanted a fifteen-year-old girl. She had avoided dark corridors.

If she pushed him away, he would let go. His hands were ready to open and set her free. Whatever else she believed, she knew this. He wanted her very much and he would let her go.

The hard, hot, animal insistence against her belly filled the center of her mind. A curious silence took possession of her. The busy niggling of thought faded away. There was only feeling. What had been fear transformed to an explicit, earthy wanting. She tightened and throbbed. A heady sweetness invaded.

LeBreton's chest rose and fell in deep, even strokes. The little motion of his breathing was a caress to her skin. The calloused palm he held on her neck slid downward. When his hand got to her bottom, he brought her an inch closer. Pressed her to him.

He waited to see what her answer would be.

She wanted this. It would be so easy, so natural, to take this pleasure. To let her body answer his. There was no one on earth to stop her.

Except herself. Except herself.

She said, "I wish . . ." *I wish I could lie with you. I am afraid and alone and I would be comforted by you.* She picked one drop out of the sea of what she wished and put it into words. "I wish I were the miller's daughter and you were the farmer's son and we could play foolish games in the stable loft. I wish you were someone I could . . ."

"Be foolish with."

"Yes." She sighed. "But I am not the miller's daughter. I have never owned such simplicity. I do not live one minute without calculation."

"Pretend I'm someone you can kiss." His lips came down softly over hers. Holding back, brushing lightly. Hinting. The taste, the possibility, was enough to hold her while he retraced the path up her backbone and slipped the calluses and strength of his hand under her wet braid and enclosed the nape of her neck.

He muttered, "We're both going to stop calculating for a minute."

He kissed across her mouth, slowly and deliberately, as if this were exotic territory and he was exploring. As if this were the first time he'd ever kissed a woman and he was getting surprised.

The whole length of his body was persuasive against her. His cock, hard in his trousers, throbbed at the cradle of her belly. His hand on her was heavy as his strength. Light as if it were part of her. He stroked with the tips of his fingers, making circles on her skin like whirlpools in a stream of moving water.

He slipped the kiss into her mouth. Kissed rows of exploration, back and forth. Wrestled a new hold on the corner of her lip. She felt herself pulled gently into his mouth. Licked. Tasted.

"Oh, my," he whispered. "My God."

She kissed him back. She felt him fighting his reaction to her. She had this much power over him. He twitched, as if shocked, when her tongue ran across his tongue.

She closed her teeth gently over his lips, capturing him for an instant. His instant of surrender overwhelmed her. They captured each other, teeth, lips, tongue, back and forth.

"You are . . . I don't know what you are." He growled it in the deep of his throat.

She unraveled. A curious liquidity, warm and quivering, spread from her belly. She pulsed inside her skin.

One of the goldfish giants of the pond surfaced and fell back with a slap of the water.

He froze. His arms tightened around her. It was as if the corners of the earth folded inward. "They could come back, any minute. Anybody could come walking by. And I've left that damn boy free to plunder France. You make me stupid."

"We make each other stupid." She resented him. She was also annoyed at her own body.

He pushed away from her. "Put your clothes on. We have to leave." Before he stomped off, he said, "We'll talk later."

Seven

DOYLE DIDN'T MIND THE HEAT HIMSELF, AND GOD
knew he didn't plan to pamper the boy, but he hated to
walk a woman through this mud.

The sky burned empty and pale blue. They went single
file across a landscape of hedgerow and long fields. First
him with Maggie, then Hawker and the animals. The boy
had fallen back a ways owing to the number and quality
of his ongoing discussions with the donkeys. Hawker was
practicing what was beginning to be an extensive vocabulary of obscenity. He hitched his trousers up with a jerk and
swaggered the way the mule boys did, enjoying himself,
playing the Game as natural as breathing.

Maggie pushed the pace. Being determined about it. A
woman with somewhere to go and something to do.

They were following the track that led to the Paris road.
Maybe she was just getting well away from Voisemont and
the people who knew her. But he thought she had herself
a destination. It might be she was leading him straight to
de Fleurignac.

The old man made the list. He knew who was slated to die. *I find him. I take the list. And I do not get myself tangled up with his daughter.*

Maggie lifted her face to the little wind that had come up and stood, eyes closed, drinking it in. She was dusty and sweaty. There was a smear of mud across her cheek. Her clothes were kitchen and cowshed wear. All that, and anyone with eyes could see what she was. Aristo.

Elegant as crystal. I keep thinking she'll break, and she doesn't.

You get to know somebody pretty well, slogging through French mud with them. Maggie was gold and grit. She set her clogs on the ruts and rocks with grim deliberation. He could have pointed her in the direction of China and she'd keep on going, one step after another, till she saw pagodas.

I don't want to like de Fleurignac's daughter. I don't want to admire her.

He wasn't sorry for what he'd do to her father. But he'd regret hurting her, if he had to.

Mistress Maggie scraped mud off her clogs on an upright rock, being a woman with a liking for lost causes, obviously. Strands of dark brown hair stuck to her forehead and her cheeks. Her clothes stuck, too, holding to the curves of her body. The tops of her breasts were stippled with little beads of sweat. Once in a while a couple of those drops got close and made friends and ran away together down the valley between her tits.

She'd be salty if he started licking her. Salty and sweet and musky. She'd taste like Maggie—like this particular woman out of all the world—with a sprinkling of dirt. There wasn't a square inch of her he didn't want to go over with his tongue.

If I hadn't tasted her, I wouldn't know. I wouldn't be thinking about it. Serves me right.

They were avoiding the main road. This cart track led to the Rouen highway, if you cut through the fields.

Keep on straight and it eventually wound toward the Paris road. They hadn't met anyone in four miles but a bashful girl with a pair of cows—the cows didn't take kindly to donkeys—and a dung cart drawn by a horse so old even the army wouldn't steal it.

Pear orchards stretched across the hilltops, rows of trees with a few brown cows grazing under them. Dun-colored fields, dotted with haystacks, alternated with the green and yellow-green waves of uncut hay. They'd cut that as soon as they had two dry days in a row.

The wheat was doing well. They'd get twenty bushels an acre in August and everybody would eat.

If the fighting in the Vendée didn't spill over into Normandy . . . If the weather cooperated . . . If they could harvest it with half the men marched off to the army.

Weedy footpaths ran between fields, up over the horizon and out of sight. Off to the west he could make out the steeple of a church. They walked the long downward slope toward a thin pinewood. It would be cooler there, out of the sun.

Behind him, Maggie hit a soft spot in the road, gave a little grunt, pulled her sabot out with a suck and a squelch, and started again. He could feel her eyes boring a hole into his back. Thinking and thinking.

He shouldn't have kissed her. *I don't chase bobtail when I'm on the job. A thousand times I've told some idiot, "Keep it in yer breeches when you're working." Now I'm the idiot.*

When he'd run away from home the first time, he'd been, what? Thirteen? He'd hid out in the rookeries and docks of London, doing heavy labor. Even that young, he'd been tall as a grown man. That intrigued women. He'd had offers enough he could have slept in a different bed every night.

Being a shy lad, he'd turned them down. Mostly.

Five years later, he'd made the rounds of the Polite World. Turned out the minor son of a major earl got the same offers. It was cleaner women, but the same hot greed.

The same curiosity to see if his cock measured up to the rest of him. Some just wanted a toss. Some of them, God help the fools, thought they could marry into the Markham family that way.

He was already working for the British Service then. He had access to levels of society most agents couldn't touch. Sometimes that meant he bedded women who played spy games for France. Women with soft bodies and skilled little hands who asked about his father's work at the War Ministry.

Copulation got to be a weary exercise when you didn't like your partner. He'd lost his taste for casual encounters. *I don't poke my staff into every woman who wanders by.*

But Lord, he wanted Maggie. He wanted to run his hands over every inch of her skin. Wanted his mouth on her. He wanted to slurp her down, like she was milk and he was a starving cat.

The squelch and shuffle stopped. When he looked back, Maggie was bent over, panting, her hands braced on her knees.

Hell. "We're far enough from the chateau. We'll rest down there." A thin rippling of water gleamed fifty yards ahead. Trees and bushes grew up around a stream. It'd be private, but with a view of the road in both directions. A good spot.

She shook her head. "I can go farther."

Right. "The donkeys can't. They need water."

"Oh." She straightened, wiping sweat off her upper lip. "Of course. Yes."

He wasn't worried about the donkeys. It takes dedication and ingenuity to kill a donkey, though Hawker was giving it a try. Any fool can founder a high-bred mare. A good horse will run her heart out and die under you.

That was Maggie. She'd keep on till she fell in her tracks.

She plodded onward, doing the last fifty yards, scrubbing

her hand, open-fingered, on her sleeve. She just absolutely did not like being dirty. "Walking this road is different from traveling by coach. I had known this, of course, in my mind." She sighed. "Now I know with my feet."

"Nothing like experience."

"There is no substitute for it, I believe. One can live too deeply in books. They are deceptive."

"I'd agree with that." What he wanted to do was start with her forehead and lick the frown off. Kiss her eyelids. Then he'd just wander down to her mouth. He could take an hour on her face, touring from place to place. She'd be wild for him before he got done with her ears.

Except he wasn't going to do anything on that agenda. He was just going to imagine it. In detail.

Maggie touched from tree trunk to tree trunk on her way down the steep of the road to the water. "I have traveled this countryside all my life," she said. "I will now carry it in the creases of my skin. This is a different way to know it, and more thorough."

The stream looked clean enough. "The boy can water the beasts. You can cool off. Wash some, if you want."

"I would like that."

Go ahead. Splash water all over you. Get your clothes wet all down you till you got no secrets at all. Let's drive the man completely out of his head.

"I will go slightly upstream," she said, "to avoid the donkeys. I am as fond of donkeys as anyone, but—I will be utterly candid—they attempt to bite me. It is the heat, I believe, that makes them irritable."

"They always do that. Remarkably even temperament in those animals."

"Doubtless. But I would argue that discomfort brings out in them a special avidity for human flesh. Hercules was sent to steal the mares of Diomedes that ate human flesh. Did you know that?"

"I'll keep it in mind if anyone tries to sell me one."

She knelt by the water. The stream was shallow and only a few feet wide, running over flat rocks, cooling the air. Gracefully, she reached up and stripped her fichu off her shoulders, unwinding it from her in a circle, uncovering white, white skin. The sun percolated through the trees to land in coin shapes all over her. She was lit up in speckled drops that slid over her neck and across the bones of her shoulders. They played peekaboo up and down the mounds of her tits. A man without his splendid self-control would have noticed she showed right down to the nipple when she leaned over.

She wet the end of the fichu in the stream and washed her face. Hawker arrived, gave one absolutely casual glance in their direction, and took the animals way off downstream to drink.

"The road'll be dry this afternoon. We'll have easier going." Doyle chose a flat gray boulder and settled down to see what else Maggie would do. Still lots of clothing on this woman.

He'd pulled his jacket off an hour ago and slung it over Dulce's back. He was walking around with his shirt open halfway down his chest. That was a fine poetical look for some men. Not him. He had too much unpoetic muscle. He was hairy, too. Even when he wasn't wearing his scar, there was nothing handsome about him. His father called him "that hairy bog jumper." They didn't get along, he and his father.

No jacket meant he wasn't carrying anything but the six-inch sticker in his waistcoat and a throwing knife in his boot. He felt a little underdressed. But he had a long view down the road. It was quiet. Only a few frogs spoke up, creaking back in the woods. He'd hear horses before they topped the rise. He'd have time to get Maggie into cover behind those bushes over there.

She made breathy sighing sounds when she washed.

Damn, but that was enticing. A man imagined her sounding like that while he did inventive things.

He was going to stop imagining.

She dribbled water here and there, which was something he could watch her do indefinitely. After a while, she sat back on her heels, pressing wet cloth to the back of her neck, and looked at him straight. Assessing. Deciding. "I am not certain where we stand. Am I your prisoner?"

"God, no." He got it out fast. He even managed to sound offended. "Walk off if you want to." He waved at the road uphill. "Go ahead. I'm not stopping you."

"I had received a different impression, somehow." But she didn't get up to leave. They'd got past the point where he had to chase her down and tackle her. Obviously his sterling character was winning her trust.

He let himself sound petulant. "I thought I was doing you a favor, taking you with me. Those Jacobins from Paris are ahead somewhere. I figured you didn't want to meet them alone."

She mulled that over a while. "I wish to avoid them."

"I don't like to deal with officials myself. Not these days. Not the bloodthirsty crew that's ruling Paris."

She held the wet cloth to her face. When she lowered it, her eyes were sober. "I do not trust them to deal fairly with one of de Fleurignac's servants. Especially one who is a foreigner." The words were lies. The fear underneath was real. "Thank you for hiding me from them."

"I was getting out of sight myself. You just got the benefit of it. You have somewhere to go?"

"I have friends. Not so far. I will go to them."

He scratched his chin. It wasn't easy to keep the right sort of stubble on his chin. It took careful shaving to look this unkempt. "What was in my mind . . . I thought I'd keep an eye on you, as long as we're walking in the same direction. There's bad men on the roads. Worse than me."

"It is possible," she agreed, dryly.

"In these towns, in every direction, they've heard about the burning in Voisemont. Everybody you pass is going to be watching for aristos escaped from the chateau. You won't look like an aristo if you're with me." He gestured, taking in Guillaume LeBreton in all his glory. "Nobody would. And nobody bothers a woman traveling with a man my size."

A damselfly went flitting over the tall weeds by the water, blue as a sapphire, bright as a jewel flying. Maggie knelt motionless on the moss by the side of the stream, watching it hover. After a while, she said, "I do not see why you would—"

"Fifty livres."

"What?"

"Fifty livres and I see you to your friend's house. To the doorstep." Nothing like asking for money to make a man look honest. Nobody trusted altruism. He stood up, doing it slowly, making sure he looked harmless, and went over to watch water running over the rocks. The damselfly got bored and flew away.

"I don't have fifty livres with me." A flicker of amusement crossed her face. "I don't have fifty sous."

"Then I'll have to trust you for the money, won't I?"

Ah, but she was tempted. One push, and she'd do it. He got down next to her on his haunches. Looked her in the eye. "You'll do some trusting of your own. You're afraid of me."

Tension buzzed like a swarm of wasps. She didn't look away. "I am frugal with trust. You will find this natural, considering the men I have met lately."

Damn, but I like you. "Does it help if I apologize? I shouldn't have touched you the way I did. I shouldn't have kissed you."

"It is not important. What happened between us was a . . . a nothing. It was the most insignificant of kisses."

"Was it now?"

"I became involved in it. For one moment only." She looked down in her lap, to where she was twisting up the linen of the fichu. She had a little blush on her, just across the top of her cheeks. "It was a small mistake."

"I'm glad to know you feel that way."

"You are pleased to be ironic. But, in truth, it was not your fault. You were under great temptation. I do not boast when I say that. I was naked, after all, and you are a man."

"Last time I took an inventory. Yes. You want me to promise it won't happen again?"

The taut line of her shoulders loosened a fraction. "It will not. Neither of us wants that. It was surprise between us, as much as anything else. There was a suddenness."

It wasn't surprise. It was damn good lust. Don't fool yourself. "I don't make a habit of assaulting women. If you were safe last night, you're safe today. You can put yourself in my hands for a few miles of road."

"That is logical. We are rational people, we two." She smoothed the wrinkles out of her damp fichu and pulled it over her shoulders, then wrapped it across her breasts. She made a crease here and there and it lay down smooth and perfect. "If you are willing to come with me on the road, I will thank you very much. I will also pay you. I've been cowardly, seeing a threat where none existed."

"Always glad to turn an honest profit. You'll need papers. I'll write some up." *I get to name her. Something pretty . . . No. Something that will annoy her. That's better.* "I got what I need in the baskets. We'll let them dry on the rock here."

"You are a forger." She smiled at him. "That is a handy skill."

Her smile was like being stroked, right on his privates. All that sensible talk, and his cock was still stupid as a barn owl.

Eight

AN HOUR ONWARD, THEY CROSSED THE CREST OF
a hill. Marguerite looked into the countryside beyond.
Gypsies had stopped by the road in the straggly trees that
marked a trickle of stream between two fields. Three wagons with canvas tops made a rough triangle surrounding
a small campfire. In the fields above, women and girls
picked blackberries in the bushes that fingered away from
the stream, their skirts and scarves vivid as poppies.

She wiped sweat off her face. This was Crow's family.
His *kumpania*.

She'd recruited Shandor—called the Crow—into La
Flèche years ago, almost at the beginning. He was head-
man of a large group, a practical man, cautious to a fault,
shrewd in keeping his people inconspicuous and safe. He
was endlessly protective of the sparrows he carried.

Today he was not following orders.

Guillaume LeBreton, walking beside her, pushed one
finger on the brim of his hat, tilting it so the men down
below would see his face. Now they wouldn't be surprised

by the scar when he came closer. He didn't slow down, approaching the Gypsies. He didn't hurry himself either. Everyone on both sides was given ample opportunity to assess and study each other to their heart's content.

Shandor had chosen a private spot to lie in wait for her. No farmhouse overlooked them. The road that led off to Paris was a mile ahead, out of sight. How she was going to discuss the business of La Flèche when she was encumbered by Citoyen LeBreton and his inquisitive hobgoblin of a servant, she did not know.

"We come upon the Children of the Road. The Egyptians. Engaged in harmless pursuits." LeBreton had hidden himself behind the facade of the big, good-natured countryman. His eyes, however, were hard and calculating. "Or not so harmless. There is something just one hair out of place about this. They're nervous. Look at the men lounging around beside that wagon. That's the one I'd search first, if I was wearing a uniform."

It was as well he was not a gendarme. She would not wish to transport sparrows past a man as discerning as Guillaume LeBreton.

So she spoke with great lightness. "They have stopped to pick blackberries. Perhaps hazelnuts, too, though it is early for that, even in a very hot year, which this has been. There are profusions of berries, anyway."

"Here, and in every hedgerow between Paris and Dieppe. They didn't unhitch the wagons to pick blackberries."

"You are a very suspicious man."

Men and boys came forward to put themselves casually between approaching strangers and the wagons. Shandor stood at the front of his men. He wore a blue vest and a red neckcloth. On every cap and hat was the red, blue, and white circlet of ribbons, the cockade of the Revolution, showing what good republicans they were.

LeBreton scratched the stubble upon his chin. She was

coming to recognize that as the accompaniment of his deeper cogitations. He spoke softly, as if to himself. "What it might be . . . Might be there's some damn thing ahead on the road and they know about it."

"There is always something unpleasant ahead on the roads these days."

Shandor knew she would come this way. He had disobeyed and stayed to talk to her, even at risk to his own people.

He was Crow. He had saved the lives of numberless men and women in the last five years. Of course he would try to save her.

As they approached the camp, the half-grown children stopped talking and edged together. The boys wore hats, like their fathers. The little girls were in blazing bright skirts and blouses, with four or five braids lost in the wildness of loose, frizzy hair. An old woman, tanned to mahogany, sat on the step of a wagon, carving with a small, bright knife.

"They're Kalderash," LeBreton said. "Coppersmiths. See the pots hung on the wagons? They make those."

She knew that. They also sharpened shovels and knives and axes. That was why Shandor's family was intact and unmolested, five years into the Revolution. His *kumpania* was known on all the roads out of Paris. Armies passed, and Shandor's people whirred away, grinding knives and sharpening bayonets. Soldiers of the Revolution lined up to take their turn. And in the wagons, under blankets, silent, the sparrows hid.

LeBreton made a sign with his hand, talking to Adrian. She would not have caught this if she had not seen him do it before. The boy twitched a stick at the donkeys' heels and followed closer.

"Maybe we'll get our fortune told," LeBreton said.

They walked into the midst of the camp. Dogs came to

sniff. Decorum tried to kick the dogs, who proved to be agile. LeBreton walked past a dozen men to stop in front of Shandor.

LeBreton said, "*Sastipe*. And good morning to you. Hot as the hinges of hell, ain't it?" He added another dozen words in what must be Romany and waited. He did not quite whistle and twiddle his fingers, but he had a great air of relaxed confidence.

Men answered him in Romany and French. Everyone agreed it was hot. Yes. Hot as the forge of the demons. Yes, it was good to stop in the shade for an hour.

She should not be surprised that LeBreton could speak a few words of their language. He was a reprobate of six or seven kinds and had doubtless led an interesting life.

The ancient grandam put her knife away and climbed down from the wagon. She hobbled to the front, acting like a force to be reckoned with. LeBreton took out a pouch of tobacco from Dulce's pack, jiggled it open, and offered it round, starting with the old woman. Adrian went off to the stream with the donkeys. In a minute he attracted a dozen half-grown boys. With his ragged clothing and dark hair, he disappeared among them. It would be one of those grubby boys who had brought her Crow's message last night.

Dulce nosed somebody into the water.

Shandor and LeBreton finished the serious business of agreeing that, yes, it's a hot day, and moved on to, those donkeys are bad-tempered devils. But so beautiful. Perhaps Shandor would take the pair in trade for a good horse or two.

Everyone laughed. Shandor sent a small boy running for his pipe and took tobacco with a liberal hand. He and LeBreton lit up from the same burning straw, passing it back and forth. They ignored her because this was the affair of men, after all, this discussing of the weather and donkeys and horses and the pleasure of smoking.

LeBreton was all that was placid and friendly. She did not trust him in this mood. Well, she did not trust him in any mood.

She tucked her apron in her waistband and knelt on one knee on the ground and was immediately surrounded by a crowd of children. Dark-eyed boys. One girl with her little sister on her hip, half as big as she was. A pair of babies, barely tottering on their feet. A pert flower of a child, six or seven, with gold bangles on her arms and rings in her ears.

They were delightful, both shy and bold. They spoke no French, nor any other language they could share with her. They giggled when she pointed at one and the other and tried to repeat their names. They were barefoot, like the children in the peasant cottages, but they seemed healthier. Strong little bodies, full of energy. And happy.

"Marguerite." She patted her chest. And then, "Maggie," because that was what LeBreton called her and she was getting used to it.

She brought this *kumpania* and these children into danger, time and time again. She sent arrogant, ungrateful men to hide in their wagons and eat their food and be impolite to their mothers and sisters. Even now, sparrows were hiding in these wagons, just a few feet away. Or they were dressed in Gypsy clothes, out there in the fields with the women, picking berries.

I risk these beautiful children to save out-of-favor politicians and the Marquise of This-and-That. It was no laughable thing to make these choices.

Shandor puffed on his pipe. "We were delayed at Vaucresson for a while. A rough road. Keeping a little to the south, though . . ."

LeBreton answered in turn. All offhanded. All as if they were talking only about washed-out roads and mud, not patrols of gendarmes. "I've heard Bois d'Arcy has bad roads, too. Just rumor."

A nod. A dozen words about crossing the Seine at Saint-Cloud. Ten words to say the Versailles road was full of troops and a prudent man would let his path wind elsewhere, however long it took. This was Crow giving her what help he could by helping LeBreton.

". . . but today should be a lucky day." Shandor drew in smoke. Exhaled. "I'll tell you what I saw this morning. I saw an egret take off from the field, fast." He swooped a gesture, like wings flapping. "One inch ahead of a pair of foxes. He got away. Flew over my wagon and headed toward Caen. Now that's a sign for you."

Shandor was saying that Egret had been threatened, but escaped. Truly, her network was exposed from Paris to the coast. It was time for her people to run, to take new names, open new waystations. Everyone left in place must be warned.

Children pressed closer. Touching her braid. Fingering the white fichu she wore around her neck. It was of poor quality, but cleaner and more fine than what their mothers wore.

In her pocket, under her skirt, she still carried the length of red string. It would talk for her. She unwound the thread and tied the ends together to make a loop and wove a cat's cradle between her hands.

She slipped it out to catch a little girl's wrist. Giggling, the girl snatched her hand back. The Gypsies made string figures by the fire at night to delight the children. These little ones all knew this game.

She pulled her net on another. Some she trapped. Some were fast as lightning. "You must be very quick to get away." She raised her voice. "You must run, or someone will trap you. See. I go one way. You go the other." That was her answer to Crow. He must leave, and she would not go with him.

She saw him hear the words and understand.

"We have a saying." Shandor was now playing the Wise Gypsy Patriarch. "The sparrows fly away to the west, but the Rom travel the whole world. Who knows where we will go next? Perhaps we will return to Paris. There's work in Paris, even in hard times."

No, Shandor. Not for you. Not anymore.

She wove the thread one last time, in a complicated pattern. A twist . . . and it became a ladder. Another twist . . . it was a net. Another brief, clever magic of woven string and she had a web that danced and changed. Even the men stopped talking to watch.

"And so . . ." She loosed a single loop and opened her hands. Everything dropped away. She held only a limp string. The children made a sound of disappointment. "It is time to stop. Let us do it before the thread breaks and disaster comes. We play out the last game and we walk away and we do not begin again."

That was how she told Crow not to return to Paris. The wagons were too easy to recognize, now that they had been betrayed. Crow's part in La Flèche was done. She would not put these children in danger again. Not to save a hundred sparrows.

Nine

Paris
La Maison de la Pomme d'Or

MADAME LET THE LAST OF THE PAPER BURN TO ASH in the saucer of her coffee cup before she spoke. "His name is William Doyle. He landed in France ten days ago. He is crafty. Knowledgeable. Very dangerous. He has come to put a stop to the assassinations in England."

Madame's sources were beyond reproach. If she said an English spy had come to France, then that was what had happened.

Justine waited silently while Madame poured coffee upon the ashes in the saucer and, with the back of the spoon, patiently destroyed all semblance of writing.

Madame said, "He must enter Paris. But it could be any day and through any gate. He might even circle the city and come from the east."

Music came faintly from the pianoforte in the parlor. It was still full daylight, but men had already come to drink with the girls. They came earlier and earlier every day. There were not many salons in Paris where the wine flowed so freely and the wit was so unfettered. In a brothel men believed their words were not immediately reported to the Secret Police.

They were correct in that, and not correct. Madame decided which indiscretions would be carried to the Secret Police. She was one of its chief agents.

"If William Doyle is so unpunctual, it would be a great waste of time to send me to watch at one of the *barrières*." Justine dared to speak so frankly to Madame. She was young, but she was not the least of Secret Police operatives. "Where shall I wait for him, this English spy?"

"I think . . . at the Hôtel de Fleurignac. De Fleurignac's home. I have a great wish to know who comes and goes from that house. William Doyle will arrive there sooner or later. Here. Take this, please." She held out the saucer.

A pitcher of clean water stood on the sideboard among the liqueurs and good wine. She poured the mess of coffee and ashes into the washbowl and rinsed the dish. She returned, drying the saucer with a soft cloth. Carefully, she set everything in place on the tray. She took it upon herself to anticipate the next request and poured new coffee. "The British are sure of this connection to de Fleurignac? Between the deaths and his visits to England?"

"It is Monsieur Doyle who has done that. He asked many skillful questions concerning the men who were killed and discovered the silly French scholar who studied each of them and filled his notebooks with their histories and spouted such absurd theories. Monsieur Doyle is entirely the best field agent of the British Service. I am gratified when our enemy sends their very best to do our work for us."

She wishes me to understand what she is saying. To show that I am clever. "William Doyle is not to be killed."

"Do not be bloodthirsty, child. There are conventions in these matters. Be glad the British observe the old customs and do not commit slaughter among our own group. In any case, we will let him find de Fleurignac's troublesome list and put a stop to the murders of young men. Perhaps he will even discover which Frenchmen loosed this atrocity upon the world. Then," Madame sipped coffee delicately, "we will see what becomes of William Doyle." She set the cup aside. "You must dress beautifully tonight. Wear the gown with gillyflowers and the blue sash. It becomes you immeasurably."

For an instant . . . a brief instant . . . she was sick and afraid. Because a year ago dressing beautifully had meant she must entertain men, as a whore does. It had meant—

"Child, I did not mean to frighten you." Madame's hand was on her arm, reassuring. "Forgive me for being clumsy. You will not do that. Never anymore. I have promised. We attend the Opéra tonight. Only that. We will go, you and I and Citoyen Soulier. For your birthday."

Joy, uncomplicated joy, filled her. Because she was safe and Madame had remembered the day for her. They would go to the play and laugh and then, perhaps, afterward Soulier would take them to the Boulevard des Italiens for ices.

"Will you buy me cakes? May I bring cakes home for Séverine?" She was impudent. If Madame worried that she had been dismayed by memories of her past, this would smooth the moment between them and make all well again.

"You must ask Soulier to buy sweets. He is the one with bottomless pockets. Now, off with you. I must dress and go downstairs before my women are induced to give themselves away entirely for free. I will send Babette to you to put ribbons and curls in your hair so all the young men will fall in love with you."

Justine went, dancing a little on the steps to the attic, to tell Séverine. It is not every day one becomes thirteen and goes to the playhouse in the company of the chief spies of France. She would wear a wide blue sash and perhaps drink absinthe at the café, if Madame was not attentive. Tomorrow she would watch the Hôtel de Fleurignac. Perhaps next week she would be allowed to kill an English spy.

Oh, but life was good.

Ten

SHE WAS SAFE. BERTILLE'S HOUSE WAS OVER THERE, across the stream. Sanctuary and friendship and a shoulder to cry on. The practicality of money and fresh clothing and help to get to Paris. She could relax.

Marguerite didn't remember the name of this rivulet that wound past Bertille's house, but it was wide enough one had to cross it stepping from flat rock to flat rock. Or one could splash through. The donkeys did not like the idea of splashing through.

"There's leeches." Adrian stood in the middle of the stream, facing the pair. "Big, ugly leeches the size of my thumbs. You keep standing here and they'll sneak up and suck your blood till you turn white." This time, when he pulled the reins, they followed. It was a strange relationship he maintained with the donkeys.

Bertille's snug stone cottage was set between her husband's workshop and the vegetable garden. A rough shed looked down from the hill above. The front of the house was bright with roses and hollyhocks. Brown chickens wandered the brick walkways, occupied with small bugs.

The chickens in the yard told her Bertille was still here. No warning had reached her. She must pack and go into hiding at once.

"That is Bertille's house." She was informative to LeBreton. To Adrian also, if he was listening. "With the cooperage to the side, you see? Where the barrels are stacked. She married a cooper, Alain Rivière. He is a dour and silent man and given to long gaps in any conversation one might hold with him, but Bertille likes him." Bertille had been her nursemaid, then her *femme de chambre*, and, always, her friend.

"You think they have fifty livres?" LeBreton sounded skeptical.

"Oh, yes."

Because Bertille was the Dove, the oldest of old hands in La Flèche, a woman who had made hundreds of journeys, leading sparrows through the dark of the streets of Paris, she would have the pouch of coin everyone in La Flèche was given. Five hundred livres, all in coin. Enough to bribe oneself free, if captured. Enough to pay for an escape, even as far as England.

"I'll be well taken care of by my friends," she said. "And you'll be paid."

Inside the cooperage yard, behind the wooden gates, Alain's big cart stood, its poles pointed up into the air. The cart hauled barrels to the makers of cider and the distillers of calvados brandy for miles around. It also led a secret life of ingenious hidden compartments and counterfeit barrels and false piles of wood. Of long, clandestine journeys to the coast. Ordinary at first glance, extraordinary upon closer inspection. It was a cart not unlike Citoyen LeBreton himself.

LeBreton looked over the house and yard, to the fields beyond. He was, she thought, a man who saw the fly upon every leaf. His face remained placid. "It's quiet."

The air lay heavy, humming faintly. In the late afternoon, no one moved anywhere within sight. The chickens of the dooryard were lackadaisical. No dog barked. Even the cows on the hill were motionless, as if they had been painted there.

Unease tickled under her skin. "Nothing is out of place. I am fond of quiet."

"Not this much quiet." Without making it obvious, he drew a circle with two fingers of his right hand. Adrian stopped talking. "If they're looking out the window, they've seen us. Any reason your friend wouldn't come out giving glad cries of welcome?"

"She is not expecting me, certainly. She might not know me at this distance. I arrive, always, in a carriage. They would wonder—"

"They'll be wondering more if we stand here talking." He made a quick hook with fingers that chopped down. Another signal to Adrian. "Let's go see your friend."

They followed the wall of the cooperage. LeBreton's strides were long and she had to push to keep up. She said, "You are right to be wary. I will go ahead alone. You will wait back there with—"

"No."

She had not yet learned the knack of giving this man orders. He was like a large rock rolling down a steep hill. Once started, difficult to control. "If there is a problem, it makes sense that I—"

"If there's a problem, it's looking out the window right now and it knows I'm here." They passed the workshop gate where the ruts of wheel tracks turned in. "Your friends have a good broad view over the countryside."

It was one of the reasons Alain liked this house. One could see visitors coming.

In the front garden, chickens scattered themselves out of LeBreton's way. The shutters of the house were closed. That was not amazing on such a warm afternoon. But Bertille did not come to the door and fling it open and rush down the path toward her.

She must be putting the baby to bed. That was why everything was quiet. She would come running in a minute, laughing.

LeBreton clumped up the path, scuffling his boots on the stone. Being loud. He banged the door. But only once. It jerked open before his fist landed again.

A soldier in full uniform stood in the doorway. The muzzle of his gun rose. Pointed at LeBreton.

Blue coat, white breeches, white shoulder belts, red cuffs. Garde Nationale. Loyal revolutionaries from Paris. Not a local gendarme.

I have walked us into disaster. Cold washed over her. Fear gripped her breath.

Behind the *garde,* Bertille's cottage was in chaos. Broken dishes, chairs overturned, something—flour—sprayed in plumes on the stone floor with dozens of boot marks. Bertille sat at the dark wood table, her arms tight around Charles, the two-year-old. He sat in her lap, pressing his face into the white of her apron. She was alive. Unhurt.

I have done this to her. I have dragged them all into danger. I did not protect her. Where were Alain and the new baby? There was an apprentice boy. Where was he?

"Ahhh . . ." LeBreton rubbed the back of his neck. His huge, tough body was awkward. His expression, sheepish. He had become the bewildered bumpkin. "You don't want to be doing that, Suzette."

She had taken a step forward, without thinking, to go to Bertille. The gun swung and pointed toward her.

Suzette? That is a ludicrous name.

The *garde* was young and scared, his finger on the trigger. He'd shoot LeBreton if any of them—herself, Bertille, LeBreton—made the smallest mistake.

She must be harmless. "What has happened here? Why do you have guns? You should not bring guns into the house. Have you no manners?" She would chatter and babble like a fool. She would be silly. A soldier might turn his back on a silly woman.

"Now, Suzette." LeBreton was placating.

There were two of them, at least. Bertille was looking at something out of sight, behind the door, letting her eyes show that someone was there.

She jostled the *garde*, knocking the barrel of the musket. *They will think I am a twittering idiot to bump into an armed soldier this way.* "I heard nothing of any fighting near here. Has someone been hurt?"

LeBreton stood upon the doorstep like a frog and did nothing. "That's a gun, love." His voice was perfect stupidity. "You got to move aside and not touch it. You don't want to get yourself shot, just by accident."

"Enough! You." The *garde* grabbed her. "Inside."

While she dithered and sputtered, she was shoved roughly into the room. She hit the table edge hard, clacking her teeth together, biting her tongue. A bowl rolled off the table and fell to the floor and broke.

She was face-to-face with Bertille. Their eyes met. And it was like old times. They had been in danger before, the two of them. They had survived. Always. *She thinks this is like the other times. She expects me to get us free.*

LeBreton lumbered forward, his hands spread and open. "There's no cause to go pushing Suzette. She don't mean no harm."

"Out of my way, ox. Over there."

"I'm coming, citoyen." LeBreton swung his head from

one side of the cottage to the other, taking in the destruction, looking puzzled. Looking like the ox he most certainly was not. "But I don't know what's going on."

The second soldier, a sergeant, had been hidden from sight by the door. He stood with his musket ready. Behind him, in the curtained alcove where the boys slept, Alain lay on the floor. His hands were tied behind his back, his face bloody and swollen. His apprentice, twelve years old, huddled at his side, also bound.

No one had been killed. Bertille had not been despoiled. These were not deserters or bandits. They were professional soldiers, disciplined, following orders. They'd come to make arrests.

This is bad. Bad as it can be.

She leaned over and clutched her belly as if she were in pain from colliding with the table. It hid her face while she thought, frantically. *They know this house is a waystation of La Flèche. They have stayed here to catch the next courier. To trap anyone who comes.* "Why have you hit me?" she whined. "What is happening? Why is that man bloody?"

"Are you hurt, Suzette?" LeBreton looked from one soldier to the other, all puzzlement. "There's no call to do that."

The sergeant snapped, "Your documents." When LeBreton didn't move quickly enough, he was hit sharply with the butt of the gun the way a man prods an animal into motion.

"You want to see my papers?"

"Yes, I want to see your papers. Dolt."

LeBreton unbuttoned his waistcoat, his elbows sticking out awkwardly. His shirt was coarse weave, cut full and loose like the smock of a laborer. He tugged it out, all the way around, being slow and clumsy about it. Next to his skin, he wore a linen money belt with flat pockets.

"Got it in here. Just a minute." He eased out a square of stained, brown leather, tied with twine. "I keep it safe, see. You can't be too careful these days. The roads are full of thieves."

The younger guard was calming down. His finger came off the trigger. The muzzle no longer pointed at LeBreton.

And she had no weapon anywhere. What was here? Wood benches. A table. Two chairs. A cupboard with dishes on the shelves. Pots on the hearth. An empty cradle. Alain had carved the cradle for Charles. Now the new baby used it. The windows were shuttered. Light came through in bright slits. Nothing she could make use of.

LeBreton put the leather packet on the table and picked at a knot in the twine. "We followed the road out of Vachielle, up over that hill there. Now that was a mistake." He picked at the knot, his face screwed up in concentration. "They said this was a shortcut. 'Suzette,' I said—I call her Suzette on account of her name being Suzanne. But I had a cow named Suzanne before I got married, and I couldn't call my wife and the cow the same name, now could I?" He worked away at the packet, his face screwed up in concentration.

"Give me that." The sergeant propped his gun against the table and unwound the twine, muttering to himself.

"I told Suzette, 'It's not much of a shortcut, if you ask me, when you have to go walking all this way uphill.'"

He was clever. But it did not matter what he said or how innocent he appeared, these men had orders to hold anyone who came into this house.

She shook with being afraid. If she stopped to think, she would be clumsy. *There is one gun pointed at us. I will get my hands on the other.*

She began a low, irritating grumble. "This way is shorter if you had not gotten us lost." No one watched her. One does not see annoying women who chatter and scold.

She inched toward the gun the sergeant had leaned against the table.

"That's Boullages ahead, ain't it?" LeBreton's accent had thickened to sludge. "If we keep on this road, we come there?"

"If you do not shut up your mouth, you will go nowhere at all."

The sergeant had the packet open. Papers were laboriously unfolded and spread flat—the passport, a creased sheet with a stamp on it, and a smaller certificate that was nearly new. The sergeant dealt with each cautiously, like a man unused to handling documents.

"Look here. This." LeBreton splayed his hand on the passport. "This is me. You see? Bon . . . i . . . face . . . Jo . . . bard." He picked it out with the pride of the illiterate. "Boniface Jobard. Resident of the Section des Marchés of the Paris Commune. And this one. That's my certificate of civism. Says I'm a good patriot and an active citoyen. My friend Louis Bulliard—"

"Be silent. I can read." The sergeant shoved LeBreton's hand aside and took up the passport and scowled at it. "I am not impressed by papers, citoyen. Bandits and counter-revolutionaries walk the road with impressive papers. I will decide for myself what you are and why you are here."

She edged along the table, as if she wanted to look at the papers also. She was close. She could put herself between the sergeant and his gun. It was one step.

"That's the sign of an honest man, that is. Not trusting papers." LeBreton turned to get confirmation from the other *garde*. Took a step toward him. "I've always said it. There is no truth to be found in papers."

They were well positioned, she and LeBreton. Each within reach of a gun. It was time to act. *We must do this now. Should I wait for his signal, or—*

At the shuttered windows, a shadow crossed the light. A leaf fell, or a bird flew through the path of the sun.

LeBreton, explaining that too much writing was the downfall of liberty, scratched his belly. His fingers bent, stretched, touched one to the other.

I had forgotten Adrian. It is about to happen. Fear crystallized into spears of ice under her skin. *Now.*

The sergeant piled documents one upon the other. "I ask myself, Citoyen Jobard, whether you are a counter-revolutionary or just a very, very stupid traveler. Where are your wife's papers?"

LeBreton took his hat off and held it in front of him. "I—"

I must give no warning.

The shutters crashed open. LeBreton dropped like a stone.

leven

THE SPACE WHERE LEBRETON HAD STOOD WAS empty. LeBreton and the *garde* rolled on the floor.

She had to stop the other man. The sergeant. Keep him from shooting LeBreton.

She hit the barrel of the musket with both hands clenched together. It fell, clattering and clattering. The *garde* grabbed after it. She kicked the gun away. It slid two feet, hit the table leg, and exploded. The noise smashed the air like a fist. The shot hit the wall, spewing plaster.

Charles screamed and struggled in Bertille's arms. In the other room, the baby began to cry. Bertille scrambled away from the table, taking the boy with her.

I have to distract him. She groped along the table and threw a china plate into the sergeant's face. It was all she had.

And it did him no harm. He brushed china chips out of his eyes, cursing. Backed away. Pulled a knife from his boot top. For a bare instant he stood there, deciding whether to kill her before he went to kill LeBreton. Then he swung at her with his empty fist, backhanded.

A white flash struck. She felt the pain. The world spun black.

When her eyes cleared, the sergeant was fending off a bowl Bertille threw. And another. LeBreton was on the floor, butting his knee into the other man's belly.

The sergeant, knife in hand, started for LeBreton's unprotected back.

No! She lifted the cradle from the hearthside and swung it with all her strength. Hit the sergeant on the back of his head. He yelled and half fell, staggering off balance.

And sprawled headlong, because LeBreton was there to kick his feet away from under him. LeBreton, pure violence that struck like a javelin. She heard the thud of his boot and an animal shriek of pain.

The *garde* sergeant lay hunched on the floor, slowly drawing together around the pain.

It was strangely still then, though Charles was sobbing against Bertille and the baby wailed in the distance. The sergeant made an odd grating noise in his throat. The other *garde* whimpered, low and continuous, in the corner.

Adrian appeared in the doorway with no sound at all. His eyes traveled the room and ended on LeBreton.

"Don't kill anybody," LeBreton said.

The boy thought it over before he nodded. She saw then that Adrian had his knife out.

"Cut those two loose." LeBreton indicated Alain and the apprentice, tied at the far end of the cottage. "I need the rope." Then he was beside her. "Your lip is bleeding."

"It is," she touched it, "not so much."

"That was a bad idea on his part." LeBreton walked over and stood looking down at the sergeant till the man looked up.

"If you'd hurt her worse, I'd have cut your hand off."
LeBreton's boot prodded the sergeant's right hand. "This
hand. The one you hit her with."

Then he went off to check on the other *garde*.

THE aftermath of battle was left to the women. They were
the sensible ones of the world and therefore left to clean up.
She worked with Bertille to pack the cart, putting this in
and leaving that behind.

Guillaume lifted large objects. Every so often he
returned to the cottage, where he had tied the two *gardes*
in chairs, and listened with unimpaired amiability while
they blustered and threatened. Then he would go back to
help Alain haul about the tools of his trade, some of which
were heavy.

Charles sat on the hearth with wide eyes, taking in the
words the soldiers used, till Bertille sent him outside. Then
Alain came in and sent his young apprentice outside, too.

Marguerite helped herself to coffee from Decorum's
pack and brought it in to grind and heat in the copper pot.
LeBreton did not seem to mind her small thefts. He doubtless committed greater ones. Frequently. She poured coffee from the pot, which would be packed last, into the cups,
which must be left behind, and brought it to everyone. She
did not serve coffee to the soldiers, who were saying filthy
things about her.

LeBreton settled himself at the table to drink coffee while he searched the belongings of the *gardes,* their
handkerchiefs and pocket knives, and most especially their
papers. He put his boots up on the long bench, which was
another thing to distress Bertille, who had a tidy soul.

When he addressed them by name—Sergeant Hachard
and Private Labadie—they became more polite. "Who sent
you to arrest the Rivières?"

That let loose threats and the promise of retribution. She would not have been so eager to make threats herself if she were tied hand and foot and Citoyen LeBreton were in charge.

"Who told you to arrest these people?" LeBreton drank coffee. He spoke like an educated man now. There was an air of authority about him, as if he had been a military officer and commanded men very much like these. "I'm going to ask that question three times. That's the limits of my patience. Then I start slicing pieces off your body. Eventually I'm going to get to the bits your wives might miss. Who do I start with?" The question was for Adrian who was walking by.

"We'll do him." Adrian meant the sergeant.

"That's a likely choice, lad. I am glad to see you understand the chain of command."

Thick, nervous silence held the *gardes*. Anticipatory silence from Adrian. Stern, uncompromising silence from LeBreton. He nudged a stack of copper pans aside to give himself room to lean back. "Sergeant Hachard, there's no reason you shouldn't tell me. You've received orders. There's nothing secret about it. Whose orders? Who told you to arrest these people?"

Adrian's knife appeared. "Can I do it now?" She was almost used to seeing the boy with a knife in his hand. The soldiers, of course, were not.

"Half minute." LeBreton shifted his boots. "Take his ears off before you start on the nose. And don't be getting blood on yourself. I'm damned if I'm going to buy you a new shirt."

The boy inspected the edge of his knife, looking critical.

"It was two men from Paris," the private blurted out. "They carried orders from the Committee of Public Safety. Twelve arrest orders. They divided them up and gave us two names." He looked around nervously. "We chased the first man yesterday and lost him. Then we came to take Bertille Rivière."

"Now that is very interesting." LeBreton took up his coffee cup again. "Tell me about these men from Paris."

And they did. Ten words were enough to tell her these were the Jacobins who had come to her chateau.

The questioning continued. Everyone packed. She carried bags and boxes out of the cottage, coming back to listen from time to time. It could not be said the men spoke freely. But then, it seemed there was very little Citoyen LeBreton expected them to know. He asked the same question many different ways.

Yes, there were twelve to arrest. No, they did not know why. They'd been denounced in Paris, most likely. Lots of folks condemned in Paris. And the men who brought the orders—? Fine revolutionary patriots, to be sure.

When she walked through the next time, carrying sheets, matters had advanced somewhat. Adrian straddled a bench. He'd found a whetstone and was honing a keen, bright edge to the knife. She brought him coffee with milk in it and sugar, the way she had seen him drink it . . . was it only this morning?

When she set the cup down beside him, fierce, dark eyes glanced at the coffee then at her. "I'm supposed to do that."

"You are engaged in being terrifying. Continue." She said it low enough she would not be overheard. When she returned, LeBreton was on his feet. ". . . bandits would be my advice. Five or six of them, at least, took you by surprise. If I were you, I'd say they were from the Vendée."

The *gardes* said nothing.

"Or you can tell everybody a woman hit you over the head with a damn cradle and you let your prisoners get away." LeBreton sounded perfectly agreeable. "I wouldn't like living with that reputation myself. I don't want folks laughing in corners every time I walk by. And what I also don't want, Citoyen Hachard . . ." He strolled closer. "What I don't want is, when I'm back in Paris, I don't want to hear that anybody's looking for a big man, with a scar like this." He drew a line down his cheek, pointing it out. "I get annoyed as sour milk when somebody talks about me."

"He gets irritated," Adrian murmured, sharpening.

The sergeant cleared his throat. "We are required to—"

"Men who annoy me wake up one morning and notice their throat's been cut." LeBreton loomed over the sergeant. He was of a size to loom with great effect.

"It's very sad," Adrian said.

LeBreton was most utterly convincing in his threats. If she did not know him somewhat, she would wholly believe he slit throats from time to time. When she next walked through the cottage, the *gardes* had been left bound and gagged, facing the wall, but with all their bodily parts intact, which must have been a great relief to them.

It was not long after that, that Citoyen LeBreton tracked her to the tiny room where she was sorting Charles's clothing.

He watched without offering to help. She said, "There are many things that must be done in this household before Bertille leaves. Surely some of them require great strength. Why do you not go do them?"

"Why did men come from Paris to arrest your friend?"

"I have not the least idea. Most likely it is nothing at all but some jealous neighbor who has denounced her in an argument over strayed cows." She folded shirts and laid them on the bed. "I do not know why *gardes* have come all the way to Normandy to fix upon Bertille and Alain. Paris is full of suspicious characters to arrest. The very dogs and cats in the street belong to secret societies. Look at you. You are a man of a thousand questionable activities and they do not come after you. That coat, behind you, on the hook. Will you hand it to me? Yes. That one."

"You're part of it, whatever it is," he said.

It was inevitable he would see this. He was not an idiot. "On the contrary. I have nothing to do with anything. I am prosaic as cucumbers. The hat as well, please." She smoothed the coat flat so it would bundle neatly and took the hat from him to set on top.

"Will you leave with your friends?"

"No." She knelt and pulled shoes out from under the bed. Two pair. She took the new pair and left the old. So much must be left behind.

He waited till she'd finished with that. "You can't stay here. You can't go back to the chateau."

She set a last pair of stockings on the pile of clothing, pulled the corners of the quilt together, and tied them. Guillaume LeBreton stood blocking the door, fixed firmly in place, like several boulders piled together.

This man could take her to Paris. With him beside her she would not have to skulk through the fields at night and take the back roads, avoiding every village. She would travel more quickly. He could probably even talk her through the gates of Paris, into the city.

She did not have to trust him. She only needed to make use of him.

And there was no one else. "You've been paid for bringing me this far. I'll pay you more to take me all the way to Paris. To my father."

LeBreton had been cool and menacing as he questioned the *garde* sergeant. Now that implacable concentration was directed toward her. She felt herself weighed and measured, plucked apart and studied. He had come to various conclusions regarding her. Nothing in his face would reveal what they were.

She would not let herself be afraid of him.

He said, "How much?"

Money. He thought first about the money. It was a pleasure to deal with a man so straightforward. She did not feel any disappointment that he was not gallant. "My father will give you twenty louis d'or."

"A hundred."

"That is an impossible price. My father is not made of money."

"Gold louis. Not paper. Not silver."

"You could smuggle giraffes across France for that price. You could—"

"And I take that ring. The one on your finger. You give that over and I hold it till I get paid."

"You put a high price on—"

"I'll get you to your father." It was said with great determination. She entirely believed him. It was that iron resolve that would get her across all the miles between here and Paris, regardless of who might be hunting her.

Sometimes only the wolf can protect you from bands of wild dogs.

She had to twist the ring back and forth to get it off. She wore it always. She had sold her jewelry, year by year, to pay for La Flèche. She had not sold this small ring. It was gold, engraved with bands of flowers. It had belonged to her mother, who died when she was born. Her mother had been pretty, from the pictures of her. She must have been patient, too, since she had been married to Papa for a decade and not murdered him. One needed great helpings of patience, dealing with men.

Finally she had it off.

LeBreton dropped her ring into the pocket of his waistcoat. "You shouldn't be wearing that anyway." He tamped the ring down firmly with his forefinger into the very bottom of the pocket. "It doesn't match what you're pretending to be."

BERTILLE washed Charles's face and went to say good-bye to her flowers and her cows. One would think she was leaving behind a cousin or two, at the least. She clucked over the state of the cottage as she made one final search for a silver spoon, unaccountably missing. LeBreton helped Alain load his anvil. Bertille washed the apprentice's face. She washed the baby. Then she washed Charles's face again. Adrian found Bertille's sewing kit.

Then it was finally time for them to leave. Bertille held her close in the garden, among the roses. "Take care."

"I am the most cautious of mortals. You know that."

"So I see." Bertille reached out to lay fingers upon her lip, where it hurt. "Put cold cloths upon this. It will not swell as much."

"That is good advice. I am sorry you must leave and lose—"

"Don't blame yourself, Marguerite. We knew this might happen. The house in Bernay is ready. La Flèche will survive this. In a week Crow will go east, beyond the fighting. Heron has his safe haven prepared. And Wren will finally go to England. You know Wren can take care of herself."

It had been Wren, four days ago, who came at midnight, sneaking up the back stairs of the chateau. Wren pursued, her sparrows in danger. Wren, desperate for help. She needed clothing. Money. Food from the kitchen.

Bags were ready for just this emergency. She took out one and then another when she heard the cry behind her.

"No. Oh, no." Jeanne stood at the window. Jeanne— the Wren—was never afraid.

She ran to see. Lights threaded the night, along the road, among the trees. Men poured across the lawn toward the chateau, shouting. They pounded the door, broke windows. Two horses, two riders, led the mob. She shouldered a bag. Handed the other to Jeanne. "Through the kitchen. We'll go out the back." There was no time for more. "I'll take care of the sparrows. You go to Heron. You know where?"

"The mill." Jeanne patted her skirt. "I'm carrying a knife. They will not take me alive."

"Don't be dramatic. If you're alive, I'll get you free."

Outside, a voice yelled for the de Fleurignac bitch. "Bring her here. Bring her to me." The torches sent shadow and light flickering across the curtains. Smoke rose from the library below.

She pushed sabots onto her feet. A pouch of coins lay in the drawer. She tossed, and Jeanne caught it neatly.

Jeanne yelled, "Marguerite!"

A man burst into the room. Tall. A coarse face. He wore the jacket and striped trousers of a sans-culottes. *A Jacobin. He was armed.*

Jeanne threw herself on him. Knocked the pistol from his hand.

He caught Jeanne. Pushed her backward, down on the writing table. His hands crushed her throat. In filthy speech from the gutters of Paris he promised death.

Papers and books scattered. The letter opener slithered off the desk, to the floor. The ivory handle glowed against the carpet. She found it, took it in her hand, and slashed him across his face.

The man screamed. Jeanne rolled away, free. The night lamp fell from the desk and smashed. The papers on the floor caught fire.

There was blood everywhere. Jeanne was on her knees, sobbing air in and out. A red mask twisted in the red light of burning. The man reared up and staggered toward her. Grabbed her and caught her. When she fought him off, her hands were red with blood. The curtains went up in flame.

"Wren is in England by now," Bertille said.

It was bright daylight around her. She was in Bertille's beautiful garden, not the chateau. She swallowed and put the memory away. "Wren is halfway to London, as you say. And you have escaped. I'll solve the rest of this." She touched Bertille's face. "Go with God. Be in his hand always. I'm glad you are out of this."

"I am Dove." Plump, comfortable, indomitable Bertille shook her head. "Remember that. I was the first. Before Jean-Paul and Wren and Crow. Before your secret signals and your safehouses and the dozens of couriers. I was there when it was only the two of us and a compartment under the seat in your coach. I am La Flèche as much as you are."

"I would rather you were safe."

"Chut. We do not do this to be safe. When I am settled in the house in Bernay, I will pass the word. If you do not send sparrows my way, I shall go to Paris and remove them myself."

"Bertille . . ."

"Now we will cry. I must leave before we do that." Bertille said that even though tears were already on her cheeks. "Take care of your great giant. He is very impressive, that one. And in the name of God, Marguerite, brush your hair. It is a shame upon the honor of French womanhood."

There was nothing to do then but watch the cart creak slowly out of sight over a hill.

Twelve

"RIGHT, THEN. PRETEND I'M A DESERTER, COME UP from the army in the Vendée."

"I would rather not."

"I spotted you." LeBreton waved in the general direction of west. "Over there. I take off after you. I'm big and I'm angry and I'm dangerous."

"That does not require great amounts of imagination to picture. Nevertheless—"

"You come panting up the hill, meaning to hide in these bushes around up here. But I catch up to you. And look what's loose here." He lifted her braid. Picked it right from her shoulder and closed his hand around it. His knuckles were scraped with dozens of fine, red-brown lines from where he had hit the *gardes*. "I grab hold of this, which any man would, by the way. You have an irresistible braid. Now what? What do you do?"

Adrian, who was keeping an eye upon the road, snorted.

She said, "I would offer you a bribe."

"I don't feel like being bribed."

"I would employ some clever stratagem. I would fool you into thinking I was the mayor's wife. I would pretend to wave at him, coming up the hill there. When you turned that way, I would hide."

"What if I found you?"

"If you are going to write the tale to your own liking, then any sort of disaster might overtake me. What if the sky poured down poison toads? What if I were abducted by Bulgarians?" She did not like to be held against her will, not even so lightly as the hold he kept upon her braid. She sparked inside with a swarm of little angers, like crackles of fire. "Very well. I would hit you." She looked directly into his eyes. "Hard. Possibly here." She doubled her hand into a fist and brought it forward slowly, to rest against his chin.

Those damned laughing eyes of his. Seconds passed while they looked at each other. Slow, important seconds. He said, "That's a butterfly landing on me."

"I know." She dropped her hand. "I am a mouse beneath the cart wheel if I meet villains upon the road. This is a sad fact of life."

They were on the hilltop that overlooked Bertille's house, in an orchard hidden by long windbreaks of hawthorn and alder. Adrian lay at length upon a horse blanket, propped on his elbows, looking through a break in the low brush with a pair of night glasses, studying to see if anyone would come to Bertille's cottage. The night glasses folded and unfolded from a metal case that pretended to be the handle of a valise. Such glasses belonged on some naval vessel, watching ships, not in the baggage of an honest seller of books. But then, LeBreton was so obviously not an honest seller of books.

"Stand there and I'll teach you how to be a mouse with fangs.

"I do not want fangs." One could not discourage LeBreton. He ignored her attempts.

He smiled, just with the corners of his eyes. The rest of his face was perfectly sober. "You are going to be dangerous. So. Let's say I've just chased you up this hill. We're pretending you don't have a cradle handy, which could happen if you were out in the countryside like this. What you do . . . No. Give me that." He took her fist and unfolded it. "If you have to hit somebody, you put the thumb out of the way so it don't snap off like a stick of barley sugar. You do like this."

She looked at what he advised to do with her thumb. "I cannot believe that is right."

"You are many things, Mistress Maggie, but a pugilist is not one of them. Now listen. You have one chance—if you're just as lucky as hell—you have one chance to hit this deserter."

"Or bandit. Let us be fair and say he could be a bandit."

"Or bandit."

"Or an officer of the dragoons. Or perhaps a persistent farm laborer. There is always that."

"So there is. Pay attention. You're going to fight this man with all the cleverness you got in you. He's coming along like this." He raised his arms up, wide. "What do you do? I'm being terrifying."

"You are ridiculous. You are like a dancing bear rearing up, saying, 'Hit me.' "

"You can't count on getting attacked by some little fellow. Now, if I'm attacking," LeBreton took the fist he'd made of her hand and held it pressed against his stomach, "you don't hit me in the belly, since that's not going to do you any good."

"I will not hit you in the belly." *I have tried that. It does not work.* "I will not hit you anywhere, Monsieur Dragoon-Brigand-Deserter. I will run."

"Run like the devil. That's your first choice. But if you can't run . . . if you're cornered . . . You take this." He opened her fist and curved her fingers together to make a claw. "You come here." He brought her fingers to his eyes. Set her fingernails to his eyelid. "You dig in. Go for both eyes if you can. He can't chase you if he can't see."

"I cannot do that. I could not."

His eyelid was soft as velvet. How amazing that this man should have any vulnerable place upon him.

"Yesterday, you would've said you couldn't hit somebody over the head with a cradle. See how wrong you can be?"

"Or you can stab them." Adrian had turned on his side to watch them and be amused. "Doesn't take much strength."

"Except she ain't going to carry a knife around in her boot, her not being a bloodthirsty blot upon the landscape like some I could mention." LeBreton let her go. She noticed, then, that he had been holding her hand all this time. "A knife just encourages you to stand and fight when a sensible person should be running. Now pay attention. If you can't get to his eyes, you go for a man here." Crudely, LeBreton reached down and cupped himself between the legs. "You kick his cock. Hard as you can. Or you reach down and grab hold of his nob and yank it right off."

I cannot do any of this. "That is a very unpleasant idea. I would rather not think about it."

"Well, just as a secret between the two of us, it's unpleasant for a man to think about, too. What I'm saying is, you can hurt somebody my size if you go about it right. Look at the boy here."

Adrian's chin lifted. His expression was inscrutable.

"I wouldn't want to face him in a fair fight, leaving aside that the term *fair fight* don't actually exist in his vocabulary. He'd hurt me, and he's smaller than you are."

"I'm nastier." Adrian went back to being attentive toward Bertille's house.

The fields behind this hill and Bertille's valley had been

left fallow. Sheep grazed there in a tight, suspicious flock. Every once in a while a fretful bleat came from that direction. Adrian inspected them with the glasses, frowning.

LeBreton was waiting to get hit.

She did not indulge him. "Let us pretend I am encouraged by the examples you present. I do not run. I perform horrible measures upon your eyes. This irks you so much you strangle me. It is a dismal prospect."

"At least you fight. Could be, that's enough. Maybe a friend shows up. Maybe your soldier brigand goes into an apoplexy and drops dead. Now." He raised his arms and shuffled forward. "Hurt me. Do it right."

He will not cease nagging at me until I fight with him. She tried to hit him.

"Try again. Go for my eyes."

He was very fast. "I am not—"

"Again." He lunged at her. She had no time to get ready. Her hands shot up.

"That's better," he said.

The next time, she feinted to the right when he came in.

"Good. Again." He circled. Closed in. He let her graze his cheek before he knocked her hands away. "This time, surprise me. Kick for the crotch."

Ten more times. Twenty more times. Sometimes she tried for the eyes, sometimes for intimate parts. By this time she was breathing hard and entirely prepared to hit him in the cock with her knee. She did not quite succeed. Not quite.

"You're getting vicious," he said. "I couldn't be prouder of you."

Adrian, who had been watching, raised his hands and clapped slowly. "That was fun. If I'd known you wanted your eyes gouged out, I'd have obliged."

"You try that, one of these days." LeBreton's hands rested on her shoulders, lightly. There was no reason to keep them there, but they stayed and stayed and she did not move away. He took the edges of her fichu where they tucked into her neckline and spread them flat against her skin. "It's all in knowing how, Maggie. The next man who corners you in a stable, you kick him in the bollocks."

She smiled at that. Then she looked into his eyes and saw herself in his thoughts.

When she was a child, she had wondered what color the eyes of dragons would be. Now she knew. They were brown, stirred with ambiguous thoughts. Thoughts that folded and fit together the way those night glasses did.

Guillaume LeBreton had dragon eyes. She was inside him there, in his mind, in that bright, hot center of him. There was no way on earth to tell what he was thinking.

Neither of them said anything. They stood this close and his hands were on her. What they weren't saying was the loudest thing in the landscape.

"When you're through doing that," Adrian said, "come over here and take a look." He gave the night glasses over to her, not LeBreton. She knelt.

LeBreton eased the brush back. "Visitors."

She put the glasses to her eyes and swept in a dizzy way along the brown and green of the road to find where the men were. Yes. She adjusted her sight, squinting, and she could see.

The sun was low in the sky to her right, round and gold as a coin. The valley was a bowl of silence tipping away into a flat distance. Tiny figures of men had come out an hour ago to dig at a ditch in a field close to the horizon. Their piles of mud marked both sides of the black slash where they had worked. A sort of punctuation.

Where the road descended the hill, two men and three horses came into sight, making their way toward Bertille's house. One slouched, thin man. One loutish, large one with a white bandage across his face, over his forehead and eye. She handed the night glasses to LeBreton.

"It's our friends from Voisemont," he said.

"Yes." The red vest and striped trousers were almost a caricature of proper sans-culottes attire. These were the Jacobins from Paris, men who carried credentials from the Committee of Public Safety.

They dismounted and entered Bertille's cottage. Within minutes, they came out again with the two *gardes* who ran to the cowshed behind the house and led their horses out. The four together rode down the road, making some haste.

Where the men were digging ditches in the field, the Jacobins stopped. Blue smocks gathered around the horses. Even from here she saw the arms spread and heads shaken. The farmers were denying all knowledge of events. They had not been in that field when Bertille and Alain drove away in quite the opposite direction.

The four men spurred onward. The soldiers rode more skillfully than the Jacobin officials.

"South and east," LeBreton said. "That means the Paris road."

The horsemen became black dots against the brown haze of fields. Now, they were in sight. Now, the road curved and they were gone.

They'd come from the Committee of Public Safety, carrying twelve arrest orders. They'd come to gather up La Flèche and destroy it. They knew her friends. Knew their names. Knew the pathways and safehouses of La Flèche. She had been betrayed, most completely.

The betrayal came from Paris. That was where she must go.

Thirteen

MARGUERITE LAY NOT FAR FROM GUILLAUME LE-Breton. The night was warm. A low haze hid the thousands of stars. The moon was half full, gauzed over, indistinct at the edges. When she turned her head to look downhill, the land was black and gray, or white, where moonlight reflected in the lines of ditches and in a small pond.

If I am taken at the gate of Paris, I will not live to see the full moon.

It was warm enough that she did not wish for a cover of any kind. The blankets Bertille had abandoned in the cowshed protected her against the spears of grass from below. They were less of a protection against the jutting stones, but she had found the greater part of those and tossed them aside. Adrian brought a bundle of cloth—men's shirts, clean and rolled—to set under her head.

Her face ached only a little from the buffet the *garde* had given her. But she could not sleep. Her thoughts were boorish company tonight and roistered in her head and kept her awake.

She stood and slipped into her sabots and crossed the ten feet that separated her blankets from Guillaume's. It was not a long way.

He lay on his back with his knees drawn up and his hands clasped behind his head. He had taken off his boots when he returned from circling the hill and assessing hazards of the surrounding fields and sent Adrian to perform that same task. His boots rested, neatly, one leaned against the other, on the edge of the blankets, within reach.

He had taken off his waistcoat and pulled his shirt from the band of his trousers so it was long and loose around him. He had large feet.

She stepped out of her shoes and walked onto the small part of the blanket he was not using to settle beside him. This was intimacy. This was how a wife came to sit with her husband in their garden, in the cool, when it was too hot to be indoors. This was the way of lovers with one another. She knew that, though she had never sat with Jean-Paul, familiar and at ease, when they had been lovers in those brief months between being children and being apart.

She would probably never have a husband and sit with him in some snug garden. The greatest likelihood was that she would be snatched from the road tomorrow and taken to the Tribunal in Paris and condemned. Or she would be recognized and taken at the *barrière* of Paris. This was her one taste of the particular fruit, intimacy.

LeBreton seemed content to be silent. She could see the outline of his features but not his exact expression. For a while, she sat, considering the night. "I have not spent a lot of time sitting on hills, looking out over the fields," she said. "It makes me feel small and rather poorly attached to the earth. It is as if one could float away altogether."

"That's poetic."

"I am fanciful sometimes. It may come from collecting old stories from the people in the countryside. I take an interest in such things and write them down. Or it may be because I have spent hours and hours of my life imagining I was somewhere else."

At Versailles, through all the long months at the King's Court, she had stood, wearing heavy, beautiful, uncomfortable clothing. Being on display. Being a de Fleurignac. There was no boredom more complete than to stand about being clever all evening. The queen's ladies said, "Oh, come. Come hear Mademoiselle de Fleurignac's latest witticism. Come hear her little fable from Normandy." They said, "So dear, so sweet, her new story."

LeBreton was still. She could see the white of his shirt rising and falling with his breath. "You lost those stories when the chateau burned."

"Some of them are copied elsewhere. Many of them."

Silence. Then he said, "It's bad to lose what you've made. You can't ever make it again the same way."

"Not quite the same."

"I had to walk away, once, and leave everything. My books. Ideas I'd written down. Essays." He didn't move, but his stillness changed in quality. "My father burned it all."

She did not rush to fill the silence up, in case LeBreton might have a use for it.

He said, "It felt like losing blood."

Wherever he came from, it had not been happy in that house. Perhaps that was where he learned to sink into impenetrable depths inside himself. Learned to study the world so carefully. Learned to see into the souls around him so well that he could select, from all her losses, the one that hurt the most. It was not comfortable to deal with a man who wielded the scalpel of such perception.

On the other hand, he also instructed her in how to remove the eyeballs of her enemies. She thought about Guillaume LeBreton for a while, but could come to no conclusions. She said, "I will take my turn at watching, when Adrian is done."

"You don't have to."

"If I am expected to claw the eyes from my enemies, I can certainly wander about in the dark for a few hours searching for them."

He sat up. They were very close, when he did that. Almost touching, body to body. He took her hand and threaded his fingers in between hers. They slid together smoothly in this way, the fingers of Marguerite de Fleurignac and Guillaume LeBreton.

She had not known what to expect when they touched so deliberately. The shiver that trickled through her was a surprise. Her body didn't know quite what to do with it.

"I'll wake you before dawn," he said. "You can have the last watch." He looked at her hand and continued to hold it, the fingers interlaced. "Generally, when women come wandering by in the middle of the night, I know what they want. Not this time."

"I am not sure, myself."

In the days of the Old Regime the great ladies of the aristocracy would take a man like this to bed. They would amuse themselves with a man of the people, unrepentantly earthy and strong. He would be a sort of plaything. She had seen gardeners and grooms and the soldiers who guarded the palace of Versailles invited into the boudoirs of the ladies of the court. She had thought it decadent at the time.

Tonight it did not feel decadent, desiring Guillaume LeBreton. Choosing him.

"Thank you for saving Bertille, and Alain, and the children," she said. "And me. If you had not been with me, I would have walked into the house alone and been taken captive. Thank you."

"You're welcome. Now, go back over and lie down. Try

to sleep." But he didn't let go of her hand. That knowledge lay between them—that he was holding her with a warm touch, soft as kid leather, hard as the knots of trees.

Men hunted La Flèche up and down the roads of Normandy. Tomorrow, she would walk between the jaws of death.

But that was tomorrow. She had tonight. "You know I am Marguerite de Fleurignac. You have always known."

"From the first minute," he said equably.

"You did not mention it."

"Seemed impolite to contradict you. And you were shy of me. Scared." He lifted their joined hands and brought her knuckles close to his mouth so that she felt his breath. "You still are. Scared. Go to bed, Mistress Maggie. It's late and we have a long way to go tomorrow."

Her fingers tightened into his. She could not see the scar that marked him. In this silver dimness, he might have been a gentleman as easily as a criminal or spy or smuggler— whichever he was. She did not care what he was. The night was heavy with possibility.

"I am not a virgin," she said.

There was enough light to see him smile. "That's a coincidence. Neither am I."

"What you are is a great treasure-house of sarcasm." She shook her hand free. "Guillaume, you understand what it is to be a de Fleurignac. I am a woman of purpose and family and duty. It is all very tiresome and dreary. Everyone in France has the *liberté* we all speak about. This is mine. This is my one small part of all that freedom. I belong to myself. I can give myself where I wish."

"Give yourself. You mean lie with me?"

"Yes."

His touch passed up the skin of her arm like a bird over water, leaving the shadow of his passage. Then the palm of his hand was warm as sunlight on her cheek. His thumb hovered soft at the curl of her nostril. Came to lie upon her lips. Softly. Softly. Who would know she was so sensitive there? "Why?"

She did not say that she had begun to ache for him at the threshold of her body, between her legs. That he was simple bread to someone who had been hungry for a long time. That he was the shelter of trees to a traveler lost in the freezing rain. That he set her free, for the space of one night. "I become one of my stories when I touch you."

He was so tall. Even sitting, he made a great shadow against the dim sky. He leaned closer and drew a line around her lips with the side of his thumb, confident and delicate. Strange to think of him knowing the shape of her lips this well.

"Does it hurt? Your lip."

"Not now."

"You have a pretty mouth," he said.

"It is not small and feminine. Monkeymouth, my aunt Sophie called me when I was small."

"There is no man on earth who'd call you that. There's no man alive who wouldn't want your mouth on him. You are beautiful."

Whatever dreadful things would happen to her in the next days, she would keep this moment in a place apart, inside herself, put away safely. Guillaume, tracing the shape of her lips and saying he found her pretty.

His fingers left her lips and slid downward slowly along her throat. She wore no fichu. She had left her vest unbuttoned. Her breasts were barely covered by the loose shift. He slipped inside her clothing, giving her time to think about it, being easy and not in any hurry.

He took her nipple between thumb and forefinger and stroked it. Her skin drew up everywhere, shivering. The shock that centered on her breast echoed low in her belly. She made some sound of surprise. Surprise at the immensity of the feeling.

"What am I going to do with you, Maggie?" he murmured.

But he would know what to do.

He said, "This is where I send you back to your blankets. Alone." But he caressed her breast.

She closed her eyes, strung too tense to move. She was plucked like strings with each small, small touch. His fingertips were harsh, blunt, rough as tree bark. So gentle on her. Barely, barely touching.

He leaned to her breast. Kissed the nipple. "I wanted this," he whispered. "Couldn't get the picture out of my head. You, by the fish fountain, dressed in nothing but morning. That's not something a man forgets."

He pulled her to him. Her cheek found bare skin where his shirt was unbuttoned. His chest was full of his heartbeat. She could become lost in this man, in territories of amazement, countries of sensation. She felt the currents of his blood. He was not merely LeBreton, villain and rogue. He was more complex than that, and simpler. Night stripped away the man and left myth. It was the myth she hungered for. This was the way the Old Gods came to the daughters of men. In dark strength, wearing the night around them like a cloak.

Closer. She would get closer to him. She would get this clothing out of the way.

"Don't move." She felt his voice in his chest when he said that. "We are going to stop this."

The heat between her legs throbbed. Her whole body shook with the pounding of her pulse. "I am willing, Guillaume."

"We're going to stop. Right now. Or else I am going to tip you back and take you on a pile of blankets on the ground with sheep and donkeys and that thrice-damned, cutthroat boy wandering past any minute." His breath rasped down into her hair. "We aren't going to do this." He let her go.

She breathed deeply. Rubbed her face, trying to scrub the feelings away. "You are very sensible."

"Right."

"I hate you for it."

"I ain't so pleased about this myself. I'm going to go stomp off downhill and kick trees."

He did not, however, kick anything. It was not his way. She heard him later, talking to the donkeys in his grit-and-sandpaper voice, sounding calm and good-humored. She was deeply asleep when he fulfilled his promise and came to wake her to take the last watch before dawn.

Fourteen

MARGUERITE HAD NEVER CONSIDERED THE PROB-
lems of getting into Paris. Transporting sparrows out was
difficult enough.

It was the hour before dawn, when the light was thin
and drawn out. Farmers lined up on the right side of the
road, two dozen ahead of them, more dozens arriving to
wait behind. All of them took their places with the resigna-
tion of long practice.

The men wore ribbons with the Revolution's colors—
blue, white, and red. Guillaume's was particularly large.
He'd pinned it on his hat this morning.

"Good for the digestion, patience." Guillaume selected
an approach to the donkeys that did not leave him vulnerable to attack and pulled a loaf of bread from under the
vegetables he'd packed into the top of the panniers. "We'll
be a while. Take some."

"I cannot eat," she said. "But thank you."

"Tired?" He touched her cheek, as if he were entirely

accustomed to doing so, and lay a finger across her mouth for an instant. Reminding her. Saying, *Speak softly.*

There was aristo in her accents. Aristos died in Paris these days.

It was also death to look discontented when standing in a bread line for one of the brown, chaff-filled "patriotic loaves." Death to mention that something—anything—was better in the old days or to step into the street without the revolutionary cockade in one's hat. Death stalked Paris, hungry as a wolf and not at all particular.

She did not whisper, which would attract attention, nor did she stay silent, which would also be noticed. She stood close to him and pitched her voice low. "If these donkeys had fewer teeth, I would lean against one of them and fall asleep."

"Come lean against me. I'd enjoy that."

He was needlessly provocative. He had not laid a finger upon her since their discussion in the fields above Bertille's house. They had slept last night within arm's reach of each other, side by side, in the leaves and moss of the woods above Chaville, and he did not touch her. She had lain awake for a long time, lying on her back looking at the sky, knowing Guillaume did the same. She would swear they breathed in unison.

Now he teased her. Perhaps he thought irritation with him would leave no room in her for being afraid. He was wrong.

Adrian and another lad his size knelt in the dirt, rolling dice in the light cast by a lantern on one of the carts. Around them, drivers gathered to watch, sucking their teeth meditatively and scratching.

Guillaume had become the quintessence of peasant this morning, communing with his donkeys, feeding them morsels of bread. An uncomplicated man. An incurious plodder. She did not know how he did this so perfectly.

She took knitting from the pocket in her apron. This was Bertille's apron and Bertille's knitting, a plain black sock, half-finished, dangling from four needles. Her Scots governess had taught her to knit, holding that it was second only to oat porridge in building character. She was rather out of practice these days, but she wrapped wool around her fingers and applied herself and became a thrifty farm-wife, working instead of standing idle.

And it kept her hands from shaking.

"Do you know one of those men at the gate?" She barely spoke it, just a whisper of words, so the men nearby would not hear. "Is that why we're here, and so early?"

"No." He glanced at the *barrière*. "Strangers to me. They look like good revolutionaries."

The gate guards were volunteer sans-culottes, drawn from the district committees of the Faubourg Saint-Antoine and the Faubourg Saint-Martin, men loyal to the radical wing of the Jacobins. The officer in charge could be seen through the window of the guardhouse, his boots up on a barrel, his chin on his chest.

She closed her eyes briefly. "I see."

"Alert, too. And they're well armed." Guillaume was all naive approval.

"It is a sight to make one proud," she agreed.

This was the way her sparrows felt at every checkpoint on the road. Afraid and helpless. Angry and trapped. She wondered if they resented their courier as much as she resented Guillaume.

She finished with one needle and switched to the next. This would be a bigger sock than she had intended, some-how. On the ground, between wagons, Adrian won again and raked in coins. There were five playing now, the two boys and three grown men. A small crowd had gathered to watch.

"I'd ask myself how the boy got money to stake himself

with." Guillaume fed Decorum a bite of bread. "But I don't want to know." He raised his voice and turned to the farmer behind them. "Citoyen. Over there. Who's that?"

Four men rode down the line of farmers and carters, kicking up dust. They were well dressed and young and rode fine horses.

"Delegates," the farmer said. "Going to the Convention." He glanced at Guillaume.

The man in line ahead of them spoke up. "They been out in the villages, enforcing the price controls, I daresay."

"Likely." There was a moment's shared appreciation. "Early at it."

"Oh, *oui*." The farmer's cart creaked as he shifted his weight. "Working night and day for the good of the common man."

She knew—everyone in line knew—where the delegates had been. Lovely, expensive women lived in the villages beyond the gates of Paris. The maximum price of the onions and cabbages was set by law. The price of women was not.

The gate opened and the *barrière* swung up. The delegates rode through with scarcely a pause and no questions asked.

The gate guard looked after them and shrugged. He turned impatiently to the first of the farmers. "Come on, then."

A rustle spread down the line. Men leaning on cart wheels or against the tail of wagons mounted the seat and took reins. Voices rose, talking to animals. Pointing out, one man to another, that the gate was open. Saying, one woman to another, that finally they could go in. The first cart pulled forward. A farmer with many chickens was admitted to inspection.

"Your papers." The gate guard held out his hand. The line trickled toward the gate. "Next. Your papers."

She edged along after Guillaume, keeping her gaze modestly lowered to her knitting. The line was moving almost at walking pace. The guards gave a perfunctory glance at passports. Wagons weren't even looked at.

"Next. Papers."

Their turn. They stepped to the *barrière*. If her description was posted in the guardhouse . . . One vigilant guard would be enough. If anyone looked at her face, at the softness of her hands. She hid them under the knitting wool as much as she could.

The guard did not even glance at their papers. Did not look at her. "Next." He greeted the farmer behind them. "Jacques. You're early."

Guillaume slapped Decorum on the rump. Adrian slipped in behind the donkeys, appearing from nowhere. She had stopped being startled by this.

"Sixteen sous," he said. "You'd think they never heard of loaded dice in this country."

"No point talking to you, is there?" Guillaume said.

Fifteen

PARIS HAD CHANGED, EVEN IN THE THREE MONTHS she'd been away. It was more shadowed. More afraid. Darker. Fear seeped from the mortar of the houses, from the cobbles of the streets. It was like coming again to the home of an old grandmother, with each visit finding her a little weaker, a little more mad.

"We'll stop for coffee," Guillaume said.

"It is just as well. I would wake up the household and worry them if I arrived at this hour."

She did not need to eat. She needed twenty more minutes with Guillaume LeBreton. She was hungry for five hundred words from him. For two accidental touches of her hand upon his. For hearing him laugh just once more.

They ate in a café in Rue de Lombard, not far from Les Halles, at the Café des Marchands. Guillaume was known here. Everyone nodded to him as he took a table. They stared at her with some interest. It was a café frequented by market men and women, all of them hungry and in a great hurry. The slices of bread in the basket on the table were of fine flour, better than she had seen in the *boulangeries* of the best streets. There was something to be said for eating in a café patronized by the violent, well-organized merchants of Les Halles. They could ignore regulations. The coffee, too, spoke to her of stores kept under the counter and sold only to special customers.

Adrian, narrow-eyed, watching everything, took a bowl of milky coffee outside and squatted by the donkeys to defend the carrots from pilferage. It was as if a cat came to a new neighborhood and was not certain he liked it.

Guillaume drank red wine. He took it in quick gulps, without tasting, the way the men around him did, as if he, too, were in a hurry, his mind on a spot in the market and the exchange of copper sous for vegetables. He ate neatly, taking a hard bite of bread and washing wine over his teeth to soften it before he chewed. It was a workingman's way of eating, crude and efficient. A stoical fueling of the body. He was intensely, alertly aware of her the whole time. She felt him thinking about her even though he did not look at her once.

He said, "Still not hungry?"

She shook her head.

He spoke, very low, "I think you're safe. There's no order posted at the *barrière*. I looked, when we passed the guardhouse. No order for your friends either."

She had seen the same thing. No arrest order. It was one more question of the many questions she was collecting. She would have liked to ask Guillaume what he thought this meant, but, of course, she could not.

So she was silent. After she'd taken a few more sips, she said, "I like this place. They serve good coffee."

"I come here when I'm in Paris. If you leave a message with these people, I'll get it."

"There will be no occasion. After today, we will not see each other again."

Soon they would leave this place and go to the Hôtel de Fleurignac. She would become Marguerite de Fleurignac again. She would become immeasurably distant from Guillaume LeBreton, seller of books, rogue and smuggler.

One cannot put the fruit back on the tree. One cannot unbreak the egg. She could not, not ever again for all of eternity, unknow what she knew of his body. Someday, when she was old, she would take this knowledge out as if it were a letter she had treasured. By then, the pain would be thin and crackly, like old paper.

She would be changed as well. She was quite certain old women did not feel this sort of pain. As if the air were knives that cut, going in and out of the throat.

She was not Marguerite de Fleurignac yet. She was still Maggie. She would not be logical.

"We cannot stay here for two hours and not invite curiosity. I have a friend who lives in this quartier, not far from here." She set her coffee down on the table and looked directly into his eyes. "She will let me use her room. Will you come with me?"

Sixteen

DOYLE LEFT HAWKER GUARDING THE BOTTOM OF the stairs and climbed three narrow flights to a room under the roof. He didn't have to meet Maggie's friend to know something about her. He summed her up in a glance around the room—young, on the small side, stylish. The clothes hanging on hooks on the wall belonged to a pretty grisette, a shopgirl, from the fashionable boulevards. She liked bright printed cloth and red ribbons in her caps.

Maggie went to draw the curtains back and open the window. "She is away, my friend Jeanne. She won't mind us coming here."

We're going to make love in her bed. Hope she won't mind that, either.

It was a clean, crowded, charming room. The window faced east. The ceiling slanted. He'd be banging his head if he wasn't careful. Sometimes there was no advantage being the size he was.

Carts and wagons clattered early in this quartier, bringing in vegetables. Not a quiet place to live—there'd be that rumble in the background all day—but somebody'd made a nest here. There were homey touches of color and a lavender smell from the bedclothes.

The friend had been gone about a week. Long enough that the room felt deserted. Not time enough for dust to settle on the table or the chest of drawers.

This Jeanne would be part of Maggie's clandestine goings-on, like the Gypsy and the cooper's wife in Normandy. They were in La Flèche, the lot of them. He'd stake money on it. Maggie would run something like La Flèche.

"I have been wise." Maggie held the curtain back. He could see the curve of her cheek, outlined by the light of the sky. "Almost all my life."

Not so wise. You're risking your neck every hour you stay in France. But he hadn't come here so they could be wise together.

The bed was neatly made, piled with blue pillows. The ropes creaked, the straws of the mattress whispered, when he sat down on the blanket to pull his boots free. The rough of his hands snagged on satin when he pushed the pillows to the side of the bed. He could hear his father calling them "peasant paws."

Maggie didn't seem to mind.

I've kept my hands off you, Maggie de Fleurignac. I am just damned tired of it.

Whatever her father had done, Maggie wasn't any part of the assassinations in England. His gut said that, and he trusted his gut. And a man couldn't walk around being tentative and cautious all the time in case the woman he wanted turned out to be murderous.

She was talking to herself or to the air outside, sounding wistful and determined. "Part of me says I do not have so many days left. I would like, just this once, to do what Marguerite wants. What Maggie wants." He could picture the smile on her. The right side of her mouth hid itself down in the corner when she made that kind of smile. "Do you know . . . I have never made love in an actual bed."

It was like standing outside a house in the cold, seeing all the warmth in the world inside there. And the door opened to welcome him in.

He said, "Come here," and she came to him.

WE *will make love now*, Marguerite thought.

She had brought him to Jeanne's rooms and climbed the stairs and closed the door behind them, knowing they would do this.

He pulled his shirt over his head and loosed his arms from the sleeves and shook it out, casually, to toss over the bedstead. He was half naked before her, wholly masculine. She knew men like him from marble statues. From pictures of heroes in books.

Jean-Paul had been fifteen when she'd been with him. A boy, rather than a man. He had been smooth and beautiful as Endymion.

Guillaume LeBreton was the Minotaur. Man and beast. Human and wild. He had never deceived her about his nature. She had known he was powerful and dangerous from the first moment she saw him. It was her choice whether she would run away or come to him.

It seemed she would approach.

He drew her closer to him so that she stood between his thighs as he sat on the bed. His hands were heavy and warm, resting at her waist. She would lean into the strength and let him take her where he would. Already, she was breathing sharp and deep. Her skin tightened in odd places. At her breasts. Up and down her arms. It felt like being afraid, this excitement. But it was not. She desired him.

They had very little time together. She must not waste it.

She helped him undress her. Ties untangled. Clothing

fell away to the floorboards. Her cap was tossed aside. Guillaume pulled down her braid and separated it into long strands with his fingers. She felt it all the way down her whole length. When he stroked her hair back from her face, the caress shuddered in the intimate core of her. Tingled at her breasts.

Then she was standing in her shift. Only her shift. She could not quite continue. It was too much. Too sudden. Her skin was too sensitive. It would sting like a shock when he touched her. She felt the imprint of his hand through the soft linen, gliding up her body, bringing the shift with it. Her breath edged raggedly, in and out. She did not try to hide what she was feeling.

This hour is mine. He is mine. Later I will—

He reached her breasts. Slipped soft linen across her, up and then down, stroking her with it. The folds caught, snagging her and tugging and stroking over her. He kissed gently at her nipples, through the fabric, back and forth from one to the other.

She gasped and arched toward him.

"Let's get rid of this." He lifted the shift up and over her head in one sudden unpeeling. Her hair fell back and swept down her skin and hid her. Then his hands discovered her breasts within the curtain of her hair. Shaped her breasts. His thumbs were eloquent on her nipples.

"You have pretty tits," he said. "Just absolutely perfect tits."

"And you are crude beyond measurement."

"Just saying the truth."

He was earthy and forthright and he did not choose to speak like a gentleman. *He could, but he chooses not to.*

I do not want a gentleman.

They shared one breath and then another, face-to-face. She was taller than he was, this way, when he sat upon the bed and she stood. He did not overwhelm her with his strength.

Every moment was her choice. Her decision. His hands slid slowly up and down her body, rasping lightly because they were the hands of a warrior. Not soft. Not pampered. He pulled her body into fascination. Enthralled her.

When she held his upper arm, her fingers didn't circle half the distance around.

I am not like my friends, who take many lovers and walk away unscathed. There will be a price for this. It will cost me dearly. "This is a mistake. But I do not care."

"A mistake. We can regret it later," he said.

"That is my intention." She had not expected the hair of his chest to be soft to the touch. Had not thought she would feel such strength beneath his skin. He held amazement within him, everywhere she laid her hands.

She bent toward his mouth. He stretched upward to her, to meet her. It was as if she attached a string to a mountain and it came to her when she pulled. His lips were smooth and hot. The trembling she felt was all her own. The doubt and the nervousness, all hers. He had no doubts at all.

A small kiss. Not hesitant, but a slow beginning of something he would not hurry. More kisses. Intense. Absorbed. Each different. He urged her head toward him the tiniest notch. Took her mouth. It was feeling and feeling again and only feeling until he was the world, and she was gasping for breath.

She could become lost in this man, as one did in the winds of a storm.

She put her hand to his cheek, studying the textures of his face. He had shaved by candlelight this morning, at the stream that ran through the field they'd slept in. Already he wore scratchy strong bristles again. He must fight continually with them.

Then, exploring, she went to touch his scar. To know what it felt like.

He caught her hand. "Leave it be." A whisper. He turned her palm over and kissed inside it. That was shivery. A wonderful distraction, as he meant it to be. "Pretend it's not there."

She had not dreamed the scar would matter to him. It did not matter to her. "I do not mind it."

"I don't either. But that's not what we're sharing today."

He stood up from the bed. They were so close his skin touched her everywhere as he rose and rose to his full height and took her against him. She felt, rather than saw, that he was undoing the buttons of his trouser band. That he was slipping his clothes off.

His cock was erect and proud and triumphant against the skin of her belly, full and heavy and male.

I was not prepared for this . . . largeness. I should have paid more attention to rude stories and jokes that dealt with this.

He was warm in all of his body, but his cock was particularly warm. She imagined it inside her, as it would soon be. *We will solve this problem of his largeness. His size cannot be . . . unmanageable. Someone would have said this to him. And I am ingenious.* She molded herself close to him and turned her cheek to be flat on his chest. There would be no space between them. She shivered everywhere, but she was not cold.

She would open to him. That was the gateway to pleasure. She would travel this country that was Guillaume.

He brought their mouths together and it was wonder and heat. Wonder that spun and buzzed and throbbed between her legs. She was lifted somehow. All unreal. All magical. She was on the bed, on blankets. The pillows scattered. He was beside her, massive as mountains. Deep beyond deep, in the cavern of his chest, Guillaume said, "This is . . . yes. This is yes."

She was a hollow of expectation, filled only with need. No trace of thought. Nothing but breath and the feeling of his skin. She could do nothing clever, only hold on to him.

He knelt between her knees. He lifted her hips in his hands. He was huge within her, entering slowly. His fingers were soft between her parted legs. There was lightning in the touch of him. She heard him saying she was beautiful. Every breath of her was lovely. This. And this. Perfect. She was a flower. He stroked and she pulsed upward toward him. Curled to him, desperate.

Pleasure gripped her, as if it were a hand that closed around her and shook her. She thrashed with it and cried out and shuddered.

She felt him inside her. Felt wild force, barely held in check. Felt him withdraw. Felt his whole body stiffen. He thrust onto her belly and threw back his head and groaned. She was held, fiercely, by all the huge strength.

Bit by bit, he collapsed upon her, breathing hard. Very heavy. Very comforting. Right and natural in her arms. She opened her eyes and she was enclosed in a warm landscape of the muscle and flesh and bone of his chest.

"I'm crushing you." He rolled to the side and settled next to her. They lay on the narrow bed together. She was tucked close to his body. One arm lay across her. The other cradled her head.

He did not take the chance of making a child. He was careful with me. That is one more truth I know about Guillaume.

He said, "Let me hold you. We have a minute for that." His breath tickled her face.

She pressed her ear against him. *I have this minute.* Her mind drifted in the sound of his heartbeat, in the stream of his life.

I have fallen in love. It does not change anything.

$\mathcal{S}$eventeen

"Street's empty." Guillaume slouched up to her. "Let's go."

Marguerite could not say how this slouching he did down the Rue Palmier was different from what he had performed in the countryside, but it was. There, he had been a shrewd peasant, a man with fields and, most probably, a local feud or two. Now he was a city man, knowledgeably sly in a way that had to do with narrow alleys and cafés on the boulevards.

He took her arm, something he had not done in the countryside. Thinking about it, she realized this, too, was a difference between the city man and the country man.

It did not disturb her that Guillaume LeBreton should change in this subtle way. She did not know all of what he was. Probably she did not want to know. But he was also the man who had made love to her an hour ago. It was that man she would say good-bye to.

"That's where they'd put somebody to watch for us. See?" Guillaume slowed.

Adrian glanced into the passageway between houses, narrow and not too clean. "Obvious. No art to that."

"Most folks are not what you'd call artistic. A better spot . . ." Guillaume looked up to the very highest attics under the roof where poor men rented cheap rooms. "Up there, up with the pigeons, in one of those windows. That's where I'd put my man. Nobody ever looks up."

The Hôtel de Fleurignac was a hundred feet ahead, on the left. It had been built sixty years ago of the cream-colored stone they mined from under the foundations of Paris. The blocks might have been quarried from under the very roots of the house, fifty feet down. Hôtel de Fleur-ignac wasn't the grandest house of the quartier, but it had not been sacked in the last four years, which was a great advantage.

Guillaume walked with the firmness of a citoyen veg-etable farmer who had business to conduct in some café or shop or at the back door of one of these mansions. They were not alone on the street. One woman passed them briskly, without nodding, carrying bread in a basket. A little servant girl, head down, wearing a floppy mobcap, swept a doorstep.

"On the other hand, if it was the Secret Police doing the watching," Guillaume continued, when they were out of earshot of the maidservant, "which it's likely to be in this town, they'd bully the patriotic citoyens of . . . ah . . . that house, I think, or the one next to it, and put their man in the front parlor. If he was careless, you might see a curtain pulled back. Maybe a light."

"There is a timber merchant living there." She could be informative, having followed the fortunes of all these houses. "He was a Dantonist, two months ago, which is no longer a desirable political association, of course. Now he is an enthusiastic follower of Robespierre. He would keep a battalion of infantry in his parlor if the police asked."

But no one would bother to watch for her. If the Committee of Public Safety wanted her, they would simply send gendarmes to pound at the door. Aristo women waited at home, terrified, until the police came to get them. She had rescued enough of them to know this. La Flèche always found them, proud and disbelieving and stupid as rabbits, hiding in their parlors.

The Hôtel de Fleurignac had not been given over to timber merchants or land speculators from Lyon. Five years ago, Lafayette himself had stationed guards to protect the house from the mob. In the disorder of the bread riots, Danton's men had been posted outside, drinking heavily and pissing in the stone flowerpots. When Lafayette had fled and Danton was dead on the guillotine, the authority of Robespierre and the Committee of Public Safety protected them. Cousin Victor arranged this protection, leaping from one party to the other as circumstances dictated.

Victor was the son of Papa's younger brother. He was the last to bear the de Fleurignac name, the others having made ill-judged stands against the march of the Revolution. His sense of timing was exquisite. He should have been *danseur noble* of the corps de ballet, he executed such clever jetés and pirouettes on the stage of politics.

"You live here." Adrian ran his eyes over the ledges and carvings and the bowed iron railings of the windows. "Nice handholds all the way up the side. Be easy to get in. Bit of a plum, really."

"You'd see that. I want you to keep walking. Make a . . ." Guillaume marked a figure eight in the air with his index finger, "up and down some streets and come by here again. Keep doing that till I'm finished."

Till I'm finished. They were almost finished with one another, she and Guillaume LeBreton.

It was good-bye to Adrian as well. She turned in the middle of the street and kissed him quickly on the forehead, astonishing and appalling him. "Be safe." It was a plea-sure to break his perfect self-containment for one instant. "If you are ever in trouble, go to the kitchen door and tell them you have a message for me. If I am alive, I will come. Remember that."

Guillaume said, "Which is better than you deserve, boy. Off with you."

She stood beside Guillaume LeBreton and watched Adrian take his grin and the two donkeys away, down the street, around the corner.

"The boy doesn't know what you're offering. What it means to be a de Fleurignac in this country. And he's talk-ing the simple truth about robbing the house."

"So I believe. I have never known a professional thief before. You must find him an interesting traveling compan-ion. Are we so very easy to rob?"

"For him. Yes."

When one had walked for days to arrive, it was a great foolishness to discover one did not want to be there at all. She crossed the empty street to go home. She had five min-utes more to be with him. Maybe ten. Some small number. She had avoided thinking about this, as one would detour around a deep swamp that one did not wish to be swallowed up by. There was no more avoiding the subject. They had arrived. If she looked down, she would see her feet sinking.

He did not take her arm again. He had assumed yet a new identity and trailed a half pace behind her, as well-trained servants did. As respectful inferiors did. It was nicely done.

She stopped at the door. Several important tasks would fall upon her shoulders the moment she stepped through. She would be Citoyenne de Fleurignac. She would much rather have stayed Maggie a little bit longer.

After a while, when she did not move, Guillaume said, "If you want that open, you'd better knock on it."

"You are a fountain of wisdom."

He showed a mild interest in the mansard roof and the carved garlands above the windows and none at all in her. This would have hurt her, if she thought his face revealed any tiny particle of what he was actually thinking.

If she were upon the most important peak of a great mountain, one of those in Switzerland or the great ranges of the East, with the ground distant below and she tripped off the edge and fell, there would be a feeling of floating and a rushing wind and she would seem to hang motionless between earth and sky. All the long minutes of falling, she would believe destruction was not inevitable. She would hold that hope in her heart till the last instant when the ground came up, quite suddenly, and all was finished.

Being with Guillaume had been such a fall. Now, she encountered the solid earth. She could not go to walk across Normandy with him again. She could not even return with him to Jeanne's small room. In every important way, they had already said farewell. She stood upon the doorstep, trying not to think about what came next. Trying to resign herself in a wise fashion. Truly, there were limits to the uses of philosophy.

"Or we can stand here a while," Guillaume said. "It's a nice day."

"One more minute. Then I'll knock." She had a stone in her chest instead of a heart. "Will you ask my father to pay you? We have not talked about this at length."

"I'm going to insist on it." He had become curiously without expression, as if even his endless invention had found its limits. "It'll look odd if I don't." Another minute. "I didn't take you with me for the money. You know that."

"I know nothing about you except an assortment of lies." She had no right to disgruntlement. She indulged in it anyway. "Now you will be finished with even the small trouble of telling lies to me. You will be pleased."

"Right. That's me, grinning like an eel."

She would not forget his voice, would she? It was like grindstones rubbing together. No one else spoke like that.

"It was good. Being with you." She spoke each word with care. Their interlude was almost over. "If matters were different, I would . . ." She pushed the air out of her lungs and stopped talking, because there was nothing to say, really. "But things are as they are."

He still kept the ring he had taken from her. Her mother's ring. She had not asked for it back and he had not offered to return it. Was she wrong to leave it with him and think he would treasure it?

She would imagine him keeping it and taking it out, sometimes. To look at. To hold his hand. There was no end to her foolishness.

"Let's get this over with." He slipped past her and raised his fist to bang on the wood, making a sound that was loud and hollow and final.

I have tasted his hands. I have bitten into the marrow of his strength. He is mine. The heart has no sense at all.

Janvier, who was Papa's steward, was already awake to open the door. He was dressed in black jacket and knee breeches and a plain linen shirt. No lace and silk livery for the servants any longer. The veneer of revolutionary ideals was thick in her father's house.

"Mademoi—Citoyenne. What?" His jaw hung open. He looked to the street. Looked in both directions and saw no carriage. No maid. No footmen unloading luggage. His eyes fixed on Guillaume's scar. "What has happened? Where is the carriage? Why are you dressed like that?"

No soldiers had come to her house to arrest her. The betrayal that struck across Normandy had not touched La Flèche in Paris. And no one had brought word of the burning of the chateau.

"You sent no message, mademoiselle. We thought you

were safe at Voisemont." Janvier retreated before her, sputtering.

"It seems I am not. Where is my father?" She must acquaint Papa with various sorts of bad news. And Victor. Victor would complain and blame her. He would have blamed her if lightning shot out of heaven and burned the chateau.

Guillaume brought his large presence into the entry hall. He stood with his hands clasped behind his back, face-to-face with a woodland nymph, naked, in gilded bronze. He studied it with a grave expression.

"The master is not . . ." Janvier searched the street again, as if he expected a carriage to suddenly appear, then closed the door. He stood, being suspicious of Guillaume.

"My father is not what?"

"He is not here. Precisely."

Fear trickled into her. "Where is he, precisely?"

Janvier said nothing. He was no fool, her father's steward, or he would never have survived being in charge of Papa's household. Like any good servant, he had a highly developed sense of when to keep silent.

Something was wrong. There was no sign of it in this calm, clean, well-ordered entry hall, but she knew. It was as if she walked the icy surface of a winter lake and heard the thin sound of ice cracking under her. "How long has my father been gone? An hour?" Janvier would tell her, eventually. Or she would find someone who would. "A day? A week?"

Had Papa been arrested? Pulled from his bed in the middle of the night and hurried away by a troop of *gardes*. It was the way of things these days. It could happen to anyone. Even Papa. Even wily, infuriating Papa.

If he was in prison, it might already be too late. It was infinitely hard to rescue men once they were in prison.

She had given Papa a hundred opportunities to leave

France and become émigré. Argued with him. Told him to go to England and be safe. He would not. She could only hope he was in Oslo again, making notes upon the nesting habits of Norwegian geese, instead of wandering some battlefront, gauging the skill of Austrian artillery officers. With Papa, one never knew.

Guillaume did not watch her directly. He looked in the long mirror and followed her with his eyes, his face without expression.

The door opened behind her. It was not her father who came from the salon. It was Victor. Who should not have been here, in her house, at this hour of the morning.

"Cousin Victor." She made the hurried small curtsy that brushed the edge of rudeness. How many times had her father told her to be polite to Victor? "Janvier has lost his tongue. Tell me. Where is Papa?"

"Where have you been, Marguerite? We heard—" Victor bit off the rest. "Why are you dressed like that?" He looked to where Guillaume was inspecting more nymphs. The way Guillaume looked at them was not the way a man looks at Renaissance art. It was in the appreciative way a man looks at statues of naked women. "Who is he?"

That was a question she'd been asking herself for a while. "I will explain to my father. Where is he? In short words, if you please. Why is he not—"

Victor cut her off. "Later."

The last time Victor had been in her house, he had not given orders. Something was dreadfully wrong. "Why are you here?"

Victor snapped, "Not in front of the servants." He scowled at Janvier—Janvier, who had known every family secret for two generations—then turned to glare at Guillaume. "You have not yet told me who this man is."

"That is a matter for my father to deal with. But if you wish to be private with me, let us do so. Come. The salon."

Act as if Guillaume is nothing. Not important. At the last minute, as if she had almost forgotten, she paused to say, "Sit down, Citoyen LeBreton, and wait. Use the wooden bench and do not touch anything. My father will pay you."

Victor did not move.

She said, "This is nothing for you to be concerned with."

"In the absence of your father . . . yes, it is my concern. The explanations will come to me. And it seems I must conduct this business for you."

A sick weariness overwhelmed her. *Guillaume must leave. I must get him out of this house. Away from Victor.*

Victor was not only her cousin and the de Fleurignac heir. He was a powerful man in his own right. A radical, a member of the Committee of Public Safety, and a friend of Robespierre himself. He was an idealist. A humorless man, self-serving as a weed, with stern morals and unshakable, very dull convictions. The opposite, in short, of Guillaume LeBreton.

Victor could have Guillaume killed by the lifting of a finger.

She sighed, noisily. "I have been in the dust of the road for four days, Cousin. I am hungry and filthy beyond endurance. You tell me Papa is in some trouble too complex to explain. Citoyen LeBreton can wait." She barely glanced over her shoulder. "Go now and come back tomorrow. We are busy."

Briefly, Guillaume looked up, straight at her. His eyes showed not a gleam of what had been between them.

"Who is he?" Victor repeated. "Explain this, Marguerite."

She threw up her hands. "Very well. Perhaps you are the one to handle this matter, after all. This is Citoyen LeBreton, a peddler of small goods about the villages. When there was disaster in Voisemont—and there has been more than you can possibly guess—he was kind enough to bring me safely through the countryside, all the way to Paris. I promised to reward him. Take money from the strongbox and pay him for me, if you please."

"A hundred louis d'or." Guillaume seated himself firmly upon the bench. He folded his arms across his chest and transformed into the Tradesman Citoyen LeBreton, his eyes filled with calculations of money and value, his hands apt to handle the shape and form of merchandise. One could see there would be an occasional short weight among Citoyen LeBreton's goods. "Gold. Not silver. Not paper."

"Patriots accept assignats." Victor was silkily threatening. "Only reactionaries and counter-revolutionaries demand coin. Do you know it is against the law to refuse assignats when they are offered?"

"The bargain was for coin."

How did Guillaume do it? A twist of his mouth. The scar revealed to the light. A change in his voice. He became a man of the alleys and dirty streets in the crowded faubourgs east and south of Paris. Even his hands, resting on his arms, looked crude and dangerous. The same hands that had been like the hands of a god upon her skin.

Do not challenge Victor. Take assignats and leave.

She did not glance once at Guillaume. She did not trust herself to lie with her face and eyes as well as he did.

"Cousin." She pushed past him impatiently. "We have troubles more important than dickering with merchants. Send Janvier to pay him and come to the salon. Please."

Important matters would appeal to Victor. He was a man with a great belief in important affairs, all with him at the center.

He nodded. "You're right. Go ahead of me."

She opened the door to the salon. Behind her, Victor spoke softly. But she heard him.

"You should beware, Citoyen LeBreton. Men mount the guillotine every day for less than this single insolence you have shown me. Janvier will bring coin. Do not let me see you again."

Eighteen

DOYLE WALKED AWAY FROM HÔTEL DE FLEURIGNAC, clicking a pouch of gold pieces.

Hawker didn't approach till he got the hand signal. Then he caught up. "You just walked off and left her?"

"Right."

"Was the father there?"

"Not a sign or a whisper. There's a cousin who's moved in. An interesting fellow. She doesn't like him."

They fell into step, the donkeys forming an auxiliary corps at the rear. The boy didn't ask for a good long time. Two hundred paces. Then he gave in. "Interesting, how?"

"The number of men he's killed." *I could drag you halfway across Paris by that curiosity of yours.* "Bit of a Utopian philosopher, Victor de Fleurignac, which these days means chopping the head off anybody who disagrees with you. About a dozen so far. He thought about adding me to his bag. He would have, if Maggie hadn't been standing right there. That is a man darkly and justifiably suspicious of me."

He took a right into the Rue Riquier, stopped, and did a check of the straps of the panniers on both donkeys. Probably they weren't being followed. Hard to tell in this part of the city.

Hawker stood alongside, fuming. "You left her with a cousin who kills people."

"Not just with his own lily-white hands, he don't. It's all clean and judicial. Orders of the Committee of Public Safety."

"You walk off and leave her because you think her father's going to show up."

"Or she'll go find him. One or the other." He patted the straps and clicked at the donkeys. "She is what we call bait."

"You do that to her. You take her upstairs with you and then you do that to her." Stomp. Stomp. Oh, the boy was outraged. "I could smell you two when you came down. Like a couple of alley cats. You grinning and her purring and stretching."

That had been good, strolling along beside her, knowing she smelled of him. "I'm hoping that cousin of hers don't have your extensive experience. Which he apparently don't, or I'd be on my way to the chop right now."

"Fine. Just fine. What about this pair?" Hawker poked an elbow back toward the donkeys. "We're through with them, aren't we? Why don't we sell them, too? Lots of good, savory meat on those bones. Donkey fricassée."

"Thought that was what you wanted."

"You don't eat your own donkey. And you don't use your own woman as . . ." Hawker kicked a loose chunk of cobble in the gutter. It rolled end over end and rapped up against a wall. "Bait. That's one of those delicate distinctions gentlemen make."

A carriage rolled past. Doyle said, "As far as eating goes, mule is better than donkey. I'll take you to a café where you can try both. There's one over on the Left Bank."

"I'd as soon not, if it's all the same to you. You could find a way to keep her if you wanted to."

"I've taken a lot of trouble to put her right where she is."

Hawker showed a line of clenched white teeth. "Piss on that."

"If she's in it with her father, planning assassinations of army officers, she deserves what she gets. If she isn't, she's still the only line we have that leads to him." It was full daylight. They'd be awake in the house in the Marais, at headquarters. "De Fleurignac knows who's marked for death. When I get my hands on him, he's going to tell me. Now, listen. You know where we are?"

"Notre Dame over there." Hawker pointed. "Hôtel de Fleurignac that way." Eyes, sharp as obsidian glass, studied him. "You didn't like leaving her."

"I don't have to like everything I do."

"When are we going to get her out of there?"

"When it's time. I'm going to wander off down that street, which happens to be the Rue Cairel. You do a little tracking after me, just for practice." He talked with his fingers, giving the same order. "If we get separated, find me on the Right Bank, downriver of the big bridge, the Pont Neuf."

Hawker said, "Yes," with his hand.

Let's see if we can lose you, boy. He strolled off, taking the donkeys, not glancing back.

"BURNED! The chateau burned! This is impossible. Impossible." Her aunt shrieked like a parrot and beat her feet upon the floor. "No! No. No. No. Impossible."

Aunt Sophie. In a world of many uncertainties, she remained predictable. It was the same shocked collapse. For a bird set free from its cage or the fall of the king. For a broken fan or the burning of a chateau.

Marguerite stood, making soothing noises, until the maids

assisted her aunt from the salon. Victor ordered scented water for his mother's eyes. A tisane of lavender and fennel. Damp cloths for her forehead. Aunt Sophie departed, in tears and hiccuping. Silence, with a sigh of relief, settled in.

It was both dim and stifling in the salon. She threw the curtains back, one after another, and opened the windows to let cooler air in. She went about extinguishing the candles, which shed little light and added to the heat.

Victor gave more instructions to Janvier. All activity would cease within the house. Complete quiet would descend in every quarter. There would be darkness in his mother's chamber, and a maid to sit with her. Pastilles would smolder. Victor considered gravely the merits of several sorts.

Cousin Victor must have invaded the Hôtel de Fleurignac in the past few weeks. In that time Aunt Sophie had splattered the salon with comfit boxes and pudgy cupids. Three clocks ticked away at three different times. Why would anyone need three clocks?

This was Republican spoil, looted from the patrician houses of Paris. She recognized some of it from the homes of her friends.

Janvier departed to oversee the brewing of tisanes. She found another clock, fairly small, on the table behind the sofa.

Victor waited till the door closed. "That was not the way to tell her. My mother is a woman of great sensitivity."

"There is no tactful way to hint that an entire building has been burned to the ground."

"There was no reason to say anything. My mother does not need to be told the full extent of this disaster." He gestured his way across the room, as if he addressed a public meeting. "My God, the loss is catastrophic. How could this have happened? The paintings alone were valued in the tens of thousands of livres. And the library. Do you know how much your father has spent on books?"

"Almost to the sou. The servants are safe. And I escaped without harm, thank you."

"Naturally, I am concerned for your welfare." His mouth thinned. The long nostrils pinched. Victor was said to be a very handsome man. She had never seen this herself. "This is your own fault, Marguerite, that the villagers were there, looting and burning. Out of control. If you had stayed in Paris, as I advised, this would not have happened."

That was the problem, dealing with Victor. He would make statements without the least thread of a logical argument anywhere. "The men who did this came from Paris."

"Exactly my point. There are political zealots who wander the countryside, stirring up mischief. You invite them by flaunting yourself at the chateau. If you had not been in the chateau, alone, without supervision, the villagers would never have rampaged loose on the estate."

"Do not blame my villagers. It was the scaff and raff of the tavern. Two men came with arrest orders from the Committee of Public Safety, rousing up—"

"Do not be ridiculous. If orders had been issued, I would have been told. Do you think no one has ever denounced your father's antics?" He paced, step by emphatic step. "I have quashed any such order. I have kept the de Fleurignacs safe. Leaving aside my affection for you . . ."

Oh, yes. Let us leave that aside.

"I cannot allow my family to be attacked. I am responsible for your actions. Do you think I can occupy the position I do and not have enemies? Your stubbornness, your father's stupidity in allowing you to live alone and go your own way has—"

"I have managed the estate at Voisemont since I was—"

"Your father's stupidity in letting you run wild has led to the loss of our estate. God knows what will be said when this becomes known. It is exactly this notoriety I wanted to avoid. If you had been in Paris, under your father's protection and under mine, none of this would have occurred."

"Where is my father?"

That stopped the stream of complaint.

Victor waited one moment too long before he answered. "I thought he was with you. At Voisemont."

Victor did not know where Papa was. If he had been arrested, Victor would have been told. It was a great load of fear removed from her heart. Papa was not scribbling mathematics on the walls of one of the prisons of Paris, annoying his fellow inmates and driving the guards to the point of murder. He was merely missing.

"Has Papa left Paris? Do you know?"

The sound she heard was of teeth grinding. Victor's teeth. "I assume so. He packed one bag and left. He did not inform me of his destination."

Almost, she could feel sorry for Victor. "He has not become émigré, if that is what you fear." Papa did not have sufficient common sense. "Whatever has become of him, it has become of him in France." Which did not limit the amount of trouble he could get up to.

"I wish I could believe that," Victor said.

"If you are concerned for him, you should have written to me for reassurance. Though you are kind to visit, of course, and your mother also. Even if it is inconvenient at the moment." She crossed the room to pull the bell rope.

She had a choice of problems. The most immediate of them was Victor. But he was not the largest.

"We will find Papa in a boat-house in Puteaux, measuring magnetism on the Seine, or in someone's mausoleum, studying the skull size of geniuses, or . . . I think it was planets in the last letter. I did not pay attention. It was nothing political."

"Everything is political, Marguerite." Victor placed himself directly before her. Too close. "What happened between you and that peasant?"

She brushed it away. "Between me and a traveling peddler? Do not be vulgar."

"You have been in the company of that scum for days."

"He is hardly scum, Victor. He is a tradesman, certainly, but they have their own virtues and codes." *Do this well. Do this very well.* "He was embarrassingly respectful. Not every petty-bourgeois feels the need to wreak violence upon the aristocracy. Some are relieved to follow orders in the old way. He only wants money. There is a piece of land in some village at the end of the earth," she let amusement infuse her voice, "and a pretty miller's daughter."

"Your father would expect me to guard your reputation."

"My father would expect you to leave that task to him. Or to me. You intrude in matters that do not concern you." Because of Victor she had denied Guillaume and insulted him and walked away. She had poisoned their farewell.

At last, he dropped his eyes. "I don't like the way he looked at you."

"His face? It is ugly indeed, but the poor man can't help his face." She turned her back on him. "I will retire now. I find myself most remarkably fatigued by this entire business. I will take coffee in my room and write letters. There are a hundred friends to be told I have returned to town." Deliberately, rudely, she yawned. "I will visit the baths this afternoon. That will refresh me. I am soiled to my very soul by the events of the last week."

"This is hardly the moment to go jauntering off to the public baths. My mother will almost certainly wish to—"

"I was not asking your permission, Cousin." She did not hurry to reach the door of the salon. She would not wish to encounter a footman with his ear still pressed to the keyhole. "Order whatever you wish for luncheon. I will be out. I need not tell you to make yourself at home."

She was tired unto the bone. Not from her journey. She could have traveled to Mongolia and back with Guillaume and not been this drained. It was the giving him up. A quarter of an hour away from him had emptied her of all joy.

It was not so hard to do one's duty. It is the afterward that eats one alive. One survives a long time after doing one's duty. Years and years.

I was born a de Fleurignac. I made myself the Finch, a leader of La Flèche. Neither of them can have anything to do with Guillaume LeBreton, not in any of his guises.

Love was painful. She would not recommend it to any of her friends.

Behind her, Victor said, "If there is something between you and the peddler, it must end."

He looked vexed. It was an expression that often visited his face. He had been a malicious boy, full of mean plots and empty bluster. Now he was an unpleasant man and his threats were entirely real.

So she spoke lightly. "Do you intend to hunt poor, grubby Citoyen LeBreton to his rooms in the Faubourg Saint-Antoine? It does not become you to be vengeful, particularly to a man who has served me well. But then, you never did know how to deal with the servants."

She must speak of a man like Guillaume LeBreton as if he were nothing. It was the only way she could protect him. "I would send a christening present to the little miller's daughter next year, if one still did that sort of thing and I could remember where he said she lived."

Nineteen

WILLIAM DOYLE FELT COMFORTABLE IN THE Marais. A man could take to the streets any time of day, dressed any way at all, and not stand out. Even the donkeys looked natural.

Hawker walked beside him, cat quiet, every muscle loose and ready, his eyes darting from side to side. "Noisy," he commented. "Lots of people."

"All kinds, which is to our advantage. And narrow streets. Good place to get lost, if you're ever running."

British Service headquarters was in the Marais. A goodly selection of humanity lived here, side by side. Rich men, in the airy, ground-floor *appartements*. Grisettes and laborers, on the higher floors, where it was cheap. Tradesmen and shopwomen passed him. Servants were out in force, walking petulant little dogs or carrying bread home to these grand houses along the way. The starveling poor would creep down from their attics later, when it got hot.

Folks who noticed him would think he was selling

vegetables at the back door of those big houses, ducking around the price controls.

I shouldn't have left her there.

Cousin Victor would guess what he and Maggie had been doing this morning. He might talk about equality and fraternity, but Victor had all the de Fleurignac pride. That was a man best avoided.

Rue Pierre-le-Sage was an alley, not wide enough for two people to walk side by side, even if they knew each other well. He and Hawker each took a donkey and led them through. A pair of shop women pushed past, one at a time, dressed in neat dark clothing, hurrying, maybe a little late for work. The distance separating him from Maggie felt like a rope playing out behind him, getting longer, but not letting go.

She'd want to boot that elegant leech-bastard cousin out of her house. One more reason she'd go to her father. The whole point in taking her to Paris was so she'd flush the old man out.

A line waited at the *boulanger* on the corner, snaking halfway down the block, everybody blinking and grumpy, hoping the bread wouldn't run out before they got to the door. Shopkeepers were setting tables of goods outside the door. The offerings were thin, so they spread the merchandise out.

He'd put her back where she belonged, with her family. He'd have men watching her. He'd know if she was in trouble. There was no call to think Victor would hurt her. She didn't act afraid of him.

It's not like I can carry her home and keep her for a pet.

The houses of the quartier showed blank faces to the street, keeping their private lives private. Passages led to courtyards inside, everything closed off by wide, high, double doors, locked tight and guarded by suspicious concierges.

British Service headquarters was partway down Rue de la Verrerie. The gate was painted blue.

He was twenty-nine years old. He'd been British Service for a dozen years, an independent agent for six. This was the first time he'd been a damn fool for a woman.

The small door in the big double gate opened a crack.

"It's me. And this one." He tugged the boy up alongside, showing him. The porter didn't mind if agents brought wild tigers to the door, but he had to see them first.

The door pulled back. The porter stood aside. They walked through a section of square dark overhang, into the courtyard. Dulce and Decorum clattered along behind.

It was quiet in here, but even this early in the morning the house was awake. The shutters on the kitchen windows were open, the sashes up. White curtains showed inside, swaying the tiniest amount. A broom leaned in the open door on the far side of the court, where the stairs ran up. Trails of water darkened the flagstones between the stone sink and the big pots of petunias and lilies set around the walls. Pools of water lay under the red geraniums on the windowsills. Dulce strolled over and started eating geraniums.

"I thought it'd be bigger, the way you talk about it." Hawker looked around, probably considering ways to burgle the place. Nothing like a lad with a trade.

Everyone here, behind every window that overlooked this courtyard, was British Service. His people. If there was any safe haven in France, this was it.

He was expected. The kitchen door opened. Helen Carruthers, Head of Section for France, known here as Hélène Cachard—old, skinny, straight-backed, white-haired, dressed in raven black, dour as always, strode out. Her shadow— Althea—round and rosy and wrapped in a red-striped dress, followed, beaming.

"You have survived, I see." Carruthers reached up, put

a hand on each of his shoulders. Gripped and released. Stepped back. "We heard about the work in London. Not badly done."

Which was the same as a crushing embrace and a hearty handshake, coming from Carruthers. He wondered what she'd heard about the job in England. Most of it, probably.

He might as well get the next part over with. "Adrian Hawkins. Hawker."

Carruthers could make silence a weapon. She could roll it up and bludgeon you with it and bury you in the garden. He was surprised the flowers didn't curl up and turn brown, the cold was so heavy in the air.

She said to Hawker, "You are not welcome here."

"I didn't ask to come." The boy used his best French. Courtly, aristocratic, polite. "Madame."

Carruthers sliced pieces off the boy with her eyes. "I have no choice but to house you. You will stay out of my sight, do you understand?" She raised her voice and beckoned a young woman over. "Claudine, take this . . . this rat to the room in the attic and leave it there. See that it remains quiet until it is needed. Other than that, I do not want to know of its existence. Guillaume, with me, please."

That went well.

HAWKER climbed the stairs to the attic, a pace behind Claudine, glad to get away from the wrought-iron wolf-bitch downstairs.

Claudine, though. He could see himself getting along with Claudine like a house afire. She was plain as a pine board, but with a nice wriggle to her hips like she was used to rocking that cradle. A knowing one, Claudine, and probably a good toss.

He loved women. It'd be a grim world if it weren't for the women in it, and ugly girls were the warm ones. The soft hammocks. The good friends. Who'd chase after pretty when there were women like this?

Claudine looked him over when they got to the top of the stairs. "Your room."

She was wondering whether to treat him like a boy or a man. He could have told her. "You are kind, mademoiselle."

"Citoyenne," she corrected primly. "I am Citoyenne Claudine. We are careful, *mon petit bonhomme*, to be excellent citizens of the Republic. You have all that you need? We will bring your belongings to you, later, when your animals are unpacked."

I do not envy the man who gets stuck with that job. He hoped nobody inventoried the counterfeit they'd be taking out of those baskets. He'd helped himself to a few bundles.

"There is water in the pitcher," Claudine said. "You may wash later at the pump in the courtyard."

That sounded like a suggestion. The British Service was about universally in love with washing. He was getting used to it.

The room had curtains and a rag rug on the floor. Looked like he wouldn't have to share the bed. Clean sheets. A bureau with a china basin and pitcher on it. And towels. Folded white towels. This was a bloody palace.

It smelled clean. He robbed houses that smelled like this. He didn't live in one.

"Nice." He'd been expecting a basement, with the possibility of chains. They knew what he was. What he'd done.

"Althea prepares the rooms. You must thank her. And Citoyenne Cachard, who ordered this for you."

Probably some trap to it then. He kept his face blank. In this household, Claudine was likely to be a woman of many talents. She might be the one they'd send to smother him in his sleep. That added a certain—what would Lazarus call it?—a certain piquancy to the situation.

"You will stay here till Citoyenne Cachard calls for you." Her eyes danced. "If you are patient, perhaps I will even feed you."

She checked to see there was water in the pitcher before she left and locked the door behind her.

The longer he lived, and he'd lived twelve or thirteen years now, the less he understood about women.

He was on his own. It behooved him . . . And wasn't that a fine word? Behooved. He wasn't sure what it meant but he'd heard Doyle use it. It behooved him to show a little initiative.

The window had a drop to the stones below that would kill a man a couple times over, doing a right painful and thorough job of it. But the roof was in reach overhead. *Once you're on the roof, the house is yours.* Lazarus said that. Unlike some of what that bastard said, that was golden truth.

Lazarus got him into this mess. It was Lazarus sent him to search Meeks Street, British Service headquarters in London. When he got into trouble, Lazarus gave him over to the Service, easy as kiss yer hand.

It started smooth, a caper like any other. He'd come down the chimney, headfirst, hanging like a spider on a silk thread. Always some fool lighting a fire in the fireplace, but this one had been out for a while. The bricks were cooled down enough he could stand to touch them. But it was always hard to breathe in chimneys. Hurt his lungs.

Light came up from the bottom, a gray square of it. They'd left a glim lit on some table when they went to bed.

He let out rope. Let out some more. The last dozen feet were hot enough to roast a haddock. He did them fast. Poked his head out. Saw an empty room. Good. Now it was just not knocking the fire dogs over when he climbed out.

He wiped his feet on the hearth rug. No point tracking ashes all over the house. Lazarus had drawn him a map of the rooms. Guesses mostly. Galba's office was in the back corner. Galba was Head of the whole damn British Service. If there was papers about Lazarus making deals with the French, they'd be in Galba's desk.

Find the papers. Get back up the chimney. Leg it out of here. He wasn't supposed to kill nobody.

Not his fault Galba walked in on him.

Claudine's sabots clicked to the bottom of the stairs. The courtyard down below was empty. He went out the window. A tight fit around the shoulders. He was putting on muscle.

He balanced on the windowsill with all that flat and hard waiting down below, hanging to the cracks in the stone with his fingertips. Holding on and reaching up to the roof, both at the same time. All a little tricky, that bit. Then he pulled himself up and over the edge of the roof. It was his roof now.

Good job. If he didn't say a word of praise to himself, who was going to?

There was nobody outside to take any notice of him. He crawled along till he could hear Doyle talking in one of the rooms below. Doyle and that woman Carruthers. *Let's go see what they have to say.*

Knowing things was like picking up diamonds and rubies off the street. Made him feel rich. It might even keep him alive long enough to see fourteen.

The drainpipe that ran down the inner corner of the building, into the courtyard, turned out to be sturdy enough to hold him. He let himself down a dozen feet, bracing against the corner wall, leaving some skin behind. His left knee was giving him trouble again. He didn't take any account of it.

Then he could hear.

". . . rabid little weasel. I'll wring his neck myself if you're too squeamish."

The Old Trout thought she was going to kill him. Not likely.

He couldn't pick all the words out when Doyle answered. ". . . falling into bad habits." Too bad he couldn't hear who was falling into what bad habits. Everybody, probably. ". . . we need . . ."

The woman was talking again. "You see only the English side of it. There were seven in the last six months in Austria. Two of them at the Theresian Military Academy. Not into their twenties. The top of their class." He could hear the chink of china on china. They were sipping tea. "It's obscene."

The Service was worried about Austrians. Seemed like de Fleurignac made himself a couple of lists. Not just the one for England.

He missed Doyle's answer. Then the old woman was talking. ". . . resources. We're keeping low to the ground while the French guillotine each other. But, certainly I can assign men to watch the de Fleurignac woman."

". . . reporting to me. I want them in place today. They follow her every time she puts a foot outside the house. I need . . ."

Easy enough to know what Doyle needed. And wasn't that a pocketful of irony? A man like Doyle could reach out and take anything he wanted. He didn't let himself take that woman.

They talked too low for him to hear. Doyle mentioned the counterfeit in the baskets, saying it was a relief to get it off his hands. Then Carruthers said, "It is not my first priority, but it will give me great pleasure to strangle the life out of that poisonous reptile you've brought among us."

That was him. A rabid weasel and a reptile, too. He was a man of parts, wasn't he?

A long rumble from Doyle. ". . . take more than that to kill Galba . . . recovered except he can't play that damned violin of his and . . ." More words he couldn't hear, and finally, ". . . is mine. Ask first. I have plans for him."

It was time to hike off. He felt the itch of it. Any thief who didn't get that feeling didn't live long. Lazarus said his instincts were good. They told him to shove off.

He could climb up, back to that room. Or he could head down, to the courtyard, and over the wall into Paris.

That was what Doyle would call a foregone conclusion.

He slipped, hand over hand, to the ground. He was flat to the wall by the privy, well hid, when Doyle stuck his head out the window and looked around. *Not bad, Mister Doyle. You are one of the best I've ever seen.*

But I'm better.

This house had more holes than a sieve. He was out of it and on the Rue de la Verrerie in three minutes. He walked off, whistling one of the songs he'd heard today. The song was about killing people.

Hell of a city, Paris.

"I don't see him." Doyle let the curtain loose. "But he's out there behind the shed. You owe me that louis."

Carruthers grimaced. "Crawled down the wall like a lizard. Nasty little monster. I'll admit I heard nothing."

"You can check his room if you want. He won't be there." He thumbed a roll open and stuffed hard cheese inside. Held it while he gulped down his tea.

"He can't be trusted, just because he was handed over to you. You know that."

"He wasn't handed over. I won him in a card game."

"He's planning to slit your throat one night, while you're sleeping."

"Then he'll do it. He hasn't tried yet." He scooped sugar lumps out of the dish on the tray and tucked them into the pocket in his breeches. "Right now, I think he's going to lead me to the man who brought the de Fleurignac list to London. He's out looking for something at any rate. I have to go. Who runs La Flèche? Do we know?"

Carruthers raised an eyebrow. "The Paris side is run by a botanist at the Jardin des Plantes. Jean-Paul Béclard. In Normandy, it's a woman. The Finch."

"Then Marguerite de Fleurignac is the Finch. I watched her hand out orders to all and sundry across the countryside. I'll tell you about it when I get back."

"In detail." Carruthers collected every secret that walked through France. Including his. "A woman of the old Normandy aristocracy. It makes sense. Yes. The de Fleurignacs have always done precisely as they pleased."

"Helen, I need to know she's safe. This isn't just the job."

He got a searching look. "I'll keep her safe."

Four words. From Carruthers, that was all he needed. "I'll leave that to you. I want Pax with me."

"He's yours. I've already told him."

His hat was on the table by the door. A glance out the window said Pax was in the courtyard, waiting, with the door to the street open. "If my rat comes back alone, don't kill him."

"If he comes back."

"Always that chance."

"Do you honestly think you can make something of that evil little animal? It's unwise to adopt baby scorpions. They grow to be venomous."

"He's going to be one of the great ones, Helen. One of us. Either that, or I'll kill him myself."

Twenty

"THE AGENT WILLIAM DOYLE GAVE ME THE SLIP in the market at Les Halles. With donkeys. He went through the stable yard of an inn and I lost sight of two donkeys among the pack animals. I am a donkey myself, Madame, and I am ashamed." Justine hung her head.

Madame laughed at her. Oh, not with her mouth. She was too kind to do that. She laughed with her eyes. "He is very good."

"I am very good as well. My heart is broken. I would have sworn there was no man I could not follow through my Paris. And now I am defeated by an Englishman." There was worse. "The boy also disappeared sometime after they left Hôtel de Fleurignac. I was not exactly following him, you understand, but it is a mortification to add upon the other one that I am not entirely certain where he went or when. I have the brains of a pineapple."

She was in the salon, which was the prettiest of several fine rooms in the brothel. All was effortlessly elegant here; the pale, cream-colored walls, the blue curtains with gold swags, the delicate mahogany furniture. No part existed by accident or failed to harmonize with the whole. Someday, she would create rooms like this.

Madame made her a cup of chocolate, made it with her own hands from hot milk Babette brought up from the kitchen. Madame had taken her own silk shawl from the arm of the sofa and pulled it over the dust and dirt of the servant dress so that Justine would not feel shabby in this beautiful room.

"When I admitted to myself that I had lost this offensive Monsieur Doyle of England—and that was not soon for I am very stubborn—and lost also two entire donkeys, I came home to confess."

Madame did not interrupt her or hurry her.

She drank chocolate and delayed one more minute. She must admit straightforwardly what she had done. "I have deserted my post. You set me to watch the *hôtel* and report on any who came to Victor de Fleurignac. Instead, I followed the Englishman. I judged you would want me to."

"Exactly well. You did exactly well. I can set any of a dozen girls to watch front doors and make reports. You are one who will know when to abandon your post to follow an order that has not been given."

"I am abashed that I lost him in the confusion of the market. I will try to do better."

Madame had set a white dish heaped with raisins upon the table. Now she nudged it forward. They were not so sweet, these raisins, but they were perfumed like dreams. They were made from the grapes of Burgundy. Burgundy had been home once.

She rescued me from hell. When I make this failure before her, she comforts me with a tiny gift from my old home. Madame made nothing of her stupidity but only smiled and tipped more chocolate from the flowered pot into the cup.

"You shall take these raisins with you and share with your sister. She will enjoy them. Now. Consider this with me. We discover that the admirable William Doyle travels in the company of the daughter of Citoyen de Fleurignac."

"They do not merely travel together. I saw her face when she looked upon him. They are lovers."

"That is ingenious of him, is it not? He seduces the daughter so she will lead him to her father."

"That would be very stupid of her."

"Alas, yes. Even clever women commit stupidities in the name of love."

"Love." Justine shrugged. "We will sell love tonight to anyone who can pay." She lived in a brothel. She could set an exact price on what happened between sweaty bodies in a bed.

A point of light slid on Madame's silver ring as she turned it upon her finger. "As you say. Let us hope this woman is not so cynical. We will wish Monsieur Doyle every success in finding de Fleurignac. Perhaps he will become so vexed he strikes de Fleurignac fatally upon the skull and rids us all of a nuisance. Perhaps he will even discover the man who stands behind de Fleurignac."

"And orders the deaths in England . . ."

"Which can only bring reprisals, if we do not put a stop to them." Madame spoke to herself, knowing her words would go not one inch further. "We have a rabid dog upon the playing field. It is, I fear, a Frenchman of some importance."

"The Secret Police have brought down important men."

"True. But I would rather the British killed him. Like Rousseau, I am a great admirer of the natural order of things." Madame had walked to the window to look out over Paris. "I have a task for you, Justine. Not an easy one."

"I will not fail you this time. I—"

Madame waved her to silence. "You have not failed me yet. Listen, child. I have learned that Marguerite de Fleurignac is the Finch."

"Finch? The de Fleurignac is Finch?" Now that it had been said, it made sense. If La Flèche was backed by one of the old nobility of Normandy, it explained many things. "And I did not discover this. Not in all the months I have been your eyes inside La Flèche."

"You have discovered other things."

"I never caught a glimpse of her. We are all a little jealous, here in Paris, because the Finch holds herself aloof. She meets only with the same few friends who were with her from the beginning."

"And thus does not show her face to spies of the Secret Police. I hope you will someday be as shrewd." The milk jug went to the tray beside the flowered bowl. Ashes, damp in that little bowl, said Madame had received messages recently, and burned them. "Here is your task. You will watch her as well as this William Doyle. When the time is right, you will approach and gain her confidence."

"I would like to meet her." She bit delicately at the edge of a raisin. "She smuggled several of the Dantonists out of Paris. In dung carts. I admired that."

"I was much amused myself. You will come to her as the Owl and give her the passwords. Try to have many convincing stories under your tongue. She will be more discerning than your Gardener, Jean-Paul. *Peste.* What is that?"

From below came a sound of tearing cloth and a shriek of outrage. Two girls of the house shouted back and forth, quarreling over a scarf no one would admit to borrowing. Madame turned, ruefully, to the door. "I will go quiet matters downstairs. No, do not get up and leave. I am not such a taskmistress as that. You shall finish this excellent chocolate and then go to your room. You will not, my poor child, wash. You must continue to be the sweepings of the street for a while. But you shall sleep for four hours. I will send Babette to wake you. Go then to the Café des Marchands and become involved in polishing some doorstep in the neighborhood. Citoyen Doyle will doubtless return there. Follow him and see what an interesting life the Englishman leads."

When Madame left, Justine did not sit to finish the chocolate but carried it up the stairs to the attic to give to Séverine. She brought the raisins in the little saucer as well.

Séverine was on the bed in their room, humming to her doll, Belle-Marie, telling it stories. They all sat together and held a small celebration on top of the blankets, passing the chocolate back and forth between them, and the raisins, making sure the doll had a portion. Séverine ate those, since Belle-Marie, for reasons of indigestion, could not finish them.

The window of her room looked out over the back of the whorehouse, where there were stables and a shed behind them. Already, men were coming and going with their horses. The business of the house had begun.

Séverine lay down, holding her Belle-Marie tight in her arms. Justine held Séverine.

She would sleep for a while, then begin her own work, when it was evening, and cooler. There would be wind moving through the streets soon. The country people called that hour between evening and night the hour between dog and wolf. She had chosen to be the wolf in life, not the tame dog.

Twenty-one

MARGUERITE RODE WITH THE CARRIAGE WINDOWS
rolled down, leaning forward on the seat, looking out at
the streets.

The sun was hot as bronze overhead. The streets were
crowded. The cafés of the Boulevard des Italiens were
filled. At first glance, nothing had changed.

Five years ago, we were not afraid.

Restauranteurs pulled tables out onto the walkway, as
always. Women in bright print dresses and wide hats drank
wine or coffee. They gathered like flocks of birds under the
trees, perched on rush-bottomed chairs, their skirts spread
wide, fanning themselves and chatting, surrounded by their
maids and their children and their dogs. Young men, the
flâneurs of the boulevards, lounged their way from group
to group. They leaned over the backs of the chairs, trading
witticisms, flirting.

It was a species of courage, this laughter and the crumbs
of biscuit shared with the strutting pigeons. A mile away,
to the east of Paris, men died on the guillotine. Death and

the most humorless brutality held the high ground. But not here. This boulevard was the front line against the barbarians who had destroyed her Paris. Wit and le bon mot and talk of the theater made a stand at these barricades. The ribbon on a bonnet, the lace of a starched cap, were the weapons.

Another jolt and the fiacre pulled to a stop in front of the Chinese Baths.

A boy from the baths ran to open the door of the carriage and let down the steps. He climbed like a squirrel to pass her payment to the driver. He followed her inside, carrying her basket, chattering about the heat. Oh yes, many fine citoyennes, many dashing young men, came today to relax in the waters. He had been busy since the morning, carrying lemonades and coffees upstairs. What heat. Everyone complained.

One entered this most fashionable of public baths between artificial hills on either side of the gate. Statues of Chinese gentlemen, holding umbrellas, sat atop promontories. The central court held a red and yellow pagoda with the café and garden where the bathers might refresh themselves. The chambers for the baths were above. The left-hand side for men. The right for women.

Whether this Chinese bath would have passed muster in Peking or Shanghai, she did not know. But it was Chinese enough for Paris. She climbed the stairs to the right-hand side and found an old friend, Olivie Garmand, the matron on duty. She stood behind the counter, neatly compact, with smooth night-black hair. In La Flèche she was called the Quail. She was as discreet and unobtrusive as her namesake.

Olivie kept the gate to one of pathways out of France. Men and women entered the baths and were not seen again till they were safe in England.

Olivie nodded, polite but not curtsying, as if she were

the most staunch of revolutionaries. "Citoyenne. It has been a long time. It is good to see you again."

"Citoyenne Olivie. Good day." She put a coin in the boy's palm and sent him away. Under cover of setting her basket on the counter, she passed the note that was ready in her hand. She whispered, "For the Gardener."

A glance along the hall. The letter disappeared. Olivie said, "How may we serve you?" and under her breath, "Are there orders?"

"None." She raised her voice. "The hot bath today, even though it is so unpleasantly hot outside."

A maidservant came then, with towels and a *robe de chambre* piled flat across her arms, holding them carefully for they were still hot from being warmed over the little braziers. Olivie, herself, led the way. They went to a cabinet far down at the end of the row, where silence and discretion were abundant. To her left was the inconspicuous door between the men's side and the women's. These rooms had seen many discreet meetings. It was a sad commentary on life that adultery and the intrigues of La Flèche had much in common.

The bathing cabinet was a bright room with huge windows covered by screens that let the light through. The walls were painted to resemble marble. The maid placed the stack of towels and the folded linen robe on the sideboard and went to prepare the tub.

Olivie, who had brought the basket, set that down also and uncovered it and began to lay out the clean clothing from inside and the hairbrush and the bottles of bath oils. "May we bring you wine? A light meal? No? You are right. It's too hot to eat. There is a compress of crushed mint leaves for the forehead, if you would like to try it." Olivie uncorked one of the bottles of bath oil. "This is nice. Neroli and coriander?"

"*Exacte*. From that shop in the Palais Royal. Near the end, next to where they sell the fans. You know the one."

Olivie sniffed again. "It would not suit me. For you, though, it is good. Fresh and forceful. Uncommon. I would have said it is not the scent of a young girl."

I am not so young. A mirror hung over the sideboard. In it she saw unremarkable brown hair. A wide, stubborn-looking mouth. Her nose was sunburned. Her eyes were sunk deep with weariness. A bruise shadowed the side of her face.

Guillaume said she was beautiful.

What part of this face is lovely? What does he see? Maybe it was Maggie that Guillaume found beautiful. She had lost Maggie in the last hours. In the mirror she saw only Marguerite.

The maid leaned over, giving the copper bathtub one last scrub. It was only to demonstrate more thoroughly that all was entirely fresh and perfect. Nothing had been skimped in cleaning before. The woman arranged cloths inside the tub so one did not rest against the hard metal and turned on the faucets, both hot and cold, before she made the silent, sagacious exit of a well-trained servant.

All was silently, gracefully done. Marguerite said, "Is she one of us? I do not recognize her."

"No. A police spy, we think. I shall set her to some distant task for the next hour or two. Something unpleasant, if I can manage it."

In Paris every café and bookshop, every corner market, was political. The Chinese Baths, as well. Here, was a stronghold of the most radical Jacobins, ardent supporters of Robespierre. It was an excellent place for La Flèche to hide, of course, in the very lap of the fanatics. But one must be circumspect in such a lap.

Olivie untied the back of her gown. "This is pretty." It was a round gown of the newest style. Soft and cool, but it had inconvenient fastenings. "I do not quite dare such fashions myself, but you have the figure for it. You have all you need?"

"Everything, except the bath itself. I am beyond filthy. I am a compendium of all the dirt in the world. I am a library of dirt. In a week or two, if I soak carefully, I will be human again."

She was left in privacy to free herself of the light stays and let her shift fall to the floor. To settle into the water and lean back and close her eyes.

There seemed to be nothing she could think about that did not hurt. So she would not think at all. She had an hour, perhaps more, before Jean-Paul crossed the Seine and came to her from the Jardin des Plantes on the Left Bank. There would be time enough to think when he got here.

Twenty-two

HAWKER STOOD FOR A BIT, TAKING EVERYTHING IN, scratching under his arm on the principle that somebody scratching looks harmless.

It was odd, being in a city where none of it was familiar. Miles of places he'd never been in every direction. The mumble of a language that wasn't English all around him. Having to think about what he said before he let it out.

And his clothes. Back home, he'd be wearing something with a bit of color in it. Men knew him in London. He had a reputation to live up to. He'd been the Hand of Lazarus for three years. He'd killed men. His mates expected a certain degree of style.

Paris was about being invisible. Blending in.

Nothing smelled right. Sour wine, instead of beer. Brandy, not gin. Garlic and some kind of herbs coming out of the chophouses. Just plain foreign.

He felt strange, walking the streets without the damned donkeys.

Funny how he'd figured it out at last. Those donkeys

were stalking horses. Nobody looked at the man driving the donkeys. All they saw was the animals. A pair of donkeys in your company and you could stop anywhere you want, as long as you wanted, and nobody thinks it's odd. You could look at the hooves. That's a job to keep a fellow occupied for the better part of the day if he does it right.

He strolled along, his thumbs hooked in his breeches. East was this way. Only took a second to figure it out from the way the shadows lay. That was another trick Doyle knew. Watch the sun. Keep a map in your head. Always know where you are. Always be thinking about which way to run. Those hard-faced coves in Meeks Street had a hundred maps with notes all over them. They'd made him study them for hours. He was a right expert in Paris before he set foot in it.

He never had to worry about maps before. Not in London.

Look like you know where you're going. That was something Doyle let drop. Just no end to what Doyle knew about this work. He called it the Game. That felt right somehow. The Game.

He'd have to learn what he could from Doyle before they parted company. Before one them got his throat cut.

Rue de Montreuil. He knew where he was. He wrapped his lips around Rue de Montreuil a couple times, practicing how to say it. They put names on the streets. Carved them right into the houses sometimes. You'd think folks who lived here would know where they was. If somebody didn't live close by and was too stupid to ask where he was, who gave a damn about them anyway?

Funny folks, the French.

Le Brochet wouldn't be hard to find. A day like this, hot as Hades, he'd be in some tavern, out of the heat, easing his throat. He'd be a hundred yards from his ken. Men like him stuck close to home and did their drinking with friends. It was dangerous, going after a cove tucked up in the middle of his mates.

DOYLE signaled Pax up to the lead position and dropped back. It'd take three men to follow somebody like Hawker. That was the Service for you. Never enough agents.

Pax set down the board he was carrying and pulled a cap out of his jacket.

Hawker looked French. Walked French. Held his hands like a Frenchman. He walked the same speed as the men in front of him. Became one more fish in the stream, a little grubbier and less interesting than the others. He had the art. You couldn't teach that.

He was headed east and down to the Seine, which meant he'd be crossing a bridge. In Paris, following somebody was all about the bridges. You could slip by your man and wait on the other bank. Your pigeon would walk right to you.

Doyle took a side street down to the river.

HAWKER ran his man to earth at L'Abondance, the tenth tavern he tried. Le Brochet was sitting in the back, with friends. Unsavory lot of friends he had. "Remember me?"

Le Brochet squinted a while. "You're the boy with Lazarus . . . Hawker. That's right. They called you the Hand. I remember you."

Except Le Brochet said, "*'awker*." When the French said his name they didn't slap a howling great *h* out in the front of it the way a nob Englishman did. They said *'awker* and made it sound right. Hell of thing when a pack of Frenchies could say his name better than Englishmen.

"You're the one brought me that girl. Polly. She was a lively piece."

"A right artist in bed, that girl." Hawker sat down with his back to the room, which marked him as a fool, except that the glasses of wine on the table were good as a mirror when it came to seeing somebody come up behind. "Let's talk."

"Alone," he added, when Le Brochet's mates didn't shove off.

Le Brochet grinned. Not one of the world's most beautiful sights. The other men wandered away, leaving them to discuss Dorcas and Fat Legs Lucy and a few more. Le Brochet had fond memories of his stay with Lazarus.

After a bit it was time to say, "Wine," to the old woman behind the counter. He used the tone Doyle had used this morning. Set the same coin down on the table. His glass got sloshed barely half full—that hadn't happened this morning—with wine of the dog piss persuasion. There was just no reason in this world not to drink gin.

"I'm on an errand," he said. "For Lazarus. Thought you might be of use to me. I need to find the man who paid Lazarus for the killing job."

Le Brochet coughed up a laugh. "Him? His kind don't come here."

"Where is he, then? There's money and I can't leave this bloody country till I've got shut of it."

"Money?" Le Brochet brightened.

"We can't do the contract. Lazarus says, 'Give it back to the man who paid. To the Frenchman. Go find him.'" If Le Brochet swallowed that story, he didn't know much about Lazarus. He touched the money belt at his waist where he had that stack of assignats folded up. Made it rustle. Let it incite a little greed. "So that's what I have to do. Trouble is, I don't know how to find the bastard."

He pretended to take a swallow and wiped his mouth with his sleeve. "Don't know where to look. And I don't like carrying this much around with me."

He touched the money again and sealed his fate. He saw Le Brochet decide to kill him.

Don't be impatient. That was what Lazarus always said. *Be generous with your time. Anything worth doing is worth taking pains over.*

He made Le Brochet work fifteen minutes to lure him out into the yard behind the inn. Made him use three "Got something to tell you" and half a dozen "Don't like to say it in here" before he let Le Brochet lead him out of the room, through the hall beside the kitchen, and into the stinking courtyard.

"This is nice and quiet." He admired the courtyard. It was private enough back here to kill five or six men. As he walked, he rolled his right sleeve up to the elbow, which would have been a warning to somebody knowledgeable.

Le Brochet moved in behind him. The slip of cloth on cloth and the change in breathing told him Le Brochet had his knife out.

If a man doesn't know how to fight with a knife, he should leave it at home. Hold a knife and you can't do anything else with that hand. Hold it stupid and it throws you off balance. A fool with a knife keeps trying to jab it at you instead of using his whole body to fight.

So the fight started with Le Brochet lurching at him. Which meant he ducked under Le Brochet's arm, slammed an elbow into that flapping mouth to keep him quiet, and kicked him in the bollocks. Took the knife away. Ten seconds' worth of fight, give or take.

He stepped over Le Brochet's back. Straddled him. Took a handful of hair and pulled his head up, throat bare. He held his knife under Le Brochet's ear. It'd be a clean stroke in, down and across. With his sleeve rolled up, he wouldn't even get his shirt messy. He'd be over the wall and out of Faubourg Saint-Marcel before the corpse stopped twitching.

Doyle won't like this.

That messed up his concentration. Le Brochet started gargling, so he pressed the knife in, just a bit, to remind the man of his own mortality.

Lazarus said to kill the cove. Clean up the loose ends. Nobody disobeyed Lazarus.

Doyle wanted the names on that list. Wanted to save men slated to die. He wouldn't mind knowing the French agents working in England either. Nobody was going to get answers out of a corpse.

Damn and rot Doyle anyway.

Le Brochet babbled, "I swear it. I was just scaring you a little. I swear to God. Sweet Saint Vincent, forgive me. I wasn't going to kill you. Wasn't going to lay a hand on you."

Unlike some, Hawker didn't get any pleasure out of men begging. That was why he was good at his job. He didn't get distracted.

Doyle would say any damn fool can kill a man. A dog can kill a man. A little bug you can't barely see can kill a man. "Shut yer trap. I can't think with you yapping."

"I got money. Jewels. Aristo stuff. The real thing. I can tell you where. Split everything with you. I wasn't going to hurt you. I swear it. By Saint Vincent. Just having a little fun. Wasn't going to—"

If I leave this garbage alive, Lazarus is going to break my neck in one snap. He's going to laugh while he does it. "Let's talk about your visit to England. Just you and me, friendly-like. You are going to tell me every man you saw. Every paper you carried. You are going to tell me every time you took a piss by the side of the road."

It took a while. His arm got tired, holding Le Brochet's hair.

"I don't know. I don't know. Just a man. A gentleman. Nothing to say about him. I swear. He met me on the street. He knew me. I didn't know him." Le Brochet sucked in blood, his face having got cut up while they were refreshing his memory. "I run messages. Carry packages. Do it all the time. He give me the money and told me where to go. Go to Lazarus. A man named Crawford. Go to this tavern. Ask for Mr. Phineas. Hand over an envelope. Then go somewhere else and ask for Mr. Tuckahoe."

He hadn't noticed what they looked like. Just men. Ordinary men. Some were French—he thought. Some were English—he thought. No, he hadn't looked at the papers he was delivering.

He remembered every girl he'd slept with in obscene detail. He hadn't noticed a damn thing about the assassins he paid to kill men.

Waste of blood, putting it in this fool. Bigger waste letting it out. Nobody's going to believe him if he talks about Lazarus.

Le Brochet panted, "Swear to God. I don't remember any more."

That was the trouble with leaving the bugger alive. You had to conduct damn, bloody conversations with him. He'd got wet and sticky with blood. For this much gore he could have just killed the cully.

Time to leave. He kicked Le Brochet in the gut, so the man didn't have a chance to poke him with some knife he'd got hidden on his verminous body. He pulled up over the wall and took off running.

A dozen streets away, he turned a corner and found a public fountain and stopped to wash the blood off. Le Brochet was yelling death threats after him in the distance.

He had the meeting places used by French spies in England. He had some descriptions that weren't worth much and a few passwords the French used. That was a start. Might be enough for the Service to track some of them down. Nobody could have got more.

Pretty good for a rabid weasel.

* * *

DOYLE uncocked the pistol and lowered it. There'd been one moment he'd almost used it. The boy had taken a while, deciding whether he was going to slit that Le Brochet's throat.

It had been close.

The attic was an oven, which was why none of the tavern girls was up here plying their trade on that filthy cot in the corner. When he stayed still, behind the shutters, he could look down into the filthy tavern yard. See and not be seen. Hear everything.

The boy got the information out of Le Brochet and let him live. There wasn't an agent in Paris who could have done a better job of it.

The tavern boiled out Le Brochet's friends and cohorts, snarling like hornets. Hawker was long gone, over the wall, down the alley.

Time to find him and take him back to Carruthers to get yelled at and cleaned up. Time for the boy to make his first report to a Head of Section.

I'm glad I didn't have to kill him.

He'd taken a risk, leaving his street rat to deal with Le Brochet. It could have been a mistake. Could have been the kind of mistake that makes a man leave the Service.

I hope you're worth it, boy.

wenty-three

THE BATHS WERE RESPECTABLE, OF COURSE. THE most proper woman might come here. But also, no one would be amazed to find improper activities. It was a fine place for secrets. Marguerite had met Jean-Paul here more times than she could count.

Boots shuffled in the corridor outside. A man's boots, not the clogs of the maidservants. There was the smallest scratch on the door.

She said, "Enter."

The high windows and the transom above the door were open to let out the steam of the bath. But no one could linger to eavesdrop in the hall or in the garden below and not be seen by Olivie. All the rooms nearby would be kept empty.

He opened the door. Familiar, reliable, dear Jean-Paul. Olivie would have told her instantly if he'd been arrested. Marguerite had known he was safe, but it was still a great joy to see him with her own eyes. All the way across Normandy, she'd been afraid for him.

When she ran to embrace him, he held her briefly and strongly and then pushed her away. "I wish you'd wear clothes."

"But I am." She was wrapped in the heavy, white linen robe of the bath. Perfectly decent. It covered her to her ankles. She wore less on the street. "Do you know, I did not expect you to grow up to be a prude. It is marriage, I think, that destroyed your sense of humor. You became very serious after you married and had children."

"I became older. Much, much older." Jean-Paul sighed and turned and closed the door behind him. "If there were churches in the city, instead of Temples of Reason, I'd light fifty candles in gratitude. Marguerite, when I heard the chateau burned, I thought you were dead."

"I was not even toasted, except a very little upon the palms of my hands, which have now healed. When I was at Bertille's house she put butter upon them, which she claims is a sovereign remedy. It makes one sticky, however."

"Gabrièlle cried for two days. I would very much like to shake you until your teeth rattle."

I am glad to see you, too, Jean-Paul. "I thought I would come to Paris and it would be too late. You would be arrested. Or dead. I feared for you."

"And I was sick with worry, knowing you were on the road, alone." He reached to her, to touch his knuckles, once, to the back of her hand. "I find you pink and well washed and happy. Naturally, I'm infuriated."

"Oh, naturally. I would like to hit you a little, too, just to relieve my feelings."

He stripped out of his jacket, setting the scene of elegant depravity in the afternoon, in case anyone should come. Because he was Jean-Paul, he arranged his coat carefully upon the back of a chair. It was a habit to drive one insane.

He was strong and slender, of course. To be a chief

botanist of the Jardin des Plantes was to move heavy exotic plant specimens all day long. He was—he had always been—beautiful to look upon, blond and fine-featured, though he was deeply scarred upon his back, of course. Uncle Arnault had done that to him when he had caught them together. Still, if she had come to the baths for dalliance, she would certainly engage in it with him.

He had not been skilled in lovemaking when they were fifteen. Probably he improved later. She had never known quite how to ask that question of Gabrièlle.

His waistcoat followed his jacket to the chair. "We have nothing but rumors here. What happened in Normandy?"

"What did not happen? The chateau burned. That is first."

"I hoped that wasn't true."

"It is wholly gone. Invading Visigoths could not have wrought a more thorough destruction. The servants are safe. The mayor will care for them. I have sent money."

He paused with his hand on the back of the chair. "You've lost your writings. Your records. Your books. I am so sorry."

"I have copies of most of it, here in Paris."

"Not all," he said.

"Not all." He knew what she had lost. Jean-Paul had gone with her to peasant huts to listen to the old women tell stories. He'd taken her seriously, when everyone else laughed. "I remember some of it almost word for word. I have already started rewriting my notes."

He slipped free the knot at his throat. "I'll help, if I can. I don't have your memory." He held the ends of his cravat, half undone, and looked at her. "When the men came to the chateau, to burn it, did they . . . Did anyone . . ."

"I was not hurt."

"You would say that, but—"

"I will intervene before you ask in plain words what will embarrass us both. No harm came to me. Not in the least.

Wren was there, you know, and we fought like Amazons. Truly. Wren will tell you about it someday. Make her dwell particularly upon the moment where I slashed the man with a letter opener. I was intrepid and resolute beyond measure."

He laughed. He sounded young as a boy and very relieved. "I don't doubt it. Where's Wren?"

"I have sent her to England. No, do not complain. She has become too well known. It is time for her to retire."

"You're taking away my right hand." He loosened his shirt and sat to take his boots off. One cannot hold a convincing *rendez-vous* in boots. "But it's time to send her away. You always know."

"We are not greedy. That is why we're alive after four years of running these risks."

"Five years. It's been five years." He grunted, struggling with his boot. "Good God. Remember how we thought this would be over in a month? How everybody would come to their senses and the deaths would stop?"

"By October. I remember you said October. We met with the others in that coffee shop, seven of us, whispering like schoolgirls, to set up the first waystations. One line to take them from Paris to the coast. We'd move fifty or sixty sparrows and disband. We'd never need to do more than that. Here. Let me." As she had done a hundred times, she knelt in front of him and took hold of his boot and pulled. She rocked back on her heels because it came off suddenly. She had tumbled backward a hundred times.

"I wish you wouldn't do that." He sounded testy, but he shifted to put the other boot in her lap.

"Gabrièlle does not pull your boots off for you in the evening?"

"Gabrièlle is seven months with child, which you would remember if you came to see us more often. I keep a husky servant for the express purpose of carrying coal and water and removing my boots at night. Will you please get up?"

"Of course." It was a pleasure to tease him. He was so respectable these days. She tied her robe with great modesty and precision, so he would notice her doing it and be exasperated at her. "What you may not have heard yet is that Jacobins from Paris led the men to the chateau, having bought them many brandies and harangued them into a mob. It is said they had official papers. We were not on such cordial terms I could ask for them."

"There's no arrest order. You know that? Even in all the confusion of the committees, they wouldn't have lost yours. I set our man to looking everywhere. There's nothing." He was up, stalking the length of the bathing cabinet. She had drawn the hanging cotton curtains all around the bathtub. He brushed his hand across the curtain each time he passed, setting it billowing. "No official papers. Not for you. Not for any of us. No denunciation to the Committee of Public Safety."

"That's what Victor says. I do not generally listen to him. But in this case—"

"He would know." Jean-Paul rolled his sleeves as he walked, to up above the elbow. One could see the thin lines of scar on his upper arms. "I hear he's moved his mother out of their rooms, into your house."

"Which charms me beyond measure. And my father has disappeared. It says much about my life that that is the least of my worries."

Jean-Paul pulled his shirt from his trousers. "I thought he'd gone to Voisemont. I assumed you had him in hiding somewhere."

"It is one of those false doctrines. I have no idea where he is. One of the few blessings of this last week is that I did not have Papa on my hands. But now he is missing and that becomes worrisome when the rest of this inexplicable disaster happens. And it is inconvenient."

"I'll let our people know. We'll try to find him for you."

"I suppose we must." She began to untangle her hair,

using the carved wood comb Papa had brought her back from England. "Victor is fiercely annoyed that the chateau is gone. It seems I am a poor guardian for the wealth of the de Fleurignacs that will someday be his." She made a face. "I should not have survived the fire, apparently, or walked across France on my own. I now have no more reputation than a stray cat in an alley."

"Your reputation is pure gold and your cousin is a pig. He was a pig when he was twelve and enjoyed beating me up. He hasn't changed."

Jean-Paul had raked his fingers into his hair. He wore the simple cravat of an artist or intellectual. It hung loose on either side of his neck, down the front of his shirt. They were a fine disheveled pair. They would look entirely guilty of adultery if anyone should come upon them.

She said, "Men came to arrest Egret. Did Crow tell you?"

"I have word from Egret himself. He's in hiding. The man has a hundred blood brothers along the coast. He'd be safe in the floods of Noah."

"They came for Bertille."

"My God. No."

"I would not sit here smiling if any of us were taken. She escaped, and the children, and Alain. None of them was hurt. She is determined to work again. Always, the same Bertille."

She had carried the knowledge for days. Now she would give him the burden of it. "The soldiers who came to take her knew her name. They knew where she lived. They knew us all—Wren, Egret, Crow. Me. Twelve of us who work in Normandy. But no one in Paris."

"Oh, Marguerite."

"It is not just one of La Flèche." Her stomach was like lead. "The traitor is mine."

"It's one of the sparrows. They go to England. They chatter."

"There is no sparrow who could put so many names together on so many different routes. Only one of us." She had hung a towel across her shoulders to keep the wet of her hair from soaking into the robe. She took it off to rub at her face. "It's someone as close as my eyelids. Who do I trust the most? That's the one who betrayed me."

"We knew this might happen someday. We're ready. Your people have taken new names. New stations. We'll start replacing the passwords. We go on."

"And the traitor goes on with us. You will have more sparrows for me soon."

"Not soon. Today. A family of five. Their arrest has been ordered for tonight. Owl is moving them into the loft at the brothel."

"I can't—"

"They leave Paris with the laundry wagons at dawn. Who will you send to meet them?" Jean-Paul's eyes fixed on the wall behind her, an imitation of white marble with black veins in it. "The son is fourteen. Old enough to go to the guillotine with his father."

The pipes in the baths were never entirely silent. One could hear the force of water in them as a burr. A throb. A low hum. "You are saying I have no choice. Even now, with this risk to all of us, we go on."

"Or I can tell the sparrows to find their own way out of France." He waited. Jean-Paul had come a long way from the boy she once knew.

Bertille had said it. No one in La Flèche did this to be safe. "Linnet. I will send Linnet. Tell Olivie to pass the message herself. With her own hand."

She brooded upon the ten thousand catastrophes that might come of this and could think of no way to avert them. Jean-Paul waited patiently for her to finish.

Her people would not draw back. Their part was to be the heroes they were. Her part was to send them into danger.

"Nothing has changed," Jean-Paul said. "Not from the first night when you named us La Flèche. We can't turn back."

"Then we are very stupid. And up to our necks in sparrows. Robespierre will make Paris a city of the dead if he has his way. Oh, I will tell you a clever scheme I came up with while I was waiting for disaster to fall upon me at the *barrière* this morning." She combed her hair and outlined a plan that involved sparrows marching out the gate at dawn, dressed in the uniform of army recruits. "The boots will be the greatest problem. There are no boots exactly like army boots."

"We can steal them."

She shook her head. "We will commission them quite openly and say they are a shipment for Lyon. You will forge some orders. No one knows what is happening in Lyon. Not even the army. They are in sufficient turmoil in Lyon that we could commission petticoats for the army and they would not—"

Very faintly, in the corridor outside she heard something. There might have been the click of opening and closing. There might have been the sound of feet.

Then the door to the room swung back. Guillaume LeBreton stood in the doorway with the light behind him.

wenty-four

GUILLAUME WORE THE WHITE ROBES OF THE house. He did not look like a man at leisure. He looked like a particularly deadly centurion at the Roman baths, one who had seen service against the barbarians until he was half a barbarian himself.

"You're in the wrong room, dolt." Jean-Paul moved in front of her. "Get out."

"Well, well, well . . ." Guillaume looked from her to Jean-Paul and then back again. "I was right about you meeting somebody. I was wrong about who. Introduce me, Maggie."

"I do not want you to know each other. Do not come in."

But he was already in. His hair slicked forward over his forehead, wet, which increased his resemblance to an ancient Roman. The scar was white, stark and shiny on his cheek. She had forgotten how intimidating he was.

Jean-Paul reached smoothly to his jacket where it was hung over the back of the chair. He came out with a long knife, the sort used in kitchens.

Jean-Paul with a knife. "Stop that." She turned the other way. "Guillaume, do not hurt him. I mean it."

"Me?" Guillaume spread his hands. They were empty, which made them no less dangerous. "I'm not carrying weapons."

"And do not look stupid. I am all out of patience with you looking stupid. Jean-Paul, will you put that away before Guillaume tears you apart."

"He won't tear me apart," Jean-Paul said.

"When did you start carrying a knife around with you? We are not bandits and Mohawks upon the streets. What do you need a knife for?"

"I use it to pry open specimen boxes," he said, being Jean-Paul and literal. "And to separate rhizomes." He was watching Guillaume, not her. She had not realized Jean-Paul could look so cold.

"Then you should leave your knife to prying boxes and not wave it in people's faces. What do you think you will do? Hold off a column of dragoons with it? You are being ridiculous."

"I've used it twice, Marguerite."

She knew, then, that he was saying he had killed. He held the knife the way that boy did. Hawker. He cradled it close to his body and pointed upward. Jean-Paul had changed one day, when she was not looking. He had become a man she did not entirely know.

Guillaume closed the door behind him. The bathing cabinet was a small room when he was in it.

"This descends to the level of farce." She stood between them. "Guillaume, you are to do nothing, do you understand? Jean-Paul, I cannot imagine why this man is here, but he is harmless to me."

Guillaume looked Jean-Paul over, being meditative and calm about it. Guillaume, being meditative, was like a mountain wondering if it should fall on someone. There was the same impassivity and inevitability. "This would be a friend of yours."

"You're the one she was with in Normandy. The book dealer." Jean-Paul ran his gaze up the mass of muscle that was Guillaume LeBreton. "You were described to me."

"Then you know I didn't hurt her. You want to put that pig-sticker away before I break your wrist?" Guillaume glanced at the knife.

"Marguerite hasn't said anything about you. Why is that, I wonder?" But Jean-Paul lowered the knife.

Guillaume said, "She didn't talk about you either. I'd guess you're an old friend."

"We are very old, very good friends. The kind of friend she entertains in private."

"I'm the kind of friend she walks across Normandy with."

They were ignoring her. "I am prepared for the scandal of meeting a man at the baths. I am not prepared for the scandal of meeting two men at the baths. It would make goats blush. I would like both of you to just go away. Now."

Guillaume settled his back against the doorjamb and folded his arms across his chest. "Fair enough. Do you need protecting from me, Maggie?"

"I am perfectly capable of dealing with you. I can deal with you with one hand tied behind my back. You are not—"

"Do you want me to go away?"

"It is finished between us."

"You said that a couple of times. Do I go or stay?"

She had no idea what she would say to him when they were alone. Sometimes one throws oneself into the river, assuming one will learn to swim after hitting the water. "Stay."

"Then I'll stay." He stepped aside, leaving an unencumbered path to the door. It did not lessen by one ounce the threat he presented. He was being symbolic. To Jean-Paul, he said, "You can leave me with her. She'll pick up that stool and knock me over the head if I annoy her."

Jean-Paul studied him. "She'll do worse than that. She'll yell and you'll have thirty half-dressed women at the door, asking what you're doing here."

"Ah. Now that would call for undiluted terror on my part, so I'm hoping she don't do it."

Jean-Paul took a moment longer. Then he made some decision that did not involve picking up his ridiculous, dangerous knife, which was good. He sat in the chair to pull his boots on. "I'm not needed here."

"Neither of you are needed," she said. "In fact, I will get dressed and go down to the gardens of the baths and sit in the shade. I will let the maids bring me medicinal teas and little iced cakes. I feel the need for soothing."

"You detest tea and cakes. Ask for lemonade." Jean-Paul did not stay to dress properly but only gathered up his clothing to carry away with him. He slipped the knife he so unexpectedly carried into the hidden sheath inside of his jacket. One could not ask one's tailor to make such an alteration. It must be Gabrièlle who sewed that for him.

"You are deserting me," she said.

"I am escaping. Call me cowardly, but I have no wish to stand between the two of you." He kissed her, unnecessarily, on the forehead and left. Smiling.

She was alone, suddenly, with Guillaume LeBreton.

He stood, being inscrutable, which was one of his talents. In the stark white robe he became dark and exotic. The long folds and draped sleeves made a mandarin of him.

How does he pass unnoticed through the streets of the city? It is as if a lion joined a pack of dogs and none of them remarked upon it. "Did you follow me from my house?"

"Something like that. You didn't make any secret where you were going."

"It was a perfectly useless thing to do, following me. It is over between us. We know it is impossible. We said farewell." She ran out of words abruptly.

"I changed my mind."

He did not move, except to breathe. He was like an idol that was made of smooth, brown stone, but also alive. His hands were in the knot of his belt. It was a little to the side and tied twice. He would take less than a moment, untying it.

She picked up her comb to have something to do with her hands. Set it down again. She would feel more comfortable if he talked more.

"I see your plan," she said. "You do not want me to regret parting with you. You have come to give me another hour of your company so I shall become delighted not to see you again. There is a logic in this. If we were to live cheek by jowl for a week, I would wish you in Parthia or on that island in the Pacific where the birds are the size of dogs and have never learned to fly."

He paid no attention to what she was saying. He loosened the knot that tied the belt of his robe.

"There is no reason to take your clothing off in that menacing and improper way. We will do nothing whatsoever that requires a lack of clothing. When I said you should stay, I . . ." *I was not looking at your body. I was not thinking about it. I cannot think clearly when you are nearby.* "I meant that we should talk."

His robe was loose in long, strong lines down his body. Like columns. He took three slow steps and he was beside her. She did not try to move. He lifted her toward him until their skin touched.

Fragile restraints broke everywhere in her mind. She placed her hands flat upon his chest and shoved cloth aside so she could kiss him there.

She could not speak. Not at all. Her muscles made decisions without consulting her brain. Her body flared into fire. Heat raced through her blood, curled low in her belly, rushed to fill the empty spaces of her mind.

He was warm and naked. Her hands fumbled with the edges of his robe, opening it upward, across his shoulders, deciphering the message of dark hairs and brown skin and the ridges of bone and muscle that were the body of Guillaume LeBreton. If she thought too much about this, she would push him away and stop this. She did not want to let him go, so she did not think.

Where had her robe gone? How had it become untied?

It did not matter in the least.

She was distracted. So distracted. It was as if her fingers could see color. The deep tans of his face. As if the rough prickles of his neck became visible when she explored him there. He was too vivid for mere feeling. He consumed every sense.

I should not do this . . . She did not say that aloud. She did not even think it loudly.

He stroked her body, all the way up and down the length of her. He spread his hands on her hips. Rough palms molded her skin, held to her bone, as if she were sculpted and he were the artist. Awe spoke from his hands. He found her beautiful. More than beautiful. It was as if he worshipped.

He was sweet and forbidden fruit. Forbidden to her in ten thousand ways. A single desperate indulgence. She had set him aside and walked away in pain, knowing the exact limits of her freedom. Now she came home to find forbidden fruit growing, unexpectedly, in her garden. Guillaume.

Kisses deep inside her mouth. Kisses that traveled happily across her lips. Kisses that strayed over her face and down her throat so that she raised her head, eyes closed, and gasped for air. Anticipated, anticipated, waited with every stitch of her being for the next small nip, the next lap of his tongue. He was a man who understood many nuances of loving a woman with his mouth. She trembled, thinking that, and pressed herself against him and she was lost in him.

He was simply so strong. She felt no effort in his muscles when she was lifted, carried, set upon the cool wood of the sideboard. Objects shuffled aside, falling to the floor. None of it important. She slid her fingers deep into his hair. It was warm, coarse in texture, smooth, reassuring to hold on to.

Her legs opened around him. The linen of his robes rubbed her inner thighs. She did not remember when she had decided to be foolish. She must have decided this.

He set her legs apart farther and touched her, intimately, drawing her into every shade of madness. Inescapable persuasion lay in every soft touch.

She could only hold on to him. Panting. No one could think at such a moment. It was a stupid moment to try to think in.

The back of her thighs were on the smooth edge of the sideboard. She slipped, slipped downward, slipped inches along him, feeling his skin to her skin. Knowing this not with her hands or with her skin but with the too-sensitive, inarticulate fire between her legs that could not tell one texture from another, only that they all were pleasure. All joyous. All demanding. All her body, committed to this pleasure, became suburbs of urgency to a city on fire.

Standing, he held her. Cupped her to him. She felt him enter her. Settle himself inch by inch inside her to the hilt. She wrapped her legs around him and hung on as he began to move. She was poised upon him, held tightly as he stroked in and out.

He stopped, buried deep, so that she clenched around him. He was huge within her. A universe within her.

He said, "We're a pair of damned idiots."

It was so exactly her own thought that she did not know whether it was his voice or her own voice in her mind. "We are stupid as guinea fowl."

His laughing was erotic inside her. Beyond erotic. Every

atom of her vibrated with it. He said, "Let's make the most of it."

I cannot stand this.

She gasped. The climax grabbed her and shook her. She arched, brought her hand to cover her own mouth, and bit down to muffle her scream.

Guillaume was motionless and powerful under her. She closed around him. Again. Again. Her breath sobbed in and out. Her head fell back limply.

He gripped to hold her. Thrust into her, oh, incredibly deeply. Thrust again. Twice more, quickly.

He pulled out and spent onto her skin and held himself against her and gasped.

Coitus interruptus. Guillaume was prudent. There would be no child. No scandal and disaster. He was careful with her when she had lost her mind. He was reason, when she had become heedless as the daisy she was named after.

He held the weight of her as if it were nothing. Held the two of them together. Then, slowly, he let her slide against him down to find the floor.

I cannot have him. I shall want him every day of my life.

When her bare feet touched the cool tiles, she let her head fall to his chest so that he would not see her face. Tears squeezed out between her eyelashes. If she brushed her face, very carefully, against his chest, he would not discover that.

They stood, holding each other without words. Then he said, "Now it smells like somebody's been making love in here. That'll keep those chambermaids from asking questions."

"You are romantic beyond words." She pushed away from him.

He set his huge hands upon her shoulders, where they were heavy and conclusive. He kissed her firmly and sweetly, taking his time. When he finished that, he held her and looked at her. "I can't take care of you, can I? I can't put myself between you and whatever it is you're facing."

"You cannot be with me at all."

He was . . . beyond all her experience. His face, craggy and brutal. His scar, dreadful and shiny and translucent. One had to know how to see him under the ugliness. When one did, there was only strength there.

That is why I love him. "I thought we had parted. I cannot say final good-byes to you again and again. I cannot even do it twice."

"No, you can't. You look different when you're wet and your hair's all plastered down, dark as ink. Your bones jut out . . ." he touched her cheeks, drew a line along her jaw, "here. And here. You're stripped down to where the beauty is."

"There is not supposed to be fondness between us."

"There is, though," he said. "Didn't anybody ever warn you about men?" Enclosing her face in his palm, he was like a man with a flower he's afraid he's going to bruise. "I'll be the first to tell you about men. You can't trust us."

She could not find a steady voice to say anything. The breath in her throat was painful. "We end this now, *mon ami.* I do not want to see you again."

The instant he delayed before he removed his hand was his answer. So eloquent, that little delay. Then he stood up and pulled his robe tight. He went out without a word, closing the door behind him as silently as the merest puff of wind.

Twenty-five

HAWKER CLIMBED FIVE FLIGHTS OF STAIRS AND pushed open the third door on the right, being cautious about it. A skinny fellow sat in a chair, leaned close to the window. Whipcord-tough muscle on every inch of him. Six feet tall. No color at all in his hair. British Service.

The cove said, "Hello, Rat."

"And a merry hello to you, too. You're . . . let me see. They were talking about some weakly animated corpse walking about. That would be . . . Pox. Pocket. No . . . Pax. That was the name."

"Paxton. I'm Paxton to you, Rat."

The Old Trout had lumbered him with that name. She said, "So, you came back, Rat." "Go wash your hands, Rat, you're dripping blood." "Close your mouth when you chew, Rat. You're not an animal." "Rat, go to de Fleurignac's and take the watch for the night." So here he was, taking the watch and being called Rat by a cove only two or three years older than him. He couldn't even stab him for it. It was a sad comedown.

The white-haired boy stood up. "They said you'd be relieving me. They didn't ask my opinion. Don't steal anything."

He offered back a couple of words he'd picked up at Le Brochet's tavern. A flavorful insult apparently. He'd have to find out what it meant.

He didn't get answered. Pax turned his back on him and stretched a few times. He gathered his bits and pieces from the table. Hat, cane, a spyglass that folded into itself, a fist-sized piece of bread. "Everybody's home. Victor de Fleurignac came in an hour ago. Doyle's woman got back from the baths about six."

"Fine." *Be interesting to see where Maggie went when she thought nobody was watching.*

"You're on duty till dawn," the boy told him. "Watch the house. Follow the de Fleurignac woman if she goes out. The night glasses are on the table. Don't break them. And don't fall asleep."

"I never fall asleep when I'm working."

"Don't start now." Pax took a last glance out the window, to the Hôtel de Fleurignac. "Remember who comes and goes. The servants, too. And don't show a light, for God's sake."

"I know what to do." *He's treating me like I'm a green 'un. He hasn't been at it so long himself.*

"There'll be lamps on the street. You'll see if anybody comes to the door. If it looks interesting, get down and follow. You're not here to sit on your arse. And don't be seen." *Pax had to run his finger down the whole catalog, didn't he?* "We have a man in that corner, down in the dogleg at the end of the street. If you go out, give him a sign as you go by."

"I'll do that. Shut the door quiet-like when you go."

He got a mean, suspicious glare out of Citoyen Ghost-hair Paxton. Then he was finally left alone.

The window had a good, straight view of Maggie's house. This was the way to spy. Inside, where nobody saw you hugging a wall and chased you away.

The wood of the chair was still warm when he sat down, which he didn't like much.

He put his elbow on the windowsill and leaned out, not worrying that somebody might see him this high up. The air smelled like city. Had some substance and weight to it. It was full of city noises, too. A proper hum and clamor going on underneath everything. It was a relief to be out of the countryside. He didn't mind admitting, all that rural quiet made his flesh creep.

The room was familiar, too. He'd lived in places like this most of his life. This was somebody's home, this attic. Home to lots of somebodys, in fact, not even counting the fleas. There were six straw mats on the floor. Six boys slept here. Looked like they shined shoes for a living.

Doyle had bribed them to keep away. That was how he worked. He didn't scare them off. He paid them.

There were two hours, more or less, of daylight. Then the night watch. He knew how to keep a watch at night. He didn't need Paxton the Pale telling him what to do. *That Paxton ain't so much. If he's Service, I could be Service.*

It wouldn't be so different from belonging to Lazarus. Except the British Service didn't kill people with quite the same verve and abandon as Lazarus. He could learn that, if he had to. He was already getting the knack of it.

Look at this morning. He hadn't killed Le Brochet, had he? He'd been downright merciful.

He'd finished with Le Brochet and got safe away. The ragtag and bobtail was running off in the wrong direction. Nothing better in this life than hearing the hounds baying to the east while you wriggled off west.

He'd kept a map in his head, like Doyle was always saying. That told him where to find a quiet street that hooked round to the side. All private. There was a fine old brass fountain at the end with the faucet shaped like a dolphin.

He pumped some water and was kind of admiring himself for being particularly clever and sluicing the blood out of his shirt. The water came out of the dolphin's mouth, like it was shooting the cat after drinking all night. Just no telling what people would want to put in the public street. That was when Doyle came up behind him, silent-like, and said, "Good. Here you are," and about scared him out of his skin.

A big man shouldn't be able to walk that quiet. Uncanny, that's what it was.

Doyle didn't have his knife out. He just walked up all easy and pleasant. "That was a nice interrogation. You wrung him dry. Why is he alive?"

Now there was no point in even speculating how Doyle got here or how he knew about Le Brochet. "I figgered it's a good idea to leave him breathing."

"Is it?" Doyle was patient as a bloody panther or something. Just ominous.

"I can always come back and kill him later."

"Good thought."

Well, Doyle would like it because that's what he'd said himself a couple of times. "It's easier to come back and kill somebody than to come back and unkill him. And if I think up some new questions later on, he's not going to be talkative if he's dead."

Doyle kept waiting, like there was more to it.

He took a deep breath. *Hell, try the truth.* "And I knew you wouldn't like it if I slit his throat."

"That's a start. Take a handful of that dirt over there and smear it down the front of your shirt to hide the blood."

Nobody seemed surprised when Doyle brought him back to the house in the Marais. The Old Trout listened to what he had to say about Le Brochet and sent him to eat in the kitchen. She called him Rat.

wenty-six

MARGUERITE FINISHED HER LETTER TO HER banker in Rouen and began one to the citoyen mayor of Voisemont. There were orders to be given about the hay harvest. A dozen women in the village had been left with no support when the army took their sons. It was all very well for the louts in the tavern to talk loudly of killing the aristos. They made no plans to pay the schoolmaster or give food to those women. She must.

There were more letters to write. Concerning the orphanage in Rouen. Concerning the factory in Lyon and fifty women out of work there. It would be some time before she could sit at peace and write fables again.

When it began to be dark, she lit candles. Four on her desk, one beside her bed, one on each end of the mantel. She pulled new paper across the desk and began another letter.

The door of her bedroom opened. She looked up and saw Victor in the mirror, carrying a cup and saucer.

People appear small in a mirror. Victor stood in the

doorway, and he was of a size she could have held him in her hand like a doll. She could have picked him up and tossed him out the window. Unfortunately, he did not live in a mirror.

"You should not come to my bedroom." She said it to his little reflection, without turning around. "It is improper, even for cousins. Your mother would comment extensively."

"I have no intention of telling her." He balanced the cup across the room and set it on the desk, at her elbow. "I wish you wouldn't fight with Maman. It would be more generous of you to give her the small signs of respect she covets. It costs you nothing." He tapped the cup. "Chamomile. Your cook says it's your favorite. I remember you used to go out into the fields with that little maid of yours, Berthe, Berenice . . ."

"Bertille."

"That's it. You'd gather flowers and stew them into some stinking mess. Chamomile was one of them." He leaned his hip against her desk and made himself comfortable, planning to stay. "We've always been honest with one another, have we not, Marguerite?"

I have avoided speaking to you. There is a difference. "I am tired tonight. Can we—"

"We are friends as well as cousins. You were a great favorite of mine, even when you were a little girl."

How strange they should look at the same childhood and see such different stories.

From family, there is no escape. If she drank the tisane he had brought, perhaps she could give him the empty cup and tell him to take it away.

"Tell me what you want." She lifted the letter she was writing to the edge of her desk to dry, then took cloth and began wiping her pen down.

"You're an intelligent woman, Marguerite. Educated. Responsible. You are a reasonable woman."

"Thank you."

"Your father is not a reasonable man."

"My father is entirely mad. He always has been." She laid the pen on the desk, next to the tisane he had brought her. "You're not telling me anything I don't know."

"Did you know he's visited England twice in the last six months? Secretly. No one goes to England but criminals and counter-revolutionaries."

She tried to remember what Papa had said about his trips to England. He had not spoken of them. Why did Papa say so little? Uneasiness ran down her spine. "When I find him, he'll have some perfectly logical explanation. He went to London to buy new boots or make an observation of the phases of the moon from the roof of St. Paul's. Next he will want to go to Milan because they have a new mechanism in the clock tower. It's always the same."

"This is why you must help me find him. You understand him better than anyone else." Victor stood with his hands behind his back, his eyes hooded. "It's for his own good. Robespierre has become suspicious of everyone these days. He sees plots everywhere, even in the wanderings of a mad old man. Even I have no way to influence him. If your father is caught leaving France, he'll be brought to Paris and condemned. You may be arrested as the daughter of an émigré. The property will be confiscated—" He glared down at her. "Your father has to be stopped."

She did not need Victor to remind her of these unpleasant possibilities. "When my father returns—"

"We can't wait. Police spies are everywhere. Your father is not inconspicuous. Think, Marguerite. Where is he? Where could he possibly be? Who would he go to?"

"Anywhere. He was in Strasbourg once, for ten weeks, measuring the river flow. He always comes back."

"He has never thought about the rest of the family. Never." Her cousin paced. His frustration rippled behind him like the wake of a black fish in a dark pond. "This time, he'll pull us all down. You haven't been in Paris these last weeks. You don't know what it's been like."

But she did know. The sparrows came, more of them, more desperate than ever, more filled with disbelief that the machinery of the Revolution should turn to rend them.

She was at her wits' end over what to do with them. Every safehouse in Paris was full. The Normandy network was a shambles. She touched across the letters she'd written. They were not yet dry enough to stack. Eventually Victor would make a salient point or go away. One must be patient.

Finally, Victor breathed out a sigh and halted. "You can't help me."

"I will ask his friends. Sometimes he tells them—"

"Let it be. I want no rumors spreading." He pinched at his shirt cuff and adjusted it a quarter inch. Nervously toyed with a button of his striped waistcoat. "I'll find him myself." Abruptly, he started for the door, as anxious to leave her room as he had been to enter it.

"Drink the tisane while it's still hot." He left without looking back at her.

When Victor had gone, she tasted the tea, but it was bitter and tepid, with a film on top, so she took one more sip and left it. The Meissen clock on the fireplace mantel chimed. Ten o'clock.

Her windows were open over the little piece of garden behind the house. The air was full of the grumble of the city. She must accustom herself to it, after weeks in the silence of the country. Wagons did not cease on the streets because honest folk had gone to their beds. Rather the opposite. Now that the streets were empty, tradesmen delivered wood and fishes and flour across Paris.

The moon was bright quarter, holding the dark of the moon in its arms. She could see only the brightest stars.

Coal smoke and the damp haze from the river hung between her and the sky.

She should ring for Agnès and change to her night shift and sleep. She was tired, as she had told Cousin Victor. There was work she must do tomorrow, and the day after that, and for many days to come.

Jean-Paul's five sparrows would leave Paris at dawn in the laundry cart. La Flèche would be loading other sparrows on to the coal barge tonight. They were already taking them aboard and hiding them. This was the third of four weeks they would use the barge. Then they would stop. Every scheme must be put away while it was still fresh, before it was detected.

However many sparrows she saved, there were always more. She was trying to dip the sea empty with a teacup.

She wished she could talk to Guillaume.

He might be looking at the moon now. He could be in the next street. Or he might be on the road to Rouen, sleeping under the sky, watching the moon rise above a dark lace of trees. In either case, he was immeasurably distant from her.

She leaned to pull the curtain. A face floated in the air before her. A white, skeletal mask of a face outside the window. Coming toward her.

She jumped back, gasping. Caught her balance. Realized what she was seeing.

Not a ghost. She laughed, yes, laughed, though she was still shaking. It was Nico. The Peltiers's monkey. He had climbed the carvings of the wall and here he was, to frighten her to death. When she held out her arms, he jumped to her and landed with a thump. He thrust his nose against her skin, licking at her cheek, sniffing and chattering.

"You will hush. I strenuously advise this." He was a capuchin monkey and wise for his breed, but he was excited. "Calm yourself. No, you do not wish to make the acquaintance of my aunt Sophie. And I am certain she does not want to meet you."

His chittering and chirping, sharp as the complaint of an exotic bird, would bring someone to her room. "You must be still." She gathered him up and stroked him and he quieted.

He was Madame Peltier's Nico. Surely he had been left safe when the Peltiers fled for Geneva. There was an old nurse who cared for him. How had he come halfway across Paris and found his way to her back garden? He knew it well, of course. He had come to visit with Sylvie Peltier for many years and played in the flowerbeds while Sylvie conducted an affair with Papa. Nico was very familiar with the walls and drain spouts of Hôtel de Fleurignac.

"You have found me. You have been nimble and clever as . . . well . . . as a monkey. Wait, I will find a nut for you. Let me look. Shhh." There were no nuts or raisins in her bedchamber, but there were anise comfits in a Limoges box on her bureau. Nico loved them.

"These cannot possibly be good for you. I have told you time and time again." But he played upon her sympathies skillfully, and in the end she gave him three. He popped two in his mouth, one in each cheek, and became silent as an apple. He held the third tightly in the hand that was not clinging to her.

When she walked back to the window to look out at the way he'd come, his arm wrapped her neck, clinging. "You were afraid out there in the dark, alone, *pauvre petit*. But now you are safe. Tomorrow you will go back to your home." He wore a red jacket, bright as cherries, with tiny gold epaulettes and the red, blue, and white cockade of the Revolution upon his chest. The jacket draped long about him, with a slit in back so his tail could move freely. "You are looking very fine, are you not? And patriotic. I do not know what it says of our life in Paris today that the sight of a monkey wearing the symbol of the Revolution seems perfectly rational."

There were wide pockets in his jacket. In one of them was a folded note.

No sane man would use a monkey to deliver a letter.

Ah well, that left the other sort, did it not? Papa. When she took the note from Nico—poor Nico, he was reluctant to let it go—she was not surprised to see the first letter of her name written on the outside. An ornate *M*.

Nico abandoned her and went to search her writing desk, stepping in the cold tea and leaving monkey paw prints across the blotter.

She unfolded the sheet. It contained two words in Papa's writing. *Tuileries* and *money*.

Papa must have released Nico into the garden and sauntered onward to—she looked at the paper again, though there was no need—the Tuileries. Papa knew she would apprehend exactly the one spot in the vast gardens. He knew she would come to him immediately.

He was mad and perfectly selfish. She disagreed with him about everything important in the world. But they understood each other completely. What a thing it was to have family.

Nico, deciding this was a night for insanity and eccentricity, ransacked the comfit box.

Twenty-seven

HAWKER PRACTICED THE ART OF BEING INCONSPIC-uous, something with which he was already moderately familiar. It was the soft belly of the night. The time for good pickings. There was dark in the corners if you were in the mood to lurk. If you didn't want to skulk, you could blend into the folks coming home from the cafés and the theater. Poor men walked the streets because their rooms were too hot to sleep in. Rich men, because they were look-ing for a woman. Anyone could be on the stroll this hour of the evening.

Back home in London, his mates would be working, breaking into a shop or lifting merchandise off some boat tied up in the Thames where the officers were careless-like.

He leaned up against a doorway, pretending to shake a pebble out of his boot. The house he had his eye on was fifty feet down Rue Honoré. Rue Saint-Honoré, they'd called it a few years back before everything in Paris got itself de-saintified.

Five men passed, each of them with something more important to do than notice him.

If he was in London right now, he'd be with Beets and Rory and Sticker and the others. When the night's job was done they'd stop at a cookshop in St. Giles for sausages before they headed back to the padding ken to hand the goods over to Lazarus. Or if they were empty-handed, they'd end up in a tavern, drinking themselves fuddled and making up excuses.

He was still working. Still robbing houses. This time he was doing it for the British Service. Life was a funny old dame.

They put streetlamps all up and down here. Some of the householders even hung a lantern by the front door. He'd have to walk through all that bloody illumination to get where he was going.

This here . . . this was Robespierre's house.

The most powerful man in France—as close to being the king as made no difference—lived in a nothing-special house, tucked up over a woodshop. If you wanted to see Robespierre, well . . . probably you trotted yourself around those piles of lumber and knocked on the door.

"He is one of the people." That's what the woman hawking newspapers said when he brought up the question of who the house belonged to. "He is ours, our Robespierre, little citoyen. He lives as we do, without bribes or favorites. He is The Incorruptible. You do well to come and see what he is."

No guards, no three hundred men in fancy uniforms riding on horses, no big iron gates closing everybody out. No crown jewels. Seemed like the French had it right somehow.

He shrugged, doing it loose in his shoulders. Practicing. It felt natural, almost, to jerk his chin up a notch, to say *no*. Turn his hand over to say *yes*. He was picking up the knack of it. Learning to look French. Why not? Maybe it'd been a Frenchman who'd fathered him.

There was more to it than shrugs. Clothes, for instance. Doyle made him change his clothes from the skin out before they crossed the Channel. He'd cut his hair. He kept telling him how to eat and how to sit and how to walk.

Ten thousand tricks. Doyle knew them all. He'd bet Doyle could tell a Frenchman from an Englishman by the smell of his farts.

The footman who'd left Maggie's house had headed straight here, easy as you please, and handed over a letter at that door down at the far end of the courtyard. He didn't wait for a reply. Be interesting to know who in Maggie's house was sending letters this time of night. Interesting to know what you put in a letter you sent to the most powerful man in France.

As to Robespierre's house . . . Doyle would say, sometimes the direct approach is best. Just walk in.

Nobody paid attention when he sauntered through the wide passageway, into the carpenter's yard. He faded into the space behind a pile of long boards somebody was going to find a use for, one of these days.

He'd wait a bit. An hour, just to be on the safe side.

This was a trusting household. No candles inside. Shutters closed and the window sashes thrown up. They were sleeping the Sleep of the Just in there. Probably they tired themselves out with being Incorruptible all day.

DOYLE found Talbot gone from Rue Palmier. Talbot wasn't the most brilliant man England ever spawned, but he was a conscientious Service agent and if he was away from his post, he'd be following someone who'd slipped into or out of Hôtel de Fleurignac. Considering the hour, that was probably somebody interesting.

In the attic lookout, Doyle found the chair empty. Hawker was gone.

The promising note was that somebody—he'd guess it was Hawker—had pulled out a brush and bootblacking from the possessions scattered around the room and written a big note on the wall. SWIVE.

He wouldn't put it past the boy to go off swiving whores, but he wasn't going to express himself in Old English. That might be his attempt at some part of the verb *suivre*—to follow—and mean that Hawker was tracking somebody.

He'd brought stew meat, wrapped up in bread, for the boy. Since Hawker wasn't in sight, he didn't mind eating it himself.

It looked like he had the night watch. That was the great joy of the Service. You never got too senior to pull the short straw. He sat in one chair and put his feet up on the other, watching Maggie's house.

Her room was at the back of the house, second floor. He couldn't see the window from here. Her bedroom would be dark, this time of night. She'd be in her bed, lying on top of the covers, letting the wind run over her. She'd have a proper bed tonight and a proper linen night shift on her, but she wouldn't be lying prim and stiff and proper. She'd be sprawled out, hugging her pillow, tucking it between her legs. She slept like a man had just finished with her. Like she was soft and satisfied and grabbing a few minutes of sleep before they started again. That was the way she always slept. He'd watched her doing it every night on the road.

That scrawny, blond man she met in the baths would be Jean-Paul Béclard, her partner in La Flèche. An old lover, obviously. A former lover, unless he missed his guess. That meant he didn't have to track the man down and beat him up in an instructive manner.

THE noise in the city leaked away. It got quiet. It was the hour for what Lazarus would call nefarious deeds.

Hawker slipped from hiding. The courtyard was full of moon and that damned lantern light from the street out front. He kept to the edges of the yard where the shadows were. He could smell dog. There was a whuffling snore from upstairs that might be a dog sleeping. Which went to show that some dogs weren't worth spit when it came to guarding a house.

The front door opened out of the work yard. It was ready to stand off battering rams. The window next to it was guarding the house with a pair of flimsy wood shutters closed with a latch. God, you'd think there weren't any thieves in this city.

Take the knife out. Slip it in between the shutters. Lift the latch. He held his breath till the shutters folded back without squeaking. He swung his feet in.

For a man who was chopping off a couple hundred heads a week, Robespierre was damn unconcerned about his own safety. Upstairs, five or six snores said they slept heavy, the way honest folks do. Seemed they had an honest dog, too.

Light came in through the shutter he'd opened. Enough to see around the room. A letter lay in the middle of the dark wood table. That'd be the one the footman brought from Maggie's house.

He nipped it up as he walked by. The door to the right let him into the kitchen, with a fire glowing on the hearth. He didn't like to put a good knife into a fire. It played hell with keeping an edge on the blade. But sometimes you do what you don't want to on a job. When the blade heated up he lifted the seal off the letter.

What he had was lots of scrawl in black ink. He couldn't read it. He couldn't read print all that well and sure as hell couldn't read twisty French handwriting. But the signature said Victor.

Take it with him, or close it up and put it back so they wouldn't know he'd been here?

Lazarus used to set him problems like this. He'd lay out the problem and give him the time it took to breathe in and out to think what to do. The next breath, Lazarus cuffed him halfway across the room if he hadn't decided.

A big, square box to the side of the hearth had sheets of fine writing paper in it, screwed up long and tight. That was to light candles with or carry fire from one room to the other. The paper had writing on it.

Not just the one letter. Lots of letters.

Just made you wonder what kind of a careless household they ran. A powerful man lived here. What were the chances those papers had something interesting on them?

He stuffed papers down his shirt. All the paper spills. The letter from Victor de Fleurignac. Then he went out the window he'd come in through.

He was out of the courtyard, out into the streets. He left the Rue Honoré as soon as he could and found the smaller ways where they didn't bother to light them, holding to the middle of the road where no one could jump him, not hurrying, walking through the dog-chewed edges of the night toward the Marais and the house with blue shutters.

Twenty-eight

MARGUERITE KNEW WHERE TO FIND PAPA. DEEP
in the park, at the end of a lane of poplars, a statue of Diana
stood naked to every weather, endlessly drawing an arrow
from her quiver. Here was an oval rose garden. They had
come here when she was very young. He had explained the
theory of numerical sequences while she sat on the grass
and collected fallen rose petals. She told him about the
fairies who lived in the rosebushes. He explained how to
calculate the orbit of the moons of Jupiter.

He was there, among the rosebushes, waiting for her.

She said, "I will tell you the bad news first. They have
burned the chateau."

But one of Papa's servants—he would not tell her
which—had already come to him with this news. The first
shock of it was over. She need only relate the whole round
tale, which did not take long. It was necessary to admit that
she had not saved his library. *I did not save my own writing. I was concerned with saving myself.* She again admitted she had not saved the library. She admitted it several

times. She agreed that, certainly, Papa would have prevented the destruction if he had been there. She heard the speech he would have made from the steps of the chateau to stop the mob. It was moving.

"They would have listened to me," he said. "You are certain you did not save any of the library?"

He was dressed oddly, even for Papa who always dressed oddly. He wore a tricorne hat and a military coat, much too large for him, dark blue. Its brass buttons glinted even in this light. The scarlet of his waistcoat was forceful enough to be seen by the light of the lanterns in the cafés across the street. His hair hung untidily around his face. Everything about him was at once shabby and flamboyant.

Papa looked up at the sky above Paris and sighed. He would have liked to ask yet again if she did not possibly save any of his books.

After a long and melancholy moment, he said, "We lay our possessions on the altar of history. It was inevitable the chateau should be destroyed. It has outlived its time. The Republic will take all the grand mansions, in the end, and put them to rational use. Schools. Prisons. Manufactories. Perhaps orphanages and hospitals."

"They did not take the chateau and put it to good use. They destroyed it to a heap of rubble."

He did not answer. He had a vast ability to hear only what he wanted to hear.

"Everyone is wondering where you have gone, Papa. Some of us are worried." She ran her fingers into her hair. "What are you doing with Nico? He should be at the Peltiers's house."

"I took him. Sylvie left him with servants, after all, and I needed him."

"You wanted a monkey?"

"I am an organ grinder. I need a monkey. It is not easy to find a monkey in Paris these days."

With Papa, one never knew how much of what he said was slyness and how much was his small madnesses and how much was rational thought expressed in his own particular dialect. A box leaned against the tree at his feet. She recognized it now by the bright colors and the hand crank. It was the box of an organ grinder. A hurdy-gurdy. "You are a street musician?"

"One must do something. If I stay in my rooms and write, they become suspicious of me. No one stays in their rooms. With Nico, I am above suspicion."

"You collect money in a hat?"

"Do not be ridiculous. The monkey does that. I play music."

"I should have seen that." She leaned against the low wall of marble that separated a walkway of raked gravel from the flowerbeds of the rose garden. Nico snuggled in the crook of her arm. He liked being scratched behind his ears and over the top of his head, so she did that. "Do you feed him properly? He looks thin."

"Of course I feed him. I feed him my own dinner. Marguerite, will you stick to the point? Did you bring money?"

She had brought all the coin she had in her room, which was a goodly amount. She never knew when La Flèche would call upon her resources. "I will give it to you when I understand what is going on."

"I am Italian. I play music upon the streets. I speak only Italian. I live among Italians of the city. I am from Padua." He brooded over that for a moment. "Padua was a mistake. It is a city I abominate. But once I had said it at random I could not take it back. I have told them my father was from Sospel, however, so I am French and have French papers."

Sometimes when she was with her father—this was one of those times—she wanted to howl like an animal and beat her fists upon the ground.

She reached into her pocket—the left pocket that held several small, useful things, not the right one that held money—and fed Nico another of the comfits he should not be eating. He had, she hoped, a digestion of iron.

Her own stomach was much disordered. She had been ill upon the cobblestones, suddenly and unexpectedly, on the way to the Tuileries. She still felt sick. It was from something she had eaten, doubtless. "You are pretending to be Italian."

"Have I not just said that? Pay better attention. Did you know, I bought papers for myself in the Rue Manon for twenty-seven livres. It is very inexpensive. I was surprised."

"There is a vigorous industry in false identity papers, Papa. We are all shocked by it. Why have you suddenly chosen to become Italian?"

"I am in hiding." He brooded. Her father brooded often and with great thoroughness. "To escape my enemies. Perhaps I should have become German. The Germans are a more serious people."

"You have no enemies, Papa. The burning of the chateau was not sanctioned by Paris. There is no arrest order for you. I asked Victor."

"They do not want to arrest me. They want to kill me. That is an entirely different matter. Even in a time of revolution, there is still murder. They tried to stab me."

"Who?"

"Two men, in an alley. I do not know them." On top of the hurdy-gurdy was a thin, braided strap. Nico's leash. He took it now and ran it through his fingers to get to the end. "They may be Martinists. Or Fouché has sent them. But it is probably the English. The English are almost certainly enraged. They might even burn the chateau." He mulled it over. "To smoke me out. Yes. It is the English." He nodded. "I hope you've brought enough money. There's a copy of

Rahn's *Teutsche Algebra* for sale in the Rue Percée that I must buy. They will not give it to me unless I bring hard cash. There are several other texts of interest."

Papa had been to England. Not once, but several times in the last year. "What did you do in England, Papa?"

"Nothing of importance. And I do not intend to go back. The food is barbarous. You should give me the money you brought and return home. It's not safe for you to be out this late at night. People watch you, and there are criminal types abroad."

There were many people abroad. Twenty yards away, bright crowds of men and women laughed and strolled in groups on the promenade, enjoying the cool of the evening. None of them came into this quiet corner.

What could Papa possibly have done?

Papa rounded the leash into his hand and whistled softly. Nico went willingly from her arms to the ground. He clambered to hang on Papa's lapels, the long tail curled up, the little paws patting and patting at the waistcoat pocket.

"What did you do in England?" She pulled out the pouch of coins and held it in her hand.

He looked away, toward the lights of the street. "My researches. My study of genius. I worked in England upon this."

His geniuses. It was another of Papa's strange intellectual exercises, like calculating the orbit of Jupiter or keeping records of rainfall. Only Papa would ask if one could select the young, the potential geniuses. Chemists, experts in physics, mathematicians, engineers, inventors of all kinds, military men, political philosophers. It was harmless, surely. He gathered information. He made lists. Papa was a great one for making lists. He would see if these Englishmen, these Germans, these Italians became famous in ten years or in twenty. He might even be right about some of them. Papa was truly brilliant.

She said, "You will not offend England by saying there are geniuses there."

"I told Victor. He took a copy to Robespierre. He was very excited. They will save a thousand lives for France, every one of those names."

She allowed her father to take the pouch from her hand. He tucked it away safely inside his waistband, looking satisfied with himself. He lifted Nico to his right shoulder and bent to retrieve the hurdy-gurdy.

"Robespierre was excited." The night stilled everywhere, as if Paris stopped and held its breath. A high-pitched buzzing sounded in her ears. "What lives? What is it that Robespierre approves? What would make men come from England, looking for you?"

I know a man who came from the coast to the chateau at Voisemont. I think he came looking for you. I think he is the Englishman you fear.

She put herself in his path and waited.

"We are at war. Soldiers of the Republic are dying every day for France. Robespierre has arranged that a few English soldiers will die before they come to a battlefield."

"Papa . . ."

"A few men. The military geniuses." He brushed at his coat. Adjusted the strap of the hurdy-gurdy. "Only men who have put on uniforms and chosen to be our enemies. He promised that. Only in countries that have declared war. Only the military."

She whispered, "Papa. What have you done?"

"I must go back to my rooms. The night is full of men who spy on us."

"Tell me where to find you."

"I have rooms on the Rue Ventadorn near the Café de Chanticleer. Ask for Citoyen Gasparini. Bring me more money when you have it." He pushed past. "Robespierre explained to me. At the cost of a few English soldiers, I am saving the lives of many Frenchmen. And the Republic." He was a few feet away when he said, "I wish I had not shown him the list."

The sound of his shuffle disappeared before his shadow got licked up by the greater shadows of the street.

Twenty-nine

HAWKER BANGED ON THE GATE OF THE HOUSE IN the Marais.

The porter at the door—didn't that man ever sleep?—let him in. Carruthers was waiting for him in the courtyard. There was nothing tougher than an old woman. This one was twigs and shoe nails, held together with sheer meanness.

"You came back. I was hoping we'd seen the last of you, Rat." Love words from Carruthers.

"I regret the necessity, madame. I had hoped to see the last of you as well." This was his aristo accent. The girl who'd taught him to speak French had been an aristo from Toulouse. "Is Citoyen LeBreton in the house?"

"You left your post."

"I left my post to follow—"

"A footman. He returned. You didn't. Where have you been for five hours, Rat?"

She wouldn't let him into the kitchen to talk about this in private. The blank stone on every side reflected her voice upward. The house was dark, but behind every window there was some Service agent, sleeping light, waking up to listen to the Old Trout.

"I am not under your command, Madame Cachard, however delightful that would be for both of us. I am Doyle's rat." He said it the way a gentleman would, using words like razors. "Did he tell you where he would be?"

Carruthers laid out a couple of silences, each with a different meaning. "The Café des Marchands. Make your excuses to him."

He knew some small number of deadly women. This one, though, froze his bones. She had the same eyes Doyle did, the same weighing look that saw everything.

Right now, she was full of contempt. "The world will be a cleaner place when somebody snaps your neck."

He wanted to shrivel up and slink out and never come back. So he grinned. "If I am a rat, madame, I'm the most dangerous rat you will encounter outside your nightmares. A good night to you." He turned his back on her and walked out the way he'd come in. He'd wipe his arse with Robespierre's papers before he gave them to that old hag.

The hell with her. The hell with the lot of them.

Thirty

MARGUERITE THOUGHT OF GOING BACK TO THE Hôtel de Fleurignac. But Victor was there, and his mother, and a houseful of servants who would look in her face and see something was wrong. They would bring her delicacies to eat and brew her tisanes. And hover.

She could not. She could not. She crossed her arms around her waist and began walking.

Papa had done something dreadful. Or, not so much done this himself as stood back and allowed his work to be used for horrible purposes. It had not been chance that brought Guillaume to the chateau at Voisemont. He'd come looking for Papa. How disappointed he must have been to find only her.

Now she must mend this.

Somewhere in her city she would find a little breeze. In some park. In some street that led down to the Seine. She would stand and let it blow into her face and watch the sun come up. Maybe that would make her feel better.

A violin played in one of the twisting streets to the left,

perhaps in a café. It was beautiful and faint, like a bird singing when the woods are utterly still. She walked for a while toward it.

If she had known where Guillaume was, if she had the least smell of a notion where he might be, she would have walked in his direction. It wouldn't have been a choice. Her feet would have started moving on their own and kept at it till they bumped into his boots.

I am a great fool. She stubbed her toes on the uneven cobbles. In the narrow and ancient streets of this quartier, stone barriers jutted into the streets so carts would not scrape the walls. That was another hazard to avoid. She seemed to be full of pain in every region inside her skin. Her stomach cramped.

He is English. Why did I not see that? He was not a smuggler, or a bookseller, or a petty criminal, or even a member of the Secret Police. He was a spy of England. He was sent to find her father and take revenge upon him.

She must have walked a long way. In some alley off the Rue d'Anduza, she leaned over and was sick, retching most miserably. But after that, she felt better. The early dawn turned chilly though, and she walked along, shivering. In the Rue Montmartre she passed cafés with every table full. Men in fine clothes idled away the end of the night, drinking cognac, talking loudly, holding the newspapers that were already circulating on the streets. Around them, at other tables, men just awakened and surly were getting ready to do the work of the world. It was as if, in these streets, humanity divided itself into Men of the Day and Men of the Night.

Guillaume was both. Day and Night. He could sit with one sort of men or the other, and they would both welcome him.

She noticed, then, where her feet had brought her. The Café des Marchands, where she had eaten with Guillaume.

Where he had told her she could leave a message for him. Where she had told him she did not need him.

I do not need you, Guillaume LeBreton. I do not want you. I do not even know your name.

She sat at one of the tables outside the café, since it was as easy to be discouraged and forlorn sitting down as wandering the streets like a ghost. When the woman paused impatiently beside her, she ordered coffee and a roll.

The coffee was laid on the table softly, so it would not spill. The roll set beside it.

"Are you well, citoyenne?" the woman asked.

She shook her head, but said nothing. The woman went away.

She did not want to eat. She wanted to be at home, in the chateau at Voisemont, at her desk, writing tales of beauty and high adventure. She did not want to live in an adventure. They hurt.

When she wiped her face with her hands, she discovered that she no longer smelled of being loved by Guillaume. She smelled like monkey.

FROM the end of the street Doyle saw Maggie, sitting at a table outside. Her head was bowed, so he couldn't see her face. She was dressed to match the café in plain, durable clothing. That could have been deliberate on her part, but it was probably wasn't.

He'd said she could find him here. He hadn't thought she would.

She'd taken the table farthest from the door, where she wouldn't be bothered by men going in and out. A cup of coffee, untouched, sat before her and a little round of bread, unbroken.

"Hello, Maggie."

Her head came up, smooth as flowing water. Strands of hair slipped and fell across one another and slid down around her face. The clear, brown eyes lifted and met his.

"I'll join you," he said.

I am drowning in this woman and I don't want to swim free. This is the one. This is the one I'll give up the Service for. Yesterday or the day before, or maybe the first time he'd seen her, he'd made the decision. While he wasn't noticing, his mind thought it out and argued it through and settled it. His Maggie. It already sounded natural.

He scraped the rush-bottomed chair back so it was up against the wall of the café and he could keep an eye on the street. He sat next to her, almost touching. She looked tired and worn out and sad. "You're up early."

"Not early. I was awake all night."

She'd walked half the city, Talbot said. Talbot had followed her, at a careful distance, all night. She'd passed a dozen cafés, talked to an organ grinder in the park, played with his monkey, scratched a cat's ears in an alley, spent time looking out at the river. If somebody was supposed to meet her, he didn't show up.

Talbot said she was sick. She'd cast up her accounts in an alley.

I want to take her home. I want to have a home to take her to. I want to put her in my bed and just hold on to her while she sleeps. I want to reach out my hand at any hour, all night long, and find her there.

He couldn't. He'd have to take her back to Hôtel de Fleurignac and leave her there. Damn, but it felt wrong. "Probably not a good idea to go walking around Paris alone at night. You meet dangerous people."

"Like you. But I met you first in broad daylight, so there are no guarantees. At Voisemont, I go walking at night." Maggie picked up the coffee and barely tasted it. "I used to go walking."

The widow who owned the Café des Marchands came out from behind the counter and brought him cut bread, a slab of hard cheese, and a cup of wine, without him having to ask. The widow liked his looks and, being in the market for another man, let him know it. She gave a shrewd glance from him to Maggie and shrugged and left.

He said, "Did you come here looking for me?"

"I don't think so. I'm not sure why I'm here." She sat staring into the cup. "It just happened somehow. Perhaps I was looking for you with some part of my soul that is very stupid and does not know it is no longer allowed to be with you. It is like a dog that cannot be told that its human is dead. It goes out on the street, taking its accustomed walk, looking everywhere for him. Does that not sound both sad and self-pitying?"

"It sounds like someone who writes down old tales. That'd make a good fable."

"Perhaps. But I came here because I do not want to go home. I could not sleep. This café was the last thing you said to me and I have not yet banished it from my mind. So my feet came in this direction without consulting me." She drank a mouthful and swallowed. "You must be careful what you say to me."

Every damn motion was beautiful. Probably she wasn't actually the loveliest creature on earth. He'd lost his objectivity.

She set the cup down. "It takes a while for me to sweep your words from the doorstep of my mind. I am led to unconsidered acts. You would not wish me to undertake such things."

"I wouldn't want that."

"I am foolish. I come to your accustomed place and still I am surprised to see you here. Every time we are together I think it will be for the last time. It utterly confounds me when I see you again."

"It's never been the last time. This isn't the last time, either."

"I think it may be. I wish I liked this coffee better." She rolled the cup between her hands. "But at least it is warm to hold. I have old friends—women I know—who have taken many lovers. They enjoy the drama of it. The flirtatious approach, the hurried, passionate meetings, the mad planning, the jealousy, the accusations . . . the inevitable betrayal. It would make me exhausted, so much emotion. I become weary just listening to them."

"I'm all for the quiet life."

She nodded. "And simplicity."

This, from his Maggie. From the woman who organized hundreds of careful, meticulously planned escapes. "Simplicity's a fine thing."

"I am a great admirer of it. For me, there have been only two lovers. To the first I brought disaster. My uncle horsewhipped him nearly to his death. The second brought devastation to me. I am not lucky at this business of taking lovers."

"Me being the second."

"Yes. I make mistakes in judgment." She didn't turn her head to meet his eyes. "I watched you walk toward me, Guillaume. You knew I would be here. I was no surprise to you."

"What's that supposed to mean?"

"Did you have me followed? You would find that easy to arrange, in your profession."

She knows. Sometime in the last day, she'd found out he was a spy. He could read that in the way the air had changed between them. She knew.

"We'll talk about that in a bit."

Not here. He was known here. He ate at Café des Marchands when he was in Paris. Rented a room six blocks north. Bought from the same firewood vendor and water seller.

Had his boots cleaned by the same grubby boy every week. Took his newspaper from the same woman at her stand at the end of the street. Folks here knew his face. "Oh. Citoyen LeBreton," they'd say. "A good patriot. He lives in my Section. He travels, selling books. I know him well."

"I will be more careful in the future when I take lovers." Maggie was letting go of him. Putting him in the past. Now he was a lover she used to have.

It's too damned late for that, Maggie. You're stuck with me.

He picked up her little roll. Offered it to her. She shook her head.

He said, "You don't take food and not eat it. Not in a place like this. Somebody's going to wonder why you have money to throw away." He finished the roll in two bites with the last of his cheese. "Drink some of that coffee, if you can stomach it. We'll walk off in a little while. You can tell me why you were out all night and I can call you a fool."

"You are all that is kind." She picked the blue and white cup off the table. "As always." She drank. "I am tempted to invent unwisdoms just so you will be pleased. I am very inventive."

Can you possibly know how much I want you? Are there any words on earth I could say that would do it justice?

"It has not been night for hours," she said. "Once there is even a hint of light in the sky, respectable women come out. These are all respectable women here in the café, except the whores, of course, and I am not dressed like a whore. Only, it has become cold. I did not expect it to be cold."

She huddled into herself. If she was feeling a chill, it wasn't in the air. The cold was inside her. Time to take her back to her house and let them put her to bed. Not his bed, unfortunately.

"Did you know? They have declared war on the prostitutes of Paris." She held the cup between her hands and gave it a lot of attention. "They have collected dozens and dozens of them from the streets and filled the prisons even more full. They are not, thank the good God, killing them. They will reform them by making them knit stockings for the army."

"Don't we all feel safer on the streets knowing that?" Maggie had paid for her food, but he dropped an extra sou on the table anyway, the way a man did when he was showing off for his particular lady. Taking her arm and giving her help out of the chair didn't fit this café or the clothes he was wearing, but any man might do that for a woman he was courting.

"It is not universally popular, this harvesting of whores, but naturally no one says this openly for fear of, as they say, sneezing into a basket, which is what one does upon the guillotine. I do not think the reformation of morals will gain much headway. Frenchmen are fond of their whores. You will sympathize."

If he'd been a lesser man, he would have sighed. "Are we going to talk about this for a while where everyone can hear, or would you like to just jump up and down and denounce the government straight out? Be a pity to get arrested for anything less."

"I am entirely in agreement. One should only take grave and important risks. In all small matters one must be exquisitely cautious. The gods do not reward frivolity."

He'd see her right to the door and turn her over to somebody who'd take care of her. Not Victor. Maggie must have somebody in that house she trusted. "Let's get you home. Maybe they haven't noticed you're out drinking coffee with disreputable men at the crack of dawn."

She walked carefully, as if she felt shaky inside. It was another reason for him to hold her.

He waited till they wouldn't be overheard. "So. What is it you think you know about me?"

Thirty-one

SHE WALKED THROUGH THE EARLIEST OF DAWN, through streets that were asleep under a white sky, side by side with Guillaume.

Papa was afraid of this man. He had cause to be. "Have you come to France to kill my father?" She was weary unto the death of lying to Guillaume LeBreton and receiving his lies in return.

"Why would you think that?"

"My father believes the English have sent men to kill him. I will not ask you to admit that you are an English spy, though I am becoming convinced of it. I will only say that you are not to kill my father. He is a great fool and half mad, but no one is to kill him for that." As an afterthought she added quickly, "You are not to allow Adrian to kill him either."

"The boy's not killing anybody. Neither am I." He fingered his scar. "If you think I'd make love to a woman and then kill her father, you don't know much about me."

"I think you would regret betraying a woman, but you would do it."

She gave Guillaume time to answer. The streets turned corners and shut the noise of the city away. At this hour, at every house they passed, lanterns were being taken in. It was the work of the first servants awake to blow out the small candles that had been left to burn in the night and save the stubs to use again. Everyone was thrifty now.

It was very quiet. Her footsteps and Guillaume's made a single cadence, like a single animal walking.

After some uncounted number of steps, Guillaume said, "I don't mean any harm to your father. Can you send a message to him?"

"No." That would be to admit she knew where he was.

"You went to talk to him. That's why you were out all night. He's still in Paris."

"Will you tell me why you are looking for him?"

"Ah. Now that I can't do."

Exchanging words with Guillaume LeBreton was like pouring water into a cup with a hole in it.

"If you will not admit to being a spy for the English and you will not tell me why you want my father, the meat of this conversation has been plucked out and we do not need to have it. I will discover the truth, eventually. I will not like you at all when I know the truth about you."

They did not return to her house directly. Guillaume chose a path of smaller streets. It might have been that he did not want to meet heavy carts and noisy carriages and these alleyways were less traveled. Now she saw this as sly and careful. He was not seen. She was not seen.

Guillaume took a hundred such precautions, because he was a spy. She had not wanted to think of this before.

He was large and comfortable to walk beside. He had decided his role of the moment permitted him to be attentive and take her arm to help her avoid the gutters in the middle of the alley. He was portraying several of the most popular masculine virtues. Two middle-aged women of great respectability nodded at him as they passed. A cat sat on a windowsill, washing. A laundry woman carried flat, white sheets, folded, in her basket. Guillaume kept his arm tightly around her, which she permitted by not thinking too deeply about the significance of it.

Somehow, at last, she was home.

Guillaume frowned down at her. Behind him the sky was the color of thin paper that has been laid on the fire, when the light glows behind it, just before it catches flame. It would be another hot day. "I don't like to leave you alone here. Come with me. I'll find somewhere to take you. We can—"

She shook her head. He knew the thousand reasons this was impossible.

"You're not well."

"Agnès will put me to bed and bring me warm bricks wrapped in cloth to hug to my stomach and I will not feel so sick. I will drink tisanes and lemonade and be better tomorrow."

"Go inside, then. God, your eyes are staring out of your face. Go to bed. Let them take care of you."

As he had upon another occasion, he reached past her and knocked on the door. The difference was, this time he kept his hand on her arm, holding on. "I'll come back tonight, around at the kitchen. Tell them to let me in when I come."

"No." The sun was everywhere, getting brighter. She didn't feel the warmth. She felt empty and ill and cold, and she was saying good-bye to Guillaume. Again. "You must not come here. Ever." *I will not let you find Papa. And I will not let Victor find you.* "My cousin," she swallowed and her mouth tasted vile, "is malicious. Whatever you are, he is dangerous to you. You must keep away from me. I will come to the café again, in a week or a month. Or someday. I will come and wait for you again. I can promise that much."

She heard the lock of the door, turning.

Guillaume's hand still rested on her arm. "It's not over between us. Think about me. I need that much."

"I have a hundred terrible things to think about. You are ninety-nine of them."

"Maggie. No. Look this way again. Look at me." He took her chin in his hand and edged her face into the sun, into a stinging assault of light. "Open your eyes. Are you using some kind of drops? Belladonna?"

The door opened behind her. "Do not be ridiculous. And let me go. I cannot stay."

"Maggie. Stay a minute. There's something wrong here."

She slipped from his hold and through the door before Janvier had it fully open, leaving behind whatever words Guillaume said to keep her there.

The halls were empty of servants. She stumbled upstairs and around, through the length of the house, to the front windows of the parlor. She threw the curtains back. She would have one last glimpse of Guillaume as he walked away.

He was a spy. He did not give one small damn about her, really. He was using her to find her father. She knew this. She knew this completely. There was no connection between them that did not involve dishonor and lies and stupidities beyond counting.

He stayed at the door for a long minute. She was in time to see him go.

Below, on a street the color of rocks, Guillaume LeBreton walked away from her. Not in a hurry, not slowly. It was as if he had twenty tasks to do this morning and he had finished three and now proceeded on to the next, at which he would also be successful. He said all that with just his steps upon the street. No one created an intelligent and eloquent walk as he did.

She held aside the red brocade curtains of the salon and pressed her face to the glass so she would see him for the longest possible moment.

I am no heartsick girl to weep at the window for what I cannot have. She cried only because she was so tired.

Because she was being foolish about Guillaume, she saw him arrested.

hirty-two

SHE SAW GUILLAUME WALK AWAY FROM HER. IN THE
entryway of the last house of the street, a little maidservant
was on her hands and knees, scrubbing the steps. Guillaume passed the girl. She raised her head to look after
him. She got suddenly to her feet.

Soldiers came around the corner. Five of them, wearing
the uniform of the Garde Nationale. City troops. Striding
ahead of them was a thin man she recognized instantly. He
had taken off the bandage, but his face was marked, red
and angry, with the slashing cut she'd given him. This was
the Jacobin who'd come to the chateau at Voisemont.

He pointed at Guillaume, and the soldiers surrounded
him.

It was like being at a play where the audience was talking loudly and no one could hear the actors. She could only
watch. Like the foolish peasant who comes to the city for
the first time and goes to the theater, she wanted to spring
from her seat and yell, "Get away. Run," and send the play

in a different direction. She wanted to jump onto the stage and save the hero of the story.

Guillaume showed empty hands and puzzlement. Protested. Every gesture portrayed innocence.

The front door of the house slammed opened. Victor was in the street, hurrying. The soldiers stopped to listen. Came to attention. Gestures and instruction from Victor. Yes and yes from the soldiers. Nods.

He is telling them to arrest Guillaume.

Guillaume was prodded roughly, boxed in by the soldiers. At the last minute, he looked back to the house. Toward her. He must have seen her in the window.

He shook his head. *No.*

He was telling her to stay quiet. Stay inside. Do nothing. That would be the order he gave. And damn him for a fool.

Then the houses on the corner cut him off from view.

Victor reeked of satisfaction. He stood shoulder to shoulder with the Jacobin who had come to Voisemont. They were complicity and familiarity, conversing amiably while they watched Guillaume being marched away. They knew each other. They were accomplices in this and God alone knew what other business.

She knew. Now she knew. *Victor sent those men to Voisemont to hurt me. Why? Why?*

The door to the parlor opened behind her. Aunt Sophie came in, scolding, filling the room with whine and confusion. With hundreds of pointless words.

Guillaume would be gone in a moment, taken to any of a dozen barracks or prisons. Lost.

I will not let this happen.

She pushed Aunt Sophie aside and went for the back stairs. The cook gaped at her as she ran through the kitchen. She ran across the garden, stumbling on the brick path, pulled up the bar on the gate to the alley and was out.

Victor must not see her. She took the long way, down the alley that led to Rue Martin. They would take Guillaume that way. She ran, as she would have run in the fields at home. Ran, half-blind in the bright sunlight.

Guillaume was there, at the end of the street, surrounded by soldiers.

She collided with someone who stepped into her path. Smaller than she was. Dark hair and a thin, keen, hungry face. A loose, dark coat. A striped waistcoat. Adrian. He grabbed her and held on, his fingers digging into her arms till it hurt. "Stop." He was unyielding as a post.

"They have Guillaume. I must go—"

"You shut your gob and listen to me. Stop. Stop now."

"They have taken—"

"I see that, damn you."

"They are taking him to prison. You don't understand. He will die."

"You can't do a bloody damn thing if they toss you in the cell next door. You were going to run right up there. Be damned if you have the sense God gave cabbages."

He was speaking in English, with an accent she could barely understand. This wasn't the sly, sullen, sarcastic boy she'd traveled halfway across France with. What faced her was sharp and brutal and utterly ruthless. He scared her.

She jerked at his hold. "I was not going to accost armed men. I'm not a fool."

"Good, then. Look at me." He was speaking French again. He squeezed her arm. Hard. "Look at me, not him. We're talking to each other, you and me. We're strolling along, out to buy eggs and feathers and baby goats. We're going in the same direction, but we don't see him. We don't look at them at all. Look at me."

You are English. "Do not instruct me in caution. We will give them time to move away. Then follow." *I was right, then. Guillaume is an English spy.*

Adrian was breathing fast. "That's better. We follow them. This is my world. I know what to do."

"And I will tell you that Paris is my world, Adrian. Now come, before they turn a corner and are lost to us."

Guillaume and his guards had turned the corner and marched onward. But they were not hard to find again, so many men, with such grim purpose. People stopped to stare after them, to point and discuss. At the Church of Saint-Grégoire a carriage waited. They put Guillaume inside. Three *gardes* accompanied him and the carriage went south.

She watched, hidden behind a corner of a house. "They could take him anywhere. There are prisons all over Paris."

"Then we stick close. Keep up, or I swear I'll leave you behind." He gave her a single, impatient look.

She did more than keep up. She knew this city, as Adrian did not. Knew when the carriage turned toward the Pont Neuf. They slipped through the slow traffic of the quay and crossed the bridge ahead of it.

At the Conciergerie Prison, the carriage stopped outside the gate. One *garde* descended. He returned in only a minute and the carriage started off again. They had been turned away. There was not room for even one more prisoner at that great stronghold.

Then deeper into the oldest parts of Paris. A long way. She knew the Sorbonne and the Section Sainte-Geneviève as one knows the tiles of one's kitchen. She took small streets in the labyrinth, making guesses how the carriage would turn. A coach could go no faster than walking pace here, and the driver wore a Phrygian cap, bright red, visible for a quarter mile.

The carriage stopped again. On Rue Tessier. This time the man returned nodding and satisfied. They were admitted. She had a glimpse of Guillaume, in the middle of *gardes*, every path of escape blocked, hurried along, into the prison.

She left Adrian outside the prison gate and staggered

away, out of sight, around the corner. In the alleyway she put a hand on the wall to hold herself up and was sick once more. Her heart beat so hard, it shook her whole body.

"They took him inside." Adrian came back to report, limping and tight lipped.

She was shaking. Whether it was fear, or running so fast across Paris, or being so sick, she could not say.

The boy said, "The carriage left. The men from the Garde went with it."

She pressed the heels of her hands hard into her belly. "I must . . . I must go into the prison and tell them it is a mistake. Convince them."

"You try to go in there, I'll hurt you."

"You don't understand." Her head was filled with a roaring darkness where she could not think or remember or make herself speak. "If I wait till he is charged and the papers are filed at the Tribunal, there will be no way out for him. For an hour, now, there may be something I can do. I will talk to them—"

Adrian put himself in front of her, inches away, grim and unboylike. "What is that place?"

"A prison. Once a convent. Now it is a prison. Wait. Don't speak for a minute. I must think."

She breathed deep, trying to set aside the fear and the sickness. Victor had done this. The accusation had already been filed, the arrest order prepared last night. It was too late to bribe and reason and plead.

"You're sick as a dog, ain't you?" the boy said. "Your eyes look funny. All dark. You eat opium?"

"No. Of course not. Let me think."

It had been too late before she drank coffee this morning. Before Guillaume escorted her home. Before Victor walked into the streets to instruct the *gardes*. The soldiers had been lying in wait. Victor expected Guillaume to come to her house, sooner or later, and had set his trap and waited.

"You pregnant?"

"What? No. It is—" Another pang hit her stomach. "I ate something that does not agree with me. Anyone might do that." She staggered when she pushed herself away from the wall. "This is the Convent of Saint-Barthélémy. They are using such houses now for prisoners, since we have no more nuns and a plentitude of prisoners."

She went to the end of the alley to see this prison where Guillaume had been taken. Where he would be held until Victor had him killed.

This was a very old convent, built like a fortress. A long, blank stone wall faced the street. Over it, she could see the roof of the church and a chapel window of red and blue glass that had escaped destruction. Spikes topped the wall. A man with a long gun patrolled the streets.

"No matter how many die, the prisons are always full. There is a dreadful mathematics to this." Her eyes hurt with the light so that she could not see clearly. Inside her, though, everything was dark and cold. "Guillaume's name is already on the rolls of the Tribunal."

"Don't faint. I'll hit you if you faint. And don't cry."

"I am not crying." She closed her eyes. "Though I may be sick again. Very possibly."

"You do that and I'm gonna walk off and leave you. I swear it. Damn it to hell and back. That old bitch is going to fry me like a kipper. She'll never believe I didn't do this on purpose."

What old bitch? But it did not matter. "This is my fault. Victor did this."

"I saw. Cod-swallowing bugger." The boy's face was blank and terrifying in the inhuman stillness that had settled there. "But Doyle's the one who stepped in it. He shouldn't have gone anywhere near your house. You want to blame somebody, blame Doyle."

"I will. I will also get him out of there." *Now I know his name. He is Doyle. Doyle.* "I must go somewhere and sit down. We cannot stay here."

They must go to one of the safe places of La Flèche. The wheels of her brain refused to turn, like a broken clockwork that stopped and stuck and would not start again. *What is close by? What is empty?* She had never permitted herself to know all the safehouses in Paris. She already carried the key to too many lives in her head.

Behind them, a voice said, "You are wise to leave here."

Marguerite turned. A neat maidservant approached them. The girl had not appeared by sorcery. She had been so ordinary, so young, they hadn't noticed her strolling toward them, basket over her arm, her white apron caught up in the waistband to keep it clean from the streets. She was a nursery maid, perhaps, barely past childhood herself. There were ten thousand like her in Paris. One did not see them, they were so common in the street.

But her eyes were not ordinary. Her eyes were deep and sardonic and knowing. Mocking. "If you stand in the street gaping the guards will come to ask what you are doing, loitering beside a prison for the enemies of the Republic."

Adrian said, "I've seen you before."

That particular tone meant he might draw his knife and do something drastic. Guillaume was not here to stop him, so she must. "Be quiet, Adrian. Do nothing unless I tell you."

"Yes, boy. Be quiet." The girl dimpled. "You saw me scrubbing a doorstep, perhaps. I have been interested in you for a while." Slanted brown eyes turned to her. "I will say, very quickly, that one may smell the roses in the gardens nearby, if the wind is right, before this bloodthirsty boy attacks me."

She is one of us. A member of La Flèche. "The roses are lovely, but it is forbidden to pick them. Who are you?"

"I am Owl. I was told to help you, if it seemed necessary. It now does. I know more passwords, if you would like to exchange them as well."

Owl. She is one of Jean-Paul's. He has spoken of her. I had not thought she would be so very young.

Adrian said, "I don't like people who take an interest in me, Owl."

"Then you must strive to be more boring, must you not? And you, citoyenne." She shifted her gaze. "If you permit, I will find a fiacre and take you to a hiding place. We will send for the Gardener."

Jean-Paul. Yes. I need Jean-Paul.

What was she to do with Adrian? La Flèche had saved dozens of Englishmen over the years. Harboring English spies was altogether different. He shouldn't see Owl or hear the passwords or go to a safehouse. She couldn't begin to think of what he should not be hearing.

How much of a spy could he be, a boy this age?

But they would arrest even a boy this young. Someone might have seen him with Guillaume.

What are they doing to Guillaume?

"The stable loft in the house of women is empty," the girl said. "We can go there. Only a few of our havens are empty today."

Adrian said, "Anyone could know six or eight words. I know them myself now. That doesn't make you anything special."

"And you are a great fool. If I wished you harm, I would raise my voice and call that guard to denounce you. It is the work of a minute. I do not have to waste my time exchanging passwords with a fool."

They would argue for an hour. "Enough. We must leave. Owl, go first, so they do not ask why we are meeting here."

"*Bien.* The guard looks this way." Owl nodded and

pointed down the street, as if she had been asked a question and answered it. "I will lead. Don't come too closely after me."

She bounced off cheerfully, the ribbons on her cap streaming behind her.

"She thinks she's clever." The boy glowered. "I'll take you anywhere you want to go. Tell me where."

Victor would already be searching. Every moment on the street, they were in danger. "We will trust her."

"You trust her. I'm not going to." They stayed till the girl was almost out of sight before they walked after her, down the street.

hirty-three

DOYLE SET HIS BACK TO THE WALL AND LET HIS legs collapse out from underneath him and slid down to sit on the floor, hugging his knees.

No one was looking. He put his head on his arm and took some breaths. His skin pulled tight over a core of ice inside. Damn, but he was afraid.

I'm going to die.

He picked the knowledge up and looked it over. His death. Here in France. Soon. *Everybody has a time and place waiting for him. This is my time. My place. Now I know.* Funny in a way. His father always said he'd hang. Looked like he was wrong about that.

No love lost between him and the earl. When he was a boy, he'd do some damn fool thing. Some typical boys' nonsense. He'd get called to his father's study and caned till he couldn't lie on his back in bed. He always wondered what he'd done to make his father hate him so much.

One day they'd been about to go through that exercise when he'd looked at his father . . . looked down at his father. The earl was shorter than he was. Neither of them said anything about it, but he never got caned again.

It had been five or six years since he'd talked to the old man. *I wonder if he still calls me "that papist mongrel."*

When he had his face blank and stupid, he lifted his head. No privacy here. No way to make any, not with men packed like herring in a barrel. They were sleeping on pallets on the floor, with just barely room to walk between. Men piled valises and clothing at the foot, marking off a bit of territory.

Twenty-five straw mats. So, about that number of men, more or less. They'd set themselves in groups with some of the pallets edged up close to each other. Friends. Factions. Tonight, when everybody lay down, he'd get a feel for the men. Figure out who the leaders were.

If he could get to the guardroom in the middle of the night and kill two or three men, he might live to get out. There might be a couple of these prisoners willing to try it.

At least they'd go down fighting.

They were handing out bread in the corridor. Men came back carrying a black-colored loaf and hunched down on their pallets to eat. Aristos on that side. Common criminals on this. He had to wonder which side they'd sort him to.

This was the refectory of the old convent, a room thirty-by-fifty feet. The paintwork and bosses on the ceiling were sixteenth century. No one had bothered to climb up to destroy any of that yet. The walls were older than the ceiling, built with limestone taken out of the quarries that ran under Paris. Big blocks of stone, an arm's-length thick, covered with a coat of plaster and whitewashed.

I am not going to gnaw my way through that.

Only one door into this room, currently open to let air in. They'd lock it at night. The lock was nothing. He could get through the lock. That would put him in the corridor outside. Whether that would do him any good remained to be seen.

What else? Four windows, high overhead and barred, which was a right discouragement any way you looked at it. He thought about the map he was piecing together in his head. Getting through one of the windows put you in the cloister garden, where you ran up against twelve-foot walls with spikes on top. And guards on the other side. Any plan that started out in the cloister was a plan that needed a bit of work.

He wiped his mouth. His beard was rough as wheat stubble. The fake scar was going to start peeling off if he kept sweating. He had three replacements in the pocket of his jacket. Maybe he'd stay alive long enough to need them.

He wished he'd had more time with Maggie. Even one more day. There was something wrong with her and he'd left her alone—

Don't think about that.

He closed his eyes, feeling the space around him. For four hundred years nuns had been eating in this room, doing needlework, keeping accounts, peeling apples. There should have been prayers lingering in the walls. The stones should have been thick with serenity. Layered deep in contemplation.

Whatever had been here once, it was stripped away. Too many men had waited for death right where he was sitting. The walls whispered desolation. The air was heavy inside his lungs, like dead men had been breathing it.

He pulled his hat off and let his head fall back against the plaster. His hair was wet with sweat. And his shirt, under the waistcoat. Fear sweat. He was used to being dirty when the job called for it, but this felt clammy and filthy.

Hell of a way for a spy to end, done in by a jealous little Frenchman, protecting his family honor.

Maggie could take care of herself. But not when she was sick. Her eyes were strange, the pupils all dilated. Something wrong. Something very wrong. He had to get out of here. Had to get to Maggie. Had to—

Put it away. Put it away till you can do something about it. Carruthers would take care of Maggie. She'd do that for him. He could trust her to do that.

There was a general shuffling in the hall outside. More men filed in the door. Twenty-three men. They sat on the mats in the clutter of their possessions, or leaned against the walls, or paced back and forth, stepping over things— all of them talking, stinking, coughing, breathing each other's breath, their bodies heating up the stifling air.

Nobody came near him. Nobody looked at him straight. Nobody stopped to talk. They knew how to treat new prisoners here. They left a man alone to make his own peace with the situation.

He needed that time.

He set his hat down beside him, deliberate and careful, keeping his breath steady. Getting through one more minute without breaking and throwing himself at the walls.

The floor under him was black oak, boards worn smooth from being scrubbed religiously for a couple centuries. There was a layer of stickiness on them now, made of fear and dust and sweat and worse than that. Nobody'd washed them since the Revolution.

Victor de Fleurignac had been waiting for him.

I played right into his hands. Love is the very devil.

Maggie. The muscles in his chest tightened and wouldn't let loose.

A guard appeared at the door, one he hadn't seen before. So the guards changed at noon. Middle-aged, medium height, fifteen stone, wearing the red Phrygian cap that showed he was a loyal revolutionary. He was better dressed than the other guards. Might mean he had a careful wife. Might mean he was a dandy among the sans-culottes. Might mean he took bribes.

And this one could read. He went through a paper, looking up, looking down, matching names and prisoners.

They feed us at midday. Then they count us. How many hours till they count again?

The guard finished and went off to check the count in the next room. There were women in there, including some nuns. He'd seen them walk by in the corridor.

Galba would be the one to tell his father that his youngest son was dead, on the public block, in France. That was a poke in the eye for the old man. A Markham, even an extra son nobody had any use for, didn't die in a public execution. Just like his father always predicted, he'd finally made himself a blot on the Markham escutcheon.

Maybe he'd take that thought to the guillotine with him and pull it out at the last minute to warm himself up, so he wouldn't start shaking at the end.

He wouldn't waste his last minutes thinking about that bitter old man. He'd be thinking about Maggie.

He swallowed. His mouth was foul and dry from being afraid. On the way in, they'd marched him past the door to the cloister and he'd seen a well out there. When they let the men out of this room, he'd get himself a drink of water out in the courtyard.

He wouldn't feel so trapped if he had sky overhead.

He'd been feeling an eye on him for a few minutes. A priest, wearing the black cassock, headed in his direction, walking crooked and painful, stopping to rest and talk with one man and then another. He'd be one of the priests who wouldn't swear to the Republic. Not too many of them left in Paris. The guillotine cut them down like ripe grain.

"A newcomer." It was a clear, educated Parisian accent. "Don't get up. I will join you, if you don't mind. We have a shortage of chairs, so the ground must serve me."

The hand that clamped down to take the support of Doyle's shoulder was surprisingly firm. There was something wrong with the man's legs, though. The weight of the priest was nothing at all—the bird bones and the tough leather flesh of the old.

Doyle reached up and grasped forearms with the man, helping him down to sit next to him. The cassock was ragged at the hem but made of heavy black silk. He'd been an aristocrat among priests.

"Father." Doyle settled back down.

The priest took three or four shallow breaths before he spoke. There was pain inside the man. You could see it in his eyes. Not much life left in him. Hardly enough to be worth the Republic's while killing him. Maybe they were hoping he'd die in prison. The priest said, "Yes. Thank you." Another breath. "Your name, my son?"

"Guillaume, *mon Père*. Guillaume LeBreton."

"By your voice, you're a long way from home, Guillaume LeBreton. I am accustomed to write letters for men who wish to send them. I'll attempt to send one for you even as far as Brittany, if this would comfort you."

"There's no one left to send it to. No one's expecting me back."

The priest touched his sleeve with a stick and tendon of a hand, half scarecrow. "Then no one there is afraid for you. It is a poor comfort, but a real one. I am Father Jérôme, a priest of Saint-Sulpice, paying for a misspent life with an uncomfortable ending." He carried a black box under his arm. When he set it across his lap it was topped with a black and white inlay of squares. Not a book. A chessboard. "I discovered, in the end, that I possessed a conscience. A most inconvenient appendage. And you? Why are you here, my son?"

"A mistake."

"We are fifty mistakes in this place." Under the murmur and cough of the other men, the priest chuckled. "Except possibly a few of our criminal brothers who admit to some small errors in honesty. We have our thieves, and our whores, and one poor forger who was unwise enough to print political writings when he was not forging. If you are a thief, I have some fine sermons about thievery."

"I'm not so lucky. Seems I've committed a crime against the Revolution. I'm that buffle-headed, I can't remember doing it."

"That is unfortunate, Guillaume. But you will find the invention of the Tribunal is nearly infinite. You will be amazed at what you've been up to." Father Jérôme shifted and sighed with the dry breath of old age. "I take confession in the hall upstairs in the evenings. The guards look the other way for an hour. You're a big block of a lad. You will help me up the stairs tonight. The pair who have been assisting me left this morning."

"They left" meant they'd gone to the Conciergerie and trial. They'd be dead by now, or on their way to it.

"Glad to. I've a broad back for it."

"We will put your back to good use then. When they count us tonight and bring the bread and soup, collect an extra loaf to be the Host. The guard will pretend not to see. Bring it upstairs with us. We will pass the climb discussing your sins, which are doubtless numerous."

"There's a few."

"You shall be my first absolution of the night. My penances are light these days. Leave me in the dark at the top of the stairs. It serves as my confessional. Those who have been called to trial tomorrow will come last. When they're finished, come for me again. I say Mass on the stairs. How long has it been since your last confession, Guillaume?"

"Years." Maybe he'd believed in a benevolent God when he was a child. Not for a long time. "That's a chessboard."

The priest sat up straighter. "Do you play?" He touched the box he held. "They allow me to keep this and my breviary. I hate to admit they're both comforts to me. My last chess partner, alas, has moved on."

"I play." He watched in silence as the priest opened the box and set the chessmen on the floor. It was an old set. Venetian papier-mâché, painted and gilded. Each man was detailed and delicate, with banners and bright robes. What was it doing in this godforsaken place? "Beautiful." He lifted the white knight.

"It was given to me by the young man who was my chess partner for a while. He had it from another man, who had it from yet another. No one knows how long the set has been moving from prisoner to prisoner." The priest lay the box flat, opened facedown, to make the board. "We will play chess on the edge of doom, you and I. There's some Christian moral in this, my young Breton, but I cannot find one that does not sound sententious. Take white, if you will." He set red men on the board with practiced speed.

"I don't mind opening the game." *What's happening to Maggie? She's sick and she's alone in that house with her cousin. I can't get to her.*

If he thought about that, he'd tear his hands apart, clawing at the stone. He had to put it away for now. Put it away.

Doyle moved out a pawn. "Tell me about the men they got guarding us. Anyone I should watch out for?"

Thirty-four

MARGUERITE SAT ON THE MAKESHIFT BED, LEAN-
ing against the wall, feeling dizzy and sick in waves. It was
better when she lay down flat, but she would not give in to
this inconvenient illness. Sitting up was a small victory.
She needed such small victories.

She let Jean-Paul take her pulse. "I will probably lose
my stomach soon. Upon you." She did not stand on ceremony with Jean-Paul. Quite aside from having been lovers,
they had played naked in the fishpond at Voisemont when
they were four.

Jean-Paul counted, holding the gold pocket watch he
had from his father.

"You do not impress me and you are not a physician."
She rested her head on the wall and held her knees close
to her so she would not slip sideways. "I will go tomorrow
and see what is what. It will not be impossible. For every
box, there is a key. I will find the key to that prison. If I did
not keep being sick and fainting, I would go today."

She endured Jean-Paul putting the back of his hand on her forehead. "You don't have a fever," he said.

"Thank you. Perhaps you will spare me an accounting of the diseases I do not have. Leprosy. Gout. The pox. I find it does not cheer me up at all."

He frowned and demanded to see her tongue. Then he held his hand to her face, covering and uncovering one of her eyes and then the other. "Have you started taking opium? It's not good for you, you know."

"Why is everyone asking if I eat opium? I do not have time to fuddle my mind with—"

"Your pupils are dilated. You've taken something. Do you still grow foxgloves in the garden behind your house?"

"They grow in abundance. And, yes, I know they are poison. But I do not graze upon the garden like a goat, so it does not matter." She pushed him away. "If you wish to convince me I am too sick to go to the prison, it's not working. Tomorrow, very early, I will go to see Guillaume and look about the walls and bars of that place."

"If your Guillaume were here, he'd tell you not to go."

"I would not listen to him, either."

"Listen to common sense then." Jean-Paul was finished poking and prying at her. He tossed his hat aside, unbuttoned his waistcoat, and fell into the armchair beside the bed that had been made for her. The chair had feather stuffing coming out everywhere and was covered with a large blanket to hide this fact. The footstool was a small crate. "Victor's going to be there, waiting for you."

"He cannot know which prison Guillaume has been taken to. Not yet. The paperwork will not come to the Tribunal until tomorrow. Tomorrow afternoon, I think."

"You're guessing."

"Sometimes, one makes educated guesses."

"And sometimes one makes stupid guesses. Lie down before you faint."

She would lie down when she had convinced Jean-Paul to do what she wanted.

The bed she sat upon was a wooden door, laid across benches and chests and pushed close to the wall. The padding beneath her was fresh hay, piled thick and covered by the coarsest of blankets, scrupulously clean. It was comfortable enough and smelled beautifully. She had slept in worse places. She did not regard the bits of hay that stuck through, into her.

Owl—her name was Justine—had brought her to one of the most secure refuges of La Flèche, a place reserved against great need. The hiding hole was up a ladder, above a shed in the stable yard of the most fashionable whorehouse in Paris. In this loft, artfully placed disorder concealed the nest within. Boxes, old trunks, and huge storage barrels lined the walls between stacks of discarded furniture. The storage room behind a notorious brothel looked very much like any other attic, in fact.

Justine had needed only ten easy, practiced minutes to set the door flat on its supports, carry hay from the stable to make a soft bed, spread cloth on a trunk to make a table, and hide the decrepitude of the large armchair under a cover.

This was the very essence of a safehouse of La Flèche. All was secret, subtle, well concealed. Lean the door back against the wall, scatter the straw, fold the blankets. There would be no sign anyone had been here.

Adrian had stationed himself at the far end of the loft at the window there. He could see the length of this attic and the ground outside as far as the fence. Justine stood on the ladder, midway between the floors. She could see the whole of the shed below and anyone who might creep in to listen. Without instruction, quite naturally, they had put themselves as sentinels where they could watch everything. It was disquieting to deal with these two silent, knowing, unchildlike children.

She must also deal with Jean-Paul. He looked tired and frustrated. His hands, clenched on the blanket where it draped the arms of the chair, were like the bony, well-carved fists of one of the ascetic saints. She would not allow her tenderness for him to turn her from her path.

He said, "There's something wrong with your pulse. I think you've been poisoned."

"I think I have eaten bad food. I will be better tomorrow. And I will be able to think again, clearly. How difficult would it be to organize a riot? A small one?"

"On Rue Tessier? It would be difficult, and it wouldn't work. Marguerite, we can't get to him. I am so very, very sorry."

"I do not need you to be sorry. I need you to help me. We have played such games before."

"Even if this could be done, we have no time to plan. We've tried last-minute rescues before. I saw Claude and Virginie die in front of me. Have you forgotten?"

That had been an old convent, too, the cobbled yard where Claude and Virginie had died. She swallowed. "Don't compare battle scars with me, Jean-Paul. I'm not discussing whether I will do this. I am telling you what I will do and asking your help."

"This is throwing your life away. And you'll take others with you."

"Then I will use only those men and women I have recruited myself. Not yours. Perhaps my people will be less prudent and cautious than you have become." At once, she was ashamed of what she'd said. "No. I take that back. Forgive me."

On the upended trunk that made a table was a basket of bread, a bottle of wine, and water in a jug. She drank some water, straight from the lip of the jug, and set it down. "I will take no risks with anyone else. There will be no deaths. I promise."

"Except possibly your own."

"Not even that. I will be careful."

A square window opened at the corner of the eaves, over the bed. The stable yard below was noisy and reassuringly normal. This was an establishment where powerful men came to carouse. It was more private than the darkest graveyard at midnight. No one saw—and most especially, no one spoke of—anything. Certainly, they would not see a woman coming and going. There was an epidemic of blindness and muteness occurring here.

Jean-Paul continued to scowl upon her. "You'd be safer in Normandy. If that man is worthy of you, he'd say the same thing. Get out of Paris. Go protect your people. Rebuild your network."

"After I finish this."

"Victor will be searching for you all over the city."

"We are experts in hiding what men like Victor want to find."

"We're not experts in storming a citadel like that convent. If you try, you'll kill yourself."

"I will not. I have never yet killed myself."

"You are stubborn as a block of wood." She knew the exact moment she had won because he kicked the crate he was using as a footstool. "You are also stupid as a cow. How are you planning to accomplish this idiocy?"

"I will think of something."

"There's a sentiment to fill the heart with terror. And I am wasting my breath. How well I know you." He stood up and reached his sleeve toward her. "Take this. Get me out of this coat. I can't think when I'm stewing hot."

She pulled at his sleeve and helped him shrug out of the coat. He tossed it over the edge of an old screen. "Convince me it can be done. And let's get the young minions out of here. The less they know, the better."

"The boy is already involved. He travels with Guillaume.

I would not have brought the girl to this place, but she seems to know it well."

Jean-Paul shifted uncomfortably.

She said, "I see. If Owl is employed here, we must put a stop to it."

He unbuttoned his cuffs and began to roll his sleeves up. "Of course."

"I mean this, Jean-Paul. I will not allow this to continue."

He sighed. "You do not change, Marguerite. And you are right. Very well, we will stop her from whoring, if that's what she does. Can we do it *after* we have rescued your Guillaume and killed ourselves doing it?"

"I can wait. I am not unreasonable."

"You are pigheaded beyond all reason."

"I am not pigheaded. I will not watch while a child that age works in a brothel. Though this particular brothel does not have the reputation of selling girls of her age."

"Who's been talking to you about whorehouses? Damn it, Marguerite, if you need to know about whorehouses, you should ask me." He stopped. "That didn't come out right. What I mean is—"

"I can hear you, you know." Justine, standing on the ladder, propped her elbows on the floor of the loft. "This is a very expensive whorehouse, monsieur. If you like, I will see that you are entertained for the evening. Not the young boy, naturally. His innocence must be maintained at all costs. But you and the charitable mademoiselle who wishes to deprive me of my livelihood may come. We cater to all tastes here."

She heard Adrian mutter, "If breaking into prison doesn't kill you lot, I might."

Jean-Paul closed his eyes briefly. "Let us proceed one catastrophe at a time. Unless you two have something to say, you should be elsewhere." He waited, then said softly, "It is not that you are young. I'd say the same to anyone in La Flèche. You should go."

Justine's chin rose. "If I have done so little—"

We have been tactless, Jean-Paul and I. They are not children. She said quickly, "I am in your debt."

And it was not a child who studied her gravely. Justine said, "I will collect payment, mademoiselle. Be sure of it." She disappeared. She could be heard, going out through the storeroom below.

Adrian was a pace behind. He swung to the ladder, agile and silent. The two clomped noisily through the storage shed and out. It was their commentary on being dismissed. It was telling Jean-Paul they'd obeyed his order.

It is a hard world where children become so subtle. "When I remove my Guillaume to safety, those two children must follow the sparrows to England. This is no life for them."

"Fine. We'll send them to England. We will put them in school where they will astonish their classmates. May we now return to the business at hand. I'll try to find someone who's been in the convent. Get a floor plan."

"Try. But we have no time. Tomorrow, I must decide how to crack this nut."

For a moment the darkness she had been holding off closed in around the edges of her vision. A soft emptiness invited her to give up. She would not, of course.

Jean-Paul said, "Sit." He pushed her shoulders. She was in the soft chair, among the feathers. "Don't stand up for a while. What do we need?"

The dizziness became manageable, though it did not go away. "Floor plans. The other houses in the street. Every house with a wall that touches the convent. Your man in the Bureau Municipal can get that. I need the distances on the street paced out. We've done this before. Maps, first of all."

Jean-Paul sat on her bed. "Maps. Distances. We can start that today. What else?"

hirty-five

CARRUTHERS GRIPPED HER HANDS TOGETHER ON the blotter of the writing desk. Her face was grim. "We know where he is, at least."

Althea set the tray down on the small table beside the empty grate. "The Convent of Saint-Barthélémy on Rue Tessier."

"I've seen the outside. An impenetrable pile of stone. Do we have any ties to the place? Anyone who knows anything about it?"

"Not yet. I've sent out word, asking." Althea poured boiling water from the black kettle into the teapot.

Carruthers's face showed every one of her years. The discipline that contained her was very apparent. Her anger, close to the surface. "Look at the guards, of course. We'll try bribery."

"We cannot get the accusation withdrawn. It was made by Victor de Fleurignac."

"This is the way we lose agents. Some fool lifts a skirt. Some pig must defend his cousin's honor." She crumpled the newspaper in front of her and tossed it into the basket by the desk. "Not for politics. Not for ideals. Not for useful intelligence. Just a woman. Even with a man like Will Doyle. Where is she?"

"Not arrested. Not returned home." Althea shrugged. "She'll be good at hiding."

"Then we will be good at finding her." Carruthers stared out into the afternoon slanting its way across the courtyard. "We have eyes inside La Flèche, of course."

"None of them close to Finch. Or we would have known who she is months ago." One lump of sugar clicked into the teacup. Thea poured tea, then dripped in three drops of milk.

"I said I'd take care of her. To do that, I need to know where she is and what she's doing."

"She will be making plans to rescue Will."

"Or betraying him further." Carruthers's lips narrowed. "Don't make Will's mistake. We have no reason to trust her."

"Everything we know about Finch says she's a good woman."

"She is a good Frenchwoman. She is an admirable leader of La Flèche. That doesn't mean she's on our side. Marguerite de Fleurignac is not one of us."

Althea stirred the cup and handed it across. "Now, Helen . . ."

"I am less enamored of young love than you are. I expected better of Doyle. I trained him better than this. What damned asinine foolery is he playing with in the middle of a job?"

"You are becoming a cynic. Will doesn't make mistakes about people. If he has put his life in her hands, they are reliable hands."

"You're a romantic, Thea." Carruthers came to her feet, impatiently, and strode to the window. She stood there, holding the delicate cup. "Very well. Let's say she's trying to save him."

"She may succeed. Finch of La Flèche is better at what she does than anyone we know. No one in the Service can match her."

"We know her work."

"If you could pick anyone to free Will, she is the one you would go to."

"Perhaps." Carruthers watched the youngest of her agents cross the courtyard. Paxton. He was seventeen. Any of her men and women might be in prison tomorrow and dead next week. She'd never thought it would be tough, unkillable Will Doyle, though. "La Flèche has tried to take men from prison before, and failed."

"They have also succeeded. Many times. She will get her Guillaume back, Helen. There is no force on earth stronger than a determined woman." Althea tidied the tea tray. When she judged sufficient time had passed, she said, "We must help her."

"She has La Flèche to draw upon." A long, reflective sip of tea. "But you're right. If we find her, if help is needed, we'll offer it. Tell the others. And we will keep her alive. For that much, she is one of ours. Who are you sending to the prison?"

"Me. I'll go myself."

"Take some of the counterfeit Will brought. Be careful, bribing. The prisons are overrun with fanatics." Below her, at the kitchen door, Claudine finished sweeping the flagstones and set the broom aside to pump water into a bucket set in the stone basin. "Idealists are the devil. Has that rat of a boy come back?"

"No."

The courtyard overflowed with red and yellow flowers and brilliant green leaves. Althea's boundless love of gardening spent itself in a few square yards. Carruthers said, "Don't take risks at the prison. I can't afford to lose you."

"We can't afford to lose William Doyle."

"I'm afraid we're going to." Carruthers's face was still as marble. "If the boy is taken, he will betray us. He may already have betrayed Guillaume." She put the teacup down, precisely and carefully, on the windowsill. "Tell the men to find Adrian Hawkins. Kill him."

Thirty-six

MARGUERITE CAME TO THE PRISON ALONE, CAR-
rying a basket, armed with money and her wits.

She was not a beautiful woman. She regretted that for
a few minutes about once a week. Right now, a plain face
served her well. The guards would interest themselves in
somebody pretty. They'd remember her. The women of La
Flèche did not try to be pretty.

At the big wooden door, she pinched her lips together.
Angrily. She held on to that look through the entry yard
and into the guardroom at the front of the prison.

They had made themselves a sty in what had once been
the visitors' parlor of the convent. It smelled of stale wine
and sweat. Revolutionary slogans and obscene drawings
scrawled the walls. Three clubs, thick and ugly, lay upon
the table. They would use those for subduing prisoners.

Guillaume did not fight when he was taken. There were
five men, armed. Did he fight here, at last, when he realized
he could not talk his way free? Did they hit him and hurt
him, where no one could see what was done?

"Guillaume LeBreton has been brought here." She made it the firmest possible statement. She did not want to be questioned about how she knew this.

"You have business with him?" Boredom filled the man at the long table. If one must deal with guards, it is good for them to be bored with you. "Show me what you're carrying."

Prison guards were of all sorts. Some were revolutionary idealists. Some small despots, puffed up in their new power. Some were men with a grudge, here to take revenge on the upper classes. Some were bullies, pure and simple, who enjoyed frightening and inflicting pain on anyone who showed fear.

She did not, therefore, show fear. She was dressed as a shopwoman, neatly but not richly. She did not come hesitant and trembling. She marched forward, enraged.

"You have arrested my man and dragged him here." She banged her basket down on the table. "*Why*, I do not know."

She jerked back the napkin that covered the basket. "He is useless." She slapped down bread. "He is a lout and a drunkard." A sausage came next, long and black and of the cheapest sort. A brown wine bottle. Then, in one handful, three meager, sour yellow plums that rolled away and wobbled to a stop. "But he is a good patriot."

"Good patriots are not denounced to the Tribunal. If Citoyen LeBreton is innocent, he will be freed."

It was treason to suggest otherwise. She glared and said nothing.

The guard helped himself to the bottle of wine and motioned her to pack the rest away.

The wine is a good test. Now I know.

She had seen four guards. The senior officer was to her right, at the end of the table, a man of straggling gray hair and deep lines across his face. He had set himself a tedious task that involved removing the small springs from inside his gun and laying them out on a white handkerchief in front of him. He looked as if he knew what he was doing.

Not that one. A man who does such intricate, careful work will think too much. He will hesitate and reconsider even when the money is in his hands. He cannot be trusted to take a proper bribe.

This other man, though, the one who searched the basket . . . He had the loose lips and complacent eye of one who indulges himself. This pilferer of cheap wine might serve her purpose.

He set his forefinger upon the *carte de sûreté* she laid down before him. It was a recent forgery, but thoroughly dry. She'd checked before she left the loft.

"You are Citoyenne LeBreton? You are his wife?"

He cannot read. "I am Citoyenne Odette Corrigou of the Section des Marchés. I am not his wife and not likely to be his wife since you have locked him up. What I am to do with a baby coming and no husband to help me, I do not know."

That was more than enough excuse to be exasperated and a good reason to visit Citoyen LeBreton in prison. Even to visit him many times. The guards would show more compassion to a girlfriend than a wife. Men generally liked their girlfriends better than their wives.

She repacked the basket. "Will you let me see him?"

The senior guard nodded that she was to be let into the prison. A morsel of sympathy showed before he turned again to his bits of metal and his gun. The guard of the soft and paunchy belly—he was called Hyppolyte by the other man—led her into the hall to the door to the inner prison. She noted the number of steps and the direction. She would make a map later.

Once, this door had separated the nuns from the outside world. Now, it marked the division between guards and prisoners.

Hyppolyte carried the bottle with him, not wishing to lose his spoils to his fellow guards.

"I would like to bring Guillaume the wine," she said. "It is one of his small pleasures." She did not care whether the wine reached Guillaume or not. She wanted to know if Hyppolyte could be bribed. A man who would take a small bribe would take a large one.

She drew a pouch from her pocket and took out a folded bill, an assignat for fifteen sous. It was counterfeit—one of many counterfeit notes Adrian had somehow produced and given over to her—but this guard did not know that. Fifteen sous would have paid nicely the whole price of such a wine. *Now we will see.*

Hyppolyte held his hand out. He took the bill and continued to hold his hand out and took the next bill as well and then the coins. When her purse was empty, he held the bottle up.

He shows me he can keep that or give it to me. Now we will see if he is sensible enough to think of future bribes.

He tossed the bottle to her. She was quick enough to catch it before it fell and broke.

I have found the man who can be bribed.

"Tell your lover to drink a toast to me." He rattled his keys and opened the door and let her into the prison. The lock turned behind her. She did not let herself think how frightening that was. Six minutes here, and already she had learned something useful.

She stayed where she was. Faintly, through the door, she heard Adrian say, "It's nothing to me, citoyen. Open it or leave it sealed. I get my tip either way." He had entered the prison behind her, carrying an entirely convincing letter addressed to an unfortunate grain merchant who had been accused of hoarding. The letter asked, Was he the Michel LaMartine who was the nephew of Naoille LaMartine of

Quesmy in Picardie? There was the matter of debt to be settled in her estate.

Adrian was saying, "I'm supposed to wait for an answer. I got all morning."

Messages went in and out of the prisons. Business was conducted. Letters written. No one looked at delivery boys. Adrian would be invisible, poking into every corner.

She found Guillaume in the third of the rooms in the long hall. This was the lodging for ordinary prisoners who could not afford to pay for better quarters. He sat on the floor, cross-legged, on a gray straw mat, talking to two other men. His head was bare. His hair chanced to fall in a shaft of sunlight. The brown of it was like the side of a chestnut, smooth and richly colored. He wore no cravat or waistcoat or coat. He had not been beaten, not that she could see.

When he saw her, he rose to his feet, simple as a peasant in trousers and his shirt. "This is a surprise." He took up his jacket as he walked by, and closed a hand around her arm and drew her away, thunderously silent, out of the open room where the men slept. "We can't talk here."

In the corridor outside, he pushed brusquely past the men and women gathered in their twos and threes and brought her to narrow stairs that led upward.

He wanted privacy and was taking her off to it, force-fully. In privacy, she could hold on to him. Just hold him. That was not possible in the midst of these bored, curious, and doomed people.

She said, "Were you hurt?" and when he did not answer, "We are of one mind here. A touch and a nod will tell me where to go with you. It is not necessary to drag me as if I were a sullen child."

His face was unrevealing, as always, and she did not have leisure to tease out signs of what he might be feeling. His muscles and the hold on her arm said he was angry. That was not entirely a surprise. He would be angry she had come here even while he was glad to see her. She was filled with joy, only to touch him, and with her own fear and anger. They were both in the grip of such conflicting emotions, it was amazing they did not fly apart like poorly wrapped parcels.

Men and women sat on the lower stairs, since there were no chairs anywhere. Guillaume glared them aside or pushed past. It was a long climb to an upper hall, dim and bare, lit by one small, high window at the end. Three men had taken the floor at the top of the stairs, casting dice. Two wore the clothing of the poor. The third, a velvet coat and knee breeches, much wrinkled.

"Out." Guillaume's tone would have dislodged hungry lions feasting upon an antelope. It had no difficulty removing three dice players from the hall.

He took her halfway down the hall before he halted and let her go. He stood, frowning at her.

"I will not stay long," she said. "We have only a few minutes together." He knew this. She was just telling him that she understood as well. "There is no need to glare at me that way."

"Tell me you're out of that house."

"My own house? Yes. Entirely. I have retreated and left it to Cousin Victor. It is very cowardly of me, but I do not have time to deal with him if I am to get you out of this place."

She laid her hand on his arm. For an instant, he held still, as if he waited while he changed inside, or made some decision, or lost some battle he held with himself.

He reached out to touch her. To take a strand of her hair that had fallen loose. He held it as if it were his first touch of any woman.

"You shouldn't have come," he said.

hirty-seven

VOICES IN THE HALL BELOW BROKE THE SMALL quiet spell they had woven between them.

Guillaume stepped away from her. Marguerite did not catch what he said. She did not think she was meant to. He reached into the jacket slung across his arm, into the pocket that was sewed on the inside, and took out the long pipe he carried with him at all times and, upon rare occasion, smoked.

He took the bowl of the pipe in the flat of his hand. Suddenly, sharply, he knocked it against the wall. It shattered. Fragments of gray-white clay flew everywhere. Among the bits of broken clay in his hand lay thin, dark shafts of metal. He tapped off the last of the clay, peeled bits of white from the small steel rods, and scraped the bent ends clean with his thumbnail.

"And we have lock picks." Adrian appeared behind them, sudden as a small djinn loose from its bottle. "All with no ingenuity from me." He glanced at the lock on the door. "I don't know why I'm risking my neck getting you out of here. You can walk out on your own."

"Guard the stairs," Guillaume grunted. "Neither of you should be here." He scattered the mess of clay chips with his boot, skidding them from one end of the hall to the other. He crouched and poked the first of his metal sticks into the door lock. Then inserted another, exactly beside it.

"I am impressed with your cleverness," she said.

"I'm just a keg and a half of clever." He rotated the picks delicately, pulling and pushing them in the lock, large, rough hands doing the deft work so naturally.

"I could do that." Adrian watched with polite interest.

"Watch the stairs." Guillaume did not look up from twisting and jiggling picks. The tiny scrape of metal on metal emerged, like the sound of steel mice.

"I could do that faster."

The lock snicked. Guillaume pushed the door open. He stepped through and pulled her in and closed Adrian's interested face outside.

Guillaume stood looking at her, breathing heavily.

"This is a linen closet," she told him. Sometimes one babbles of the obvious when there are too many important things to say and one does not know where to begin.

"I know. I talked to one of the nuns. Three of them are locked up downstairs."

This room was lit by a pair of small, barred windows, high above her head. They had not encouraged the nuns to gaze out upon the city, had they? A low, solid table ran down the center of the room. The shelves on both sides were stacked with neat supplies of sheets and pillowcases and towels. "This will go to the army, I suppose, when some- one remembers it. That is why it has not been despoiled. It is surprising, really, the way in which—"

His hand fell upon her, no heavier than a shaft of sunlight.

Like sunlight, falling suddenly in the eyes, it shocked her. Could anything be more loud than his plans for her? He turned her and his touch stayed on her, heavy and slow and full of intention.

He took up her fichu and pulled it away from her breasts. The knot she had made in it disappeared in a weak fashion, as if it had not been there at all. "Chipper as a squirrel, ain't you?"

"I am generally cheerful in the mornings."

He was vast and beautiful. He could have been one of the first men on earth, the men who lay with goddesses in the morning of the world.

If Greek goddesses could see him like this, they would want him. "It is part of one's nature, whether one will be lively soon after awakening. The learned speak of the humors of the body. I do not know myself." She met his eyes steadily. She wanted to be unclothed by him. Slowly. Wanted him to continue in this deliberate way he had begun.

"Humors. That'd be it." With his fingertips, he enjoyed her hair. It fell into his hands, came loose, wrapped him where he held it. He would get to her clothes eventually. They had very little time, but he was going to make excellent use of it.

"I had a cat once," she told him, "who was mad as Caligula. Each day at dawn it woke me, attacking my feet under the covers. It had much of the humor of Mercury . . ." Her fichu fell in a swirl to the floor. Her composure was lost with it. She was hot and unsettled inside and not sure what to do, except talk, which was not right either, but she could not seem to make herself stop. "I was speaking of Mercury. Much of the humor of Mercury in my cat. Did you know Mercury is the god of both thieves and travelers? That is why one is so often robbed when one travels."

"Is that so?" He could have been one of the stone dolmens of the countryside, given life. He was as hard and solid as such stones. Adamant. Determined. In the light from those windows, golden dust motes swirled around his head, circling him as if they had volition and enjoyed him.

His palms lay on the top of her breasts, where her skin was bare. He was . . . not uncertain—nothing he had done since she had first seen him had ever held uncertainty—but holding himself in check. The tendons and bones of his hands spoke of a tension beyond description. He waited, as horses wait, quivering at the starting gate, plucked by anticipation, filled with controlled strength.

"I am here," she said simply, "because I want you."

"Say that. I need to hear that." His fingers were at the buttons of her jacket. Buttons that opened as if they melted. He slid the jacket away. Her breasts, covered by her shifts, ached and anticipated. A single pull, and the bows of her stays came undone. The thin ribbon slipped from the holes. And her stays were gone, too.

"I want this. Want you." *Did I tie the lacing so loosely this morning because I hoped he would do this?*

He skimmed the neckline of her shift down, uncovering her breasts. Setting her skin free so he could touch it.

She whispered, "Yes," and he poured over her like night falling, smooth and powerful. Enclosing everything. Shutting out the world.

She was in a space filled only with him. His hair fell like a caress on her face. His mouth touched warm and soft on her forehead and her eyebrows. He worked his way in kisses across her eyes. Over her cheekbones. His breath was hot in the curve of her ear. The sound was like the sea on rocks.

The universe wheeled around her and she was the center of it all. She and Guillaume, at the still center. He lifted her from the floor and pressed her to him. Then down to the table.

However carefully he held her, his was the advance of a male animal upon the female. She was mate, she was pleasure, she was the woman he wanted. He desired her with all the single-minded determination that was Guillaume. All his huge, immediate physicality. All his strength.

But he worshipped also. He exhaled pleasure, deep in his throat, when he kissed the skin of her shoulder. He nudged her chin to the side so he could taste her ear. Pressed her face against his shirt so he could lift her hair and lean to tongue down the back of her neck, little bone by little bone. It was as if every inch of her body was his estate and he would know every furrow of it. Every hill. Every valley. As if no part of her was overlooked or unimportant.

It was magic, to be worshipped. Exciting beyond all experience to know how much he wanted her. Her body was ready for him, more than ready for him, when he loosened the band of his trousers and undid the buttons and lifted her to the edge of the table. He raised her close to him, guiding himself into her, until they fit. Until they were together and joined.

She gripped his shirt at the shoulders where it fell downward in a great sweep. Held on. She breathed deeply, deeply and fast. Fire within her. Guillaume within her.

They were both on the knife edge of pleasure. So close. He was making it last for her. Giving them minute after minute to be like this, locked as one. Every iota of their bodies prickled and hummed together.

"Good?" he whispered. They poised, so ready that even that brushing of his breath across her ear set off shocks.

"Very good." Vibrations from her own voice buzzed and tugged at her. She was dizzy with wanting him. So filled with wanting it pushed at her skin.

His hands cupped her bottom, held her close to him, rocking slightly. It was not a gentle hold that cradled her. He had hands like the sinews of trees.

His shirt was open to the level of his heart. She set her mouth upon him, not licking or kissing, just putting her mouth to his skin and the hair of his chest, breathing him

in, feeling the texture of him with the inside of her mouth.
When she closed her teeth down on the tendons of his neck,
holding on, he swelled and throbbed inside her. The power
within him wound more tensely.

She wrapped her legs around him. Pushed herself even
tighter to him. Crossed her ankles around him so she held
him within her, deep in her. Her arms, too, she wrapped
wholly around him to clasp together at his back. She held
every inch of him as close as she could.

"*Mon coeur. Mon âme.*" She said words into his flesh,
into his skin, against the great expanse of his chest, to
his heart. Said them to the beating center of his life. "*Je
t'aime, Guillaume.*"

He said, softly, "My name is William. Marry me."

She was breathing shallowly, in fast, quick pants. Sharp
peaks had begun inside her, hitting like drumbeats. *He
proposes at a time like this.*

He stroked hair back from her face. "I'm English. Good
English family. English, Irish, French, mongrel. But all
good family. The scar's not real. I can take it off. I—"

"Yes." She bit him again, on his chest, and held on.

He rumbled something out. Some word. Some claim.
Thrust into her triumphantly. Thrust into her again and
again.

She held him with her legs through the long trembling
moments of heat and surging power. It was like being part
of an earthquake. She moved upon him. Stroked herself
with him. Waves of pleasure flowed from him, into her.

He is mine.

He threw his head back. His whole body stiffened. He
pulled her to him and he cried out and came within her.

And held her while she pulsed around him. Held her
while dark red pleasure pulsed behind her eyelids. While
she shuddered in every part of her body, he wrapped her to
him, enclosed, safe, and warm.

It could not last forever. Slowly she let go of pleasure. Let it slip away from her.

Guillaume laid her back upon the table. He smoothed her skirt down, but didn't do a thing about covering her breasts. He lay beside her on the broad table, leaning on his elbow, his hand on the curve of her breast. He looked, if she might put it so bluntly, pleased with himself.

He ran his thumb across her nipple and she jerked everywhere. She tightened and thrilled inside as if she had not just barely relaxed from passion. It was embarrassing.

"You are light in the darkness, Maggie. I'm holding you to what you said. We're getting married." He stood up, buttoning his trousers fast, then took her hands and pulled her to her feet.

She was not fully coherent. There were no words in her and very few thoughts.

"Let's get you dressed some. Damn, but I hate covering you up." He found her stays where he'd dropped them on the floor. Swift, skilled, matter-of-fact, he pulled them around her and began lacing up. "If it was anything less than keeping you alive, we'd do that again. Fact is, we'd do it half a dozen times, getting more and more inventive. No. You just stand there. I'll do the finding clothing part."

"I would like to make love again. Can we not?"

"No. Other arm now. Good." He pulled the jacket up and began buttoning.

"This scrambling into clothing is very undignified. I am not in the mood to be active just at the moment. I would much prefer to lie back and stretch like a satisfied animal. Purring, perhaps. In fact, I would like to—"

"You have any objections to marrying me?"

"There is no need—"

"There is every damn *need*, woman. What we're talking about is whether you're going to do it." He tied a fast, lopsided bow in the drawstring at the neck of her shift. "There.

Neat as a magpie." He flipped the fichu around her neck and tucked the ends down her front with a grand impersonality. She had not been so efficiently or quickly dressed since she was a child. "Your cap's run away somewhere."

She didn't remember losing it. And her mind . . . And her mind. "My cap is under the table. You have had a little practice in helping ladies dress. I find that attractive in a man. It argues a certain thoroughness."

"Oh, I'm thorough. That's what I'm scared of. I'll get that for you. And that's the last of it. Damn, but you're fine."

"I am what the cat drags in." She combed her hair with her fingers, making it lie down neat. She was barely done when he fished out her cap and dropped it on her head.

"You are the most beautiful woman on earth. We're going downstairs now and getting married. I think I can manage it."

"Now? At this moment?"

"At this moment." His face was sober, utterly. "I have money. Enough to keep you. I'm not just . . ." He gestured to his clothes. Himself. "I'm not just this. My family's not the equal of the de Fleurignacs. But—"

"I know what you are. You are the son of some house of great respectability that has not the least idea what to do with you. The de Fleurignac who rode to the Crusades was exactly a man like you. He besieged any number of cities with great success and carried a sword as tall as I am. He also wrote poetry. I am not entirely an idiot, Guillaume."

"I didn't fool you for a minute, did I?"

"Not so many minutes. And we will speak of marriage at some time in the future when your life is in less danger."

"We're not going to talk about it. I want you gone from here before Victor arrives. What possessed you to put yourself right in his path?"

"I am not in his path. It will be a miracle, a black and unlikely miracle, if he locates you before this afternoon."

"You shouldn't have taken the chance." Guillaume was not angry, precisely, but he was in a mood that did not lend itself to rational discussion. He stopped before opening the door. "Why did you come here, Maggie? You know better."

"I am planning to rescue you. This will take some work on both our parts. The first—"

"God's frogs." He stomped out.

"I do not yet know how I will do it, but I am very good at such things. It has been my work for years, this rescuing of people."

"You're not rescuing anybody. You're leaving Paris." He got to where Adrian sat cross-legged at the top of the stairs. "He'll take you to London." Guillaume scowled as he pushed past and headed down. "Hawker, you get her out of here, you understand me? Out of this damned deathtrap of a city. Out of France. Put her in a sack and carry her if you have to."

"Understood." He scrambled nimbly to the side, just in case. He was a boy who had dodged many informative blows in his time. "Now?"

"In a minute. First I have to marry her."

"Fine with me." The boy followed them down the stairs.

$\mathcal{T}$hirty-eight

"I HAVE SAID I WILL MARRY YOU." SHE WOULD HAVE preferred to stay in the room upstairs and make love, but it was not prudent. She could be as prudent as any number of Guillaume LeBretons. "You will admit there are minor difficulties."

"That's not going to stop us."

The cloister was square, open to the sky, the carved stone arches and columns beautiful. It lay at the heart of the old convent, between the chapel on one side and the refectory and dormitories on the other. A well stood in the center with a roof over it. Two men were taking turns lowering a bucket, yard by yard into the well, and winding the windlass to bring it up again, full.

The chain shrieked. The bucket clanked and clattered. The men splashed across the courtyard to spill pails of water into a long trough on the shadowed side. A dozen girls and women had rolled their sleeves back to wash clothing. It was an agreement that the garden was left to the women in the morning, Guillaume told her. It was the men's turn in the evening.

Guillaume intruded into this world of women and laid claim to a corner of this courtyard. He cordoned an invisible barrier around them by sheer force of will. In ten minutes, he had gathered a crippled priest, a cheerful middle-aged nun, the stiff, acerbic Marquise de Barillon, who remembered her, with disapproval, from Versailles, and Adrian.

It very much looked as if she was getting married. Almost immediately. She was willing, but she had not quite prepared for this in her mind.

Thirty feet away, women worked in line at the long trough, chatting to one another, as the women might in any village washerie. Here was a nun, elbow to elbow with a prostitute. A brown countrywoman splashed suds next to the soft, pink descendent of seven generations of nobility. They washed their clothing. They washed themselves. An old woman combed her long gray hair out over her back to dry. The courage of women expressed itself in these hundreds of small braveries. It was wholly admirable.

She would need small braveries of her own. It was not that she had not thought about marriage. But she had expected to be dutiful about it and somewhat resigned, as was proper for a woman of her class. She had not expected to marry the man she wanted. In prison.

She could not even contemplate the unlikelihood of marrying an English spy.

Père Jérôme read the service. She would be no less married if he gabbled out nonsense syllables by rote, but it was comforting to have this madness done by a scholarly priest who understood the words he spoke.

She had confessed to him ten minutes ago, standing beside the pear tree in the corner where they would not be overheard. It had been a hurried but sincere confession of her attempt to murder the Jacobin who attacked her at the chateau and the matter of making love to Guillaume. With two mortal sins to lift from her conscience, she had not added the details of her uncharitable thoughts toward her aunt, and the telling of many lies, and other small faults. Her brain had run perfectly dry and she could not even remember them.

The priest was not as shocked as she had expected. But then, he had come to her fresh from confessing Guillaume.

Latin whispered in the thick air. The low stone walls and the bushes and trees everywhere were spread with linen, drying. The sun fell blinding white, giving the cloister the look of an etching. There were no degrees of shade, no soft compromise, only a stark confrontation of opposites, black shadow and bright light, one against the other, with no mediation between them. July, in Paris, had been like that.

The planted beds on the four sides of the courtyard were abundant with flowers. Someone, perhaps a succession of these women, had been watering them right along.

She had always thought there would be a procession to the church and a silk canopy over her head. They would dance afterward and everyone would eat a great deal and become silly from the wine. She would be wearing a much prettier dress. The priest did not speak the whole Mass, only the consecration of the bread and wine. It was as if they stood on a battlefield and he performed the most necessary things.

When Death reached out, ready to close his fist, one saw what was necessary and important. Marguerite de Fleurignac could indeed marry Guillaume. She would choose. *This is what I want.*

The women at their washing looked and then looked away with only quick glances back. They did not allow themselves to show curiosity about the ceremony going on across the cloister, though certainly they would talk about it at length, later.

Guillaume stood beside her, patient and serious. The

sun slid over his great brutal strength. The scar was counterfeit, he said, but it seemed part of him. She would miss it. She had not seen him as marred for a long time. The line on his cheek was part of him, as if a lightning bolt slashed a tree, marking it but not making it less. She would someday see him without it, and he would be altogether different. Yet another Guillaume for her to know.

She knelt to take the small tearing off of dark bread from the hands of the priest. Guillaume did the same. Then, coming forward, the marquise and the nun.

The wine was sour stuff. The cheap glass was accidentally elegant in its simplicity. It was their wedding, so the priest gave wine as well as bread. When she had drunk, and Guillaume also, the priest wiped the lip of the glass with a white cloth and finished what was left of the wine to the dregs, making a face when he did so, but conscientious. His cuffs were deeply frayed. He had been in prison long enough to become shabby.

Father Jérôme set the cup down and lay folded cloth across it. "Another forbidden Mass in Paris. I like spitting in Robespierre's eye. We may be interrupted at any moment, so I will spare you my homily on the sacred nature of marriage. It is somewhat boring."

He opened his breviary so Guillaume could lay a gold ring upon the open pages.

"To the marriage, then. Guillaume, *vis accípere Marguerite hic præséntem in tuam—*"

Guillaume interrupted. "William. I am William Doyle Vaudreuil Markham."

That is his true name, so our marriage will be valid. If anyone reports this, he condemns himself utterly. He does not hesitate.

Father Jérôme nodded. Truly, nothing surprised him. "William, *vis accípere Marguerite . . .*"

Guillaume said, "*Volo.*" *I do.*

"Marguerite, do you take William . . ."

It was her turn to decide and agree and become. Behind her, Adrian and the nun and Madame la Marquise de Barillon stood quietly.

I should make Guillaume worry, just the smallest amount. He deserves it.

But she did not. *"Volo."*

". . . faithful to her in all things as a man should be faithful to his wife, according to the command of God?"

Guillaume made his response, serious and grave, not taking his eyes off the priest.

He is not what I expected. Not what I have dreamed of. In a dozen ways, he is more powerful than any man I have known.

At Versailles, she had lived among the great men of France, the brilliant, influential men who ruled half the world. Men of privilege and ancient title, of wit and dashing charm. Guillaume was the warrior who enters the king's hall in black armor and throws down his gauntlet. Beside Guillaume, the men of the court looked like vicious children, playing corrupt games.

He had become distant and strange to her, even while he took the ring from the priest's hand and slid it on her finger. Guillaume married her with her mother's ring, the wedding band of her grandmother, which he had extorted from her. Guillaume, who was William Doyle and other names she could not recall. Who was a spy. Who was English. Who must be dissuaded from menacing Papa. Who must be rescued from this prison and from death.

She was married. Somewhere between one word and the next, it had happened. She changed her name. Her nation. She was becoming English in this very moment. It swept across her, inch by inch. It was like being transformed to a tree or a statue of gold or a red deer by some careless spell.

When she glanced up, Guillaume was laughing at her

silently, with every obscure and sneaky particle of himself. Perhaps he knew what she was thinking. She was wedding a mountain of slyness.

I do not know how to not love him. He was breath to her lungs, the fire of her nerves, the light of her eyes.

Father Jérôme said, "*Dóminus vobíscum.*"

I will not let Guillaume die. I will get him out of this dreadful place. All that I have been, all that I have done for these five years in La Flèche leads me to this moment. I will pluck him away from this prison.

"Whatever the fashion in civil law this week," the priest said, "in God's eyes, you are married."

"Good." Pounding impatience, barely held in check, radiated from Guillaume. In most marriages, it would be the eagerness of a husband to bear his wife away to the wedding bed. Here, it was Guillaume's determination to be rid of her. "We need this written down."

The priest opened the breviary. "In the back. Here. My brothers at Saint-Sulpice will add your names to the parish registry. I will write marriage lines for your lady as well. I need paper."

Guillaume gestured to Adrian. "Inside. Sharpish. Find paper. I want you two out of here."

"I'll do better than that." Adrian was already jerking his shirt free as he walked, headed behind a stone column. "Let me not show this to the whole bloody world. I have . . ."

Under the boy's shirt, a wide band of linen wrapped his chest and belly. A money belt, of sorts. He pulled loose an end and unwound. "I have paper."

"Helped yourself to some money, I see." Guillaume didn't sound disapproving.

"Irresistible temptation. You knew the minute I lifted it." Adrian glanced around. Nobody was watching. He passed across a thick stack of assignats. "I'd give you the lot, but we're going to need them. This is your paper. I collected it a night back. Decided I didn't want to hand it over to that woman you work for."

"I don't work for her," Guillaume said.

"Of course you don't. And if that woman doesn't terrify you, you lack imagination." He unfolded a dozen creased sheets of pale cream writing paper. "Here. Wedding present."

Guillaume peeled off the top sheet. It was clean on one side. He smoothed it flat against the nearest column and passed it to the priest. "Use this. Marriage lines for Marguerite."

"I will write that with some dispatch." The priest sat on the low wall. "This is no place for your wife."

Guillaume took up her left hand and looked at the ring upon it. "If I live, and you want it, I'll give you another ring."

"I am content."

"Then I'll give you rubies to go with it." He kissed her knuckles, where her ring was. "It'll have to do. Hawker—Adrian—will take you to friends of mine. They'll keep you safe."

"I have my own friends in this city. I have not been transformed into a ninny by marrying you."

The grin was so fast it didn't twitch his features, just glinted in his eyes, like sun on water. Then it was gone. "A month from now, I want you in London."

"I do not—"

"Maggie, listen. Go to England. To a man named Galba, in London. Hawker knows him." Another gleam of a smile. "At Meeks Street, number seven. If there's a child . . ." His hands tightened. She felt the trembling of his tendons, deep in his flesh where it didn't show. "If there's a child, Galba will make it right. He'll make him legitimate."

"When I go to London, you will be with me and deal

with any small legalities." She pounded her certainty into the rocks of reality as if it were an iron stake.

"If it's a girl, name her Camilla. That was my mother's name."

Do not say this as if you will not be there. "Camilla. William, if it is a boy."

The priest sat on the stone bench and wrote. The ink bottle rattled ever so slightly when he took more ink.

The round, bustling nun picked up the papers Adrian had left on the wall. "These are very dirty." She shuffled through them, frowning. "There is writing on them. Let me run inside and find you clean sheets."

"This will do." The priest left off writing. "Madame, if you will sign in this book and upon this paper I have prepared." He held the last page of the breviary open for her. The Parish of Saint-Sulpice and the date, in the old style, was written.

When one married a man like Guillaume, one must not expect an ordinary marriage register in the corner of the parish church and a procession of giggling girls and dancing and little cakes. She wrote her new name in an old breviary with a sputtering quill, then signed marriage lines that had been written on the back of some discarded letter.

"Guillaume, my son. Your signature."

He took her place and signed the book quickly, with his English name.

The marquise signed as witness. "I do not say your father will disapprove. De Fleurignac was always an oddity." She considered Guillaume. "I'm not certain I disapprove either."

"Sister Anne. If you would." The priest was patient with the nun's observation that the breviary was not a marriage register and that banns had not been called. That the paper was dirty and creased. He looked up. "And you."

"Me?" Adrian's voice cracked.

"You." The priest filled the pen with new ink and wiped the clinging drop off on the lip of the bottle. "Here."

Adrian held the pen as if it might turn and bite him. He drew his name, letter by letter, slowly.

The priest makes him a witness because he may live. Everyone else who signs, perhaps, will not.

"It is done." The priest gave her the marriage lines. She held the paper by the edges. The signatures had not dried. On the back there was writing. Lines and lines of it.

Guillaume was giving orders to Adrian. He could as easily have saved his breath. "If she's in Paris when they chop me, you make sure she don't see it. Lock her up somewhere. You'll figure out a way to do it."

"You want to order me to stuff the moon in a box, you go right ahead," Adrian said. "Don't expect anything to come of it."

He had a realistic view of the situation, Adrian. And what was this, written here on the back of her marriage lines?

". . . a false idolatry that tolerates corruption, weakness, vice, and prejudice in men unworthy of the ideals of the Revolution." There was more of it. ". . . monsters who have plunged patriots into dungeons and carried terror into all ranks and conditions . . . demands that we expunge from our midst those who prepare political counter-revolution by . . ."

Then came names. Names added, scratched out, added again. Joseph Fouché, Tallien, Vadier, d'Herbois. A dozen more.

She said, "This is very strange, this paper. I know who these men are, of course. Where did you get this, Adrian?"

Guillaume took it from her, frowned at it, then stuffed it back in her hand and went to find the other papers where they lay on the stone wall, fluttering like feathers on the wing of a bird. For a while he stood, going through one page after the other. He became very still. A less intelligent wife would have annoyed him with questions. She was not such a fool.

Guillaume looked at the boy. "Talk."

It was a short explanation.

"Let me get this straight. You walked into Robespierre's kitchen."

"I wanted to know—"

"You walked out with his next speech." Guillaume was shuffling from one paper to the next. "These are the names."

Adrian said, "What names?"

She explained it to herself, as well as him, seeing the possibilities as she spoke. "He has said he will denounce his enemies to the Convention. Robespierre said this. Tomorrow or the next day everyone is expecting him to stand before the Convention and call for their deaths. All of Paris is waiting to see who he will name."

"Lots of men want to know if their name is here. In this speech." Guillaume gathered the papers together.

"Robespierre is not sure himself. Look. He thinks of one and then another and then marks that one out."

"There's what? . . . Seven . . . eight names."

She said, "We can warn them. They have time to run."

"I don't want them to run. I want them to turn and fight." Thumb and forefinger, Guillaume considered the page he held. Assessed the paper. "Look at the names. These are men who'll fight if they're cornered. If they see their death written out and there are enough of them . . ."

She met his eyes and knew what he was thinking. What he planned to do. "You will send copies of these," she gestured to the pages he held, "to Fouché, Tallien, Vadier. All the men he names and crosses off and writes again."

Guillaume nodded.

"It is more than that. You have the skill to add any names you want to these papers. You can send them to anyone, even Robespierre's allies. No one feels safe. Each of them will feel the blade on his neck. His allies and his enemies, both, will conspire against him."

"If I can get this to them before Robespierre walks into the Convention and gives his speech."

Robespierre had not made the Terror by himself, but he drove it onward, cracking the whip. He had taken Papa's work—Papa's silly, harmless musings on the growth of genius—and twisted it to evil. Made Papa part of the cowardly assassination of young men.

It would be fitting to take Robespierre's speech, in his own writing, and destroy him with it.

She said, "Varenne. Add Varenne. And Barère."

He was already nodding. "Hawker, go inside. Find a man called Ladislaus. He's a forger. I need him." He jerked his thumb. "On the double. Run."

Thirty-nine

MARGUERITE CLEARED A PATH IN THE LONG LOFT
at the whorehouse so she could pace back and forth and
think. She could not think sitting in one spot. "We have two
days, maybe three, before Guillaume is taken to trial."

Jean-Paul said, "Two days. Victor will make sure of
that."

No time. She walked and turned and walked again. "We
have two days, then. The easy way, the obvious, is to bribe
a guard. We enlist his aid. We provide some small excuse
for a guard to walk Guillaume out the gate."

Jean-Paul sat in the armchair at the end of the loft. He
had been there a long grumpy hour. "Release orders."

"They would send back to check such orders if they did
not come with the regular messenger."

"Transfer orders. That's the next obvious choice. We
wave some paper at the guards and hope they deliver Guillaume into our hands. We need a carriage. A horse. We can
steal those. Two men to play guards and a driver. We've
done this before. Many times."

At the end of her path she confronted a stack of crates and a decrepit chair. She came back again. "We did that five years ago, in the first chaos of the Revolution. All was in disorder. We could have fooled prison guards with chalk scrawled on a schoolgirl's slate. It's not the same now."

"The basic principle hasn't changed. Men look at a paper and do what they're told."

"When we played that game, we were the first. Too many romantic fools have traipsed in and out of Paris since then and bragged to half of Europe when they succeeded. The easy subterfuges are known."

"Then we will find something that is not known to everyone."

"It is not known to me, either." She walked again, letting her mind revisit each corner she had seen in the prison. The answer was there, somewhere.

A small child, no more than four, sat on a box, watching her. She belonged to one of the whores of the house, doubtless, and was left to run free in the stable yard during the day. It was good to see that the mother kept her close, clean and well fed. There was love in the carefully combed hair and the little necklace of coral beads. But it was sad to see a child who would grow to take up her mother's profession.

"What do you think?" she asked the girl. Her name was Séverine. "Shall we knock on the front gate with forged papers and obvious ploys?"

The blond head shook gravely. "No."

"You are right. We have not survived by being dashing heroes with colorful disguises. We are like mice. There is no one more unobtrusive than a mouse." She began pacing again. "I must find a mouse hole into that prison. There has to be one."

Jean-Paul rose to take another look at the sketches and plans and maps spread out across her bed. He did not approve of what she was doing. He would risk his life to help her. Was that not the definition of a friend? And he did not approve of her marriage. He called Guillaume "that great rack of muscle" and "that walking lump," which lifted her heart utterly. After all, who would want an old lover to endorse one's marriage?

He arranged the sketches into a new order. When she came near, he picked up one on the left. "The baker."

"The baker."

"The wall he shares with the convent is covered by his ovens. We'd have to take them apart to get through. He employs three boys, who sleep in the shop."

"That is not promising."

"Here," he held up the next paper, "we have Citoyen Vilmorin who lives with his good wife and two children. His garden backs to the church. It's all open space, over-looked by three houses. He has a cellar of beaten earth. If there's a crypt beneath the church—and we don't know that—it's thirty feet from his basement wall."

"We have dug tunnels. We have knocked holes in walls. It is not impossible."

But there is no time to dig tunnels. We both know this.

I can think of nothing. This time, when it means so much, my mind is empty.

Jean-Paul took up the next sketch. "The Widow Desault. Lives alone with a dog of noble aspect. Shares a wall with the convent. Again, it's the chapel wall. Some of the guards are sleeping in the chapel apparently. This next one . . ."

He went through them all, one after another. He had done masterful work, he and the others. A dozen members of La Flèche had been at it all night and all morning. Her own plan of the prison lay on the makeshift table. The corridors and the cloister and the cells were laid out, each with the distances she had counted off. Adrian's contribution was exact and careful, adding rooms she had not seen.

It can't be done. Not through the walls. Not tunneling under the earth. There is no time.

She would not let herself despair. She started walking. Jean-Paul went to sit in his chair, glaring out the window.

Séverine said, "Is your friend in very much trouble? The one who is a walking lump?"

"As much as can be."

The child said, "The times are difficult. We must all be patient and clever."

"You speak a great truth. I will not be patient, exactly, but I will try to be clever. If I were Sinbad and I did not have my roc handy—"

"What's a roc?"

She stopped and knelt down. "That is a good question. A roc is a great white bird with wide wings. They would stretch from one side of the market square to the other if a roc landed there. They eat only elephants and ginger, and if you ask one nicely, he will give you a ride upon his back. They are especially fond of little girls who dress in blue. Did you know that? Is that why you wore a blue dress today?"

The child folded her giggle up inside herself and enjoyed it there. She was not shy, but she was careful and self-contained and did not laugh out loud. "I wore my blue dress because my green one is being washed."

"That is also a very good reason. But as I say, if I were Sinbad, who was a sailor, and I did not have my roc at hand, I would fly out in a balloon, way up over Paris. I would look down and toss out my anchor . . ." She pantomimed tossing an anchor. "And let down a long, long ladder. My great lump of a man would climb up to me and we would sail away."

Séverine approved this. Jean-Paul grunted and got up to sort through the sketches and plans again. He would not be blighting. He knew that her mind held a great deal of nonsense.

She got up to pace.

They could tunnel a foot an hour, in good soil. Shovels, boards, teams of men, burlap bags, bribery, silence . . . but it was never that easy. Thirty feet might take a day and a half. Or a week.

She had planned many rescues. She knew in her bones what was possible. What was impossible.

Jean-Paul put the sketches away. They'd be burned, now that they had both seen them.

She said, "We don't have time to dig into the prison. None of the walls will work."

"I know."

Séverine also followed her with her eyes. "Will you tell me another—"

She had heard nothing in the storeroom below, but suddenly Adrian hauled himself up through the trapdoor.

He crawled out onto the loft floor, one-handed, his other arm wrapped in a fold of his jacket. When he opened that up, he was bloody.

"Adrian." She pulled him the last of the way up. "What is this? Show me."

She pulled open his coat so she could see. His sleeve was ripped in thin slashes. When she eased his coat down from his shoulders, the arm of his shirt was soaked red. He was bleeding, drop by drop onto the floor.

"You've left a trail," Jean-Paul snapped. He swung past them out the trapdoor and down the ladder.

"I didn't," Adrian called after him. He grumbled the same thing to her. "I didn't leave a trail. I'm not an idiot. I wrapped it up good half a mile before I got here. Not a drop. I wouldn't lead them here."

She said, "Of course. I'm sure you were careful."

It was startling to turn and find Séverine holding the heavy water pitcher with both hands. Setting it down carefully. Running back for the basin and towels.

What kind of life does she live, this small child, that she knows immediately what must be done when a man is stabbed?

Adrian peeled his sleeve back and uncovered four long parallel slashes on the outside of his right forearm. Shallow, clean cuts. The coat had protected him from worse.

He was stoic and entirely adult while she examined the wounds. He didn't wince when she washed and washed and made certain all was clean. Water trickled over him and fell red into the basin. His face was so studiously blank he might have been somewhere else entirely.

When she tried to rip a towel to make bandages, he produced a knife from behind his back and offered it to her. That was a clever trick. She tied pads over the worst of the cuts. "I won't need to sew this, if you keep it bound tightly."

There was boy in him still. She saw it in the way he accepted her words without a blink, trusting her to know these things.

"You are carrying a knife." Séverine came closer, fascinated.

This wasn't the sort of thing a child should be seeing. It was too late to do anything about it. She wrapped linen around everything and tied it in place.

With perfect gravity, Adrian said, "I have several knives, but Maggie only needs one at a time. So that's all I gave her. Does Justine carry a knife?"

Séverine regarded him with a closed expression and said nothing.

"You've already learned the first rule. Say nothing." Adrian tilted his head, watching. "You don't answer any questions about Justine."

Marguerite tied the last knot. "Justine?"

"She's Justine's sister. See the eyes. And her mouth. Can't be a daughter. Has to be her sister."

She could see it, now that he pointed it out. Séverine had more gold in her hair than Justine. Her eyes were green, not brown. But they were sisters.

There were two of them she must take away from this house. Both Justine and this beautiful child. When she had freed Guillaume, she would set about it.

The clatter and squeak was Jean-Paul, climbing the ladder. He boosted himself out, sat on the floor, and swung his legs around. "You're right. You left no trail."

Adrian showed his teeth and didn't answer.

"We get these bloody rags out of here." Jean-Paul was already gathering them up. "And make sure there's nothing splattered on the floor. Why were you fighting?"

"Me? I'm innocent as an egg. I was trying not to fight. Not my fault somebody wants to poke holes in me."

"Who?"

"He's named Paxton." There was a cold bleakness in the way the boy said that.

Another Englishman. The Englishmen in France seemed a bloodthirsty crew. "In a city of so many Frenchmen I would think it was one of them trying to kill you. Why is Citoyen Paxton poking holes in you?"

"Now that is something I didn't get around to asking him, being busy jumping around and staying alive at the time." He took his knife back from her, since she was no longer using it, and handed it, hilt first, to Séverine. "Here. You can play with this if you don't cut yourself. It's sharp. Make marks on the floor."

Séverine proceeded to do exactly that, kneeling, using both hands to hold the knife. She cut slanting lines on the boards.

I should probably put a stop to that.

"Look. You want me to deliver this message from Doyle or not?" Adrian said it exactly as if she had been shushing him to silence for the last ten minutes.

"Speak, by all means."

"He says, 'Maggie. It's done. I've played Cadmus with the boy's papers. Stay off the streets.'"

Guillaume could send her such a message, knowing she would understand.

Adrian pulled the damp red sleeve down to cover the bandage she'd put on him. He didn't look up from doing that while he said to Jean-Paul, "If you don't keep your hand off Doyle's woman, I'll take that knife back and gut you with it." He sounded perfectly friendly.

Jean-Paul, who should have known not to take this threat seriously, nonetheless removed his hand from her back. "What did you do with the body? Can it be traced here?"

Adrian did up the button on his sleeve, left-handed. "I didn't kill anybody. I ran like a rabbit, is what I did. I have papers to deliver." He lifted his coat from the floorboards, showing the slashed and bloody sleeve. "I can't do it wearing this."

"What papers?" Jean-Paul returned from pouring the basin of bloody water very carefully out the window, along the ivy and bricks. "What does Cadmus have to do with this? Marguerite?"

It took several minutes to explain.

"... drafts of the speech that Robespierre will deliver to the Convention, tomorrow or the next day. All of Paris is waiting for this speech, wondering who Robespierre will condemn next. Most especially, his enemies want to know this. Guillaume ..." *Even in prison, he is dangerous.* "Guillaume has made copies of these papers and added a name or two that perhaps Robespierre did not exactly mention. He sends these to ... How many?"

Adrian said, "Twenty copies. I've got six more to deliver. Who's Cadmus?"

"He is in a story. The hero, Cadmus—I will tell you frankly this seems an unwise thing to do—Cadmus sowed the earth with the teeth of a dragon. From this seed, warriors sprang up."

Adrian was patient, waiting for her to get to the point.

"Always before, Robespierre attacked his enemies one or two at a time, without warning. That is his plan again. But this time, there will be twenty men in fear of their lives. Those are the dragon teeth you carry. That is the battle Guillaume arranges."

Jean-Paul let out a slow whistle. "I can imagine the names. They'll see a draft in Robespierre's hand. They'll be desperate. If they work together . . ."

"Robespierre will fall. The Terror will end."

But it will be too late to save Guillaume. He knows this. However many he saves, he will not save himself.

"It just might work." Jean-Paul was a man of swift action, when it was needed. He pulled his coat off. Tossed it to Adrian. "Wear this. It'll cover that shirt so the blood doesn't show. I'll send Justine to help you find the last six men."

"I don't need her." The coat was too large, but a young messenger boy might buy such a garment in the market for used clothing. "This'll do till I can get something that fits."

"You are welcome." Jean-Paul spoke ironically, but his eyes glowed. "Go. Deliver the papers. Change the course of history while I sit in my shirtsleeves and scrub your blood from the floor." He knelt to be level with Séverine. "I will return this one inside, to her house. And I will collect this toy from her." He took the knife and passed it to Adrian. "If your history is anything to go by, you'll need it again."

Adrian made the knife disappear. "I could have stayed in London if I'd wanted a pack of people trying to kill me. Didn't have to come to Paris for that." He grinned, and he was gone in an instant. A mere creak on the stairs. Utterly silent in the shed below.

Her Guillaume sowed dragons' teeth today. They would see what came of it.

She stood in the middle of the broken and discarded furniture of the loft, feeling helpless. Useless. Guillaume was trapped behind guards and walls and she could not get him out. She couldn't even visit the prison again. Victor would have set watch by now.

She would have gone into Hades, itself, like Orpheus seeking his Eurydice. There was nowhere she would not have gone to find Guillaume. No journey to the underworld she would not undertake.

Jean-Paul picked Séverine up, promising her that the boy with the cut arm would be perfectly safe. And yes, he would come back soon.

No journey to . . .

The large map of Paris was still spread across her pillow. She took it up, knowing it would not tell her what she needed to know. There was a map that did. "Wait."

Jean-Paul turned back.

"There is a way."

Jean-Paul looked from the map to her. "What? What are you thinking?"

"I'm thinking about building stones and magnetism. About history and washing clothes." She let the map go. "I never expected to say these words, but I need my father."

Forty

DOYLE MUTTERED, "I CAN'T TELL YOU WHAT I DON'T know, you bleating goat."

The guard grinned behind Victor's back. But a nod from Victor, and the same guard slammed Doyle against the wall, making sure it hurt.

"Where is she?" Victor demanded.

"Don't know. Don't give a damn." He'd cut his lip, kissing the wall. He couldn't pick that one pain out of the pack, but he tasted blood.

That was the wrong answer. Victor motioned. The guard hit him against the wall again. They'd been doing this a while. There just aren't any good ways to chat with a man who plans to kill you.

Victor said, "Where is she?"

"If your cousin run off, she didn't run with me."

"You have chosen a bad moment to be amusing, citoyen. Guard, bring him in here."

It looked like they were going to skip right past bribes

and threats and persuasion and go directly to breaking bones.

The guardroom had one door into the prison. Locked. One door, closed but not locked, leading out to the street. One door leading from the guardroom to a front courtyard the size of a handkerchief. There was a little window that let you see into that courtyard.

The guards made themselves comfortable here. Empty wine bottles lined up in ranks on the shelf over the chimney. Dirty cups scattered the hearth. Uniform jackets hung on the backs of chairs. The table was cluttered with cudgels and manacles and old newspapers. They'd leaned their guns up in the corner. Four standard infantry muskets, in only moderately good condition, loaded, muzzles crossed.

Victor wore a black coat and breeches with white knee stockings. Likely he'd come straight from the Convention. In this company he was a pale, smooth-curried spittle of a man. A well-bred lapdog. Next to the sans-culottes guards, he looked flimsy as thin paper.

"Secure him." Victor pointed.

They'd tied his wrists behind him when they hauled him out of the cells. That was one more disadvantage to walking around, the size he was—all this mistrust on the part of the authorities. The guards cleared off the biggest chair and manhandled him down. They left his hands trussed up at his back, coiled rope around his chest, and pulled it tight, being rough but impersonal. They didn't waste malice on somebody who'd be dead in a handful of days.

There was slack in the ropes. The chair wasn't solid as rock. Give him half an hour to himself and he'd get loose. Unfortunately, Victor had plans for his next half hour.

"It is done." A bushy mustache walked into his line of sight, hauling a grizzled guard along with it.

"Leave him with me," Victor said.

"We have no orders to give a prisoner into your charge."
That one was a soldier. A veteran of the colonial wars, he'd
guess. Wasted on prison duty.

"I said go."

"It is a bad precedent. Without orders—"

"I am from the Committee of Public Safety, a friend of
Robespierre. That is the only order you need."

It got quiet. One man whispered to the next. Laid a
warning hand on the sleeve. The senior guard hesitated,
then nodded, and the men jostled out, silent. The door
didn't click behind the last man.

They'd left the door open a crack. Done that on purpose. There'd be a man left picking his teeth in the hall,
innocent-like, keeping an ear on events. They all reported
to somebody. The Secret Police. The royalists. The military. There were no secrets in Paris.

Victor strolled over to appreciate the selection of clubs
and bludgeons laid out on the table. He picked out a sturdy
length of wood that had started life as a table leg.

This is where I get hurt. It said everything he needed to
know about Victor that the man only came close when he
had a weapon in his hands and his opponent was tied up.

The club swooped back and forth. Victor faced him.
"My cousin has not left Paris. You are going to tell me
exactly where she is."

"Citoyenne de Fleurignac? I left her at your house.
That's the last I—"

Victor swung the club.

Pain. God, the pain. Couldn't get his breath. It took
three tries before he could talk. "Listen, you cod-sucking
pig, I don't know where she is. It's not my fault you can't
keep hold of—"

That got him a fist across his face. "Where is my cousin?"

*Ask question. Get no answer. Apply beating. Ask the
question again.*

He spat out a mouthful of blood, getting some on Victor's fine white shirt. "Your cousin is nothing to me. Never touched her. Never wanted to. Don't know where she is now."

He saw the club coming, twisted, and took the hit on the flesh of his arm. He yelled so they'd hear it on the street.

"If you do not tell me where she is, you will die. Before you die, I will break every bone in your body."

"I don't know where she is." He slumped, groaning. Being stoic just encouraged folks to beat the hell out of you. "I don't know . . . where . . . she is." *The minute I lift my head he's going to hit me again.* "Damnation, man. How many times do I got to say it? I don't know where she's run off to."

Victor drew back and swung in a wide arc.

"I don't know—" Pain tore the words apart. The idiot was going to kill him by accident. "Hell in a bucket."

He's going to break my damned ribs. Send bones into my lungs. I'll drown in my own blood and he'll be surprised.

God, I hate amateurs.

He coughed. Agony shot into his side. Pain like white ice. "Wait. Just a minute. Wait." *Say something he wants to hear. While he's listening, he's not hitting.* "Listen. I brought her home at dawn, but it's not what you think. I found her in the Tuileries, out where she shouldn't be. I took her home. That's all. I left her on your doorstep. I never touched her. That's twice I've collected yer wandering girl for you. You should be thanking me for—"

He caught this one on his arm. He yelled, making it loud.

"When she left the prison, where did she go? Where did Marguerite go?"

Give it a count of three. One. Two. Three. Look up. He put the right amount of startled on his face. "The prison? Your cousin? She weren't here. That was my Odette." He let bloody saliva dribble out of his mouth.

Victor's pale green eyes flicked over him, flicked away fastidiously. "What do you mean?"

You don't like looking at that, do you? You got a weak stomach for torture.

His half brothers used to hurt him this bad every time they came home from Eton. They'd race in, howling, and pull out the cricket bats, and track him down. Teach the bog-trotter not to be uppity. They didn't mind admiring their handiwork.

"It was . . ." He let his voice drop weakly. Panted. "Was Odette Corrigou. My woman. Works for a seamstress on Rue de Roule. Nothing to do with you." He bit his lip to coax some more blood out. Nothing like leaking blood to make a man look sincere. He kept his breath shallow, skimming under the pain. "She's a good woman, my Odette. Good Bretonne woman. Comes from—"

"Lies."

Pain. White hot. Blood red. "My cousin visited you here. She told you where she's hiding. Where her father's hiding. Tell me."

"It was my woman." That was truth. His woman. His Maggie. Always and for all time, his. "Just my woman."

You'll never touch Maggie. You'll never get close to her.

Hawker would be delivering those dragons' teeth across Paris. Twenty powerful men had just got themselves terrified. They'd bring down the whole bloody French government. *Including you, Cousin Victor. Including you.*

And Maggie would be safe.

His breath cut like a knife going in and coming out, bright and sharp. He let his head loll back, mumbling as if he were losing consciousness.

Victor lowered the club. His eyes slunk away.

Look at me. Damn you for a bloody incompetent coward. Look at the man you're torturing. You think the answers are written on that wall? If you were paying attention to the man you're beating up, you'd know I'm not broken. God save us from idiots.

Victor crossed to the plank table and dropped the club clattering among the wine bottles. "You're really quite good. I could almost believe you."

Victor had taken his gloves off for the dirty work of beating a prisoner. He picked them up from the table and shook them out. "I discovered Marguerite's involvement with La Flèche some weeks ago. Émigrés in London talk of nothing but their escape from France. I recognized Marguerite's rabble of lowborn friends in the reports of our spies. She is fortunate no one realizes what she has done. You are one of her flock of traitors, I think. Heron, perhaps. I could never decide who Heron was."

Doyle kept his head down, concentrating on being stupid. Staying alive.

"You and the others who betray France will be swept away like the garbage you are. But I will keep my cousin's name out of this. You make a mistake when you keep her from me. I am the only chance Marguerite has."

A chance to get killed. But he didn't say that. He didn't say anything.

"I have men searching for her. I've discovered Marguerite's secrets before. I will do so again. Someone saw her leave this place. Someone knows where she went." The gloves were kid leather, bone white. Pristine. Victor tapped his fingers in. First one hand, then the other. "It cannot be too difficult to find one woman."

You have not one crumb off the loaf of an idea of what she is, do you? He lifted his head. "Nothing to do with me. Told you that."

"I'm not an idiot, Citoyen LeBreton." A thin smile appeared. "Did you think I wouldn't know my cousin had been with a man? You should not have touched a de Fleurignac. It was the worst mistake you ever made."

It was the best thing that ever happened to me.

Victor finished with his gloves. "I will return in a day or two to tell you I have found her." He paused and pretended to reconsider. "But no. Of course not. There will be no reason to return. You will be dead."

Forty-one

"AND THEN?" MADAME STOOD ON THE STAIRS above her. She was dressed severely in black. Her hair was caught up with silver butterflies, on pins. She wore silver rings upon her hands.

Justine made her report concisely, as she had been taught. "He delivered the last of the papers to Tallien and to Vadier."

"Who are great enemies of Robespierre."

"*C'est sûr.*" Madame would find this amusing. "The so-clever Adrian took me with him for the last deliveries. He said if he did not, I would only follow him, and this would save us both a great deal of trouble."

Madame smiled at her. "And did you discover what is in these papers?"

"Alas, no." Really, these English were not trivial opponents. "I did not see them. I wheedled and cajoled and the boy was not moved in the least. I think these are matters of great gravity."

Madame waited, her hand on the railing.

"The Gardener has told me to stay inside for the next

days. I am on no account to go about in the city alone. He is afraid there will be riots."

"Because of these letters. Someone is meddling with grave business indeed. The Gardener is not precisely a fool, so I shall second his orders. Be prudent, Justine. If you hear disorder, take care to be elsewhere."

It is good to have someone to tell me to be careful. "The boy was hurt, delivering these letters. Attacked by someone. He was not candid about that, either." She said the last part very quickly. "I have put him into my room for tonight. I hope you do not mind."

Madame studied the rings upon her hand. They were heavy bands, intricately worked. "I have learned more about this Adrian since we last spoke. He is Hawker the Hand of London, a dangerous playmate for you. He has killed more men than you have hair ribbons."

She had suspected something of the sort. There was that in his eyes sometimes that spoke of such things. "I do not underestimate him. I am not . . . I do not interest myself in him except for the de Fleurignac matter, you understand. I made a pallet for him upon the floor beside me in case he should develop a fever and need to be watched. Events will be complicated enough without that boy becoming ill."

Madame coughed delicately. "They have a plan to rescue William Doyle from prison, then?"

"They do not speak of it to me. I will go tomorrow and insert myself into their affairs and tell you what is afoot. It will be interesting to see Marguerite de Fleurignac concocting one of her plans. I have admired them for years and will now see one from beginning to end. It is strange to assist in freeing an English spy from prison. Yet, next week you may send me to see him arrested again."

"It is amusing beyond measure," Madame said. "Life is an ever-laden table of delights, is it not?"

"Most certainly."

Madame walked downward, past her, on the stairs. When they were level, she stopped. The silver butterflies she wore in her hair were on small springs. With every movement they vibrated, as if they were alive. "I do not forget how dangerous this is for you. Do not think for a moment that I do this lightly."

"I do not mind danger."

One brush of fingers on her cheek. *She is careful never to touch because of what has been done to me.* "Are you quite sure I cannot send you and your sister to safety? There is a school in Dresden run by good friends of mine. They have a house on the river . . . No? I am not entirely happy to send a young girl to do this work."

But Madame's own daughter was part of their work. Not a small player of the Game, either. Everyone knew she had been ordered to safety abroad and had refused to go. She was given dangerous assignments, even upon the battle-field. *And she is younger than me.* "I want to be here. To do this. I feel alive when I do this."

One of the girls of the house had taken up a song. That was Péronette, who had a most lovely voice. Madame looked toward the sound and then back to Justine. "We are much alike, you and I." She made a shooing motion. "Go tend your young spy. I will tell Babette to look at his wound. Yes, I know you are capable of caring for any injury short of a beheading, but we will indulge Babette by letting her cluck over your handsome boy."

What was there to say? That lethal, sly boy was not hers, of course, but denial is always unconvincing. So she shook her head and tripped upstairs to see what searches he performed among her belongings.

"Justine."

She turned back.

"The British Service brought him to Paris, but Adrian Hawkins is not theirs. He has no reason to be loyal to them and some small cause to hate them. Recruit him for France, if you can. He would be most useful to us."

That would be interesting. "I shall attempt it."

Forty-two

THIS WAS WHAT HELL HAD BEEN LIKE WHEN IT was first constructed and lay empty, before the demons moved in with their cauldrons of fire and their pitchforks. Hell would have smelled like wet rocks, Marguerite thought, before it filled with the fumes of sulfur and whatever devils smell like.

They carried candles, bringing five small points of light with them. Of all the uncanny occurrences since she had descended to this place, the strangest rested here in her hand. The candle flame stood upward, only stirring when her breath fell across it. Here, there were no currents of air, no connection to the winds under the heavens.

These were the quarries under Paris. The miles of excavation that had built the city.

The rock around her was damp, full of minerals, without the least trace of life. This was the Kingdom of Darkness. Their candles did not challenge it at all.

"Hold still." Papa was testy. He was the only one of them who did not carry a candle. He demanded the light of hers so he could study his maps and open the case of the compass and complain. He had nothing good to say about the compass she'd bought for him. "You make the needle jump."

"I do not make the needle jump. I am not touching it."

"It is not needed that you touch it. Your animal energies work upon it. If you will hold your breath and not think we will do very much better. The principals involved are quite . . ."

He went on in that vein.

Now she must listen to Papa explain that the human body exerts influence upon the magnetic force. She did not believe it and she did not care. But his voice was company. Nobody else felt like chattering in these looming hollows and narrow passageways. They went forward, six people and five small lights.

The stone underfoot was rough and marked with drag-lines where the quarrymen moved the huge blocks out on sledges. Sometimes they splashed through shallow pools of water, completely clear when they approached, murky white after they had walked through them. As they made their way across the galleries of excavation, pillars emerged before them in the blackness. Pillars that grew like monstrous tree trunks from the stone below to hold the stone roof up. It would take the joined hands of ten men to go around these trunks of stone. The roof was low, arched from pillar to pillar. The light of their candles flickered across it making random pockets of dimness and shadow.

Justine had found boots for her. Men's boots. What strange and useful things one could come across in a brothel. If she and the others disappeared forever into these caverns, someone would find her ordinary shoes in the cellar of a café near the Sorbonne, neatly together, at the top of the stairs that wound downward into the rock.

She walked beside René Petitot, one of the Gardener's

people. She knew him by reputation, of course. He was Poulet in La Flèche, the chicken, a man of the most reckless exploits. He and a few others were the small band who knew the shy, secret openings to the quarries beneath the city. They led sparrows through the labyrinth of the old and new mines, to come forth in the night in some stoneworker's yard far beyond the walls of Paris.

Poulet, now that she met him, turned out to be a dandy, a thin man who wore a brown velvet coat and ruffles at his cuffs to explore the quarries below Paris. He said, "Your father thinks he can find one place—one single spot—in the caverns?"

"He'll find it." *He must find it.*

Poulet said, "It's harder than you think. I can show you a few landmarks. But there's nothing close to the Rue Tessier and the convent. It's not easy to know where you are, down here."

They entered a passage that led between excavations. It was not so wide here. The walls were stone blocks, fixed with mortar, looking exactly like the stone buildings of the city above. That was to be expected. The city of Paris was born here. In this stone.

They went one by one, following Justine's light in the lead and then Papa's voice, which was explaining that magnetism came in colors. Was it possible she had misheard that? Jean-Paul came last of them, making certain no one wandered off into the dark. To either side, as they passed, great arched caverns opened like mouths.

It was not icy beneath the earth. Not shivering cold. It was more like the chill of death, when what was alive becomes empty of spirit. But nothing here had ever been touched by life. The rocks, never covered with seeds and flowers. The pools of water, never drunk from. The air, never drawn into lungs. All was devoid of meaning, as if it were a book written in nonsense syllables.

I have risked everything on this throw of the dice. If I am right, I will save Guillaume. If I am wrong . . .

If I am wrong, I will be near him when he goes to die.

Poulet faced resolutely ahead. "I'll bring you as close as I can. The maps of the quarries are a wish and a guess, mostly. The maps of the streets of Paris aren't reliable. Matching one to the other . . ."

He wishes to tell me we may fail. I already know that.

She cupped her hand near the candle for the comfort of it. To hold on to the light. "My father spent an entire winter, six years ago, measuring distances in Paris. He went with a gang of three men and lengths of chain. He was famous for a time." She had been briefly, humiliatingly notorious as his daughter. "Then he dropped heavy weights off of high buildings with great exactitude. Gravity is stronger near water, he thinks. Or weaker. I never got it straight."

"I know he is your father, but—"

"He is mad. There is no one who knows it better than I do. But he is an accurate madman. Madness will not keep him from finding the Convent of Saint-Barthélémy for me."

Papa had come to the end of his discussion of magnetism and paused to consult the plaque on the wall. Justine obligingly held a candle for him.

87 G 1777.

The numbers were cut into stone on the wall at this corner, cut deep, and then each line fixed in emphatic black. Beneath the number was another carved message. Papa read out loud, "RUE JACQUES."

They were sixty feet below the Rue Jacques. It had been Rue Saint-Jacques before. The revolutionaries had come so far, all this way, to eradicate the Saint from the Jacques, though no one walked these underground tracks but the Inspectorate of Mines and smugglers of taxable goods. And La Flèche, leading sparrows out of Paris.

Papa read each plaque aloud as they passed, being a

man given to stating the obvious, when he was not saying mad things. "45 G 1777."

Poulet glanced at the carved plaque, then upward to the stone that arched overhead. There were symbols there in chalk. Greek letters and an arrow. Nothing obvious. He said, "It's only pockets of mining this far north. They haven't dug everywhere. If they didn't quarry under the Rue Tessier, there's nothing we can do. You know that."

"Yes."

They were close. Rue Saint-Jacques was close. There had been mining here, everywhere. As she passed archways, she could feel deep caverns beyond that swallowed the edges of her father's voice. The scrape of grit under their boots shushed away and died in there.

They stopped at 37 Rue Jacques. Papa held the compass in one hand and the map in the other and shuffled in an odd dance, fitting compass to map, the direction of a vibrating needle to reality. These were his own maps of Paris, hand-drawn. They were extraordinarily accurate maps, but they only showed the tallest 156 buildings in Paris.

Adrian and Jean-Paul, who hauled the heavy loads, stood with their packs pressed against the wall, resting. Picks and shovels clicked against the rock. Papa tapped the compass and frowned at a solid wall.

Do not let that be the direction of the convent. Not there. Not into solid rock. Please. There are so many excavations. Let there be one under Rue Tessier.

"We must go around." With a spurt of decision, Papa led the way back as they had come, speaking all the while of magnetism. It came in lines, apparently. They were hot upon the trail of one.

It does not matter that he is mad. It does not matter whether I have been logical, or wise, or if I have made a reasonable decision. Guillaume's life rests only on whether I have been lucky.

Poulet reached up to run his fingers along the roof of the passage as they walked. "You know we can't dig through this. It'd take months to chisel upward, and they'd catch us at it. It's not a path into the prisons. If we can't find the well . . ."

"I am hoping rather desperately that we do find the well."

Papa stopped. He closed the compass and put it away. There was a great finality in the click of closing that brass case that held the compass.

"Here?" she asked.

"It cannot be known. It is a mistake to think everything can be known. Heraclitus wrote upon this. The fluxes of the lines of force within the earth—"

"Papa, is it here? This place?"

"I am telling you—one cannot know."

Nothing could be more certain than the pointing of a compass. Long after she was dead and gone, a compass would point to the north. "If one cannot know, can one guess?"

"If it is a guess you want . . ." He shrugged. "Go fifty paces. That way." He pointed. "The front gate of the convent is within a hundred yards of whatever rock you stand upon, fifty paces down that line." He pursed his lips. "Probably."

She carried her candle into the darkness, counting. *I must believe this.*

Jean-Paul followed. The circle of his candle overlapped her own. Where she stopped, he set down his pack and concerned himself with the practicalities of taking out candles and lighting them. They had brought a huge supply. One cannot bring too many candles into the quarries, just as one cannot carry too much water into a desert.

The convent was above them. Guillaume was sixty feet away, in the sunlight.

"We are beneath the Convent of Saint-Barthélémy." She didn't have to raise her voice to be heard. They came close to her. Small flames showed their faces, their hands, their chests. "There is a well in the convent. I watched them draw water only a few hours ago. It is a well from centuries ago. The well shaft reaches through this quarry into the water that lies below. It is not far from where we stand." *If I say this strongly enough, I will make it true.* "All this digging," she waved the hand that did not hold her candle, "came later. Long after the well."

So much silence. It is a small world that contains only six people and an immense darkness and the horrible finality of rock. One could not imagine how much darkness spread beyond them in every direction. Oceans of dark.

"This is the story of this place," she said. "When quarry workmen find wells, they back away. They leave the stone untouched all around the well. They make it one of these pillars. Or they build around the well shaft with cut stone and mortar. Our well, the well of the convent, lies within one of these thick walls or these columns of stone."

No one spoke. There was nothing to say. She finished, most simply, "We will find it."

Adrian dropped his pack at her feet. Like Jean-Paul, like Justine and Poulet, he began to light candles and secure them to the floor with drippings of their own wax. Five candles. A dozen. Two dozen. A circle of light grew around their supplies, small and stubborn as stars in the sky. They invaded the darkness, and made camp, and these were their sentinels.

Adrian came to her when he was done. "So I'm looking for a patched-up hole in one of these big pillars, or a bit of wall that doesn't make sense. Right?"

"Just so." They might spend a week looking. Guillaume had one day. Perhaps two. Did everyone here know how small the chances were?

"What kind of idiots build a city on eggshells? Somebody sneezes and the whole place is going to fall in." Adrian went off, shaking his head. "Paris."

Poulet drank wine from his flask, corked it, and stowed it in the leather pack he carried. He raised his voice. "Don't go where you can't see somebody's light. If you get lost, sit down and wait. I might even come looking for you. *Bon courage.*"

The first hour was spent searching every pillar and wall of that gallery, minutely, for any sign. They moved beyond, then, and lit their way into the next gallery and searched that.

In the fifth hour, they stopped to eat in a domed niche cut within the rocks. They ate on the circles of steps that led down to where water lived within the rocks. Eight feet below them lay a round pool, the drinking water, and perhaps the footbath, of the old quarrymen. It was water of such complete clarity it almost did not exist, except that it reflected back the flame of their candles. They ate the excellent tarts and cheeses served in the whorehouse and drank wine and spoke very little to one another.

Papa was tiring. She had made him bring a warm coat, but he was chilled. It would be late afternoon in the outside world.

Their tenth hour under the earth, six o'clock in the evening, they had traced and retraced and circled the center of their search and were in a new gallery. Bats spiraled upward and escaped through some vent in the arched ceiling. A weak shaft of light infiltrated from far above and struck all the way down to the cavern floor, fresh and beautiful as a spring in the desert.

It was a ventilation shaft, drilled in the rock. She went to it as if pulled by strings and stood in the light and looked up. She had been in darkness for a century.

"I'll track this, up top, and find it," Poulet said. "It'll show exactly where we are. But that's going to take a day or two. It probably comes up in somebody's garden."

They stood, all of them, looking up.

"It'll be big enough for a man to go through, lowered by a rope. Always good to have one more entrance," Poulet said.

They were close. She knew it. If she could tear these rock walls and rock stanchions apart, she'd find it. *We will not be in time. I made a mistake, trying this.*

Jean-Paul came up beside her. "We can do the ploy with a prison transfer, just after dawn. We have time to forge the papers if we head back now. We'll use Harrier's carriage and he'll go as driver. I still play a convincing guard."

You will not risk your life—you, who have a wife and a child and another baby coming. "No."

"Marguerite . . ."

"I have decided, Jean-Paul. It is this or nothing. We are committed."

They did not discuss it, but none of them moved from the spot. They would look further, but they all knew it was pointless.

A wind exhaled from the quarries, beginning who knew where, and leaving through that hole far above. The thin flowing of air would have been imperceptible anywhere else. Here, she could hear it whisper past her ears.

This is the kingdom of utter silence. Noise is a visitor here. In her hand, the candle flickered as she exhaled.

And she knew.

She said, "A well is not merely a hole in the ground. It is for bringing up water. The chain clinks of metal. The bucket splashes at the bottom. The load squeals going up again. We've been wrong. We do not look for the well. We listen for it."

Perhaps they were not cautious. Perhaps they raced too quickly from one chamber to another, to listen, with ears to the rock. But no harm came of it.

Justine was the one who heard. Less than thirty feet from where they had dropped their packs she heard the faint, sharp creaking of the chain behind a wall of mortared stone blocks.

Adrian ran for the picks and crowbars. It took five minutes to break the mortar and pry a stone loose. Carefully. Quietly.

Jean-Paul whispered, "If this is the well, they can hear us down here. I don't want them wondering why the frogs are talking."

He took the block out and stepped back. In that hand-width of opening, they saw the void behind. There was the most fragile and imaginary suggestion of light.

"We've done it," she said.

Forty-three

WHEN THE OPENING WAS LARGE ENOUGH, SHE leaned into the well and twisted around to look upward to the coin-sized circle of light above. Only a sou-sized coin, but it dazzled. Contrast is everything.

They spoke in whispers. Every few minutes, the bucket came down the shaft and went up again, full.

She chose a spot away from the opening of the well so her candles would not spill light into the well shaft, in case someone should look down. There was a corner where a block wall met another wall. This was where she would wait.

"I want to say you can't stay here." Jean-Paul sighed. "But you'll do exactly what you want."

"There is nothing useful for me to accomplish above ground. Victor is on the hunt for me. I'm in danger from him every step I take on the street. I endanger anyone with me." That wasn't why she had to stay. Jean-Paul would know that.

"In La Flèche, we don't make grand gestures, Margue-rite."

"This one, I will make."

He knew the futility of arguing with her.

She settled in to wait. Poulet came and kissed her on both cheeks and left his coat behind for her to wrap herself in and sit upon. He unpacked candles and flint and tinder and set them next to her. Also his flask of wine and all the food they had not eaten.

Jean-Paul left his gold watch, his father's watch, putting it into her hand as if it were a casual nothing. He unrolled a ball of twine, beginning at her feet, that would lead all the way out. "In case," he said. He left his coat also and would not be talked into keeping it.

Papa gave her the sticky dates he had found in the bottom of his pocket, wrapped in a handkerchief. He had been struck by several interesting observations of the magnetic waves beneath the ground. He began to describe them to her.

But he proved perfectly willing to talk about his list of geniuses. The very one he gave Robespierre. Yes. There was a copy in the library at home. Not in his desk. He had left it in a book . . . He would find it for her.

She pointed out that Victor had tried to poison her. Victor was very likely the man who had set assassins on his trail. And Victor was currently encamped at Hôtel de Fleurignac.

"I see." Papa absentmindedly ate one of the dates he'd given her.

Justine, wide-eyed and unafraid, small and competent, took charge of Papa and led him away.

Adrian stayed till last. "Don't worry if we're late."

"I am not addicted to worrying. I have a number of candles to keep me company."

"We have to fetch rope and the ladder rungs from the

workshop in the Jardin des Plantes. Get them across town to the café. Bring everything all the way down here. It'll take a while."

"So I should think."

"There might be gusts of wind coming out of that well shaft, the way it comes down a chimney sometimes. Set some of the candles where they can't get blown out." He pointed. "Over there."

"That is wise. Thank you."

"Don't wander off and get lost. You need to piss, do it here." Earthy, practical words in the lyric, slurring pronunciation of the South.

"That is good advice, Adrian. I am sufficiently afraid of this huge darkness that I will not be careless with it."

"Put those coats over you before you feel the cold. You don't notice it, but it'll eat your strength up if you don't cover up."

"I will."

"Probably not. I know I can't make you." His lips quirked. "Nobody tells you what to do but Doyle. And not him, much. I'll let him know you're here, waiting, keeping the gate. It'll give him incentive. I'm leaving this coat behind because it's got bloodstains inside. I can't be seen in something like that. You want a knife? I got extras."

"You are kind, Adrian, but it would be of no use to me."

"My friends call me Hawker."

"Then I will call you Hawker."

He stayed an instant, looking at her closely, then followed the others, leaving her in this empire of dark and uneasy silences.

Sound travels a long way in the rock. She heard their footsteps for a long while before the quiet closed over everything and she was alone. Poulet's coat was the warmest. It smelled strongly of the musky scent he wore, but she did not mind. She wrapped herself in it and put Jean-Paul's coat and Adrian's—Hawker's—under her and lapped them around her legs and was comforted. Time passed slowly.

Sometimes the bucket fell with a splash, came up with the chain rattling, and fell again. It was a connection with the world above. Sometimes, when the bucket was quiet a while, there came a sudden, astonishing plink as a single drop fell all the way down to the water.

It wasn't fear of Victor that kept her here, or common sense of any kind. She kept a vigil, as if she had lit candles in a church and waited beside them the night through. Guillaume was a hundred feet away. She sat on his doorstep, with leagues of dark around her, keeping him company.

From the brown cloth bag she had carried with her, she brought small matters to keep herself occupied. A book. Knitting. One does not need a great deal of light to knit stockings. One does it by feel and by counting. The sonnets were by the Englishman, Shakespeare, and so familiar she did not need to see the writing well.

She had also brought a small bottle of glue and two brushes and papers of gold leaf. She took off the boots and began the business of gilding her toenails. The small toe, she did first, since it required the most contortion. Then the next toe. This was an exacting process and long, since everything must dry thoroughly before she applied the next layer of gold. She went about it with great patience.

If Guillaume lived through the night and escaped, and she lived, she would surprise him with these gold toenails. It would drive him mad with passion. It would be very satisfying to be in bed with Guillaume when he was mad with passion. It was a thought to keep one warm even deep underground.

Forty-four

IN THE ATTIC ROOM OF THE BROTHEL, THE SMALL fry slept on top of the covers of the bed, sprawled out like a drunk soldier, limp as a dead fish. She'd probably spent a long day doing whatever it was kids did. Digging holes under the bushes out back. Eating worms. Getting underfoot of the horses and narrowly escaping death. Hard work.

"Is she supposed to look like that?" Hawker said.

"Yes. You may be grateful she is not snoring," Justine said. "What are you thinking, 'awker? Are you worried about tonight?"

"Trying not to be. I'll learn to love bumping around in the dark, eventually. Go down there for a stroll on Sunday afternoons."

"I will not join you there myself, thank you. They are putting old bones in those caverns, did you know? It is only in a single spot out of many miles of quarries, but one would not wish to stumble upon it by accident. They have taken bones from the ancient churchyards and put them in a cavern, piles and piles of them. I believe they sometimes stack them neatly." She thought about it. "For some reason that is even more distressing. They move them in carts in the middle of the night."

"You could tell me anything about this city and I'd believe it." He'd taken London for granted all these years. It might be damp and filthy, and the next time he poked a nose in London, Lazarus was going to have him killed. But at least they didn't go carting the dead around like cordwood. And London was solid underfoot. "Do you really eat donkey?"

"I do not, though one never knows what adventures await one in life. I will give you warning if I plan to serve you donkey."

Doyle was going to feed him donkey. He just knew it. "Some folks go eating their way through the animal kingdom without any regard for common sense or decency. They'd dine on griffins and bats if somebody didn't stop them."

"I will not serve you bats, either." She cleaned the table where they'd been eating, brushing crumbs into her hand and walking over to toss them out the window. There wasn't a scrap of food left. There was good food in Paris, at least in the whorehouses.

It was a well-run house. He'd only seen the back end of it—the kitchen and the stable yard and the stairs up to the attic—but everything looked rich and smelled clean. The girls laughed a lot, even when there weren't any men around.

Justine was the youngest of the women by a couple years, so it wasn't that kind of brothel. The kid on the bed, Séverine, would be left alone. Made his stomach heave, what they did with little kids, some places.

"Who takes care of . . ." He waved his hand at the bed but didn't say the name. The ruckus downstairs wouldn't wake her. Saying her name might. ". . . the sprat while you're out gallivanting around the city?"

"You need not concern yourself about Séverine." Justine unfolded a strip of white silk embroidered with flowers, snapped it briskly, laid it down the center of the table, and stroked it smooth. "We all watch after her."

You'd kill for the kid, wouldn't you? Die for her. Cheat, steal, lie, whore yourself. You'd do anything. Lazarus would call that kid your ruling weakness. So now I know.

"You and the whores are raising her."

"I do not let her see any of what happens in this house. She would not understand anyway. You do not need to reform us."

"That's Maggie does that. Not me."

"Then do not. I have the greatest dislike of being reformed."

She'd rousted a dozen books off the table so they could eat. Now she set them back standing in a row, pushed up against the wall. She studied the effect. "Séverine is young. She will forget."

"She won't." He could say that, because he knew. "Don't fool yourself. She sees everything that goes on here. Ask her, if you don't believe me."

She kept at her tidying and ignored him.

Her books were substantial, with leather covers, not the cheap bound paper they hawked up and down the streets. They'd been looted from some nob's library, maybe, when the mob tore it apart. "LeBreton says the revolution heats up the kettle of idealism by burning books under it. He always has something pithy to say."

"Well, no one will burn these."

"Where'd you get the books? Steal them?" He liked to think she'd had the initiative, but she probably just bought them. He came over to open one. Lots of writing. He recognized some of the words.

"They are lent to me by a friend. You will be careful with that."

"My hands are clean." For God's sake, she acted like he wasn't good enough to even touch one.

"I didn't mean that. It's just . . . no one comes here. I have lost the knack of hospitality."

No. Men didn't come to this narrow broom closet of a room. No sign of it. Whatever Justine did in this house, it wasn't making the beast with two backs in this room. Interesting to speculate on just what she did do for a living. If Doyle was alive tomorrow, he'd ask him what he thought.

He held the book up, asking permission.

He felt silly, sitting on the froufrou, dainty bit of a chair she had, so he took the book with him and sat with his back to the wall under the window where the light was good.

She'd set him a mat here, last night, on the clear space under the window. He didn't need watching over for a few scratches on his arm, and he didn't need it washed and rebandaged this morning. But if a girl offered, he wasn't going to turn it down. That was what you might call one of the guiding principles of his life.

He'd found out last night that Justine snored. A burring, feminine little snore. Kind of pleasant.

The book he'd picked had small print, but there were pictures. That helped. He couldn't figure a lot of words. Pictures let him know the general territory he was walking around in.

Halebarde. He put his finger under the text and started working his way along. *Arme offensive composée d'un long bâton d'environ cinq piéds, qui a un crochet ou un fer* . . . And there was one of those words that didn't seem to mean anything much. Even if he could figure out how to say it, likely as not he'd never need it.

Justine sat down beside him and took the book away. "You cannot pronounce French at all. You speak as if you came from the smallest hill village of Gascony. I think you are very stupid. And whoever sent you to France is even more stupid. Listen to me." She read it off, making the words sound Parisian. "This is Diderot. The *Encyclopédie*. Everything there is to know is in here."

Now that was interesting. He'd like to know everything there was to know. "Read some more."

It turned out a *halebarde* was a stick with an iron hook on the end. Not useful just at the moment, since no one was waving one in his face, but it might come in handy someday. He said the words after her, memorizing and trying to get them right.

She didn't sound like Daisy, who'd taught him to speak French. From Gascony, Daisy was. He could learn two accents. He'd sort them apart in his head when he was talking.

He put his arm behind Justine's back so she could lean on him, instead of on the wall, him being softer and warmer than plaster. He wasn't pushing. She could take him up on the offer or leave it.

After a few minutes, Justine leaned against him and set the book half in her lap, half in his.

They'd got to "*halibran,*" which was a baby duck and another word he was going to have only moderate use for, when she stopped and looked sideways at him. "Guillaume LeBreton was well when you went to see him?"

"Well enough." Doyle had got himself beat up in prison, but he was walking around. He'd do. "We didn't take time to chat."

They'd had three minutes' meeting in the open corridor. Time to pass over a ball of twine and tell him to send it down the well. To say the rescue was planned for midnight. That Maggie was waiting for him in the dark. Time to point out that nobody on earth was going to talk Maggie out of doing whatever she set her mind to and they were all just helpless corks bobbing in her wake and Doyle might as well get resigned to it.

Then he'd slipped off to deliver another puzzling communication to the merchant they'd made use of before. More questions about inheritance from a relative he had never heard of, this relative being a figment of the imagination.

"Will this work? Can your LeBreton do this?" Justine asked.

"If he can pick two locks and get to the courtyard and he doesn't come across something more interesting to do. He said he's bringing other people out with him."

"That is unwise." Justine frowned. "And it makes our part more difficult."

"Which I am sure is an object of great importance to him. Anyway, I didn't have time to talk him out of it."

"You think he will be there, at midnight."

"I think he has to be." There was no one else he could say this to, so he said it to her. "He told me his name was read out. They're coming for him in the morning. If we don't get him out tonight, he'll die on the guillotine tomorrow, round about teatime."

orty-five

MARGUERITE PUT THREE LAYERS OF GOLD LEAF
upon each toenail, stopping in between to knit and read
poetry and let everything dry. She heard the voices before
the tramp and shuffle of boots because they did not trouble to keep themselves quiet. Then the click and clank of
metal they carried also announced their coming.

When she held Jean-Paul's watch to the candle she
saw that it was eleven o'clock. Time had passed more
quickly than she had thought.

They were stars in the dark, the men who came with
their lanterns, and there were a dozen of them. Two of them
hefted huge coils of rope. Others carried lumpy sacks.

"My Marguerite." Poulet came in front of the others and
dropped down to sit cross-legged beside her. "You must put
your shoes on or my friends will go mad with desire. You
have the most exquisite feet."

"I am told that," she said. "It pleases my vanity no end."

His friends were young, all of them. Her own age,
or younger. They dressed with great aplomb and style,

expensively, in an extravagance of fashion that put large brass buttons upon their coats and spread lapels like wings across their breasts. Two of them wore gold hoops in the left ear, like pirates.

They were not very good at being silent. They had dined well and smelled of wine and some of them were a little tipsy. When she listened to them speak, it was obvious that every one of them had been in these caverns many times before. They came to the quarries for the adventure of it. Because it was forbidden and dangerous.

They were not of La Flèche. They told her their names, carelessly, openly. They made her feel old.

In a while, when they would not be silent, Poulet took them into the next chamber to lay out ropes and rungs and assemble the ladder Jean-Paul had designed for this endeavor. Jean-Paul himself came not many minutes later, with Hawker and three more of these young men, and went off to supervise.

She sat with her back to the wall of the well, waiting and listening.

Lights appeared, the furtive, faint glows of dark lanterns, and with them, a third group of men.

They approached silently, only their lights revealing that they were there. These were suspicious men who studied her and every corner of the cavern, and slid off in twos and threes to investigate the distant voices Jean-Paul supervised.

Justine was with them. "I brought friends." She stood, frowning. First one man and then another came up to whisper in her ear. She nodded. The men, and their lights, retreated to separate, distant corners of the cavern.

None of them was well dressed, none laughed or made jokes, and none of them told their names. However, several also smelled of wine.

Justine sat beside her in a companionable way. "They

are smugglers, but they are also friends of mine. They can be trusted."

"I had thought they might be. The traders of the coast are remarkably similar to your friends." She passed Poulet's flask across. Justine thanked her and drank and cleaned the mouth of the flask politely against her sleeve before she gave it back.

"What is the time?" Justine asked.

"Twenty minutes short of midnight. The ladder is almost ready, I think."

Justine nodded.

There were a few minutes to wait so she spoke of what was puzzling her. "Why did you bring me smugglers? It is not that I am ungrateful, but I do not know precisely what to do with them."

"I am almost sure we will need them." Justine laughed softly.

Forty-six

LET'S HOPE THIS WORKS. I AM TRAILING A THUN-dering herd of guesses.

Doyle lined men and women up across the courtyard and down the cloister, touching a shoulder to say "Keep quiet." Touching an arm to say, "Wait." They'd be scared, pulled out of sleep in the middle of the night. His lieutenants, three men and one woman, were holding their sections of the line tight and quiet.

Five minutes to go. He pulled the healthy, young ones out of line and moved them up first. These were the ones he could move fastest. The ones who had the best chance.

Two candles stood on the rim of the well. Little lights that wouldn't be seen on the other side of the wall. Everything else was black. Nobody whispered. Nobody shuffled his feet. Nobody even breathed loud. Guards were patrolling twenty feet away, beyond the wall.

The great danger was a *mouton,* a spy among the prisoners, who'd give them away. They'd left one tied hand and foot in the cells—the man they all knew about. Now everybody was on the lookout for another, watching the man next to him.

Ladislaus, the Polish forger, carried a watch. The candle gave enough light to read the hands. Midnight.

The bucket was by the well, upside down. They weren't going to use that tonight. Bucket and chain made an unholy racket. He'd send a scout down, sneaky and quiet. Strong, brown string, the kind gardeners used to tie up plants.

Hawker hadn't had time to explain. He'd passed over the ball of twine and said, "Get to the well at midnight. We'll be down in the bottom. Maggie's taken it into her head she has to be waiting for you."

He knew Maggie's plan. Knew it just as if she were standing here telling him the whole thing. He could have sat five hundred years in this lockup without thinking of the quarries. Maggie thought of them right off.

He'd filled a handkerchief with dirt and tied it to the end of the twine. Another handkerchief was tied on, floating out free, making a big white flag. Nothing more useful than handkerchiefs. He walked past men and women, up to the well, and let his bait down over the rim, into the cup of dark. Fishing for a way out. He hoped they were ready, down there, for the crowd he was bringing with him.

He played out a dozen yards, then another ten, keeping track, feeling the rough edges of the well shaft as the bag caught and bounced over the stone. *She's down there right now. I'm sending this down to her.*

When he hit the water, he'd bring it back up and try again. They might not be ready yet.

There's just no end to what could go wrong.

Hand over hand, slow and easy. Then he felt someone take hold of the other end. Felt the twitches that meant somebody working. Then three hard tugs.

He took back his sixty feet of twine, pulled in rope that had been tied to it, then reeled in still heavier cordage.

Ladislaus helped him bring up the last of it. It came slowly, bumping awkwardly. What they had was heavy burlap bundles wrapped around big iron hooks. The hook went over the rim of the well. The rope ladder trailed down from that, disappearing into the depth and the dark.

He barely had the hooks secure when he felt the jerks of somebody climbing up. A minute later, a head poked out. Hawker. He came aloft scowling at the line of men and women, disapproving as a cat in a glue factory. A bare whisper of sound. "You lost me ten sous."

The first man in line was a soldier from the Vendée. A bandit, they called him in Paris. He didn't need help getting over the rim. He knew how to follow orders and he was fast. A good choice for the first man out.

"Did I now?" He counted off thirty seconds under his breath and tapped the next man. The one after that was a woman. She already had her skirts tied up high over her knees.

Hawker whispered, "I said you'd bring a friend or two. Maybe five. Maybe six." The woman put her hands on Hawker's shoulder as he lifted her up to the edge, found a rung for her foot, and started down. "Jean-Paul bet me you'd empty out the whole damn prison."

"Ah."

"I told him," Hawker managed to pack a huge freight of sarcasm into a whisper, "you wouldn't do anything that stupid."

"We all make mistakes." He gave the nod. Hawker put his arm out to help. The next man scrambled over the side.

THEY'D come to about the last of them. A scared girl. Hawker swung her across and prodded her over the edge of the well. She stuck there, holding on and whimpering. Hawker pried her fingers loose from his shirt and stuffed her down the well. It was catch on to the ladder then, or fall, so she grabbed the ladder.

Sister Anne, who was helping them, leaned over to coo and coddle. Pat, pat on the head. Pat the cheek. Whisper. Whisper. "Go, my child. All will be well. They're waiting for you below. Go now."

"Move before I hit you," Hawker said.

Between them, they got the girl started. He motioned Hawker in after the girl. Hawker would get her to the bottom in one piece, if anyone could. It might involve tromping on her fingers to keep her moving, but he'd do it.

It had taken them an hour to get everyone out. Now it was only Father Jérôme and Sister Anne. The other two nuns were inside, too weak to walk. He'd have to leave them behind.

The nun had been useful, helping him move the women along. "Tuck your hem in your waistband, Sister. If your foot gets caught in your skirt, just hold on and kick it free."

"Oh my, no. I'm not going."

I don't have time for this. "There's no choice, Sister. It's the only way out. It's easy once you're over the rim."

The prison was too quiet, now that they'd emptied it out. None of the coughing and snoring that went on every night. Pretty soon, one of the guards was going to sense something wrong.

She laid her hand on his arm. "My dear boy, surely you realize I never intended to leave. I can't."

Maggie's down there, and God knows what's happening to her. "If you stay behind, you're going to die."

The priest's voice came, very calm. "Guillaume, it has already been decided. The sister and I will stay behind."

"Father, we don't—"

"The Sister will stay because it is her duty."

"I could not possibly leave Sister Scholastica and Sister Benedict behind. There is no one to care for them.

And they don't understand what is happening." A breathy pause. "Someone must be with them when we are taken to the guillotine. They are really too old and frail to face it alone."

He closed his eyes. "Oh, damn."

"They have been my sisters for thirty years. Of course we will go together." She patted him, exactly the way she had patted the terrified girl on the rim of the well. "You must hurry and leave so I can return to them. They wake in the night sometimes, thinking it is Matins, and it frightens them that we're not in the right place."

"You can't—"

"She can and will." Father Jérôme hitched his steps toward the well. "Her work is here. You have work to do elsewhere and must get on with it."

"Father . . . You know what I'm trying to do with those papers. Even if it works, it may not work fast enough to save you. They could take you out of here tomorrow."

"That is now, and always has been, in the hands of God. To be practical, I do not believe even your great strength can play Aeneas and carry me out of Troy. Not with that cracked rib. There are some dozens of men and women at the bottom of this infernal pit. They are your responsibility now. You must go to them."

"I can carry you. I'm strong enough."

"We shall not attempt to find out. This is for you." The box fit into his hands, corners and smoothness and the faint ridges of the inlaid squares. The chessmen. "I am delighted to say there will be no one left for me to pass it to. And it is time for me to return to bed. I am composing an edifying speech to deliver on the scaffold."

"A man doesn't throw his life away to make a point."

"On the contrary. That is exactly what a man does. Put that away safely. You'll need both hands to climb with."

"At least send out that silly nun. You can order her to go."

"But I will not do so." The priest propped himself against the upright timber of the windlass. "She also will make her final point. Did you think bravery was the sole province of the wise? Go with God, my son."

There was nothing else for it. He climbed into the well. Put his hands on the rungs. Started down.

Above him, the priest said, "I regret not finishing the last game with you. I would have won."

Nun and priest were lit by the candles as they leaned over the rim of the well. He could see those candles all the way down. When he reached the bottom, when he was with Maggie, the ladder lifted once, to confirm it was empty. Then it fell, rung and ropes, plummeting into the water, forever concealing the path of their escape.

Forty-seven

MARGUERITE SAID, "THEY'LL BE SAFE. EVERYONE who leads them has done this, or something like this, before."

"You have interesting friends," Guillaume said.

The last of Justine's smugglers departed, taking with them the last of the prisoners—a dark-haired Polish man, a quivering seamstress, and a tight-lipped, frightened counter-revolutionary from Nantes.

La Flèche would be busy for weeks, spiriting this many men and women out of Paris.

Voices became a scratching on the surface of the silence and then silence itself. The great cavern was empty. Now it belonged to Guillaume and to her. Candles burned at the far edges of the stone galleries, small lights left behind, floating in the darkness. In a few hours, they would burn down and flicker out, one by one, and the dark would come back.

"You're cold. Every part of you is cold to the bone." He touched her face. Her upper arms.

"A little chilled. I don't feel it." There had been no time

in the noise and confusion of the rescue to hold him. Now she did. She pulled close to him and pressed to his chest. She did it carefully, because he had been hurt. The first men to descend the ladder in the well shaft had come out speaking of Guillaume. How he had given them their lives and how he had been beaten in prison.

He stroked her hair. Soft. Soft. Tucking it behind her ears where it had come loose.

"Victor hurt you. Everyone heard it happening." She drew away from him to look down at his body. Her hand hovered over his ribs, without touching them. "I wasn't fast enough to spare you this."

"My own fault, for getting arrested. If I hadn't walked off and left you alone with him it wouldn't have happened. I should have kept you with me. Protected you."

"I am pleased to be protected, as any woman would be. But it also happens I am well able to decide when I shall go to my own house and when I will be carried off by a handsome seller of political texts."

"You can do any damn thing you decide to." He put his hands down upon her shoulders. "Keep away from Cousin Victor. He knows you're in La Flèche."

That was hard news, though it explained Victor's behavior, which had puzzled her. "He knows and you know and your colleague Hawker as well and these many odd men who came to take the sparrows away. I am utterly revealed. If I were one of my couriers I would send myself to England."

"If you don't, Victor's going to try to lock you up someplace to keep you from making trouble for him. He might have worse in mind. There's not much I'd put past him."

"That is what Jean-Paul says. He says that Victor poisoned me with foxglove leaves."

Guillaume's hold tightened. "I'll have to make sure he doesn't do that again, won't I?"

"You sound very threatening, I think, but I shall handle my Cousin Victor. It was the night I was so sick and came to find you in the café—that night—I drank some of a tisane Victor brought me. But I withhold judgment in the matter. I do not say Victor would not poison me, because he is a man lacking the most elementary scruples, but there is no real proof that—"

He kissed her, swiftly. Claiming her mouth, once, and letting go. "I'm going to kill him."

"It is a thoughtful offer, but no. I have no proof, only guesses and the evidence of his character. If one set about murdering all the men who are without scruple, one would depopulate Europe. Let us instead go find hot coffee and a bed. As it happens, I have never gone to bed with a married man."

He continued to hold her and look at her, his face serious. "Why did you stay here in the quarries all night?"

He knew very well why she had stayed. "I was waiting for you. I will always be waiting for you."

"You . . ." He breathed out. "Damn."

She had deprived him of speech. That was satisfying. She said, "Make love to me."

He shook his head. "Not here. Not underground. And I'm filthy."

"Then we will go somewhere else and wash you. Then we will make love." She picked up the end of the twine that would lead them out of the dark. Poulet's coat was lined with silk and smelled of musk. She put it around Guillaume's shoulders to keep him warm and they left the dark.

Forty-eight

MARGUERITE FOLLOWED THE PATHWAY OF TWINE
Jean-Paul had threaded for her through the galleries and
corridors. Guillaume carried the lantern. She gathered in
the thread of their way, winding up the labyrinth. It was as
if she were Ariadne and had rescued the Minotaur instead
of Theseus. That was a slight rewriting of the old tale, but
she was in the mood for rewriting sad endings. The ball
had become huge by the time she reached the inconspicuous stairway that led upward.

It did not amaze her to find Hawker sitting upright, doz-
ing, at the top of the stone stairs. He pretended he had not
been sleeping.

"About time." Hawker rubbed his sleeve over his face.
"Means I don't have to go down and fetch you. Anybody
else coming?"

"We're the last." Guillaume closed the lattice door that
blocked off the stairs and began to shift barrels in front of
it. He could do this by himself, even when he was hurt, but
she helped him anyway.

He stopped once, suddenly, in the middle of rolling a barrel on its edge from one place to another, and said, "Every breath I draw from now on, I owe to you."

"It is not—"

"I want to say it." He let the barrel down gently, in place, exactly where it belonged.

She changed from boots to shoes. Guillaume blew the lanterns out, all except one, and left them behind on the table. She was on the narrow ladder that led to the café when he said one of several things that had been resting, silent, between them. "The priest and the nuns didn't come."

She had seen that and had said nothing. "I wondered."

"They chose not to."

"They may survive. Jean-Paul's friends were full of news. There were accusations in the Convention yesterday. Robespierre is isolated and the delegates seething like a stew. He may fall. It could be today or tomorrow. Soon enough to save them."

"I hope so." But he was somber inside, preparing for the worst. Guillaume would be hurt to the soul that he had to leave people behind. It would never be enough for him to save almost everyone.

They opened the door to a café, disturbing a small gray moth. Outside, it was the darkest time of night, long before the streets would begin to wake. Guillaume took a deep breath and started off. She didn't know where they were going, but she was willing enough to follow.

Did anyone at all see them go past? Were there eyes behind the closed shutters? No one challenged them, in any case. They stopped once and huddled together in the alcove of a doorway while boots marched on a street nearby.

They crossed the Pont Neuf, walking side by side with Hawker far behind, keeping some careful watch upon all the streets. The water emanated cool. Profoundly black, it held the light of the bridge lanterns, rippling in the water.

There were no stars, and it was the dark of the moon. Perhaps this meant misfortune for someone tonight. If so, she hoped it would be for their enemies.

"I have found your list for you," she said. No one would overhear, on the bridge. "It is that you have been seeking up and down the countryside. The list that my father was so infinitely stupid to make."

"Ah." Guillaume slowed. "That list."

"I have finally spoken to my father. He was one of the men who came to free you tonight, which should make you feel cordial toward him. He will find the list and give it to you. You are not kill him, do you understand? He had no idea what would be done with it."

"I won't hurt him."

"Good. Cousin Victor is responsible for this stupidity. And Robespierre. Robespierre, you may hurt as much as you want."

"I'm going to take you up on that."

In the Marais, Guillaume thumped on a substantial door in a quiet, shuttered street. After a time, light came to the grille. The portal door was thrown back. They entered quickly. Hawker slipped in after them.

They made little noise, but as they walked in, two candles flickered into being on an upper floor and crossed the spaces of the windows. Light blossomed behind shutters on all sides. Then the ground floor lit.

The porter who had opened the door for them set his lantern on the stone bench and clasped Guillaume's hand in both of his and pumped it hard. He murmured, "We were afraid for you" and "There seemed no way."

It was a welcome home. This, then, was Guillaume's.

The door across the courtyard opened to show a wide kitchen behind. A tall old woman with her white hair in long braids strode toward them, a peignoir of Chinese crimson silk, unbelted, sweeping behind.

"You're safe." A dumpling of a woman detoured around the gaunt old one and ran ahead to grab Guillaume's shoulders and hug him firmly. She released him to look up and down his whole length.

The white-haired woman held up a candle. "Guillaume. Alive. At least relatively unharmed." The candle shifted to the left. "And Marguerite de Fleurignac." It was a statement, not a question. Steely eyes considered her, then traveled to Hawker. "And you." The gaze returned to Guillaume and warmed, fractionally. "I was not optimistic. This once, I am glad to be proved wrong. Come inside, all of you. I need to know what's going on."

"Give me a minute to wash the prison off of me." Guillaume unbuttoned his waistcoat and dropped it and his jacket on the bench as he passed. He headed for the square stone basin at the side of the courtyard. "Maggie, go ahead to the kitchen. Make them give you something hot to drink. Hawker, take the stairway straight behind you. One flight up and second door left. I have clean towels in my room. Bring some."

Guillaume sent Hawker into the heart of the house to tell the disdainful old woman the boy was under his protection.

"Hawker." Her voice stopped him. The dark head, sleek as a seal, went up. "Present me to Madame."

His eyes locked with hers. He knew what she was doing. Every one of them understood. They all held conversations in glances and the twitch of an eyebrow.

"Of course." Hawker slid into place between her and the old woman. Straight-backed, formal, mocking, he gave the smallest bow and spoke like a young Gascon nobleman. "Madame Cachard, permit me to present to you Mademoiselle Marguerite de Fleurignac. You will have heard of her father, perhaps, the former Marquis de—"

"My wife," Guillaume interrupted. He'd pulled his shirt

off over his head. He stood, half-naked, in the open air. "She's not mademoiselle anything." He stripped the shirt down off his arms and bunched it together and tossed it across the bench.

"Fine. You do the pretty. Don't expect me to know what to call her." Hawker stalked off through the courtyard, skirting pots of sprawling geraniums, headed for a door in the corner. "Let me know what name you're using today."

The door slammed behind him, which doubtless relieved his feelings. There was no one asleep in this house, in any case.

"You are married?" Madame Cachard did not sound approving.

If this woman disapproved of Guillaume's marriage, she would have to deal with his wife. "We are." Even without her fan—oh, but she was fluent with a fan—she needed only two words to tell another woman to keep her nose from beneath this particular basket lid.

Madame Cachard raised her eyebrows. Guillaume sat to pull his boots off. "Let's delve into my private life later, Helen. I need to know what's happening in Paris."

"As do we all, after this grenade you've tossed into the middle of French politics. What the devil have you been about?" The old woman's eyes rested on Guillaume and then on her. "You will also explain how you got out of prison. Wash, get dressed, and come inside." She raised her voice. "You will all join me in the kitchen in a quarter hour, *if* you please. The world is rolling hotfoot to hell and I need reports. You won't discover anything interesting in bed."

A man's laughter rolled out from above, and an answering chuckle and a murmur of talk. The old woman lifted her candle. "I shall spare my aging eyes the sight of Guillaume LeBreton in all his naked glory. Don't cover those ribs till Thea sees them. She may decide bandages are called for." She started to turn, then stopped. "You were right about the boy."

"I told you so."

"Give him to me."

Guillaume pulled his boots off while he thought. "He's yours. He needs to stay out of England for a few years."

"We will allow him to menace the populations of Europe for a while. I will begin the process of civilizing him. It will be an arduous undertaking." She swept off, upright and grand in her crimson robe.

Guillaume stood up, grinning. "Hawker's in for an interesting time."

"Madame Cachard as well, I think."

"Oh yes."

She came closer to him. For his disguises, Guillaume had built himself the callouses of a poor man, the brown neck and shoulders and chest, as if he worked on the land, bare-backed, under the sun. He could pass for a peasant or sailor and be completely convincing. She had watched him do it again and again in the short time she had known him. He shaped his lies even with his muscles and bones.

But the strength of him was real. She had read the textures and surfaces of his body. When she was lost in sensation and could think only of pleasure, her skin continued to discover him. At least some of what she had learned must be truth.

He unbuttoned his trousers.

"You cannot become naked here," she said.

"There's a screen over there. Blow that lantern out and come over here and we'll both go be naked behind it. Nobody can see."

Perhaps he was right. The light of the lantern barely touched him and the night was all around. He'd stripped his trousers down and stood in his *caleçons*, barefoot in the courtyard. Then he removed the last of his clothing. It seemed he could indeed wear nothing at all. He was matter-of-fact about his nakedness, as men are who spend their lives on board ship, or traveling, or in armies, where no privacy is possible.

He said, "I was hoping for a chance at you before the day starts. If you're keeping your clothes on, I won't get one, will I?" He hefted the bucket into the bottom of the deep stone basin and pumped water.

"I do not shed my clothing in the middle of a courtyard with everyone stirring and coming to breakfast. I am more modest than you. Frogs in a duck pond are more modest than you."

"Now you see, that philosopher fellow Zeno would disagree with you. He'd say being naked is more modest than going around all dressed up. He had a whole set of reasons."

"That is a pernicious doctrine. One can tell you have been to university. Only the very educated believe such nonsense."

"I'm just saying that to get you out of your skirts. Too bad it's not working."

It was certain Guillaume had been to . . . not Oxford. He had been at Cambridge, where they were liberal and mathematical. If she went to Cambridge town and asked after a giant who was brilliant and curious about every-thing, who laughed largely and had a huge, sly sense of humor, they would remember him.

The bucket was full. He lifted it with both hands and dumped water over himself in a great downpour, shivering as it streamed down him, shaking his head fiercely to get the hair out of his eyes.

I would love him for the beauty of his body if I did not already love him for his calculating sneaky mind. If I did not love his body, I would love his great heart. I would love the strength of him.

He scooped soap from a jar. It was the harsh jelly of lye soap, intended for clothing or pots or scrubbing floors. He washed with wide motions back and forth across his chest. When he came to his face, before he closed his eyes and lathered, he stopped to peel away the false scar he wore on his cheek, scraping it away with his fingernails.

He was without concealment now. Naked indeed. Water ran off him, along the flagstones, down into the shallow channel that led out into the street. All this time he looked at her with hot eyes. Wanting her.

Voices murmured in the night. Scuffles and creaks came from bedrooms of people getting up from bed and dressing. The household was roused. She smelled coffee being ground in the kitchen. She was not alone with Guillaume. "You are all spies here, are you not? Everyone I will meet in this house is a spy."

He didn't hesitate at all. "Yes."

With that one word, he said, "We are married." He said, "Husband and wife trust each other." He said, "There are no secrets between us." One word, and he said all that to her.

"I had not expected to marry a spy."

"Does it bother you?" He studied her while he filled the bucket again.

"I am unsettled by it." She felt shy of him. Not because he was English, and in the habit of lying to her, and a spy. Because he was her husband. She did not know how to deal with a husband. Probably Beauty dealt very well with the Beast, but could not imagine what to say to the handsome prince he turned into. Her problem was compounded in that her Beast did not turn into a handsome prince. He turned into a tricky fox. As always, when dealing with Guillaume, matters were complex. "I do not mind that you are a spy. I have sent men out of France who were probably spies. I do not ask. They would only lie."

No one would have seen the brief pause unless they were watching him closely and knew him well. "Spies do that."

"I have told a few lies in my own time. I have less fondness for candor than some people, having a father who is most perfectly candid and would drive a lesser woman to murder. And I do not mind that you are English. I am entirely in charity with England. You give refuge to our squabbling idealists and our aristocrats, who are perfectly useless to you and expensive as well. I do not like it that England wishes to give us another fat Bourbon king, but I am even less fond of Robespierre. I think perhaps there is no government I would like."

"I'm sure there's a good reason we can't get rid of all of them. It'll come to mind in a minute."

"You do not seem very English, in any case. You make a convincing Frenchman."

"I'm about half French, if you add it up. Does that help any, or are you still feeling strange?"

"I will feel strange for a time. Being in love with you is shedding the skin of my soul, as a snake sheds its skin. I feel tender and naked. I would rather not love you, in fact, but I have no choice in the matter."

"I don't have any problems at all, loving you. It's pure pleasure." He filled another bucket and poured it over himself. This time, she got wet, too, she was so close to him. She cupped her hand to take some of the water that spilled off his body. It was chillingly cold, but she splashed it on her face.

She was disconcerted when he leaned down to nip at her ear and kiss her there, quick and playful.

His teeth, closing on her ear, tightened her skin up, sent a hot pulse of lightning within her, down to her toes.

A little breathless, she said, "Will we live in this house? I can deal with your Madame Cachard, if I must."

"We'll live in England, at least at first, since they're

holding a war in France and half the people in Paris know you're running La Flèche. I'll buy a place near London. Hampstead, maybe. They're always after me to work in London. Training. Analysis. I'll be Head of Section eventually, if I stay—"

"No."

She felt the sigh he did not allow himself. "Then I won't," he said. "There's enough work in this world for a man that he doesn't have to go spying. There's a paper on Celtic languages I've been meaning to write, if I ever got the time. I can—"

"I mean, no, you will work as you always have. You will travel about, poking and prying into the affairs of the world, and bring balance to the fate of nations and spin peace out of your own strength. You will do the work you were born to do. I will not make you less than you are."

His lips and his breath were warm on the top of her head. His hair hung down, just touching her forehead, chilly from being washed. He was entirely motionless. It was like being held by one of the tall stones in Brittany, the menhirs, that mark the hilltops. "You'll send me off? Let me work?"

"Do you think I want a great lummox like you about and underfoot all day long, every day? I shall breathe a sigh of relief, very secretly, when you go away. Then, in a short time, I will forget how annoying you are and welcome you back with great enthusiasm when you come home."

"I like the welcoming-home idea. And the enthusiasm part."

She stood on tiptoe to kiss his face where his scar would have been. Where it would be, when he went on his travels again. He tasted like harsh soap. It was a masculine flavor but not romantic. She liked it on him. "Think of my enthusiasm, at night, when you are in dangerous places. You will know that I am waiting for you. I shall, of course, take lovers, but I will shove them swiftly out of the house when you arrive. You must pretend not to notice their coattails disappearing around the corner."

"Right." His hands were confident and amused, drawing her in. "Good thing I'm not a jealous man."

"I will make a home for you, Guillaume, not a cage. You will go away always, to your work and your wandering. If you will leave your heart with me, I will care for it like diamonds."

When Hawker appeared with clothing they were standing, silent. Guillaume was naked and his arms were around her.

"Anybody'd think you don't have a bed," Hawker said.

"I am very fond of beds," she said. "Perhaps if you take me to one I will show you my toenails. I have gilded them for you. Although I believe there are affairs of state to discuss in the kitchen."

"Damn affairs of state." Guillaume carried her away upstairs.

Forty-nine

RUMOR ENTERED THE HOUSE IN THE MARAIS WITH the dawn and returned again and again all day. Somehow everyone in Paris knew Robespierre would condemn his enemies in the Convention. English spies took a great and immediate interest in this.

Marguerite worked beside Althea, cooking omelets, toasting bread, and slicing ham for men and women who came to the kitchen and spoke, very fast, very excitedly, to Carruthers and ate what was put before them and departed.

By late afternoon, the kitchen held seven men and five women. That was too many to sit down. Three men and Hawker stood with their backs to the wall. The woman Carruthers—Madame Cochard—was at the head of the table, as she had been for some hours, collecting reports.

". . . shouted him down when he tried to speak. Half the deputies are out for his head. Robespierre was so angry he lost his voice. The Convention is in an uproar."

"Somebody said, 'The blood of Danton is choking him.'"

"That's a good one. That's good."

"The chairman kept pounding the gavel. Keeping Robespierre from saying anything. From naming any more counter-revolutionaries."

Althea poured new coffee into cups and laid them down. "They're all in this. Everyone Doyle warned. Both the Left and the Right."

A woman, small and dark as a Gypsy, said, "They planned last night. A dozen of them met in the Tuileries." She turned in her chair to look behind her, to Guillaume. "Fouché was brandishing that forgery of yours like he thought it up himself. That was well done. Well done."

Carruthers narrowed her eyes at Guillaume. "Next time you decide to topple the government of France," there was an edge to her voice, "warn me."

Laughter broke out around the room.

Carruthers lifted her hand. Silence fell. "The tumbrels were stopped by a mob in the Faubourg Saint-Antoine. That's the temper of the streets. Did they get the prisoners free? Does anyone know?"

Around the table, head shakes. Hawker spoke up. "The mob was pushed back. Horses. Guns. The tumbrels went through."

Silence for a moment. "Damn," from one man.

"That'll be the last of them."

"The mob has spoken. We're done with this killing."

Carruthers said, "The Garde Nationale's ordered to report to the Place de Grève. Robespierre's been taken to the Luxembourg Prison. Anything else?"

A square, nondescript man, dressed like a storekeeper, spoke up from beside the door. "The prison turned him away. He's at the mayor's office on Quai des Orfèvres with troops around him. The streets say the Garde's going to march on the Convention."

"Then I need you there, at the Convention. Gaspard—"

On the other side of the room, a man nodded.

"To the mayor's office. The rest of you make a round of the Section offices. Everything depends on whether Robespierre can get the Sections behind him. Stay in pairs. If there's fighting, try not to get your heads blown off."

They laughed. Men and women finished coffee in a single swallow, grabbed a plum from the bowl on the table, and left. There was a quiet, competent recklessness about them, as if they could be sent into hell to fetch one particular piece of charcoal from the furnaces and they'd make a good job of it.

Hawker clattered dishes, carrying them to the scullery.

"There are waiters in Paris who could clear this off and no one would see them." Carruthers was making notes on the pages she'd spread in the clear spaces of the table. "They'd be invisible."

"I could pick their pockets while they were doing it." The rattling ceased. He wrapped an imaginary apron around his middle and became the serving boy in a café, deft, practiced, silent. They were chameleons, these Englishmen.

Guillaume was the most changeable of them all. He'd been out since early morning, gathering facts and rumors. He wore the crumpled blue smock of a market laborer. Althea had cut his hair short and rubbed in powdered ash. He was gray-haired now. The scar was gone. Every long crease of his face was a separate and deep seam. His eyes hid in a network of wrinkles. She did not know how he managed that.

She had watched him leave this morning to walk the streets of the city. He changed, even as the porter opened the gate. He became another man. Abruptly, between one step and the next, there was something wrong about his left shoulder and arm, as if they had been pasted together hastily and jiggled before the parts dried. He looked clumsy. He did not look in the least like Guillaume LeBreton.

It could not be easy for a man to play so many parts, so long. In the home that she would make for him, he would be only Guillaume. Only himself.

Guillaume set his empty cup in Hawker's hands. "I'll go back to the stalls of Les Halles. The market men know what's happening, if anyone does, and know it first."

"Far be it from me," Carruthers said, "to give orders to an Independent Agent, but I could use you here, winnowing reports. I have plenty of eyes and ears walking around. I'll send the boy out to the markets," she looked at Hawker, "and see what he can drag back for me."

"Good enough. I'll—"

The door pushed open. A young man came in, moving quickly. He was sixteen or seventeen, pale-haired, with a scholar's face. His eyes skipped from one person to another, lingered on Hawker, then went back to Carruthers. "The man I was watching . . ."

"Victor de Fleurignac." Carruthers hooked a chair with her foot and scooted it back for him to sit in. "You can talk. And you don't have to kill Hawker after all. He's mine now." She gave a tight smile. "We're all relieved. What about Victor de Fleurignac?"

"Fouché visited just after nine this morning. Stayed twenty minutes. Three messengers came between ten o'clock and noon. Then nothing. An hour ago the old man showed up. The older de Fleurignac. The marquis. He opened the door with a key and let himself in. He hadn't come out when I left."

Fifty

DOYLE COUNTED DOZENS OF MEN OUT ON THE streets all walking fast, going different directions. There were no carriages, no carts, no wagons. No women but the one walking at his side. Everyone expected fighting to break out when troops from the Convention came to arrest Robespierre. Maybe a good, rousing riot.

He'd brought Hawker and young Pax with him, which was half an army. Maggie strode beside him like a Valkyrie. He didn't envy Cousin Victor when he faced Maggie. If Victor had hurt her father, she'd probably tear him apart with her bare hands.

That's another reason I'm going to kill Victor. So she doesn't have to. He didn't want her to carry around the knowledge that she'd killed somebody.

The shops were closed and locked up and barred, with the owners inside, armed and waiting, ready to fight off the mob if looting started. But the cafés and taverns were open, packed so that men stood up to drink. Everybody had a newspaper, reading, trading them back and forth. Arguing. Spreading rumors. He could hear them as they walked by.

"Robespierre's called the Sections to rise in his defense."

"The Garde is marching against the Convention. My brother-in-law told me."

"They're ordered to their barracks."

"The Gendarmerie's out. They've lined up in front of the Convention. They have cannon."

". . . declared him outlaw. Declared Robespierre himself outlaw."

Nobody knew what was happening.

The *pop pop* of gunfire sounded from the direction of the Seine. That'd be from the Hôtel de Ville. But it was troops firing into the air, not a real battle. There was a different rhythm to a real fight. They'd have people running away in this direction if anyone was getting hurt.

The rumbling in the air that sounded like thunder a long way off—that was the mob.

The tocsin sounded again, starting at Notre Dame in the center of Paris, spreading out. The church bells, as many as had been left hanging in the bell towers, had been ringing for an hour now, sounding the alarm. No one knew what to do about it though. Everybody who owned a uniform had put it on and headed into the streets, waiting for somebody to pass out orders.

Twice they passed small troops of *gardes* marching in formation.

Maggie stalked along, keeping an eye on the streets, listening, but not panicked. He had to remember she'd been in this city through four years of violent revolution. She was a veteran of riot.

"Papa picks this moment to come out of hiding," she fumed. "Paris is a powder keg and a thousand men have fuses in their pockets. I have told him Victor is our enemy.

So today, he goes home. When I am through strangling Victor, I will strangle Papa."

A new sound prickled the air when they turned onto Rue Palmier. Someone was playing Bach. The Italian Concerto. Fine playing. It was very fine playing indeed. "That would be your father."

She nodded brusquely and speeded up. "Papa's there. He would play Bach at the world's ending."

De Fleurignac has all his fingers working. At least we're not going to walk in on a corpse.

"In case you're wondering," she stopped at her door, "I don't play like that."

He didn't have to knock. The majordomo, Janvier, threw the door open before they got to it. "Thank God you've come. He's going to send the master to the asylum at Charenton."

"Who? Victor?" Maggie swept ahead of him, past the steward, into the foyer. "I will not allow Victor to send Papa to a madhouse. Why is Papa here? Did he say?"

"He came to challenge Victor to a duel."

She growled, a deep, feline, impatient sound. "Papa will not be permitted to kill Victor, either. They will lock him away if he begins killing people."

Janvier said, "I hid his swords in the kitchen, behind the brooms."

The entry hall was empty. No voices anywhere in the house. No footsteps. Nothing to hear but music and distant gunfire. Janvier had got the servants out of the way. Good. He took hold of Maggie's arm before she went charging into the salon. "Not yet. Your father duels?"

"He's a brilliant swordsman." Whenever she talked about her father she got a little crease between her eyes. "I've kept him from slicing up any number of rival mathematicians over the years. And political philosophers. And a few poets."

"I don't kill people. Not unless I have to. I generally don't have to." *You'll never have to worry about me, the way you worry about your father. You'll see.*

Hawker and Pax did a little cross-and-jostle work over who'd go through the door first. Hawker won that round. Once in, they separated just as far as the entry hall would let them and stood glaring at each other.

"There has been no duel. Monsieur Victor said he would not fight with a madman." Janvier closed the door softly. "They argued loudly, all up and down the house. Madame Sophie retired to her rooms, discomposed. And your father began to play the pianoforte, as you hear. Angrily. Victor sent for his two men, the *canailles* who do his bidding about town. They have just arrived. Mademoiselle, they have brought pistols."

That would be their old friends, the Jacobins who'd chased them across Normandy. The ones who'd hauled him off to prison. And they were armed. It just kept getting better and better.

"I hid the master's gun in the pantry. I can bring it to you, mademoiselle. Or to you, monsieur."

Doyle had his own gun. That was why he was wearing this damned uncomfortable coat.

I don't want to kill a man in front of Maggie.

"Let's play this a different way." He waved Pax close. "Section headquarters. You know it?" Pax nodded. "They'll have some pack of *gardes* milling around. Tell them Robespierre's man, Deputy Victor de Fleurignac, is here, in this house."

Maggie said sharply, "No."

Pax hesitated.

"Go," he told him. "Do it."

Pax yanked the door open and pounded out into the street, already running.

He watched Maggie take hold of anger in both hands and wrestle it down. The air shimmered around her. "I will decide what is done to my cousin Victor."

But they both knew what had to be done. "He plans to kill your father. That's why he sent for his jackals. His men are here to say your father went mad and attacked."

Her throat worked. "We are safe while Papa is playing. It demonstrates that his hands are occupied with the music and not with strangling Victor."

"He'll come to the end of this piece in five or six minutes. I have to be in there when he finishes."

"We will both go in. Victor won't kill Papa if I'm here to accuse him. And he does not dare kill all of us."

"That's what I'm hoping. Can I convince you to wait out here?"

"No." She stared, unblinking, at the salon door. "I understand why you sent for the *gardes*. You think Victor must die and you want our hands clean. You think he'll try again to kill Papa, if he fails today."

"Your father. You. Me. Your friends in La Flèche. Probably some other folks along the way. He's got a taste for it now. He's not going to stop." When a dog goes bad, it has to be put down. Anybody in sheep country could tell you that.

"I have known Victor all my life. All my cousins, even the most distant ones, are gone. He is the last of the de Fleurignacs." She breathed deeply, painfully. "Family is everything. I will tell him the Garde is coming to arrest him. I will give him a chance to escape." Even as she spoke, she shook her head. "It will not save him. He will not run. You heard what your Paxton said. Fouché was here this morning. It must be that Victor has made some pact between them and changed sides yet again. He will trust Fouché and Fouché will betray him. When Robespierre is arrested, Victor will follow him to the guillotine. We will be his death, you and I."

"If he stays after you warn him, he's made his own death. Some men, even you can't save. Let's go." He turned to Janvier. "Keep the servants away. Don't let her aunt come down, whatever happens."

Janvier's half bow acknowledged authority. "*Oui*, monsieur. Madame Sophie has taken sleeping powders and—"

Maggie stopped. "*Mon Dieu*. Aunt Sophie."

"One thing at a time, love. Let's deal with Victor. Maybe he'll take off for Kiev and save us all some trouble."

The doors to the salon opened smoothly. Maggie walked in beside him. Hawker fell into step behind, soundless, a stoppered bottle of excitement, his hands a twitch away from his knives. Hawker didn't need to be told to protect Maggie. He'd just do it.

Four men waited for them in the salon. Maggie's father was bent over the pianoforte, oblivious, deep in the final chords of the third movement. Victor stood by the hearth, pretending he was in control of the situation, looking as menacing as a man can when he's standing next to a gaggle of china shepherds and woolly lambs. He wasn't carrying any obvious weapons. The two henchmen were off to the side, both armed. The one Maggie had slashed across the face was going to be fairly grotesque even when the scar healed.

That is a man who wants revenge. I'll get rid of him first.

Hawker slipped into place between Maggie and the pistol scarface was bringing up to point. He did it so smoothly, it looked accidental.

Bach wound to a conclusion. Maggie's father set his hands on his knees, shook himself, and took note of what was going on. "What are you doing here, Marguerite? No. Never mind. It's not important. Run and fetch me my swords, girl. I am going to skewer your cousin like a suckling pig."

"We have discussed this, Papa." Ignoring guns, ignoring Victor, she stood over her father and put her hands on her hips. "There will be no more dueling. Why did you come here? Victor is trying to kill us, for heaven's sake."

"I am not," Victor snapped.

She ignored that, too. "You have walked into his hands. Do you have any least vestige of a reason for doing this?"

"I'd be a poor father if I didn't gut him for you. He won't duel, though. My brother's child, and there's no honor in him."

"Of course there is no honor in him. A man of honor does not feed me poison in my evening tea. He does not bring armed men, capable of countless evil deeds, into my salon. He does not let them point pistols at me. He does not . . ." She threw her hands up.

"I rescind my challenge." The old man frowned. "I will hire assassins instead. I have made the acquaintance of several Italians who are suitable."

"De Fleurignacs do not hire assassins. It is not honorable to ask someone to do your killing for you."

The marquis appeared struck by this. "You are right. If Victor will not with duel with me, I will use poisonous reptiles. It should not be difficult to find one. I'll ask Jean-Paul what he recommends."

"You're not going to kill anyone with snakes, Papa. And Jean-Paul will not help you. Besides, I think it would not work. Snakes are unreliable."

Damn, but this is like marrying into the Borgias. He picked up a statue, a bronze Pan. Heavy. Very pastoral. He didn't look at the scarface Jacobin who was edging sideways, trying to get a clear shot at Maggie.

This is risky as hell. I wish she wasn't here.

Behind him, Victor said, "Who is this man you've brought here? Whoever you are, get out. You're meddling with family matters that are none of your concern."

Everybody ignored him. He left his post by the fireplace

and came closer, trying to get a look. "I know you. I've seen you before. Where do I know you from?"

The gun was still pointed at Maggie. *Not yet. Not yet.* Without turning, he said, "I'm Maggie's husband."

"She's not—" Victor straightened. "You're him. Without the scar. You're the prisoner. You're LeBreton." He whirled, shouted and pointed. "Kill him. Kill this one. He's an escaped prisoner. Shoot."

The gun wavered away from Maggie.

Now. He threw the statue. It hit the gun and knocked it aside.

He grabbed a silver box from the table as he lunged by. Brought it down on the Jacobin's face and heard him scream. He grabbed the man's gun hand. Cracked the elbow over his knee and heard it break.

The pistol bounced away on the carpet. The Jacobin's eyes rolled up in his head. Without a sound, he went white and crumpled.

One down.

He let his man slide limp and roll onto the carpet. Hawker had dealt with the other one. The thin melancholy Jacobin had his hands in the air, gun pointed at the ceiling. Hawker's knife pricked his throat.

Maggie scooped the gun up from the floor, fast about it. Not getting in Hawker's way or joggling his knife, she helped herself to the pistol the other man held. She took a place, straight and intent and merciless as a Fury, confronting Victor. The gun in her left hand pointed to the floor. The other was steady and unwavering on her cousin.

"Marguerite, put that down." Victor held his hands up, palms outward, placating. "Be careful. It's loaded."

Maggie didn't turn a hair. She looked good, armed.

She said, "Of course it is loaded. Why would I point a gun at you that isn't loaded?" Her father padded up behind her. "No, Papa, I will not give you a gun. I will keep both of them. If I want him dead, I'll do it myself. I am perfectly capable of pulling a trigger."

Some low complaining from her father.

"Neither of us will kill him. Even animals do not rend their own families. Because he has become a viper, shall we do the same?"

"That's enough. Stop this," Victor said.

Didn't the man see Maggie's face? He might as well have been arguing with a fire.

Slowly, Maggie took one step and then another toward her cousin. "What am I to do with you? Even when the world becomes sane again, you will not. You will always be malignant."

"You bring this brigand into my home to attack my men. You hold a gun pointed at me. You're as mad as your father. I'm the one who's saved this family, year after year. I am the de Fleurignac heir. I am—"

"It's over, Victor." Distaste, sadness, and anger warred in her voice. "I have asked myself why you did this. Maybe you were afraid. You feared for you life at the hands of your revolutionary friends. Maybe it was greed for the inheritance." She shook her head. "It doesn't matter. You will never get close to us again, Victor. Not to Papa. Not to me. It is the end between us. You will leave, now, and you will not come back to the house again."

"You are so sure of yourself. I wouldn't be." Behind a tight mask of rage, Victor was thinking about killing them. Planning how and in what order. How he'd get away with it.

Armed men rattle and clank when they walk. A small troop was coming up Rue Palmier, getting closer. Pax had done his work.

Doyle said, "Maggie, we have company."

She'd heard it, too. "We have sent for the Garde, you

know. You have time to get away, if you leave now. Take the back way out, through the kitchen. I will delay them."

"They won't arrest me. I'm a friend of Robes—" Victor realized that wasn't going to work. "I am a friend of Fouché."

"Fouché is nobody's friend. Run, Victor." Even now, she'd save the bastard if she could. "If you stay, the laws you have made will eat you up. Hide in the country. In a few months they'll forget you. Everyone is sick of bloodshed."

"I have nothing to be afraid of." A muscle twitched at the corner of Victor's eye. "Fouché promised I won't be arrested."

You're about to find out. The Jacobin on the floor was down with his arm broken and a cracked head. He wouldn't be a problem. The other one hadn't hurt anybody that he knew of.

He caught Hawker's eye. "Let that one go." Hawker lowered his knife. The man took one quick look around the salon and scuttled for the door. His feet clattered out the back way, taking the escape Victor had refused.

One less to keep an eye on. "Your man has more sense than you do."

Victor was tempted. Then he set his shoulders back and decided to be a fool. "You're the ones who should run. A madman . . . an escaped prisoner of the Republic." He gave Maggie a contemptuous smile. "And a bored noblewoman who dabbles in counter-revolution. A leader of La Flèche. If they arrest me, I will trade you for my freedom. I can name a dozen enemies of the Republic, starting with the servants in this house. The gardener's son, Jean-Paul. I know all of you. I have you in the palm of my hand."

"You have a froth of conjecture." Maggie held the gun steady. "The men who have come to the door will not be impressed. It is your last chance."

"It's too late anyway." Doyle came to stand beside her. "They're on the doorstep. Give me those pistols. I don't want to have to explain them to the military."

She let him take them. He knocked the powder out of the pan, onto the floor, as he walked across the room. He dropped both guns inside the pianoforte and closed the lid. He didn't pay attention to Maggie's father saying what that did to the strings.

In the foyer, Janvier's image crossed the tall mirrors to answer the knocking at the front door.

One more piece of business to take care of. Victor was right about one thing. He could still spit venom. Doyle stepped around the Jacobin on the floor. "I've been looking forward to talking to you, Victor, when I wasn't tied up."

Victor edged sideways. "They have come for you, Guillaume LeBreton. Not for me. Your name, your description, is all over Paris. I saw to that."

"But they're looking for a man with a scar." He took another step closer. "Like this fellow on the floor. Not me."

"You'll see. You will discover who they listen to. A hulking bandit or—Keep away from me." Victor sprinted sideways. Grabbed Maggie from behind. Wrapped his arm around her throat. A little blade appeared suddenly in his hand. He brought it up under her breast, sticking it in so the cloth parted. Pointed it to her heart.

"Don't." Doyle snapped the order before Hawker could throw. "Leave him to me."

I'm going to get his blood on Maggie. Damn. I didn't want her to see this. He drew his knife.

Maggie twisted inside the arm that held her. She reached up and behind and found Victor's face and raked at his eye.

Victor screamed. She jerked free and swirled back, out of danger.

"Nice work." That was beautifully done. Smooth as silk. He'd taught her exactly that move, and she did him proud.

"Thank you. I am not a cat one grabs by the scruff of the neck," she said.

Victor was sobbing. "Took my eye out. She took my eye out. She's killed me. My eye. I'm bleeding. I'm—"

"Your eye is fine. The rest of you, though . . ." He punched, short and fast, into Victor's belly. Victor's words cut off in a shriek.

He said, softly, so only Victor heard him, "That's for taking a club to me when I was tied up." He knocked Victor's elegant little dagger out of reach on the floor.

At the street door, men demanded Citoyen Victor de Fleurignac. "He is one of the followers of the tyrant Robespierre. He is to be arrested." When Janvier protested, he was answered, "It is the order of the Convention."

Plenty of time to finish this. He hit Victor with his left, into the ribs. Holding back, because this was a flimsy small fellow. "That's for sending assassins after an old man."

Victor gurgled.

"I don't think anyone's in the mood to listen to you today. But just to make sure . . ." Precisely, scientifically, he struck upward and broke the man's jaw.

Victor swayed against the wall.

"That one was for sending soldiers to arrest a woman with a baby." He set one hand in the other and rubbed his knuckles. "But this one . . . This is for Maggie."

He snapped his knee up fast, hard into the bastard's crotch. Then he turned away and let the pig fall where he would.

At the front door Janvier said, "Victor de Fleurignac is in the salon. I will take you to him."

Fifty-one

MARGUERITE LEFT THE HÔTEL DE FLEURIGNAC, walking beside Guillaume in the Paris dawn, trailed by a pair of donkeys and Adrian. It was a familiar feeling.

Much had changed. Guillaume did not wear his scar today, continuing to disguise himself as himself. The lack of a scar made him look dull and honest, which was misleading, to say the least.

The Garde Nationale would take no interest in missing prisoners today, not when the great Robespierre himself was so newly dead and no one sure who would be ruling France next week. Still, it was unwise to match too closely the description of an escaped prisoner. One does not thumb one's nose at Fate.

Of Victor, she had no news whatsoever. The prisons had swallowed him and all was in confusion there. As far as she was concerned, he could continue to live.

Guillaume traveled as a Breton merchant, she as his wife, returning home from settling some business in Rheims. They had packed to portray a dull and solid respectability.

Guillaume told her to bring only her most plain and ordinary shifts and stockings and stays. He would buy her new, indecent ones in England, he said.

Her name was Martine, this time, for this trip. She preferred that to Suzette.

Hawker checked the straps on Dulce, who was eating a carrot and pretending to be the most docile creature in creation. "You'll clean up the mess in England." He didn't look at Guillaume. "You have the names now."

"Just a matter of time," Guillaume said. "We'll find our assassins. I'll pass along your regards to Lazarus. If he hasn't killed anybody, he's of no interest to us."

"I don't think he's killed anybody on that list." There were more straps for him to go over, pulling on each one and tucking it tight. The donkeys carried a pair of valises, one on each side, and a complicated set of bags tied on top of that. Lots of straps. "I wouldn't go so far as to promise he hasn't killed anybody at all."

"He won't come looking for you in France. You don't belong to him anymore."

"Right." Hawker sounded skeptical. The last adjustments to the packs were firm and brisk. "Bread and wine, cheese. You can buy more when you're out in the countryside and the food gets better." He turned and grinned suddenly. "I don't have to tell you that."

"No," Guillaume said calmly. "But I don't mind. You coming with us partway?"

"As far as the *barrière*. Just seeing you off. Then it's back to tell Citoyenne Cachard you're safe on your way." His voice was a shade too casual as he added, "She has work for me."

Hawker clucked the donkeys into motion. It could not be said he strutted, but he was very pleased with himself. He wore knee breeches and a striped vest and a shirt of smooth, close-woven linen. Better clothing than Guillaume. When someone saw them on the street, Hawker would look like the son of some rich merchant house, walking with the family steward.

The fine clothes, oddly, made Hawker look younger. Close to his true age. They did not succeed in making him look like a schoolboy, though. A magic cloak gifted to him by the Queen of the Fairies would not make Hawker look like a schoolboy.

"Let's hope they don't change governments again before I get you out of the city." Guillaume studied the street behind them, looked down the Rue de Laval, ahead. To a suspicious mind, the quiet itself must seem vaguely ominous.

The city waited. Violent men woke to the promise of a hot day and tried to decide whether it was worth rioting in such heat. Delegates to the Convention poured their morning chocolate and gave thanks they had not yet perished on the guillotine. Officers of the Garde Nationale pondered the difficulty of keeping order in the city without inadvertently arresting the men who might be in power tomorrow.

And Robespierre was dead.

No tumbrels rolled to the guillotine. The nuns and priest at the Convent of Saint-Barthélémy were safe. Even Victor would escape death if nobody noticed him.

It was a good day to leave Paris. The *barrières* would be lightly manned and the guards uncertain and distracted.

Guillaume tilted his new hat back on his head. It was very much in the style of his old one but less decrepit. Hawker paused at the corner to metaphorically sniff the air. He was the first to see Justine. She sat on the steps of a house, the child, Séverine, in her arms. She lifted her chin as they approached.

"Good day to you, citoyens. It is a pleasant day to be walking free under the sun, is it not?"

"Very," Guillaume said amiably. "You're waiting for us?"

"For Marguerite, though this is a matter of interest to you as well."

It would be a matter of some importance. When the city might explode into riot at any minute, Justine would not stroll about in the dawn to wave good-bye. She would not bring the child.

Séverine lay, sleepy-eyed, in Justine's lap, wrapped tight in her arms. She wore a dress of printed cotton. Justine, in dark serge, could have been a nursemaid looking after her mistress's daughter.

Séverine stood up on her sister's lap. "Justine said you would tell me stories."

"Perhaps one." If there was time. If Justine walked along beside them for a while.

"She likes you," Justine said abruptly. "She is very smart, you know. She can already read a little. And I have spoken to her in English since she was very small. She speaks it somewhat. Also some German, though my own accent is not good."

"She's a lovely child."

"She is, isn't she?" She had never seen Justine tentative or unsure. She was now. "She has never been sick. Not once, since she was little. No matter where we lived or what we had to eat, she was . . . oh, strong and happy and uncomplaining and so good."

"I could tell that. She climbed into the loft the first day I was there, feeling so ill. I was comforted by her."

Justine stroked her sister's hair and then lifted her up. Held her out to be taken. "She sings beautifully. No one has ever taught her, but she does it anyway."

Séverine smelled sweetly of lavender and fresh starch and raspberry jam. *This is a gentle moment to take away with me, holding this child.*

Justine folded her empty arms. "You were right. A

whorehouse is no home for a child. France is no place for her. A war is coming."

"I fear you are correct."

Justine's eyes were resolute. "I told you I would ask a favor of you. In return for," she became lightly derisive as she flashed her eyes toward Guillaume, "this one's life. I have spared it several times and helped you save it once. You recall?"

She said, "Yes. Of course."

Guillaume said nothing. He watched Justine.

"That is what I ask in return for the debt. You will take Séverine as your own. You will take her away from France and keep her in safety. You will watch over her. You, yourself."

Yes! And then, *No. It cannot be right to do this.* She fitted Séverine to her. The child was heavy and solid. Precisely right.

"She will be no trouble on the road." Justine spoke quickly. "She has learned to be quiet. She will go with you willingly when I tell her she must. She knows to say nothing at all and to answer to any name she is given. You can leave her to wait for you in any place, and she will wait. Wait a day or more, if necessary. She—"

Guillaume said, "You're giving your sister to us?"

"I give her to Marguerite," Justine said tartly. "Though I suppose that means I give her to you as well."

"It does indeed. If we take Séverine—"

"You must." Impatient now, Justine reached for the brown leather bag at the side of these stairs. "You may call her something else." A shadow of a smile. "Something English."

"She has a name. I'm not going to take it from her." Guillaume rasped fingernails on his chin. "This is what you want for taking Maggie to safety when she was sick and needed you?"

Justine bowed her head, once, sharply. Perhaps she didn't trust herself to speak.

"Maggie. What do you say?"

"Yes." *The child needs me. They both do. I would save them both if I could.* "Oh, yes."

"Then we do it." Deliberately, Guillaume put his hand on the child's head. "Séverine is mine. I'll treat her no differently than a child of my blood, born in wedlock. I'll set her welfare before my own life." He looked directly at Justine. "I'll love her as a father. You have my word."

Justine's lips worked. Perhaps it was only now becoming real for her.

"If you come in a few years and want to take her back, expect a fight. I don't part with my daughter easily." He took his hand away. "Is that what you want?"

Justine's eyes were bright and sad and . . . hard. Full of tears and determination. "Yes."

This should not be. "How can I take your sister and leave you behind? Do you think I wouldn't welcome you? Come with us."

"Maggie . . . no. She can't." Guillaume touched her arm. "She's Secret Police."

"What?"

"Best explanation."

"But . . . But . . ." It did not make sense. "She is Owl. She's of La Flèche. She is—"

"She's one more reason Jean-Paul has to close down that whole damned leaky organization. It's served its purpose. I told him that."

Secret Police? Justine's face, by its blankness, said Guillaume was right.

Guillaume said softly, "Maggie, when she gives the child to me, it means no one will ever use Séverine against her. No one on either side will ever touch her. That's what we're doing for her."

Justine nodded. Her face did not look young at all.

There is unending cruelty in the world. I will not let it destroy this little one. "Séverine is my daughter, flesh of my flesh. As if I had carried her within my own body. I swear it."

She felt the words resonate inside the child she held. Séverine would remember this someday.

Quickly, Justine turned away to add a valise to the others on the donkey's back. "I have packed clothing for her. Things she will need." She studied valises and bags resolutely. "Her . . . doll."

"Some people," Hawker said, "wouldn't leave this to the last minute." He rearranged this and that on Dulce and rolled a blanket to make a riding nest to fit a small child. "She's going to make them conspicuous."

"What is more inconspicuous than a child? Would anyone suspect a family traveling across the countryside with a small child? No and no. Everyone should take an infant or two with them upon their missions. She is a better companion than you, in fact, because she has been trained to keep her mouth closed and follow orders, which you have not."

"I follow orders. It's that hair of hers. Might as well attach a red flag. That has to . . . Here." Hawker unwound a leather thong from one of the bags and held it in his teeth and went to Séverine. Skillfully, he plaited a thick braid and tied it with leather. "That's better." He frowned at the effect. "She's dressed too well. You should dirty her up. Put some mud on her."

"I am pleased to know she will not be in your hands, Citoyen Hawker." Justine's touch was light on the child's back. One touch, very quick. "I have already said my good-bye to her. She will be a good child. She cannot—" The pause came while she was turned away from them. "She cannot eat strawberries. They make her turn red with blotches."

"I will not feed her strawberries." She tried to fit all the other things that needed to be said inside the words.

Justine had already taken the first steps away when Guillaume said, "One last thing."

She turned back. "What?"

"What is her true name? All her name. The name of your parents?" When there was no immediate answer, he said, "Don't plan to tell her later. You know what's coming in France. You may not live."

No answer.

"It'll stay with the five of us. You. Me. Hawker. Maggie. The child herself, if she remembers." He waited. "Don't leave her wondering for her whole life."

Justine's voice was hollow as an echo. "Her parents were the Comte and Comtesse de Cabrillac. They died in the courtyard of the Abbaye Prison two years ago. She doesn't remember seeing it. So far as I know, no one of our family on either side remains."

"Only you."

"Only me. Tell her, someday, that I did not abandon her. When she's old enough, tell her I will wade the rivers of hell to come to her if she should ever have need." That quickly, she was gone, walking down the street with the careful, unobtrusive stride of the experienced agent, her head high.

"Well, damn," Hawker said.

Guillaume took his hat off to watch her go. "I made the promise for you, Hawk. That information doesn't go beyond your lips. Not to anyone."

"Not to Cachard?"

"Not even there. That's an order. Congratulations. You have your first secret."

Hawker said, "I have lots of secrets. Why don't we go before all Paris wakes up? The idea was to get you out the gates at first light." He looked toward Maggie. "She's heavy. You want to set the girl here on Dulce?"

"No need." Guillaume reached out. "I'll carry her."

A small hesitation. Then Séverine's arms wrapped around him.

She walked beside Guillaume. Séverine, pressed against his chest, stared out at her gravely. This was the foundation of the home she would build. Guillaume's strength. His kindness. Even a young child knew, without doubt.

Very low, she began, "Do you know . . . in the city of Paris there are magic birds? You can see them in the trees sometimes, just for a moment, if you look quickly." She looked up as she spoke, at the trees. "They are red as rubies and green as emeralds. Some are golden. The golden ones are the smallest. They are the bravest and most wise."

There was a little stir. Séverine said, "Golden?"

"They are the gold that is found in streams in the far country of Armenia where water has washed over the river gold for years upon years. A gold as soft as the warmth of a fire. That is the gold of those birds' feathers."

She took up the thick, gold-brown braid that curled down Séverine's back and tucked it in front of her, against Guillaume's waistcoat. "Now, it happened that one of these magic birds, a young girl bird, was chosen to make a long journey. It was an important journey, and she was a little worried . . ."

Keep reading for a glittering excerpt
from Book Two in the Spymaster series
by Joanna Bourne

The Spymaster's Lady

Available now from Headline Eternal

One

SHE WAS WILLING TO DIE, OF COURSE, BUT SHE HAD not planned to do it so soon, or in such a prolonged and uncomfortable fashion, or at the hands of her own countrymen.

She slumped against the wall, which was of cut stone and immensely solid, as prison walls often are. "I do not have the plans. I never had them."

"I am not a patient man. Where are the plans?"

"I do not have—"

The openhanded slap whipped out of the darkness. For one instant she slipped over the edge of consciousness. Then she was back again, in the dark and in pain, with Leblanc.

"Just so." He touched her cheek where he had hit her and turned her toward him. He did it gently. He had much practice in hurting women. "We continue. This time you will be more helpful."

"Please. I am trying."

"You will tell me where you have hidden the plans, Annique."

"They are a mad dream, these Albion plans. A chimera. I never saw them." Even as she said it, the Albion plans were clear in her mind. She had held the many pages in her hands, the dog-eared edges, maps covered with smudges and fingerprints, the lists in small, neat writing. *I will not think of this. If I remember, it will show on my face.*

"Vauban gave you the plans in Bruges. What did he tell you to do with them?"

He told me to take them to England. "Why would he give me plans? I am not a valise to go carrying papers about the countryside."

His fist closed on her throat. Pain exploded. Pain that stopped her breath. She dug her fingers into the wall and held on. With such a useful stone wall to hold on to, she would not fall down.

Leblanc released her. "Let us begin again, at Bruges. You were there. You admit that."

"I was there. Yes. I reported to Vauban. I was a pair of eyes watching the British. Nothing more. I have told you and told you." The fingers on her chin tightened. A new pain.

"Vauban left Bruges empty-handed. He went back to Paris without the plans. He must have given them to you. Vauban trusted you."

He trusted me with treason. She wouldn't think that. Wouldn't remember.

Her voice had gone hoarse a long time ago. "The papers never came to us. Never." She tried to swallow, but her throat was too dry. "You hold my life in your hands, sir. If I had the Albion plans, I would lay them at your feet to buy it back."

Leblanc swore softly, cursing her. Cursing Vauban, who was far away and safe. "The old man didn't hide them. He was too carefully watched. What happened to them?"

"Look to your own associates. Or maybe the British took them. I never saw them. I swear it."

Leblanc nudged her chin upward. "You swear? Little Cub, I have watched you lie and lie with that angel face since you were a child. Do not attempt to lie to me."

"I would not dare. I have served you well. Do you think I'm such a fool I've stopped being afraid of you?" She let tears brim into her eyes. It was a most useful skill and one she had practiced assiduously.

"Almost, one might believe you."

He plays with me. She squeezed her lids and let tears slide in cold tracks down her cheeks.

"Almost." He slowly scratched a line upon her cheek with his thumbnail, following a tear. "But, alas, not quite. You will be more honest before morning, I think."

"I am honest to you now."

"Perhaps. We will discuss this at length when my guests have departed. Did you know? Fouché comes to my little soiree tonight. A great honor. He comes to me from meetings with Bonaparte. He comes directly to me, to speak of what the First Consul has said. I am becoming the great man in Paris these days."

What would I say if I were innocent? "Take me to Fouché. He will believe me."

"You will see Fouché when I am satisfied your pretty little mouth is speaking the truth. Until then . . ." He reached to the nape of her neck to loosen her dress, pulling the first tie free. "You will make yourself agreeable, eh? I have heard you can be most amusing."

"I will . . . try to please you." *I will survive this. I can survive whatever he does to me.*

"You will try very, very hard before I am finished with you."

"Please." He wanted to see fear. She would grovel at once, as was politic. "Please. I will do what you want, but not here. Not in a dirty cell with men watching. I hear them breathing. Do not make me do this in front of them."

"It is only the English dogs. I kennel some spies here till I dispose of them." His fingers hooked the rough material of her dress at the bodice and pulled it down, uncovering her. "Perhaps I like them to watch."

She breathed in the air he had used, hot and moist, smelling of wintergreen. His hand crawled inside the bodice of her dress to take hold of her breast. His fingers were smooth and dry, like dead sticks, and he hurt her again and again.

She would not be sick upon Leblanc in his evening clothes. This was no time for her stomach to decide to be sincere.

She pressed against the wall at her back and tried to become nothing. She was darkness. Emptiness. She did not exist at all. It did not work, of course, but it was a goal to fix the mind upon.

At last, he stopped. "I will enjoy using you."

She did not try to speak. There was no earthly use in doing so.

He hurt her one final time, pinching her mouth between thumb and forefinger, breaking the skin of her dry lips and leaving a taste of blood.

"You have not amused me yet." He released her abruptly. She heard the scrape and click as he lifted his lantern from the table. "But you will."

The door clanged shut behind him. His footsteps faded in the corridor, going toward the stairs and upward.

"PIG." She whispered it to the closed door, though that was an insult to pigs, who were, in general, amiable.

She could hear the other prisoners, the English spies, making small sounds on the other side of the cell, but it was dark, and they could no longer see her. She scrubbed her mouth with the back of her hand and swallowed the sick bile in her throat. It was amazingly filthy being touched by Leblanc. It was like being crawled upon by slugs. She did not think she would become even slightly accustomed to it in the days she had left.

She pulled her dress into decency and let herself fold onto the dirt floor, feeling miserable. This was the end then. The choice that had tormented her for so long— what should be done with the Albion plans that had been entrusted to her—was made. All her logic and reasoning, all her searchings of the heart, had come to nothing. Leblanc had won. She would withstand his persuasions for only a day or two. Then he would wrest the Albion plans from her memory and commit God knew what greedy betrayals with them.

Her old mentor Vauban would be disappointed in her when he heard. He waited in his small stone house in Normandy for her to send word. He had left the decision to her, what should be done with the plans, but he had not intended that she give them to Leblanc. She had failed him. She had failed everyone.

She took a deep breath and let it out slowly. It was strange to know her remaining breaths were numbered in some tens of thousands. Forty thousand? Fifty? Perhaps when she was in unbearable pain later on tonight, she would start counting.

She pulled her shoes off, one and then the other. She had been in prisons twice before in her life, both times completely harrowing. At least she had been above ground then, and she had been able to see. Maman had been with her, that first time. Now Maman was dead in a stupid accident that should not have killed a dog. *Maman, Maman, how I miss you.* There was no one in this world to help her.

In the darkness, one feels very alone. She had never become used to this.

The English spy spoke, deep and slow, out of the dark.

"I would stand and greet you politely." Chain clinked. "But I'm forced to be rude."

It was a measure of how lonely she was that the voice of an enemy English came like a warm handclasp. "There is much of that in my life lately. Rudeness."

"It seems you have annoyed Leblanc." He spoke the rich French of the South, without the least trace of a foreign accent.

"You also, it would seem."

"He doesn't plan to let any of us leave here alive."

"That is most likely." She rolled off her stockings, tucked them into her sleeve so she would not lose them, and slipped the shoes back on. One cannot go barefoot. Even in the anteroom to hell, one must be practical.

"Shall we prove him wrong, you and I?"

He did not sound resigned to death, which was admirable in its way, though not very realistic. It was an altogether English way of seeing things.

In the face of such bravery, she could not sit upon the floor and wail. French honor demanded a Frenchwoman meet death as courageously as any English. French honor always seemed to be demanding things of her. Bravery, of a sort, was a coin she was used to counterfeiting. Besides, the plan she was weaving might work. She might overcome Leblanc and escape the chateau and deal with these Albion plans that were the cause of so much trouble to her. And assuredly pigs might grow wings and fly around steeples all over town.

The English was waiting for an answer. She pulled herself to her feet. "I would be delighted to disappoint Leblanc in any way. Do you know where we are? I was not able to tell when I was brought here, but I hope very much this is the chateau in Garches."

"A strange thing to hope, but yes, this is Garches, the house of the Secret Police."

"Good, then. I know this place."

"That will prove useful. After we deal with these chains," he clinked metallically, "and that locked door. We can help each other."

He made many assumptions. "There is always the possibility."

"We can be allies." The spy chose his words carefully, hoping to charm her so she would be a tool for him. He slipped velvet upon his voice. Underneath, though, she heard an uncompromising sternness and great anger. There was nothing she did not know about such hard, calculating men.

Leblanc took much upon himself to capture British agents in this way. It was an old custom of both French and British secret services that they were not bloodthirsty with one another's agents. This was one of many rules Leblanc broke nowadays.

She worked her way along the wall, picking at the rocks, stealing the gravel that had come loose in the cracks and putting it into her stocking to make her little cosh. It was a weapon easy to use when one could not see. One of her great favorites.

There was a whisper of movement. A younger voice, very weak, spoke. "Somebody's here."

Her English spy answered, "Just a girl Leblanc brought in. Nothing to worry about."

". . . more questions?"

"Not yet. It's late at night. We have hours before they come for us. Hours."

"Good. I'll be ready . . . when the chance comes."

"It'll be soon now, Adrian. We'll get free. Wait."

The mindless optimism of the English. Who could comprehend it? Had not her own mother told her they were all mad?

It was a tidy small prison Leblanc kept. So few loose stones. It took a while before the cosh was heavy enough. She tied the end of the stocking and tucked it into the pocket hidden beneath her skirt. Then she continued to explore the walls, finding nothing at all interesting. There is not so much to discover about rooms that are used as prisons. This one had been a wine cellar before the Revolution. It still smelled of old wood and good wine as well as less wholesome things. Halfway around the cell she came to where the Englishmen were chained, so she stopped to let her hands have a look at them as well.

The one who lay upon the ground was young, younger than she was. Seventeen? Eighteen? He had the body of an acrobat, one of those slight, tightly constructed people. He had been wounded. She could smell the gunpowder on his clothes and the wound going bad. She would wager money there was metal still inside him. When she ran her fingers across his face, his lips were dry and cracked, and he was burning hot. High fever.

They had chained him to the wall with an excellent chain, but a large, old-fashioned padlock. That would have to be picked if they were to escape. She searched his boots and the seams of his clothing, just in case Leblanc's men had missed some small, useful object. There was nothing at all, naturally, but one must always check.

"Nice . . ." he murmured when she ran her hands over him. "Later, sweetheart. Too tired . . ." Not so young a boy then. He spoke in English. There might be an innocent reason for an English to be in France, in these days when their countries were not exactly at war, but somehow she was sure Leblanc spoke truly. This was a spy. "So tired." Then he said clearly, "Tell Lazarus I won't do that anymore. Never. Tell him."

"We shall speak of it," she said softly, "later," which was a promise hard to fulfill, since she did not expect to have so very many laters. Though perhaps a few more than this boy.

He struggled to sit up. "Queen's Knight Three. I have to go. They're waiting for me to deliver the Red Knight."

He was speaking what he should not, almost certainly, and he would injure himself, thrashing about. She pushed him gently back down.

Strong arms intervened. "Quiet. That's all done." The other man held the boy, muffling his words.

He need not have worried. She was no longer interested in such secrets. In truth, she would as soon not learn them.

"Tell the others."

"I will. Everyone got away safe. Rest now."

The boy had knocked over the water jug, struggling. Her hands found it, rolled on its side, empty. It was perfectly dry inside. The thought of water stabbed sour pinpricks in her mouth. She was so thirsty.

Nothing is worse than thirst. Not hunger. Not even pain. Maybe it was as well there was no water to tempt her. Perhaps she would have become an animal and stolen from these men, who suffered more than she did. It was better not to know how low she could have fallen. "When was the last time they gave you water?"

"Two days ago."

"You have not much longer to wait, then. Leblanc will keep me alive for a while, in the hopes I may be useful to him. And to play with." *In the end, he will kill me. Even when I give him the Albion plans—every word, every map, every list—he will still kill me. I know what he did in Bruges. He cannot let me live.*

"His habits are known."

He was large, the English spy of the deep voice and iron sternness. She sensed a huge presence even before she touched him. Her hands brought her more details. The big man had folded his coat under the boy, accepting another measure of discomfort to keep his friend off the cold floor. It was a very British courage, that small act. She felt his fierce, protective concentration surrounding the boy, as if force of will alone were enough to hold life in him. It would be a brave man indeed who dared to die when this man had forbidden it.

She reached tentatively and discovered soft linen and long, sinewy courses of muscle down his chest and then, where his shirt lay open at the neck, a disconcerting resilience of masculine skin. She would have pulled away, but his hand came to cover hers, pressing it down over his heart. She felt the beat under her palm, startling and alive. Such power and strength.

He said, "I know what Leblanc does to women. I'm sorry you've fallen into his hands. Believe that."

"Me, I am also extremely sorry." This one was determined to be nice to her, was he not? She took her hand back. She would free him, if she could, and then they would see exactly how delightful he was. "These locks," she jiggled his manacle, "are very clumsy. One twiddle, and I could get them off. You do not have a small length of wire about you, do you?"

She could hear the smile in his voice. "What do you think?"

"I do not expect it to be so simple. Life is not, in my experience."

"Mine also. Did Leblanc hurt you?"

"Not so much."

He touched her throat where she was sore and bruised. "No woman should fall into Leblanc's hands. We'll get out of here. There's some way out. We'll find it." He gripped her shoulder, heavy and reassuring.

She should get up and search the cell. But somehow she found herself just sitting next to him, resting. Her breath trickled out of her. Some of the fear that had companioned her for weeks drained away, too. How long had it been since anyone had offered her comfort? How strange to find it here, in this fearful place, at the hands of an enemy.

After what seemed a long time, she roused herself.

"There is another problem. Your friend cannot walk from here, even if I get him free of the chain."

"He'll make it. Better men than Leblanc have tried to kill him." Not everyone would have heard the anguish beneath the surface of that voice, but she did. They both knew this Adrian was dying. In a dozen hours, in at most another day, his wound and thirst and the damp chill of the stones would finish him off.

The boy spoke up in a thin thread of polished Gascon French. "It is . . . one small bullet hole. A nothing." He was very weak, very gallant. "It's the . . . infernal boredom . . . I can't stand."

"If we only had a deck of cards," the big man said.

"I'll bring some . . . next time."

They would have made good Frenchmen, these two. It was a pity Leblanc would soon take her from this cell. One could find worse companions for the long journey into the dark. At least the two of them would be together when they died. She would be wholly alone.

But it was better not to speculate upon how Leblanc would break her to his will and kill her, which could only lead to melancholy. It was time to slide from beneath the touch of this English spy and be busy again. She could not sit forever, hoping courage would seep out of his skin and into her.

She stood, and immediately felt cold. It was as if she had left a warm and accustomed shelter when she left the man's side. That was most silly. This was no shelter, and he did not like her much despite the soft voice he used. What lay between them was an untrusting vigilance one might have carved slices of.

Perhaps he knew who she was. Or perhaps he was one of those earnest men who go about spying in total seriousness. He would die for his country in a straightforward English fashion in this musty place and hate her because she was French. To see the world so simply was undoubtedly an English trait.

So be it. As it happened, she was not an amicable friend of big English spies. A French trait, doubtless.

She shrugged, which he would not see, and began working her way around the rest of the cell, inspecting the floor and every inch of the wall as high as she could reach. "In your time here, has Henri Bréval visited the cell?"

"He came twice with Leblanc, once alone, asking questions."

"He has the key? He himself? That is good then."

"You think so?"

"I have some hopes of Henri." There was not a rusted nail, not a shard of glass. There was nothing useful anywhere. She must place her hope in Henri's stupidity, which was nearly limitless. "If Fouché is indeed upstairs drinking wine and playing cards, Leblanc will not leave his side. One does not neglect the head of the Secret Police to disport oneself with a woman. But Henri, who takes note of him? He may seize the moment. He wishes to use me, you understand, and he has had no chance yet."

"I see." They were most noncommittal words.

Was it possible he believed she would welcome Henri? What dreadful taste he thought she had. "Leblanc does not let many people know about this room. It is very secret what he does here."

"So Henri may come sneaking down alone. You plan to take him." He said it calmly, as if it were not remarkable that she should attack a man like Henri Bréval. She was almost certain he knew what she was.

"I can't help you," the chain that bound him rattled, "unless you get him close."

"Henri is not so stupid. Not quite. But I have a small plan."

"Then all I can do is wish you well."

He seemed a man with an excellent grasp of essentials. He would be useful to her if she could get his chains off. That she would accomplish once those pigs became like the proverb and grew wings and went flying.

Exploring the cell further, she stubbed her toe upon a table, empty of even a spoon. There were also chairs, which presented more opportunity. She was working at the pegs that held a chair together when she heard footsteps.

"We have a visitor," the big English said.

"I hear." One man descended the steps into the cellar. Henri. It must be Henri. She set the chair upright, out of her way, and drew her cosh into her hand and turned toward the sound of footsteps. A shudder ran along her spine, but it was only the cold of the room. It was not fear. She could not afford to be afraid. "It is one man. Alone."

"Leblanc or Henri, do you think?"

"It is Henri. He walks more heavily. Now you will shut up quietly and not distract me." She prayed it was Henri. Not Leblanc. She had no chance against Leblanc.

The Englishman was perfectly still, but he charged the air with a hungry, controlled rage. It was as if she had a wolf chained to that wall behind her. His presence tugged and tugged at her attention when it was desperately important to keep her mind on Henri.

Henri. She licked her lips and grimly concentrated on Henri, an unpleasant subject, but one of great immediacy. There were twenty steps on the small curved staircase that led from kitchen to cellar. She counted the last of them, footstep by footstep. Then he was in the corridor that led to the cell.

Henri had always thought her reputation inflated. When he had brought her the long way to Paris to turn her over to Leblanc, she had played the spineless fool for him, begging humbly for food and water, stumbling, making him feel powerful. She was so diminished in her darkness he thought her completely harmless. He had become contemptuous.

Let him come just a little close, and he would discover how harmless she was. Most surely he would.

She knew the honey to trap him. She would portray for him the Silly Young Harlot. It was an old favorite role of hers. She had acted it a hundred times.

She licked her lips and let them pout, open and loose. What else? She pulled strands of hair down around her face. Her dress was already torn at the neckline. She found the spot and ripped the tear wider. Good. He would see only that bare skin. She could hold a dozen coshes and he would never notice.

Quickly. Quickly. He was coming closer. She took another deep breath and let the role close around her like a familiar garment. She became the Harlot. Yielding, easy to daunt, out of her depth in this game of intrigue and lies. Henri liked victims. She would set the most perfect victim before him and hope he took the bait.

Hid beneath layer upon layer of soft and foolish Harlot, she waited. Her fist, holding the cosh, never wavered. She would not allow herself to be afraid. It was another role she had crafted; the Brave Spy. She had played this one so long it fit like her skin.

Probably, at the center of her being, under all the pretense, the real Annique was a quivering mouse. She would not go prying in there and find out.

THE grilled window in the door glowed ghostly pale, then brightened as a lantern came closer. Grey could see again. The details of his cell emerged. Rough blocks of stone, a table, two chairs. And the girl.

She faced the door, stiff and silent and totally intent upon the man out in the corridor. Not a move out of her. Not the twitch of a fingernail. Her eyes, set in deep smudges of exhaustion, were half-closed and unfocused. She didn't once glance in his direction.

He watched her draw a deep breath, never taking her attention from that small barred window in the door. Her lips shaped words silently, praying or talking to herself. Maybe cursing. Again, she combed her fingers through her hair in staccato, purposeful, elegant flicks that left wild elflocks hanging across her face.

She was totally feminine in every movement, indefinably French. With her coloring—black hair, pale skin, eyes of that dark indigo blue—she had to be pure Celt. She'd be from the west of France. Brittany, maybe. Annique was a Breton name. She carried the magic of the Celt in her, used it to weave that fascination the great courtesans created. Even as he watched, she licked her lips again and wriggled deliberately, sensually. A man couldn't look away.

She'd torn her own dress. The curve of her breast showed white against the dark fabric—a whore, bringing out her wares. She was a whore, a liar, and a killer . . . and his life depended on her. "Good luck," he whispered.

She didn't turn. She gave one quick, dismissive shake of her head. "Be still. You are not part of this."

That was the final twist of the knife. He was helpless. He measured out his twenty inches of chain, picturing just how far a fast kick could reach. But Henri wasn't going to wander that close. She'd have to subdue Henri Bréval on her own, without even a toothpick to fight with.

There were red marks on her skin where Leblanc had been tormenting her and the tracks of tears on her cheeks. She couldn't have looked more harmless. That was another lie, of course.

He knew this woman. He'd recognized her the moment

Leblanc pushed her stumbling into this cell. Feature by feature, that face was etched in his memory. He'd seen her the day he found his men, ambushed, twisted and bloody, dead in a cornfield near Bruges. If he'd had any doubt, the mention of the Albion plans would have convinced him. The Albion plans had been used to lure them to Bruges.

He'd been tracking this spy across Europe for the last six months. What bloody irony to meet her here.

He'd have his revenge. Leblanc was an artist in human degradation. Pretty Annique wouldn't die easily or cleanly or with any of that beauty intact. His men would be avenged.

If he got out of here . . . No, *when* he got out of here, Annique would come with him. He'd take her to England. He'd find out every damn thing she knew about what happened at Bruges. He'd get the Albion plans from her. Then he'd take his own vengeance.

She'd be supremely useful to British intelligence. Besides, he wouldn't leave a rabid hyena to Leblanc.

The peephole went bright as Henri held the lantern up. His heavy, florid face pressed to the grill. "Leblanc is furious with you."

"Please." The girl wilted visibly, leaning on the table for support, a sweet, succulent curve of entrapped femininity. "Oh, please." The drab blue of her dress and the crude cut of the garment marked her as a servant and accessible. Somehow her disheveled hair, falling forward over her face, had become sensuality itself. "This is all a mistake. A mistake. I swear . . ."

Henri laced fingers through the bars. "You'll talk to him in the end, Annique. You'll beg to talk. You know what he'll do to you."

There was a sniffle. "Leblanc . . . He does not believe me. He will hurt me terribly. Tell him I know nothing more. Please, Henri. Tell him." Her voice had changed completely. She sounded younger, subtly less refined, and very frightened. It was a masterful performance.

"He'll hurt you no matter what I tell him." Henri gloated.

The girl's face sank into her upturned palm. Her hair spilled in dark rivers through her fingers. "I cannot bear it. He will use me . . . like a grunting animal. I am not meant to be used by peasants."

Clever. Clever. He saw what she was doing. Henri's voice marked him as Parisian, a man of the city streets. Leblanc, for all his surface polish, was the son of a pig farmer. And Henri worked for Leblanc.

Henri's spite snaked out into the cell. "You were always Vauban's pet—Vauban and his elite cadre. Vauban and his important missions. You were too good for the rest of us. But tonight the so-special Annique that nobody could touch becomes a blind puppet for Leblanc to play with. If you'd been kind to me before, maybe I'd help you now."

"Leblanc has become Fouché's favorite. With the head of the Secret Police behind him, he can do anything. You cannot help me. You would not dare defy him." She rubbed her eyes with the back of her hand. "I will do whatever he wishes. I have no choice."

"I'll have you when he's through with you."

She went on speaking. She might not have heard Henri. "He will make me oil my body and do the Gypsy dances I learned when I was a child. I will dance in the firelight for him with nothing but a thin bit of silken cloth upon me. Red silk. He . . . he prefers red. He has told me."

Grey wrapped the chain around his hand, gripping tight, seized by the image of a slim body writhing naked, silhouetted in the golden glow of fire. He wasn't the only one. Henri gripped the crossed bars of the grill and pressed his face close, salivating.

Annique, eyes downcast, swayed as if she were already

undulating in the sensual dance she described. "I will draw the crimson silk from my body and caress him with it. The silk will be warm and damp with the heat of the dance. With my heat." Her left hand stroked down her body, intimately.

Grey ached from a dozen beatings, thirst was a torment every second, and he knew exactly what she was doing. He still went hard as a rock. He was helpless to stop it. God, but she was good.

Huskily, dreamily, she continued. "He will lie upon his bed and call me to him. At first, only to touch. Then to put my mouth upon him, wherever he directs. I have been trained to be skillful with my mouth. I will have no choice, you see, but to do as he demands of me."

Henri clanked and fumbled with the lock. In a great hurry, was Henri. If the Frenchman was half as aroused by Annique's little act as Grey was, it was a wonder he could get the door open at all.

The door banged back against the stone wall. "You must not come in here, Henri," she said softly, not moving, "or touch me in any way without the permission of Leblanc."

"Damn Leblanc." Henri slapped the lantern down and cornered her against the table. His fist twisted into her skirt and pulled it up. He grabbed the white shift beneath.

"You should not . . . You must not . . ." She struggled, pushing futilely at his hands with no more strength than a tiny, captured bird.

"No." He threw himself at Henri. And jerked short on his iron leash. The circle of pain at his wrist brought him back to reality. He couldn't get to her. He couldn't fight Henri for her. There wasn't a bloody thing he could do but watch.

"Do not . . ." Her flailing arm hit the lantern. It tilted and skidded off the table and clattered to the floor and extinguished. Darkness was instant and absolute.

"Stupid bitch," Henri snarled. "You . . ."

There was a small squashed thud. Henri yelped in pain. More thuds—one, two, three. The table scraped sideways. Something large and soft fell.

No movement. He heard Annique breathing hard, the smallness of it and the contralto gasps uniquely hers.

Planned. She'd planned it all. He crouched, tense as stretched cord, and acknowledged how well he'd been fooled. She'd planned this from start to finish. She'd manipulated both of them with that damned act of hers.

There was a long silence, broken by intriguing rustling sounds and Annique grunting from time to time. Her footsteps, when she walked toward him, were sure and unhesitating. She came in a straight line across the cell as if it were not dark as a tomb.

"What did you do to Henri?" The issue, he thought, had never really been in doubt.

"I hit him upon the head with a sock full of rocks." She seemed to think it over while she sat down beside him. "At least I am almost sure I hit his head once. I hit him many places. Anyway, he is quiet."

"Dead?"

"He is breathing. But one can never tell with head wounds. I may have yet another complicated explanation to make to God when I show up at his doorstep, which, considering all things, may be at any moment. I hope I have not killed him, quite, though he undoubtedly deserves it. I will leave that to someone else to do, another day. There are many people who would enjoy killing him. Several dozen I can call to mind at once."

She baffled him. There was ruthlessness there, but it was a kind of blithe toughness, clean as a fresh wind. He didn't catch a whiff of the evil that killed men in cold blood, from ambush. He had to keep reminding himself what she was. "You did more than knock him over the head. What was the rest of it, afterwards?"

"You desire the whole report?" She sounded amused. "But you are a spymaster, I think, Englishman. No one else asks such questions so calmly, as if by right. Very well, I shall report to you the whole report—that I have tied Henri up and helped myself to his money. There was an interesting packet of papers in a pocket he may have thought was secret. You may have them if you like. Me, I am no longer in the business of collecting secret papers."

Her hands patted over him lightly. "I have also found a so-handy stickpin, and if you will lift your pretty iron cuff here. Yes. Just so. Now hold still. I am not a fishwife that I can filet this silly lock while you wriggle about. You will make me regret that I am being noble and saving your life if you do not behave sensibly."

"I am at your disposal." He offered his chained wrist. At the same time he reached out and touched her hair, ready to grab her if she tried to leave without freeing him.

She put herself right in his power—a man twice her size, twice her strength, and an enemy. She had to know what her writhing and whispering did to a man. Revenge and anger and lust churned in his body like molten iron. The wonder was it didn't burn through his skin and set this soft hair on fire.

"Ah. We proceed," she said in the darkness. "This lock is not so complicated as it pretends to be. We are discussing matters."

She edged closer and shifted the manacle to a different angle, brushing against his thigh. With every accidental contact, his groin tightened and throbbed. All he could think of was her soft voice saying, "I will oil my body and dance in the firelight." He was no Henri. He wasn't going to touch her. But how did he get a picture like that out of his head?

"And . . . it is done." The lock fell open.

She made it seem easy. It wasn't. He rubbed his wrist. "I thank you."

He stood and stretched to his full height, welcoming the pain of muscles uncramping. Free. Savage exultation flooded him. He was free. He bunched and unbunched his fists, glorying in the surge of power that swept him. He felt like he could take these stones apart with his bare hands. It was dark as the pit of hell and they were twenty feet under a stronghold of the French Secret Police. But the door hung open. He'd get them out of here—Adrian and this remarkable, treacherous woman—or die trying. If they didn't escape, it would be better for all of them to die in the attempt.

While that woman worked on Adrian's manacle, he groped his way across the cell to Henri, who was, as she had said, breathing. The Frenchman was tied, hand and foot, with his stockings and gagged with his own cravat. A thorough woman. Checking the bonds was an academic exercise. There was indeed a secret pocket in the jacket. He helped himself to the papers, then tugged Henri's pants down to his ankles, leaving him half naked.

"What do you busy yourself with?" She'd heard him shifting Henri about. "I find myself inquisitive this evening."

"I'm giving Henri something to discuss with Leblanc when they next meet." It might buy them ten minutes while Henri explained his plans for the girl. "I may eventually regret leaving him alive."

"If we are very lucky, you will have an eventually in which to do so." There was a final, small, decisive click. "That is your Adrian's lock open. He cannot walk from here, you know."

"I'll carry him. Do you have a plan for getting out of the chateau with an unconscious man and no weapons and half the Secret Police of France upstairs?"

"But certainly. We will not discuss it here, though. Bring your friend and come, please, if you are fond of living."

He put an arm under Adrian's good shoulder and hauled

him upright. The boy couldn't stand without help, but he could walk when held up. He was conversing with unseen people in a variety of languages.

"Don't die on me now, Hawker," he said. "Don't you dare die on me."